What They Knew

A native of Dundee, Marion Todd studied music with the Open University and worked for many years as a piano teacher and jobbing accompanist. A spell as a hotel lounge pianist provided rich fodder for her writing and she began experimenting with a variety of genres. Early success saw her winning first prize in the *Family Circle Magazine* short story for children national competition and she followed this up by writing short stories and articles for her local newspaper.

Life (and children) intervened and, for a few years, Marion's writing was put on hold. During this time, she worked as a college lecturer, plantswoman and candle-maker. But, as a keen reader of crime fiction, the lure of the genre was strong, and she began writing her debut crime novel. Now a full-time writer, Marion lives in North-east Fife, overlooking the River Tay. She can often be found working out plots for her novels while tussling with her jungle-like garden and walking her daughter's unruly but lovable dog.

D0492502

Also by Marion Todd

Detective Clare Mackay

See Them Run
In Plain Sight
Lies to Tell
What They Knew

MARION TODD
What they knew

CANELO CRIME

First published in the United Kingdom in 2021 by

Canelo
31 Helen Road
Oxford OX2 0DF
United Kingdom

A CIP catalogue record for this book is available from the British Library.

Print ISBN 978 1 80032 203 5
Ebook ISBN 978 1 80032 102 1

Look for more great books at www.canelo.co

Printed and bound in Great Britain by Clays Ltd, Elcograf S.p.A.

For my brothers, Iain, Stuart and Kenneth,
who field my endless questions about crime
without raising an eyebrow between them

Thursday, 31ˢᵗ December

Chapter 1

Alison Reid studied the changes she'd made to her dating profile on Attracto while Jools Holland played boogie-woogie piano on the annual Hootenanny TV show. She had turned the volume down low to concentrate on the task and she could only just hear the tinkling of piano keys as she scrolled through.

'Bo-ring,' the girls at work had said when they'd seen her first attempt; and when she compared it with other profiles on Attracto, she had to admit they were right. There had been a couple of messages from men on the site and one promise of a date but nothing had come of it.

'You need to change that profile,' the girls had said. They were full of suggestions, some of which had made Alison blush, but she jotted down the better ones and promised she would update it over the festive break. And she had determined to do it before the new year dawned.

It had taken an hour or two but she was pretty pleased with her evening's work. Out had gone:

Thirty-something who enjoys country walks

and in had come:

World's worst skier – but I have a Roomba!

The photo was new too – taken at her work desk, with the background blurred. Fay had brought in Velcro rollers to give Alison's usually straight bob a tousled look and Kezia had taken dozens of photos which she had uploaded to her office computer. She and Fay then played about with filters until they were satisfied with the result.

'There,' Kezia had said, turning her monitor round so Alison could see. 'Don't you look fab?'

Alison had to admit the photo was a huge improvement. Instinctively she'd put a hand up to her hair, patting the unfamiliar style as she stared at the screen, taking in her new look. But she stopped short of letting the girls loose on her profile. 'I'll do it myself, at home,' she had said.

'We'll be checking,' Kezia warned and Alison had assured her she would do as they suggested.

A blast of jazz trumpet from the TV momentarily distracted her and she checked her watch. Her guest was late. But it didn't matter. She turned back to the laptop, running her eye over her profile again. She hadn't made all the changes the girls had suggested but she was pretty happy with it. She glanced at the clock. Five minutes to midnight. Five minutes until the new year and Alison was determined that this year was going to be different.

She clicked the Update button and rose from the table. Glancing at the TV screen she saw the large studio clock on the Hootenanny, the hands approaching twelve. She should have poured a drink, really, but she wanted to wait for her guest. She thought back to the plans they had made a few days earlier. She hoped her directions had been clear enough.

A sharp trill on the doorbell took her attention from the screen and she quickly closed the laptop.

Ten, nine, eight, seven…

The Hootenanny audience were counting down, as Alison moved into the hall. She crept up to the door and put her eye to the spy glass that gave her a wide-angled view of the doorstep and beyond. It was dark of course, only a few streetlights casting a dull glow on the houses opposite. But her outside light shone down on the person who stood on the threshold. She scrutinised the face for something familiar. She was faintly nervous, but not quite sure why.

Happy New Year, Jools announced, and the sound of a pipe band playing Auld Lang Syne drifted into the hall. A new year. She took her courage in both hands and opened the door.

A smile spread across the visitor's face. 'Alison – so sorry I'm late. Forgive me?'

Alison stood for a moment, hesitant, then she returned the smile. 'Of course,' she said. Then she stepped aside to admit her guest.

The visitor held out a bottle of red wine. 'Let's toast the new year. I hope red's okay. It's a good one.'

In the kitchen Alison switched on the oven to preheat, uncorked the wine and took glasses out of the cupboard while her visitor waited on the living room sofa.

'Can't beat the Hootenanny,' the visitor said, as Alison appeared with two glasses of wine. She set these down on the coffee table. 'I've put some food in to heat. Just veggie sausage rolls but they're pretty good. Quite like the real thing.'

'Sounds great.'

She chose a seat opposite her visitor and made to raise her glass.

The visitor took the other glass then said, 'Sorry – I hope this doesn't sound cheeky but I don't suppose you've got any food we can have now. Crisps? Or nuts? I missed dinner and I'm starving.'

'I'm sure I have something,' Alison said. She rose from her seat and went back into the kitchen.

As soon as she was out of sight the visitor slipped a small tablet silently into Alison's glass, swirling it around to help it dissolve.

Alison returned, bearing a bowl of pistachios and another of Bombay Mix. 'Is this okay? The hot food shouldn't be too long.'

'Perfect.' The visitor picked up the other glass. 'Cheers. Here's to us.'

On the TV, Jools was chatting to some celebrity.

'Who is that?' the visitor asked but Alison shook her head.

'Soap star, I think. Not sure, really.'

The visitor indicated Alison's glass. 'Drink up. It's bad luck if we don't finish the bottle.'

As Alison drained her glass and held it out for a refill the visitor checked the time. Half an hour ought to be long enough. Just thirty more minutes and then the fun would start.

–

It was just after one o'clock when the visitor left, taking the wine bottle and both glasses. No point in leaving DNA evidence or fingerprints. A few snowflakes began drifting down from the sky, settling on the pavement outside the house where Alison Reid had lived for the past five years and where, this evening, she had died. Not quite the start to the new year she had planned.

Sunday, 3rd January

Chapter 2

Clare stood ankle deep in snow in a field to the south of St Andrews, her collar turned up against a biting north-easterly wind. The snow had finally stopped the previous afternoon and, as the skies cleared, the mercury had dropped, giving the white blanket a crisp coating that crunched satisfyingly underfoot. Although it was now almost nine thirty, a watery sun was still struggling to peep over the horizon. Out to the east the grey North Sea merged with the sky making it difficult to see where the sea ended and the sky began. The fields around her were plump with their wintry coating and the trees hung with snow, softening the bare branches. Overhead a lone buzzard was circling, its eagle eye alert for any small movement on the ground. It was an idyllic view – redolent of the Christmas cards Clare had hurriedly stuck onto the door frames on Christmas Eve. And yet, as she looked without enthusiasm at her companions on this wintry morning, she thought, if this wasn't hell, she could probably see it from here.

Benjy strained on his lead as a middle-aged woman in a Barbour jacket and Hunter wellies went past, picking her way carefully through the snow. A handsome German pointer trotted obediently beside her paying Benjy no heed. They took up their place, a few yards from Clare, and stood waiting for the class to begin.

Clare's feet were starting to feel cold and she flexed them inside her boots, thinking longingly of the cosy cottage she had just left. It was the first proper snow of the winter, and she cursed herself for not digging out her thermal socks. There was snow in Boston, too. She knew that now, thanks to the new year text message from Geoffrey Dark, her on-off partner (boyfriend seemed too juvenile a word). The new year message that hadn't actually arrived until late last night. It had been full of news – the parties, fireworks over the harbour, skating in the park… Oh yes, Clare thought. Lots of news. But very little else. Very little about us, she thought.

Her own new year had been tame, by comparison: a glass or three of red in front of the Hootenanny with only Benjy for company, and bed by one o'clock.

Two more women arrived with a pair of German Shepherds. Clare recognised the dogs as Zander and Leila, although she'd no idea what the women's names were. To her relief, she saw the familiar figure of Ralph, the exuberant and completely wild Border collie, coming through the gate into the field. Clare was always pleased to see Ralph at the classes. Not only could he be relied on to be far more disruptive than Benjy, but his owner – one of the few men who attended the dog training – was particularly easy on the eye, as far as she could tell from the other side of the training field. He had a new hat today, Clare noticed. A soft grey beanie with a Nordic pattern. A Christmas present, she assumed. On some men it might have seemed girlish and wrong. But, with his swarthy complexion and stylish clothes, he somehow carried it off. Clare studied the other dog owners. Mostly swathed in long padded Puffa coats and ski jackets. Ralph's owner, by contrast, cut a striking figure against the grey sea in a dark brown pea coat, a scarf with a fine stripe knotted casually at his neck. Clare noticed most of the other women glanced across at him, although that could have been due to Ralph's boisterous attempts to round up their own dogs.

'A happy new year to you all,' boomed Isobel, the dog trainer. 'I'm glad to see so many of you back here, despite the weather. So… let's begin with a clockwise circuit please.'

The owners began moving round in a well-practised routine. Most of the dogs walked obediently, paying heed to their owners' instructions while Benjy and Ralph, distracted by the presence of so many other dogs, barked, tugged and jumped around, to Isobel's obvious impatience.

'Benjy's mummy,' she bellowed across the field, as Benjy made to run across to greet Ralph.

Clare thought she saw Ralph's owner laugh and she could only hope Isobel would refer to him as Ralph's daddy before the morning was out. He really was very good-looking but he probably had an equally attractive wife or girlfriend. All the good ones did. But you never could tell...

As she led Benjy round the perimeter of the training area she thought again about Geoff.

Admittedly he had come for Christmas. Joined Clare and her family on Christmas Day at her parents' house in Glasgow. Then he'd driven back with her to Daisy Cottage for a few days. And it had been fun. He was fun. Full of life and vigour.

And then, two days before new year, he had breezed out of her life again – places to go and people to see. Back into a taxi – no need to drive me, Clare – then onto a plane and back to his job in Boston. The job that was supposed to have been a secondment but that was feeling increasingly permanent as time went on. He had repeated his offer for her to join him, as he did now and then. But they both knew she wouldn't go and the offers were becoming more casual and less frequent.

As she came to a halt with the rest of the group to await the next instruction, Clare wondered if this would be the year she finally found someone to settle down with. She had thought Geoffrey was that person. But that was before he'd decided to move to Boston.

And then there was her fling with her boss, DCI Alastair Gibson. They had been rubbing along quite well together and then Clare had ended up in hospital and Geoff had flown back to be at her side. Al Gibson had melted into the background and they had never really given their relationship a proper chance.

Isobel barked the next instruction and half of the owners turned to begin walking their dogs in the opposite direction, while Benjy, Ralph and a few others were instructed to stand still. This sent Benjy into transports of delight as he tugged and strained towards each dog that passed. Clare stood watching him and quite suddenly she came to a decision. It was time to stop messing about. She would end things once and for all with Geoffrey and take it from there. 'Before I'm too old to care,' she said aloud. At the sound of her voice Benjy looked up and sniffed at the pocket where she kept the dog treats and she bent to ruffle his neck, suddenly grateful for his unconditional love and affection.

Monday, 4th January

Chapter 3

Clare was just returning from her morning walk with Benjy when she felt the phone buzz in her pocket. The temperature had risen, and all round her snow was starting to melt. Walking through the wood she'd heard the sound of water running off an adjacent field while the trees dripped steadily as snow slipped from the branches.

She fished in her pocket for the phone and glanced at the display. Jim, her desk sergeant. Clare's first thought was for Jim's wife Mary whose health had been poor since her stroke. Jim wouldn't be at work today – there was only a skeleton staff covering the public holiday. Unless...

She swiped the phone. 'Jim?'

'Clare – sorry to disturb you on your last day off...'

'It's not Mary, is it?'

'No, Clare. She's fine, thanks. It's work, I'm afraid. We've had a call-out. Woman found dead in her bath this morning. Robbie attended but he thinks you should take a look.'

Robbie was one of the younger uniformed officers but generally pretty reliable and Clare wondered why he thought this particular death suspicious. 'Locus?'

'Lindsay Gardens. It's off Canongate.'

'I know it, Jim. I'll be there in half an hour.'

Clare ended the call and took out her door key. She stepped out of her wellies, banging them together to shake off the wet snow then put them down in a corner of the kitchen. Benjy made to wander through to his favoured spot on the sofa but she grabbed his collar and subjected him to a thorough drying.

He bore this patiently for a minute then wriggled out of her clutches and padded through to the sitting room. Clare threw the wet towel into the washing machine and went upstairs to change into her work clothes. She sent a quick message to her nearest neighbour and dog walker Moira asking if she could look in on Benjy later, then she headed out to the car.

A snow plough had been along the road leaving it passable. The snow from the road was banked up on the verges and melting fast now. Clare reckoned there would be some flooding if the thaw continued. She drove on through the slush that remained, spraying it left and right, but as she neared the town the roads were clearer and the pavements gritted. All round her drains had been overwhelmed and water was running along the channels at the side of the roads. As Bogward Road gave onto Canongate she passed a large area of grass peppered with snowmen. A clutch of children brightly kitted out in hats and scarves were wandering along the pavement trailing sledges in their wake, probably heading for the gentle incline on Hallow Hill.

Lindsay Gardens was a quiet residential street, many of the houses decked out with Christmas decorations. A few had bushes hung with strands of lights and one garden had a family of reindeer arranged in a semi-circle. The pavements were a messy mix of slush and dirty-brown grit, marked with foot-prints and the snow now appeared more nuisance than novelty.

She pulled in behind a marked police car and nodded to a uniformed officer standing in the drive of a 1970s-built house. A low wall bordered a patch of snow-covered garden to the front with a path leading to a half-glass door. The house itself was a two-storey semi, clad in a brown-coloured stone, unremarkable but in good order. As she stepped out of the car, Clare wondered who the owner was and what had caused her to be found dead in her bathtub.

She took a white forensic suit, overshoes and gloves from the boot of her car, noting as she did so that the curtains were drawn on the front room windows. She made her way up the drive, dodging past drips as the snow melted off the brown roof tiles. Jim was waiting at the door to meet her.

'Fill me in please, Jim.'

'Woman, early thirties we think, found submerged in the bath.'

'Name?'

'Alison Reid.'

'Any evidence of a struggle?'

Jim shook his head. 'There's no water splashed around the room. Mind you, we've no idea how long she's been there. It could have dried up.'

'It's not just a drunken accident? Falling asleep in the bath.'

'I don't think so. You'll see what I mean…'

Clare stepped carefully into her forensic suit and pulled on a pair of gloves. 'Who found her?'

'Next-door neighbour.' Jim glanced at his notebook. 'A Mrs Tanya Sullivan. Sara took her back round to her own house. I said you'd probably want to speak to her, yourself.'

Clare nodded at this. Sara, her young PC, could be relied on to soothe even the most frantic of witnesses. She pulled the hood over her head. 'Any sign of SOCO?'

'Shouldn't be too long. I asked for Raymond but with it being a public holiday it'll be whoever's on duty.'

'Have you had a look yourself, Jim?'

He shook his head. 'Didn't want to contaminate the site.'

'I'll just pop my head round the bathroom door, then,' Clare said. 'Have a quick look before SOCO arrive.'

'Robbie said to take a look at her neck…'

Clare stepped carefully up the hall, her eyes roving round for anything that seemed out of place. But nothing struck her as unusual. The house was a model of order. The bathroom door stood open and she peered in, studying the room with a practised eye. It was simply decorated with a white suite and tiles, a single row of narrow Delft blue ceramic strips providing a contrast. On the floor was a small pile of clothes, presumably what the victim had been wearing before entering the bath. Other than that, the room was immaculate. As she took it all in, Clare wondered idly why the bathroom at Daisy Cottage always seemed so disorganised.

A shower cabinet to the left partly blocked the view of the bath and Clare stepped further into the room to view the victim. Alison Reid lay, partly submerged, her head to the side, facing towards Clare. The skin on her hands was shrivelled and Clare thought she must have been in the water for some time. Overnight at the very least. Her hair, which Clare guessed was shoulder length, now partly obscured her face and her abdomen had risen to the surface, causing the water level to drop, judging by a slight tidemark near the top. Clare took another step towards the body and bent to examine it more closely. She remembered Jim's words and peered at Alison's neck. Her hair was in the way but she was sure there were marks on the neck. Had Alison been strangled when she was taking a bath? Clare looked round. The window was closed and, from what she'd seen so far, there was no evidence of an intruder. So what had happened here?

Her thoughts were interrupted by a shout from Jim.

'That's SOCO arrived.'

She stepped carefully back out of the room, retracing her steps and moved down the hall. Out in the street Jim and the uniformed officer who'd been guarding the door were setting up a cordon with blue and white tape. The SOCO team were unloading equipment from their van and Clare went to greet them. She was relieved to see Raymond Curtice had drawn the short straw and was donning a white forensic suit.

'Raymond,' she said, smiling. 'Sorry to drag you out.'

'Ach it's no problem, Clare. I was starting to get cabin fever anyway. So what do we have?'

'Woman, early thirties, dead in the bath. Possible marks on her neck. No sign of a break-in as far as I can tell but I've only had a peep into the bathroom.'

'Anything particular you want us to focus on?'

Clare considered this. 'I'm not sure. I'd like to come back in with you, once I've spoken to the woman next door. Have a proper look round.'

'She the one who found her?'

'Yep. And, if you have even a vague idea of how long she's been there…' Clare knew she was chancing her arm. Raymond always told her it wasn't his job.

He shook his head. 'It doesn't matter how many times I tell you, does it?'

Clare grinned. 'Thanks, Raymond.'

As she left him to his work she saw a red Golf GTi draw up behind the SOCO's van. Chris West, her detective sergeant.

He jumped out of the car and ambled up the path, pulling on his jacket. Clare thought his work trousers were a bit tighter than usual. He'd obviously had a good Christmas. He rolled his eyes at Clare. 'We very nearly made it through the holiday…'

'And a happy new year to you too,' Clare said, pulling off her white suit. 'Come on – we've a distraught neighbour to interview.'

'Oh goodie.'

Chapter 4

A figure standing at the window of the house next door drew back as Clare and Chris began making their way up the garden path. The front door opened as they approached and Sara stood there in her stocking soles.

As she stood back to admit them she said, 'Mrs Sullivan had new carpets for Christmas so she'd prefer if we took off our shoes.'

Clare glanced at the pristine cream carpet that ran up the hall and she removed her mules, avoiding Chris's eye. She waited until he had stepped out of his shoes – without bothering to unlace them – and indicated to Sara that she could leave. 'See if Jim needs any help.'

Sara stepped back into her shoes and escaped, closing the front door behind her. Clare turned and saw a middle-aged woman standing at what she guessed was the sitting room door. She was dressed in a pair of dark blue tracksuit bottoms and a red Christmas jumper depicting Santa in wraparound sunglasses. She was pale and there were mascara smudges below her eyes. She introduced herself as Tanya Sullivan and led them into a square sitting room, also with the new cream carpet. The room was light and airy, with dark blue leather sofas and an artificial Christmas tree in one corner. The walls were covered with photos of what Clare guessed were grandchildren, the same children photographed at every age from just a few months old up to early teens. There was a large television screen, mounted on the wall. Clare glanced at it and thought about her own new TV, a Christmas treat to herself. Too big for the room maybe but it seemed a good idea at the time. She'd considered mounting it on the wall but Geoff had said that was naff. She studied Tanya Sullivan's TV for a few moments. Was it naff, having it up there? She couldn't decide.

A half-drunk mug of something sat on a coffee table and Tanya lifted it. 'I'll just...' she began, then she said, 'I suppose you'll be wanting a drink. Coffee okay?'

Clare smiled. 'Only if you're making it.'

Tanya nodded. 'I'll just put the kettle on.'

She returned a few seconds later and indicated one of the sofas. 'Please, sit down.' She took a seat opposite them and clutched her hands.

'Mrs Sullivan...' Clare began.

'Tanya's fine.'

Clare nodded. 'Tanya – perhaps you could tell us what happened this morning.'

Tanya swallowed and looked from Clare to Chris. Then she seemed to gather her wits. 'I hadn't seen Alison, you know. Not for a few days. And we always wished each other a happy new year.'

'Can you recall when you last saw her?' Clare asked.

Tanya nodded. 'Two days before new year. I knocked on her door to offer her some Christmas cake. I always have loads and, with her being on her own...'

'She lived alone?'

'Yes. Anyway, she thanked me for the cake, said she'd see me after the new year and that was that.'

'And today?' Clare prompted.

'Well, I noticed her curtains were still drawn. So I thought I ought to check. See everything was all right, you know?'

'You have a key?' Clare asked.

Tanya nodded. 'Just for emergencies.' She glanced across at Chris. 'I'd only go in if I thought there was a problem.'

Chris smiled. 'Of course.'

'So, I put my key in the door and called out. Just hello, so she wouldn't get a fright. But there was no answer so I went up the hall, and then I saw the tree.'

'The Christmas tree?' Clare asked.

'Yes. The sitting room was in darkness, you know? But the tree lights were on. And I knew something was wrong.'

'What made you think that?'

'Oh, Alison was always so careful. Always turned the plugs off when she went out. She wouldn't have gone to bed and left the tree lights on.'

Clare nodded. 'Where did you go next, Tanya?'

Tanya was warming to her subject now. 'I looked in the kitchen, just to make sure she wasn't there – or out in the garden, that sort of thing. Then I went back into the hall and I noticed it felt a bit odd.'

'In what way?'

'Sort of damp,' Tanya said. 'Like when a pan's been boiling on the cooker. I thought maybe there was a leak, or something. So I went to the bathroom...' she broke off.

Clare nudged Chris. 'Why don't you go and make us some coffee, Chris.'

He took the hint and rose, heading for the kitchen.

Clare waited until he had left the room then said, 'Did you enter the bathroom, Tanya?'

The woman nodded. 'I just peeped in. I thought maybe Alison had run a bath and forgotten it. And then I saw...'

Clare waited.

Tanya hesitated then swallowed again and said, 'I saw Alison. In the bath. But... she looked odd. I mean I'd never seen her without her clothes on, obviously, but she was... rounder, somehow. Her stomach, I mean. Bigger, you know?'

Clare nodded. 'And did you notice anything else about the room? Anything out of place?'

Tanya shook her head. 'No. Only...'

Clare waited.

'Her clothes – they were on the floor, in a bit of a heap, you know? As if she'd taken them off in a hurry. And her trousers were outside in. And that wasn't like her. Not Alison.'

Clare leaned forward. 'Not like her how, Tanya? In what way?'

'Oh, she was as neat as a new pin. Not a thing out of place. And there was a laundry basket in the bathroom. I don't think she'd have left a pile of clothes on the floor.'

Clare thought of her dog-walking clothes, currently lying in a heap on her bedroom floor and she wondered if Tanya was making too much of this. If Alison had been drunk and decided to take a bath… maybe it was a drunken accident after all.

'And that's another thing,' Tanya was saying.

'Sorry, what did you say?'

'Towel. I said she didn't have one. I think she kept her towels in the cupboard opposite but it's too far to reach from the bath. She'd have left one handy, don't you think? But there was only a small hand towel on a rail. You don't take a bath without leaving a towel close by, Inspector, do you?'

You might if you're drunk, Clare thought but didn't say. She smiled. 'Thanks, Tanya. That's all really helpful. Just a few more questions, if you're up to it.'

The sitting room door opened and Chris appeared, bearing a tray with mugs. 'I've brought the cake you left out,' he said hopefully.

Tanya beamed. 'Everyone likes my Christmas cake, Sergeant. I made it in October, you know, and I've been feeding it brandy ever since.'

'It sounds amazing,' Chris said, setting down the tray. Tanya picked up a knife he'd brought and began cutting pieces of cake.

Clare rolled her eyes at him but he spread his hands in response. When the coffee and cake was handed out she went on. 'How long have you known Alison?'

Tanya considered. 'Five years, I'd say, Inspector. Since she moved here. After her divorce, you know.'

22

'She was married?'

Tanya nodded. 'She and her husband had a big house in the town.'

'Don't suppose you know where?'

'Buchanan Gardens. Lovely big house it is. Near that student place – the apartments.'

'David Russell Apartments?' Clare said.

'That's the one. The ex-husband still lives there, I think.'

'Do you happen to know the number?'

Tanya shook her head.

'Not to worry. We'll find it.' Clare took another bite of cake. It was very good. 'This is delicious,' she said, earning herself a smile from Tanya. Then she went on. 'I don't suppose you know the ex-husband's name?'

Tanya's lips tightened. 'Miles Sharp,' she said. 'Sharp by name and sharp by nature, if you ask me. Not that I've met him, but from what Alison said…'

'Were they married long?'

'I'm not sure, Inspector. But she's been here about five years. I think she came when she and Miles separated.'

'Was it an amicable split?' Clare asked.

'Depends if you mind your husband carrying on with someone else.'

'Mr Sharp was having an affair?'

'He certainly was! With the other partner in his office. Sharp and Lafferty,' she added. 'They're accountants. Office in Hope Street.'

Clare knew the street. 'So, Mr Sharp – he was a partner?'

'That's right. And Alison, well she worked there. That's how they met. She was a junior accountant and they fell in love. Next thing she knew he'd whisked her off to New York and proposed to her in Central Park. I think they were married a few months later.'

'But it didn't last?'

'If you ask me, Inspector, his kind can't keep it in their trousers. They were only married a few years when he started sniffing round Cheryl Lafferty.' Tanya held out the plate of cake and Chris took a second piece. She offered it to Clare who waved it away. 'Next thing Alison knew, he wants a divorce and Cheryl's sporting a huge diamond ring.'

Clare sipped her coffee then said, 'That must have been difficult for Alison.'

'I'll say.' Tanya cradled her mug. 'Poor Alison moved out of that lovely house and he'd moved that Cheryl in before Alison had got to the end of the street!'

Clare noticed Tanya's lips tighten again and she wondered if that Cheryl was as black as she was being painted.

'I think that's why she changed jobs,' Tanya went on.

'Where did she move to?'

'A smaller office in Market Street. Crossford Financial.'

'And was she still there?'

Tanya nodded. 'I think she liked it. Not as fancy as Sharp and Lafferty but friendly. Nice people, she said.' Tanya lifted the coffee mug to her lips then put it down again. 'I wonder if she never got over it – Miles, I mean. Do you think that's why…'

'Did Alison have anyone else in her life?' Clare said quickly, before Tanya could speculate any further. 'Another boyfriend – partner – that sort of thing?'

'Not that I saw,' Tanya said. 'She lived very quietly, poor thing.'

Clare thought it was no wonder Alison kept to herself with a neighbour like Tanya. 'What about family? Did she have anyone to stay for Christmas?'

'No. The dad's dead, you know. And the mother's in a care home.' She moved closer to Clare and mouthed 'Early onset dementia,' as though this was something to be talked of only in hushed tones.

Clare was growing weary of this gossipy neighbour. 'Do you know which care home?'

Tanya frowned.

At last, Clare thought. Something she doesn't know.

'I think… possibly Pitlethie,' Tanya said after a short pause. 'It's in Leuchars. About quarter of an hour from here. Out past the primary school. A new build. Only been open a few years.' She nodded as if to confirm this. 'Yes, Pitlethie.'

Clare noted this down then said, 'Just one more question, Tanya. Have you seen anyone hanging around the street, recently? Anyone unusual or unfamiliar?'

Tanya's eyes widened. 'You think someone did that to her? That it wasn't suicide?'

'It's just routine,' Clare said, keeping her tone light. 'We always have to ask these things. So… can you recall anything?'

Tanya sat back in her chair and appeared to consider this. Then she said, 'Nothing comes to mind, Inspector. But I'll have a think. I mean, if it was murder…'

Clare decided she'd had quite enough of Tanya Sullivan and she rose from the sofa. 'I'll leave you my card, Mrs Sullivan. If you do remember anything else…'

'Oh, I'll be sure to let you know, Inspector. Don't worry about that.' She picked up the cake knife again. 'I'll just give you some cake to take away. I know how hard you police officers work.'

Chris's face lit up and Clare dragged him to the door to retrieve their shoes.

Chapter 5

They walked back down the path, picking their steps as the snow gradually turned to slush.

'You want to head over to the care home?' Chris said.

Clare considered this. 'I'm not sure. If the mother isn't capable of understanding what's happened...'

'Maybe worth speaking to the matron, or whatever they're called these days.'

Clare nodded. 'Can you call the home, please? Find out if it's worth us sending someone over.'

'Yeah, sure. What about the ex-husband? Want to call in on him?'

Clare frowned. 'I'm not sure. If it's five years since they divorced, would he know anything?'

'If the mother's not able to tell us anything it might be worth speaking to him.'

'Fair point. Can you get onto the control room then? See if they can find the number in Buchanan Gardens. Remember he's a partner in Sharp and Lafferty. Might help track him down.' She glanced back at Alison's front door. 'I just want a quick word with Raymond.'

Clare went through the tedious but necessary process of suiting up again then she stepped back into Alison Reid's house. Raymond was standing just outside the bathroom door directing the police photographer while his team were waiting to take swabs from around the bath.

'Anything significant?' she asked.

'Not much yet,' he said. 'Place is pretty tidy. No evidence of forced entry. Some snacks in bowls on a coffee table so we'll take them away and check for DNA. I'm not convinced it is a suspicious death but we'll check anyway. There is one thing, though...'

'Yes?'

'In the kitchen – we found a cork from a wine bottle. And the corkscrew sitting beside it.'

'Do you think she got drunk and fell asleep in the bath?'

'As to that, you'll have to wait for the post-mortem. See how much alcohol's in her system. But that's not what I meant.'

Clare waited.

'We've had a good look round and can't find the bottle. No glasses in the sink either – or the dishwasher.'

'Neighbour says she was very tidy. She'll have washed up. Put the glasses away, no?'

'If she was that tidy, Clare, why leave the cork and corkscrew out? And would someone drunk enough to fall asleep in the bath manage to wash and dry her wine glass, never mind dispose of the bottle?'

Clare considered this for a moment then said, 'What about recycling? She might have a bag of bottles somewhere.'

'Way ahead of you. There's a bag in the utility room but only one bottle and it's a screw cap. And no bottle in the fridge or anywhere else, as far as we can see.'

'Checked the bin?'

'Yep. Nothing there, although we've not been right through the contents yet. But the cork and corkscrew being on the kitchen table suggests she had the wine recently. So even if she did put the bottle in the bin it would be at the top.'

Clare fell silent again. Was there something here? Or was Raymond reading too much into a carelessly discarded wine cork? If Tanya Sullivan was to be believed, Alison Reid wasn't the carelessly discarding type. 'Okay, Raymond. Best check the rest of the bin. Let me know if you find the bottle. What about the body?'

'You've had a look, yeah?'

'Just a peep. Fully suited up, of course.'

He laughed. 'I'm not accusing you, Clare.'

'So?'

'Well, it'll be the pathologist's call but I'd say she's been there a maybe a couple of days. The abdomen's distended which suggests putrefaction and there's a tidemark round the bath above the current water level.'

'The body gases have raised her up, allowing the water level to drop.'

'You're learning! We'll make a scientist of you yet, Clare.'

'And her neck – any thoughts on the marks?'

Raymond's brow clouded. 'It'll be easier to see once they have her at the mortuary. But there definitely is some bruising.'

'So she could have been strangled...'

Raymond hesitated. Then he said, 'I think you need the pathologist's opinion on that, Clare. I wouldn't like to commit myself. The bruising – I'm not sure it's enough for strangulation, unless she really was so drunk that she didn't put up a struggle. But even then...'

'Okay, Raymond. Thanks for that. Let me know if there's anything else once you're done please.'

'Will do, Clare.'

'Mind if I just...'

'As long as you're careful. You know the drill. Touch nothing, take nothing.'

Leaving Raymond to his photographer, Clare moved carefully through the house. The safety conscious part of her wanted to switch off the Christmas tree lights but she resisted the urge. The sitting room was tidy enough, similar in size to Tanya Sullivan's house next door but Clare couldn't help thinking how two people can make the same room look quite different. Instead of the large dark blue sofas there was a small two-seater in a dark red fabric, dotted with cushions, and two occasional chairs, different from the two-seater. There was a TV set but it sat inconspicuously in a corner, the remote control on a nearby shelf. One wall was lined with bookcases and Clare's eyes flicked across, taking in Alison's eclectic choice of reading matter: from Jane Austen to Kingsley Amis; Lonely Planet travel guides, political biographies and books by Ben Goldacre. Clare thought she might have liked Alison Reid.

She turned away from the bookcases and her eye fell on the coffee table – solid oak with chunky legs. It was clutter-free, apart from a copy of the Christmas Radio Times and two bowls of snacks. She wondered about that. There were pistachios in a bowl but no empty shells. Peering down at the carpet she could see a few crumbs had been dropped from the Bombay Mix. Maybe they would get something from the bowls. She had to hope so. She looked round the room once more then moved through to the dining room. The table was clear, apart from a laptop and a poinsettia, now drooping for the want of water. A light wood sideboard stood against one wall and Clare saw that none of the furniture matched. The sideboard didn't look new and she wondered if it was a family heirloom or if Alison had been reduced to furnishing this house from one of the growing number of second-hand shops. Maybe Miles Sharp had played awkward when it had come to dividing up their possessions. Or maybe she preferred recycled furniture. Judging by the contents of her bookshelves, Alison Reid was someone who cared about the planet.

She glanced in the kitchen and saw it was serviceable enough. Probably the original cupboards from when the house was built. It was miles away from Tanya Sullivan's kitchen with its integrated appliances and modern units, but it was clean and well cared for. A SOCO officer was bagging the wine cork and the corkscrew and Clare drew back so she wasn't in his way. Something caught her eye and she bent to peer at the oven.

'Something in there, I think,' she said and the SOCO officer nodded.

She made her way back out into the hall and ascended the stairs. There were two rooms furnished as bedrooms and a smaller one which appeared to be a study. Clare stepped carefully into the room. It was built into the eaves and surprisingly bright for such a small space. The only window was a small Velux above Clare's head. She looked up and saw snow sliding slowly down the glass, allowing a shaft of sunlight into the room. A bookcase stood against the wall below the window, filled with books which Clare assumed were related to her work. There were tax manuals, books on accounting principles and a guide to Excel spreadsheets. A Pukka pad sat on the desk with a tray of pens and paperclips to the side. Clare smiled at a coaster bearing the words,

There are 3 kinds of accountants in the world:

Those who can count and those who can't

To the right of the desk was a sturdy shelf holding a row of neatly labelled lever arch files. Clare studied the labels: Bank Statements, Bills, Legal Correspondence, Training Courses... all perfectly normal. She stepped carefully back out of the room and opened a door to the right.

Alison's bedroom was painted in a pale lavender shade, carpeted in a grey flecked pattern. The matching bedding and curtains were a deeper shade of lilac and Clare thought they were vaguely familiar. Marks & Spencer, maybe? She wasn't sure. She glanced round the room and saw it was as tidy as the rest of the house. A paperback sat on a bedside table, alongside a radio alarm clock and a pair of reading glasses. A cream dressing gown hung on a hook on the back of the door, reminding Clare of Tanya's comment about Alison's clothes, carelessly discarded on the bathroom floor.

The other room had a bed and a chest of drawers but otherwise was unfurnished. Looking round, Clare thought Alison couldn't have had many house guests.

She made her way back down the stairs, reflecting on the house and its occupant, now lying dead in the bath. Nothing in these rooms particularly matched. Some of the furniture had seen better days. And yet Clare thought she would have felt more at home here in these simply put-together rooms than in the newly carpeted house next door.

Outside, Chris was on the phone, scribbling something on his hand. As Clare approached he ended the call.

'Got the address for Miles Sharp.'

'And the care home?'

He shook his head. 'I spoke to the manager. The mother's dementia is pretty advanced. She doesn't think the news would sink in. I've asked her to let us know if there's any change.'

Clare glanced at her watch. It was eleven already. 'Alison Reid's work won't be open until tomorrow at the earliest. Let's call on the ex-husband. I'm not sure how much he'll be able to help after five years but it's worth a shot.'

Chapter 6

Buchanan Gardens was a pleasant road to the west of St Andrews, dotted with individually designed houses set in substantial gardens. Tall trees screened the houses from passers-by and Claire drove slowly along while Chris looked for the house Alison Reid had once shared with Miles Sharp. Clare presumed he shared it with Cheryl Lafferty, now. The new Mrs Sharp.

'Here,' Chris said suddenly. 'Just reverse back and it's that one there – behind the fence.'

Clare backed the car up and, seeing there was no gate on the drive, pulled it in off the road. She crunched over the gravel, past a substantial double garage until she was opposite the front door. They stepped out of the car and surveyed the house. It was a fairly new building but had been designed to look as if it dated from the 1920s. It was finished in a white render and the substantial arched front entrance was bordered on either side by two bow walls with leaded windows. The upper floor windows were hooded by canopies, probably zinc, Clare thought. And above the front door was a rose window in stained glass.

'Pseudo Arts and Crafts,' Clare muttered, locking the car.

'Eh?'

'The house. They've tried to make it look like an Arts and Crafts house but they've tried a bit too hard.'

'Listen to you,' Chris said. 'Dating an expert in architecture is finally starting to rub off on you.'

Clare's brow creased as she thought of Geoffrey, now back in Boston. She really must do something about it. End it, once

32

and for all. But if she did end things with Geoff, what would she have left?

She turned her attention back to the house. A woman with blonde hair was standing at a window, openly observing them. 'Come on – let's see if the Sharps are at home.'

As they moved towards the entrance the woman disappeared. Clare rang the bell and, after a few seconds, the blonde woman opened the door. She glanced over their heads to Clare's car then back at Clare. Her expression was not encouraging.

'Yes?'

This, Clare decided must be the new Mrs Sharp – Cheryl Lafferty, who had been carrying on with Miles Sharp under his wife's nose. She was younger than Alison. Late twenties, maybe. Her blonde hair was thick and lustrous, curling down past her shoulders. She had an attractive face but her lips were pressed together and her eyes hostile. She was dressed simply but expensively in a cream polo neck, camel-coloured trousers and brown suede boots. Her left hand rested on the edge of the door as if barring the way and Clare couldn't help but notice the enormous diamond ring next to a white-gold wedding band.

She held out her warrant card and introduced herself and Chris.

The woman stood her ground. 'You've still not said why you're here.'

'Are you Mrs Sharp? Mrs Cheryl Sharp?'

'What if I am?'

They had only been on the doorstep a few seconds and already Clare was tiring of Cheryl Sharp's hostility. 'Is Mr Sharp at home?'

'Yes.'

'We'd like to speak to him,' Clare said.

Cheryl hesitated then she stood back to admit them. 'You'd better come in, then.'

As they entered the hall, a bundle of something small and white came barking towards them.

'Pixie,' Cheryl snapped, 'behave!'

Pixie stopped in her tracks but continued to snarl at Clare and Chris as Cheryl led them into a sitting room. It was a large square room with two corner sofas arranged around an enormous coffee table on which lay a stack of celebrity gossip magazines. A Harrods Christmas coffee mug sat on a gold hexagonal coaster, a half-eaten box of chocolates next to it.

'Sit down, if you want,' Cheryl said, without enthusiasm. 'I'll get him.'

She left the room but Pixie stood her ground, emitting the odd growl.

Chris fixed the dog with his eye. 'Come anywhere near me,' he said, his voice low, 'and I'll kick you right across that sofa.'

While Chris psyched out the dog, Clare studied the room. The laminate flooring was broken up with thick rugs in geometric patterns. Cream-shaded lamps burned on small tables, giving the room a warm glow. There were abstract prints on the walls and Clare inclined her head, trying to work out what they were meant to be; but she could make nothing of them. She couldn't help comparing this expensively furnished house with Alison Reid's, just a few miles away. Alison's furniture was perhaps second-hand – it had certainly seen better days – but her sitting room, easily half the size of this room, was somehow more interesting. There was that wall of books, the ill-matched but attractive selection of cushions, and a sense of it being a home. Not a show house like this, but a home.

Her eye fell on a side table on which stood a framed photograph taken at Miles and Cheryl's wedding. Cheryl was turned away from the camera, her arm on Miles's shoulder, presumably to show off the back of her dress which was cut away in a deep V, down to her waist. Clare moved closer to study the photo but the door opened, interrupting her perusal. Miles Sharp entered, with Cheryl behind. Pixie started to yap and Cheryl moved to pick her up, making soothing sounds.

He strode across the room, hand held out. His smile was as broad as it was insincere. He was a little taller than Clare and perhaps a few years older. Older than Cheryl, certainly. Early forties, maybe. His hair was surprisingly dark – no stranger to the dye bottle, then – and his face, bony and lined, bore evidence of regular sunbed use. He was casually dressed in navy jeans and a fine grey sweater with a tiny Ralph Lauren logo. He indicated one of the sofas and sat down on the arm of the other. Clare wondered if he had deliberately taken up a higher position. A man used to dominating the room.

'Officers, this is an unexpected pleasure. How can I help? No trouble at the office, I hope?' The smile was still fixed, his words glib and practised.

Cheryl, still holding Pixie, sat down next to her husband, her mouth set in a hard line.

Clare watched the pair carefully. Then she said, 'I'm afraid I have some bad news, Mr Sharp. About your ex-wife, Alison.'

There was the tiniest flicker of something in Miles Sharp's eyes. Clare wasn't sure what it was, but it was definitely there. And then it was gone.

'Alison?' he said. 'But I'm not sure how that concerns...'

'I'm afraid Alison was found dead this morning.'

For a moment Miles Sharp seemed at a loss. Then he opened his mouth to speak but Cheryl cut across him.

'Sorry, Inspector, but I don't really see how this concerns Miles. It's five years since they were divorced. So it's really nothing to do with us, is it?' She stuck out her chin, her expression obdurate.

Clare regarded her. There was clearly no love lost here but, even so, it was a pretty hard-headed reaction. Miles, on the other hand, seemed to be struggling for the right response. And then he recovered himself.

'What my wife means, officers, is that we didn't really have anything to do with Alison. Not for some years now. I mean it's very sad of course.' He turned to Cheryl and took her hand. 'I'm sure we're both very sorry to hear it, aren't we honey?'

Cheryl said nothing.

'We'll send flowers,' he said suddenly. 'For old times' sake. I mean she was my wife for a few years…' He seemed to be running out of things to say.

Clare forced a smile. 'I do realise it's some years since you were married to Alison,' she said smoothly, 'but I'm afraid her mother is too ill to help us with our enquiries so we're trying to find out as much as we can from those who knew her well.'

This seemed to relax Miles and he smiled back. 'Of course, Inspector. Please ask anything you wish.'

Clare flicked a glance at Cheryl then turned back to Miles. 'I understand Alison worked for you at Sharp and Lafferty but that she subsequently left to work with another firm.'

Miles Sharp spread his hands. 'You can imagine how awkward it was, Inspector. With the divorce and all that…'

'And of course you were engaged in a relationship with Mrs Sharp at the time,' Clare said smoothly, 'were you not?'

'So?' Cheryl said. 'Not a crime, is it? People get married, they split up. It wasn't my fault Miles looked elsewhere, you know.'

Oh wasn't it, Clare thought. She could just picture it. Miles with the wandering eye was easy prey for someone like Cheryl. She had set her cap at him and she didn't care who she hurt in the process.

'And like I said,' Cheryl went on, 'it's nothing to do with us.'

Miles was frowning. Perhaps the penny had dropped, Clare thought.

'What is it,' he said, choosing his words carefully, 'that you want from me? Was Alison's death not…' he tailed off, apparently struggling for the right words.

Clare waited a few seconds before answering, watching them. She saw Cheryl flick a glance at her husband.

'It's possible Alison's death wasn't due to natural causes,' she said. 'We won't know for sure until the post-mortem has been carried out but, in the meantime, we're trying to find out a bit more about her. She lived alone, you see, so we need your help to build up a picture of her life. Perhaps you could start by telling me the last time you saw Alison.'

And there it was again. That flicker in Miles's eyes. Was he hiding something?

He scratched his head. 'That's a tough one. I'm not really sure. Maybe at a conference?'

'And when was that, sir?' Chris said, his tone pleasant.

Miles turned to look at Chris. 'Erm, you know, I'm not even sure it was a conference. Perhaps I saw her in the supermarket. Saturday morning shopping. Or at the recycling place. We like to do our bit for the planet, don't we honey?'

Somehow, Clare couldn't imagine the Sharps carting bags of recycling to the supermarket on a Saturday morning. But she nodded in agreement. 'And did you speak to Alison?' she asked. 'At the recycling point?'

Miles spread his hands. 'I'm sorry – I really can't remember.'

Clare tried another tack. 'Did you share this house with Alison when you were married?'

Miles nodded, on surer ground now. 'Yes. We bought it together. Pricey, mind you. But we were lucky. Got in early with a decent offer.'

'And when you divorced,' Clare went on. 'You stayed?'

'Yes. Alison – she seemed less bothered about it. Just wanted it all signed and sealed. So I offered to buy her out. All legal and above board, of course. Half the market value.'

'And you were seeing Mrs Sharp at that time? You were in a relationship?'

Miles shifted on his seat. 'Well...'

'I don't see why this is such a big deal,' Cheryl interrupted. 'They were married and now they're not. She was dead boring, if you must know. She was boring, and he was bored with her. There's nothing wrong with realising a relationship is dead and moving on to a better one. So yes, we had an affair while Miles and Alison were still married. It happens, Inspector. Get over it.'

Clare felt Chris shift in his chair beside her but she continued to smile. 'And how did Alison feel about it?'

Miles shot a glance at his wife. 'What Cheryl means, Inspector, is that Alison and I, we knew we weren't happy. That it wasn't working. And sometimes it takes something – or someone – to force you into facing it. Cheryl – she did us all a favour, Alison included.'

Clare doubted Alison Reid had seen it that way but she simply smiled at him. 'That's fine, Mr Sharp. I'm just trying to build up a picture here. And we won't keep you much longer. Just a couple more questions, then we'll be on our way.'

Miles put a hand on his wife's shoulder and squeezed it. 'We'll help in any way we can.'

'When did Alison leave the firm?'

'Pretty much as soon as we started divorce proceedings,' Miles said. 'Five or six years ago.' He put a suntanned hand to his chin and rubbed it. 'It was awkward, you know. I offered to help her find something but she said she'd manage. She had holidays to take and I wanted to make things easy so I gave her two months' salary and she left that day.'

'More than he needed to,' Cheryl said. 'Really generous.'

Clare nodded. And then she turned to Cheryl. 'And you, Mrs Sharp, when did you last see Alison?'

The hesitation was just long enough. Cheryl looked down at the dog on her lap and began fondling Pixie's ears. 'Oh, I'm not sure. I mean it's not like we were friends.'

'But you have seen her recently?'

Cheryl had gathered her wits now and she lifted her gaze to meet Clare's. 'I really can't remember, Inspector. Like Miles, I probably met her in the supermarket. It's not like there's lots of choice in St Andrews. We all tend to shop in the same places.'

Clare rose and fished a card from her pocket. 'We won't keep you any longer then. Thank you for your time and, if you do remember anything else, please call me.'

Cheryl remained seated with the dog while Miles showed them out, closing the sitting room door behind him.

'Erm, I don't suppose you know anything about the funeral, Inspector?'

'Sorry, I don't.'

He rubbed his chin again. 'I wonder if I should be doing something about it – I mean with her mother's dementia...'

Clare smiled. 'We'd better get on, Mr Sharp. Thanks again for your time.'

They walked towards the car and Clare knew without looking that he was watching them leave. As they pulled on seat belts, Chris glanced back.

'Still watching,' he said.

'I bet he is.' She threw the car into reverse, backing up until she could swing round and out of the drive. 'He's torn between not wanting us to know he's seen Alison recently – 'cause I'm pretty sure he has seen her – and wondering if she's left him anything in her will. That house in Lindsay Gardens isn't a patch on the Sharps' house but you know what prices in St Andrews are like.'

'You reckon he might fall heir to the house?'

Clare pulled out into the road and turned the car back towards the town centre. 'Not a hope. The care home will swallow up anything that's left.'

'Yeah, suppose.'

'Fancy some lunch?'

'Definitely.'

They drove along in silence for a few minutes then Chris said, 'Shifty pair, aren't they?'

'Yeah. And he seemed to know about Alison's mum's dementia.'

'You did mention it.'

'Nope. I said she was ill. I didn't say what was wrong.'

Chris thought for a moment. 'Neither you did. You reckon they're lying about when they last saw Alison?'

'Definitely. The question is: what are they hiding and how do we find out?'

Chapter 7

They stopped at a sandwich shop to pick up a quick lunch.

'No mayo on mine,' Clare called as Chris jumped out of the car. While she waited, she took the chance to call Jim. 'How are things, Jim?'

'All fine, Clare. The body's been removed now and SOCO reckon they'll finish by the end of the day.'

'Okay but I want a cop on the door, day and night. Just until we have the result of the PM.'

'Will do.'

'Anything else I should know?'

'SOCO are asking if you want Alison Reid's laptop and mobile.'

'Yes please. I'm just grabbing a bit of lunch just now. If you could let them know I'll pick them up shortly?'

Chris opened the car door and a blast of cold air came in with him. Clare started the engine again, turning up the heater.

'Chicken satay or brisket with cheddar?' he said, pulling on his seat belt. 'Both no mayo.'

'Ooh they sound amazing.' Clare pulled the car away and headed down towards Golf Place and turned into the car park in front of the Golf Museum. This early in January, with snow still on the ground, it was almost empty and she drove to the far end, parking in front of a shallow inlet, bounded by rocks. The tide was out and the wet sand was dotted with little birds rushing about the water line.

'Sanderlings,' Clare said, killing the engine.

'I've never heard of them. How do you know? Oh wait – don't tell me: Geoff was a twitcher as well as an expert on fake 1920s houses.'

'Why do you always assume I learned everything from Geoff?' She reached across him into the glove box and took out a folded tea towel. She spread this over her knee, protecting her work suit from the sandwich. 'I knew stuff before I met him, you know.'

'You're a dab hand with a knife and fork now, though,' Chris said. 'Give the lad some credit.'

Chris dodged the back of Clare's hand and reached into the brown paper bag for the sandwiches. 'Chicken satay?' he said.

'Mm. Please. My shout next time.'

'Aye, so you say.'

Clare bit into the sandwich and almost as soon as she did a large grey and white herring gull appeared in front of them, perched on the railing. It looked pointedly into the car, as the wind ruffled its feathers, its yellow beak a splash of colour in an otherwise grey vista.

'Not a chance,' Chris said to the gull, biting into his brisket and cheese roll. The gull was not deterred and continued to scope him out, shifting occasionally on its feet.

'You're not doing Veganuary, then?' Clare asked.

Chris shook his head, his mouth full of sandwich. 'Sara is, though,' he said wiping a smear of relish off his chin.

'Ooh, lucky you.'

'No milk for the coffee. She's bought this oat milk instead. It's okay but I miss the real stuff.'

Clare laughed. 'Are you sure you two are compatible?'

Chris hesitated and Clare put down her sandwich. 'Oh no, Chris. I've not put my foot in it, have I? You two are okay...'

Chris's face began to redden. 'Actually, we're more than okay...'

Clare waited, unsure what was coming.

'I'm not supposed to tell anyone – but we're engaged!'

'Oh, wow, Chris. That's wonderful news. When did this happen? Did she say yes right away? When are you going to tell everyone? When's the wedding?'

'Godsake, Clare – calm down! Okay, I proposed on Hogmanay but we don't have a date yet. She said yes right away and she's going to announce it tomorrow; and if you let on I've told you she'll kill me.' He smiled. 'Satisfied?'

'Yes, thank you sergeant. But, seriously Chris, I am so happy for you both. It couldn't happen to a nicer couple. Well, Sara's nice, at least...'

Chris ignored this. 'I've booked a party but it's a surprise so you mustn't tell her.'

'Scout's honour. Where is it?'

'The Kenlybank Hotel. Saturday the sixteenth. You'll come, yeah?'

'You bet. The Kenlybank, eh? Very posh.'

'Nah. It's their smaller function room. Still big enough for a ceilidh though.'

Clare hesitated, then Chris spoke again.

'I know what you're thinking. You're remembering that murder at the hotel. With the Land Rover.'

'It had crossed my mind.'

'Clare, we're police officers. If we avoided everywhere there was an incident we'd never leave our front doors. It's a lovely hotel and we'll have a great night.'

She smiled at him and gave him a gentle punch on the arm. 'Yes we will. Just try not to have any of your guests killed. It does put a damper on things...'

They gathered up the rubbish and Chris went to put it in a nearby bin, followed a little too closely by the hopeful gull. Clare started the engine and put the heater up to high again. The snow was certainly melting but it was still bloody cold.

'Where now?' Chris said, jumping back in and rubbing his hands together to warm them up.

'I want to go back to Lindsay Gardens. They've got Alison's laptop and mobile. Might be something that helps fill in the gaps.' Clare pulled on her seat belt. 'Then you, Sergeant West, can run them down to Tech Support for me.'

He sighed. 'It's always me, isn't it?'

'I know. Aren't you lucky?'

Chapter 8

It was growing dark by the time Chris returned to the station. Clare had arrived just before him and was in the kitchen making a coffee when he appeared.

'Laptop and mobile dropped off okay?' she asked.

'Yeah. Skeleton staff at Tech Support until tomorrow but they'll check them as soon as they can.'

Clare nodded. 'I managed to track down Alison Reid's solicitor. So at least he can take charge of the funeral, once we release the body.'

'Suppose that's something,' Chris said, rubbing his hands together. 'The temperature's fairly dropping out there.'

Clare glanced out of the window. The sun was low in the sky now, casting an orange glow out to the north-west. 'Yeah,' she agreed. 'Going to be another cold one.'

'So,' Chris said, hovering in the kitchen doorway. 'What now?'

Clare sipped at her coffee. 'Not much more we can do until we have the post-mortem report.'

'Does that mean…'

'Go on,' Clare said. 'Get off home. But in early tomorrow, mind.'

Clare took the mug into her office, flicking on the light. The cold hit her and she bent to turn her radiator up high. Then she sat at the desk and switched on her computer. As she waited for it to warm up she leafed through the mail on her desk. There was nothing that looked like it couldn't wait until tomorrow and she turned to her monitor, clicking to check her emails.

As she waited for her Inbox to load she felt vaguely unsettled. Perhaps it was the cold – she wasn't sure. But, after two weeks away, the station seemed a strange place. Almost as though she didn't belong here. Maybe she'd feel different tomorrow. The holiday would be properly over by then.

Her Inbox finally stopped loading and she ran an eye idly down the messages looking for anything that needed her attention; but it was mostly requests for crime statistics and reports that were now overdue. There was one that caught her eye and she clicked to read it. The subject was:

Admin Assistant: Zoe McManus

'Yippee,' Clare said to herself. She'd been asking for a civilian member of staff for months and her request had finally been granted. She read,

> Zoe McManus will be attached to St Andrews station for an initial period of twelve months, from Tuesday, 5th January.
>
> Zoe will report at 9:00 a.m. She has already undertaken the Civilian Induction Programme. Please ensure she also receives local orientation training, as appropriate.

Things were looking up. She scanned the rest of the emails and, finding nothing urgent, closed down her computer. She rinsed her cup in the kitchen then walked back out to the front office, stopping only to ask Gillian, one of the uniformed PCs, to have the car park gritted. That done, she emerged into the dying January light. It hadn't been a long day – not by major enquiry standards – but it had been mentally exhausting. The circumstances of Alison Reid's life and death, her poor mother, lost to dementia, and the mean-spiritedness of Cheryl Sharp – it all felt a bit overwhelming now and she was surprised to find tears pricking her eyes. Maybe it was the come-down after Christmas, or perhaps it was the knowledge that, before the night was out, she was going to end her relationship with Geoffrey Dark. Geoff, the man who at one time she had thought was about to propose. But instead he had gone off to Boston, leaving Clare to wonder if she'd ever really known him at all.

She picked her way across the slushy car park towards her car. Chris was right. The slush was crisping up already and it would certainly freeze tonight. Pulling out of the car park, she felt the back wheels of the car slip, then the juddering of the ABS. As she turned onto Largo Road she saw the welcome sight of a yellow lorry heading towards her, spraying its mix of grit and salt across the road. She hoped it had come from the Craigtoun Road – her route back to Daisy Cottage. The slush she had driven through that morning would soon turn to ice. The car thermometer was reading minus one now and she felt sure the temperature would drop further as the night went on.

As she drove, her mind drifted back to Christmas. She'd been so excited about Geoff coming back from Boston and, unusually, she'd opted to take the full two weeks' holiday. It was normally a busy time at work but she reckoned she deserved a proper break.

And it had been a break. She and Geoff had travelled through to Clare's family in Glasgow on Christmas Eve, laden with gifts, crackers, an enormous ham – Clare's contribution to the meal – and a bottle of Glenfiddich which Geoff had brought. Clare's mother had been delighted with the ham, baked in a Cumberland sauce glaze and studded with cloves. Clare hadn't the heart to tell her she'd bought it ready-baked from a deli in St Andrews. If it made her mother happy to think she was turning into a domestic goddess who was she to disabuse her of the notion? Geoff had been all charm and relaxed good humour. He had that happy knack of slipping easily into any gathering and Clare had basked in her parents' approval. Even James, her little nephew, now formally diagnosed with autism, was mostly on good form and it had been the happiest Christmas Clare could recall.

Or at least that's how she hoped it had looked to her family. She couldn't put her finger on what the problem was but it was something to do with Geoff lending himself to her family for a few days. He wasn't giving himself to them, or even to Clare – not in the way that Chris and Sara would when they stood up to make their vows. Rather, he was like one of those bright butterflies, touching down on a flower for a short time before fluttering away again.

After Christmas he'd come back with her to Daisy Cottage and spread himself around for a few days, as though it was the happiest place in the world for him. But, as the days wore on, she knew he would soon be off, just like the butterfly; off to another garden.

And now, it was time to stop dithering. Time to do what she'd known she must do for some time. She turned the car into her drive and killed the engine. She would tell him tonight.

Benjy was thrilled at her return, and he brought her a towel from the kitchen to demonstrate this, shaking it from side to side, as though it was a rabbit he was trying to stun. She retrieved the towel, earning herself a volley of sharp barks in protest.

'Really?' she said, in the sternest voice she could manage. 'Is that any way to speak to your mother?'

She put the towel straight into the washing machine and opened the freezer to find something to defrost for her evening meal. Her mother, as usual, had sent her back with a dozen homemade meals that could be heated from frozen and she took out a chicken pie, topped with cheesy mashed potato. There was half a bag of carrots in the fridge and she laid these out beside the frozen pie to cook later. Still full of chicken satay from lunchtime, she flopped down on the sofa, kicking her shoes across the room. Benjy leapt up to join her and she lay there for a few minutes, going back over her day.

Had there been something iffy about Miles and Cheryl Sharp? Or was she looking for something that wasn't there?

Maybe her dislike of the couple was clouding her judgement. But then she thought back to the moment she had asked each of them when they had last seen Alison, and she felt sure one or both of them was hiding something. The question was what? Was marriage to Cheryl more than Miles had bargained for, causing him to seek tea and sympathy from his ex-wife? Or more than that? She couldn't see Miles admitting to anything and Alison certainly couldn't tell them. She had to hope the laptop and phone would yield something.

Her phone pinged, cutting across her thoughts. A message from Chris.

> Forgot to remind you –
>
> Not a word about U NO WOT!!!
>
> See you tomorrow
>
> C

Clare found she was smiling. She was so happy for Chris and Sara. They'd been through a lot together and now they were settling down for a lifetime of happiness. She sat up on the sofa and swung her legs round to stand.

In the kitchen she took a bottle of Chianti from the wine rack and uncorked it. She poured herself a large glass and drank half of it down then checked her watch. It would be mid-morning in Boston. She picked up her phone, swiping until she found Geoffrey's number and she clicked to dial. He answered after a few rings, full of bonhomie. She listened to him for a few seconds then she said, 'Geoff, I think it's time we talked properly. About us...'

Tuesday, 5th January

Chapter 9

Clare arrived at the station just after half past eight to find it full of chatter. A small group had collected round Sara who was proudly showing off a diamond solitaire ring. She did her best to look surprised and gave her PC a warm hug.

'Oh Sara! What a wonderful start to the new year. I'm thrilled for you both.' She had obviously done a good job of hiding her knowledge of the engagement, earning a grateful smile from Chris. 'So when's the wedding?' she went on.

'No plans yet, boss. We just want to enjoy being engaged, don't we?'

In the midst of all the excitement, Clare didn't notice the front door opening and a young woman walking in. Suddenly the hubbub died down and Clare turned to see her. She was about twenty-five with curly hair, as red as a postbox. She wore false eyelashes and killer red lipstick, and was swathed in a pink faux-fur coat. In the sober surroundings of the station, the only other spark of colour Chris's green tie, she cut a striking figure. The crowd round Sara melted away and Gillian, at the front desk, smiled at the woman.

'Hi there. Can I help?'

The woman looked round and flushed a little, no doubt conscious that she had interrupted something. 'Zoe McManus. I'm starting work here today.'

Clare regarded Zoe with something approaching dismay. She had hoped for someone older with a couple of decades' clerical experience behind them. Zoe seemed as if she might be more interested in having her nails done. But Clare wasn't about to look a gift horse in the mouth. 'Hi Zoe, I'm Clare – the DI here. Let's grab a hot drink and we can chat in my office.'

Over mugs of tea Zoe told Clare she'd worked for Police Scotland for the past two years. 'And in a solicitor's office before that.'

'And you've used the online systems before?'

'Oh yeah. They're fine. Pretty easy once you get to know them.'

'Are you living locally, Zoe?'

'Yeah, flat in town. Just renting.'

They exchanged a few more pleasantries then Clare said, 'If you've finished your tea I'll take you to meet Jim Douglas. He's the station sergeant and he's been here for ever. Anything you want to know – just ask Jim.'

Having left Zoe in Jim's capable hands, Clare sought out Chris. 'If you can tear yourself away from your lovely bride-to-be, we have a call to pay.'

Chris picked up his coat and followed Clare out to the car. After the early frost it had clouded over and it looked as if it might snow again. 'Bloody January,' he said, climbing into the car. 'Where are we going anyway?'

'Crossford Financial,' Clare said, turning up the fan heater to clear the windscreen which had started to ice up again. 'Alison Reid's employer.'

The windscreen cleared and Clare turned the car north, heading for Market Street. The roads had been gritted but the pavements were still icy. As they drove up the gentle incline on Bridge Street she saw more than one pedestrian stagger as they lost their footing. 'Can you message Jim and ask him to get onto the council about the pavements please? Before the hospital's queued out the door.'

While Chris sent Jim a message Clare scanned Market Street for a parking space. Crossford Financial was a small office next to a gift shop and she managed to squeeze into a space just a few doors further on. The pavements in Market Street were well-trodden and some thoughtful shopkeepers had attacked the ice with snow shovels.

'Sara seems happy,' Clare said as they walked back towards Crossford's office.

'Well of course she is. She gets to spend the rest of her life washing my socks.'

'You wish!'

'Good reaction to her news, by the way,' Chris said. 'Remind me never to play poker with you.'

Clare pushed open the door and approached the reception desk. She produced her warrant card and asked to speak to whoever was in charge.

'That would be Mr Crossford,' the receptionist said. 'I'll just see if he's available.'

While they waited, Clare looked round the office. It had clearly been part of a house at one time. There was ornate cornicing around the ceiling and in the centre was the original plaster rose. The skirting boards were deep too and a door behind the receptionist was panelled in the Victorian style. Then she gave herself a shake. She had to stop viewing everything through Geoffrey's eyes. That part of her life was over now. The conversation had been less awkward than she'd expected. He had seemed surprised but not unduly upset.

If you're sure that's what you want, Clare?

I'm not sure it's what I want, Geoff, but it seems the sensible thing to do.

She tore herself away from analysing the architecture of the room and studied the posters on the wall. One said,

Let Us Help You Find

The Right Mortgage for You.

She nudged Chris. 'You two thought about buying somewhere?'

He was prevented from answering by the panelled door opening. A man with wavy brown hair in a checked suit appeared. He smiled when he saw Clare and Chris and moved forward to greet them. He looked as if smiling came easily and Clare couldn't help comparing him with Miles Sharp whose default expression, she suspected, was a scowl. She began to understand why Alison Reid had chosen to work for this man who, on first meeting, seemed warm and friendly.

'Good morning, officers. I'm Derek Crossford. I understand you wanted to see me?'

Clare noticed the receptionist had stopped typing and was pretending to arrange some papers on her desk. 'Is there somewhere we could talk?'

Derek Crossford led them through the door and down a short passage to his office at the back of the building. It was a small room but there were comfortable chairs and a mahogany side table with a coffee machine, kettle and an impressive selection of teas. Derek indicated the table. 'Can I offer you something to drink?'

Clare waved this away. 'Thanks, but we won't keep you long. It's about one of your employees – Alison Reid.'

Derek Crossford put a hand to his face and rubbed it. 'She's not turned up this morning. I'm guessing you're here because there's something wrong.'

'I'm afraid I have some very bad news. Alison was found dead at home, yesterday.'

The colour drained from his face and he seemed to be struggling to speak. Then, finally he said, 'Alison? Dead?' His voice was hoarse and the shock genuine. 'But she's so young…' He looked from Clare to Chris. 'I can't take it in. Can… can I ask what happened?'

'We're still awaiting the outcome of the post-mortem but, for now, we are treating Alison's death as unexplained.'

Derek rose from his desk. 'I think I'll have that coffee, if you don't mind. Are you sure I can't persuade you?'

'Actually,' Clare said glancing at Chris who was doing his best puppy-dog eyes at her, 'that would be lovely. Milk, no sugar for us both.'

Over cups of coffee, Derek Crossford explained that Alison had been with them for around five years.

'And how was she? As an employee, I mean,' Clare asked.

Derek almost seemed to be surprised by the question. 'Oh, she was excellent. Hardworking, reliable – to be honest, Inspector, I was surprised she wanted to work here. She could easily have gone to one of the larger firms for a far better salary.'

'And yet she stayed five years?'

'She did. I think…' he broke off, apparently choosing his words, '…I think she found it – easy to be here, if that makes sense.' He hesitated again, glancing down at his coffee cup, then raised his eyes to meet Clare's. 'I'm not one for gossip, Inspector. But St Andrews is a small town. And Alison's ex-husband – well, he has a bit of a reputation, you know? With the ladies, I mean… and I think she found the divorce quite hard. Quite public.' He glanced round the room. 'We're a small firm, you see. Here, she could slip under the radar. Come in, do her job, go home.'

Clare studied Derek Crossford as he spoke. He had kind eyes and she could see why Alison Reid had felt comfortable working for him. He wasn't as flash as Miles Sharp – probably drove an old Volvo – but perhaps that was why Alison chose to bury herself in this tiny business. Maybe you can have too much flash. 'Did she talk about her private life?'

'Not to me, anyway.'

'Did she socialise with the other members of staff? Go for drinks or have people to her house?'

Derek spread his hands. 'I really don't know, Inspector. But I can ask Kathy on reception. She might know. Although…' he broke off.

'Yes?'

'Now I come to think of it, I did go to her house once – Lindsay Gardens. Both houses actually.'

'Do you mind if I ask why?'

'It was a bookcase. Miles was getting rid of it and Alison decided she would take it. But she couldn't get it in her car. I've a Volvo Estate so I offered to help her move it.'

Clare suppressed a smile at the mention of Derek Crossford's car. Maybe she was psychic! 'So you went to Miles Sharp's house in Buchanan Gardens?'

'That's right. He met us at the door. The bookcase was in the hall and he helped me carry it out to my car. Then I drove it round to Lindsay Gardens and Alison and I lugged it into her house between us. Pretty heavy but we managed it in the end.'

Clare glanced down at the wedding band on Derek Crossford's left hand. 'I'm sorry to ask, Mr Crossford, but was there anything between you and Alison? More than colleagues, I mean?'

He looked surprised. 'Of course not. I'm happily married, Inspector, and Alison wasn't that kind of person. I really liked her as a colleague and a friend. But that's as far as it went.'

Clare smiled. 'Thank you. I don't suppose you know if she had anyone else in her life?'

He shook his head. 'We never really had that kind of conversation. But Kathy – our receptionist – she might know. Would you like me to call her in?'

'Please.'

Derek Crossford picked up the phone to speak to his receptionist. A few seconds later the door opened and the woman who had greeted Clare and Chris entered.

'Kathy, these officers are here to ask about Alison. Perhaps you could answer a few questions?'

Kathy gaped. 'Is something wrong? Is Alison in some kind of trouble?'

Clare indicated a seat. Kathy hesitated then, with a glance at her boss, she sat down slowly, perching on the edge of the chair.

'I'm afraid Alison was found dead yesterday morning,' Clare said.

Kathy gasped, and put a hand to her mouth. Her face drained of colour.

'I'm so sorry. I realise it must be a dreadful shock. But we're trying to get a picture of Alison – what her life was like,' Clare said. 'If you feel up to it, of course.'

Kathy nodded mutely, and Clare went on.

'Did Alison have any close friends? Or a boyfriend? Anyone she saw regularly?'

Kathy shook her head. 'Not that I ever saw, Inspector. I mean, she kept herself to herself here, but I think she was a bit of a loner anyway. Mind you...' she broke off.

'Yes?'

Kathy glanced at her boss then said, 'A couple of the girls were trying to get her to start dating again. I think they gave Alison a kind of makeover. In the lunchbreak, of course.' She looked at Derek Crossford again and seemed relieved when he waved this away with a hand gesture.

'Maybe we could have a quick word with them,' Clare said, and Derek Crossford suppressed a smile.

'I'm guessing it's Fay and Kezia?' he said, and Kathy nodded.

'Did she talk about what she did away from the office at all?' Clare went on. 'Evenings? Or weekends? Holidays, even?'

Kathy was quiet for a moment, then she said, 'She read a lot. Always talking about books. And sometimes she mentioned a TV programme she'd seen. But never anything I was watching. She went on a river cruise once. Some historical theme, it was. Guest speakers and the like.'

Clare smiled. 'Thanks so much, Kathy. That's really helpful.'

Kathy glanced at Derek Crossford and she made to rise from her seat. 'Well, if there's nothing else?'

'Perhaps you could ask the other two ladies to join us,' Clare said. Kathy glanced across at her boss.

'Of course,' he said, and Kathy went to fetch her colleagues.

There was a quiet tap on the door a few minutes later and two young women in their mid-twenties entered. They eyed Clare and Chris, then their boss.

'Nothing to worry about, ladies,' Derek Crossford said. 'Inspector Mackay just wants to ask you a few questions.'

Fay and Kezia confirmed what Kathy had said. They had persuaded Alison to let them do her hair and make-up for her dating profile.

'She looked lovely,' Fay said, and Kezia nodded.

'Which dating site was it?' Clare asked.

'Attracto,' Kezia said. 'She was going to update her profile over Christmas,' she added.

'Do you know if she went on any dates?'

The pair glanced at each other then back at Clare. 'Don't think so,' Kezia said. 'She told us she'd send a WhatsApp if she had a date.'

They learned little more from Fay and Kezia and the pair escaped with evident relief.

Clare waited until they had closed the door behind them then she turned back to Derek Crossford. 'There is one more thing, Mr Crossford...'

'Anything at all, Inspector. Under the circumstances I'll be happy to help.'

'Could we have access to Alison's computer and her diary?'

Derek looked doubtful and Clare went on.

'At this stage we don't have a warrant so you are within your rights to refuse. But we're having difficulty piecing together Alison's last movements. It's just possible there might be something among her work files that could help us. If we can get into her account...'

He was silent for a few moments, then said, 'Of course. Everything we do here is above board, Inspector. We have nothing to hide. And if it helps you find out what happened to that poor lass...'

'Thank you, Mr Crossford. We're very grateful.'

He rose and said, 'Bring your coffees if you like. Her office is just next door.' He led them into a room, similar in size but without the tea and coffee-making facilities. He went round the desk and switched on Alison's computer. 'I have Administrator permissions so I can access all accounts on our network. Obviously it's rarely necessary but...' He tapped at the keyboard then walked back round the desk. 'I'll leave you to it, officers. Just shout if you need any help.'

Chapter 10

They studied the desktop shortcuts on Alison Reid's computer.

'What are we looking for?' Chris said, peering over Clare's shoulder.

'Anything personal, anything out of the ordinary and anything that includes that shifty pair in Buchanan Gardens.' She opened Alison's email and typed Cheryl into the search box. There were eleven results and Clare scanned them. None appeared to have anything to do with Cheryl Sharp. She repeated the search with Lafferty, then Miles but there was nothing that seemed to be connected to the couple.

She tried again with Christmas and Weekend but, again, she found nothing to help fill in the gaps in the weeks leading up to Alison's death. She turned instead to Alison's diary and navigated her way to the week before Christmas. There were reminders about clients' tax returns and the January deadline, an entry on the eighteenth of December for the Crossford Staff Christmas Lunch and a series of appointments with names and phone numbers.

'Check when her last day at work was,' Chris suggested.

Clare moved to the end of December and began working back.

'Looks like the twenty-third,' she said. 'See?' and she indicated the date.

'WFH?,' Chris said.

'Working from home. See how she's put AL against the rest of December?'

Chris nodded. 'Annual leave.'

Clare moved to the documents folder and again performed a search for Miles and Cheryl Sharp but there was nothing. She spent a few more minutes browsing through the list of documents and finally she checked the Pictures folder. There were a few publicity shots of the Crossford staff, formal posed photos taken at desks, and a folder entitled Summer BBQ. Clare opened it to find a dozen or so photos of staff members, casually dressed in summer clothes, tucking into burgers, kebabs and plastic cups of beer. She recognised Kathy, Fay and Kezia in some of the photos but there seemed to be none of Alison. Maybe she had been the photographer.

She rose from her chair. 'Want a look?' she said.

Chris sat down and began scrolling through the files. After a few minutes he too rose. 'Nothing here.'

'I agree,' Clare said. 'Shut it down and let's get back to the station.'

–

As they drove down Bridge Street tiny flakes of snow began to settle on the windscreen. Clare flicked the wipers on to clear them, but by the time they reached the station larger flakes were falling steadily, straight down, the black road surface gradually turning white.

They ran across the car park, into the warmth and light of the station. Jim was settled at the public enquiry desk which, unusually, was absent of callers.

'How's Zoe doing?' Clare asked, as she shrugged off her coat, shaking it to dislodge a few snowflakes.

'Pretty good, from what I can see,' Jim said. 'She's already input the reports that came in over the holiday weekend and she's going through the lost property lists now. She seems to know what she's about.'

'Keep an eye, all the same,' Clare said. 'She wouldn't be the first to be overburdened with confidence.'

'Call for you, boss,' Sara said. 'Neil Grant.'

The pathologist. 'That was quick,' Clare said. 'Put it through to my office, would you Sara?'

Clare flicked the light on in her office, glad to feel the warmth from the radiator, and she shook the mouse to bring her computer to life. She pulled the blinds back from the window for a few seconds and watched the progress of the snow. It was lying all right. The street lights had come on, even though it was still morning. There was going to be precious little daylight today. She just hoped she'd get home to Daisy Cottage okay. She turned back to her desk and sat down, clicking the phone to speaker.

'Neil,' she said. 'Happy new year to you.'

'And to you too, Clare. Good time over Christmas?'

'Yes, thanks. It's a distant memory now, though. So I presume this is Alison Reid? Our body from yesterday.'

'God, no, Clare. I've not even looked at her yet. Still wading through the holiday backlog.'

'Oh.' Clare couldn't keep the disappointment from her tone. She had hoped to tie up Alison's death quickly. 'So, if it's not Alison...'

'It's one that came in just before the new year. A woman in her early thirties.'

'Sorry Neil – I was off for the whole two weeks and I've not caught up yet. Can you fill me in?'

'Sure. A woman found face down in the Kinness Burn. Early hours of the twenty-ninth.'

'Name?'

'Ingrid McKinnie. I think it was the Dundee Inspector who dealt with it.'

Clare pulled the keyboard towards her and typed Ingrid's name into the search box. Within a few seconds the report appeared. 'Says here it was a suspected drowning with alcohol as a possible contributing factor. Does the PM confirm that?'

'It can be hard to tell, sometimes. As to whether she'd been drinking, there was food and alcohol in her stomach.'

'But she did drown?'

Neil hesitated. 'I can't be absolutely sure. Drowning – well it can leave certain clues: bloody froth in the airways, for example. But not always. Sometimes, Clare, it's a diagnosis by default – when nothing else makes sense.'

'Why do I sense a but...'

'Because I don't think she did drown. I think she was dead by the time she hit the water.'

Clare waited.

'She had Rohypnol in her system.'

'So she was drugged.'

'She was.'

'Any evidence of sexual assault?'

'Not that we can tell. I mean, she had been in the water a few hours but not fully submerged. I can't be certain but I'd say she probably wasn't assaulted. The semen tests came back negative.'

Clare thought for a moment, then she said, 'I can't see why someone would drug a woman and not assault her.' She scrolled through the incident report as she was speaking. 'It looks like her handbag was found by the body – money in the purse. It doesn't make sense, Neil.'

'I agree. It's an odd one. There are some marks on the neck but...'

'Eh?' Clare was suddenly alert. This was sounding familiar. 'What kind of marks?'

'Some slight bruising round the neck.'

'Consistent with strangulation?'

Neil hesitated then said, 'Possibly. But it's not heavy bruising. Certainly no evidence of a struggle.'

'Which would make sense if she was drugged.'

'True. But, even then, I'd expect to see a bit more bruising, and petechial haemorrhages – you know, those little pinpoint bruises around the face and eyes.'

'So what's your thinking?'

'I'm going to check a couple of things and come back to you, Clare. I just wanted to give you the heads-up that it probably wasn't a drowning.'

'Neil...' she broke off, trying to order her thoughts.

'Yeah?'

'I don't suppose you could put yesterday's death to the head of the queue? Raymond mentioned she had some bruising to her neck too.'

'Will do. Just remind me of her name again?'

'Alison Reid.'

'Okay, Clare. Back as soon as I can.'

'Thanks, Neil.'

She sat for a few minutes, thinking about Ingrid McKinnie and Alison Reid. Could their deaths be connected? It didn't sound likely. Ingrid had died possibly on her way home from a night out, whereas Alison seemed to live a quiet life. Ingrid was found outdoors, fully clothed, partly submerged in the Kinness Burn, the narrow stream that flows through St Andrews down to the harbour. Alison was found at home, naked, in her own bath. It didn't make sense to connect the two deaths.

Looking again at the incident report she saw that Ingrid's home was in Lamond Drive. Not too far from the burn. If she'd been out partying she was probably on her way home from one of the bars in South Street. Maybe some bloke chatted her up in the pub then slipped the Rohypnol into her glass. He could have walked her as far as the burn then realised she was nearly unconscious and left her to die. Could she have died of exposure? Neil would surely have said. But maybe he couldn't be sure. Alcohol was a factor in fatal hypothermia. She knew that much. It lowered the body temperature without the victim realising. Was that what had happened here?

Suddenly Clare thought she would very much like to talk this over with DCI Alastair Gibson. She hadn't seen so much of him lately, not since their burgeoning relationship had fizzled out, with Geoffrey's sudden return from Boston. They hadn't really spoken of it since, and now Clare thought these two sudden deaths would be a good excuse to give him a call. She reached for the phone and dialled his work number. And then she listened to the message saying he was on annual leave until Wednesday, with the usual option to leave a message. She ended the call and sat for a few minutes, turning it over in her head. She looked at her phone contacts. She had his home number but somehow she didn't feel comfortable using it. She clicked to dial his work number again and waited for the message prompt.

'Oh, hi, Al. Hope you're having a lovely break. I just wondered... if you're not too busy when you come back... I've a bit of an odd case I'd like to talk over. Only if you're not busy... erm, hope you're well. And happy new year.'

She put down the phone, thinking how stupid her message would sound when he heard it. He might even have been listening – screening his work calls from home so he'd know what was waiting for him in the morning. Maybe he would call her back. She stared at the phone for a few minutes then turned and looked out of the window. The snow was lying thickly now and she let out a sigh. January was such a long month.

Chapter 11

'She's doing great,' Jim said, nodding towards Zoe. 'I've checked what she's done this morning and it's all fine. What's more she's zipping through it. You want to hang on to this one, Clare.'

'I will, don't you worry. I'll have a chat to her in a bit. Just to let her know we appreciate her work.'

The station door opened and a snow-clad Sara entered, stamping snow off her shoes.

'My feet are wringing,' she said. 'Just as well I have a change in my locker.'

'Don't tell me you've been out on patrol in this weather?' Clare said.

Sara took off her outdoor coat and gave it a shake. 'Nope. Shoplifters again.'

'Really? I'd have thought Christmas would have seen an end to it.'

Clare followed Sara to the staff room where she took a change of shoes and socks from her locker. 'Where was it this time?'

'Pizzazz. Little boutique on South Street. Nice clothes. Manager reckons at least two dresses and a cashmere cardigan. Getting on for a hundred and fifty pounds' worth, she thought.'

'Any CCTV?'

Sara pulled off her wet socks and put them on the radiator to dry. 'Yes, I've copied it. Give me a few minutes to sort my feet out and I'll let you see it.'

'Get yourself a hot drink first,' Clare said, and she went off to chat to Zoe.

'See here,' Sara said, pointing at a grainy image of a woman in a long padded coat and a Baker Boy hat, pulled down over her eyes. She had a scarf wrapped round her neck making it impossible to see her hair.

'She seems to know where the cameras are,' Clare said. 'See how she looks down when she passes them.'

'Yep and she's carrying that big bag.'

'Probably a Faraday cage.' Seeing Sara's expression, she explained. 'Shoplifters use them to avoid setting off security alarms. They line the inside of the bag with foil – bit of parcel tape to hold it in place. The foil stops the security tag triggering the sensors at the door.'

'One of the other shops mentioned a woman with a big bag,' Sara said.

'The bigger stores are wise to it. When they spot customers carrying a bulky bag they usually keep an eye on them. Sometimes, just having a member of staff hovering is enough to put them off. Send them elsewhere. But the smaller shops don't generally have the staff for that which is why they're targeted. How many reports is that now?'

Sara thought for a moment. 'I'll have to check but I think it's six or seven.'

Clare frowned. 'We'll have to do something about it; or word will get out the town's an easy target.' She wandered over to the window and opened the blinds to peer out at the snow. 'I reckon some of the shops might close early today – if the snow doesn't stop. But tomorrow I'd like a few bodies out round the town, being visible. Call into the high-end shops, let them know we're here. And get as much CCTV footage as you can. There might be something to help identify the culprit.'

By mid-afternoon the snow was lying several inches deep. Clare checked the forecast and saw it was due to keep snowing for the rest of the day. She went to find Zoe.

'I know your flat's in the town, Zoe, but I think you should pack up now and head home. The snow's on for the next few hours and you've done a power of work already.'

'I don't mind staying,' Zoe said.

Clare smiled. 'Thanks, but I'll be happier if you go now. There's nothing that can't wait until tomorrow.'

'You're the boss,' Zoe said, shutting down her computer. 'See you in the morning.'

By four o'clock Clare was starting to worry that she might not get back to Daisy Cottage. 'Jim, I'm going to head off home. And I want any officers from out of town to get away too. The local lads can turn out if anything happens. But I reckon most folk will be staying indoors so hopefully it'll be a quiet evening.'

She went out to the car park to find Robbie shovelling snow away from the entrance. She waved a thank-you to him, put her bag in the car and took a collapsible spade from the boot. She spent a few minutes clearing the snow from around the tyres then she scraped the windows clear and jumped into the car. Her hair was white with large snowflakes and she was longing to be home. It was almost dark now and she switched on the car headlights. As she backed carefully out of her space she felt the tyres slip a little, but she made it out of the car park and was soon driving slowly along a snow-clad Largo Road. Her wipers squeaked rhythmically as they cleared the windscreen and she was struck by how silent the world became when traffic noise was muffled by snow. A lone figure – a man, possibly – was walking along the pavement, hood up and head down. His long coat was flecked with white, hands driven deep into his pockets and Clare hoped he didn't have much further to go.

As she neared the roundabout at the top of the road, she was relieved to see there were no other cars. She knew if she was forced to stop that she'd end up having to dig around the tyres to get going again. She turned the car gently, feeling the back wheels slip and she eased off the accelerator then touched it lightly, gaining traction.

The roads in the Bogward housing estate were little better but her heart rose when she saw a snow plough heading towards her, spraying snow left and right. She slowed to allow it to pass then steered her car across to the path it had cleared.

There were few other cars on the road and her progress was steady, if slow. After what seemed like an eternity, she reached her drive heaving a sigh of relief. Daisy Cottage was like a Christmas card, its red-brick walls dusted with snow, the roof clad with a thick layer of white. As she approached the wooden portico that sheltered the front door, she heard Benjy's welcoming bark and she put her key in the door, thankful to be home for the night.

She had left the heating on low for Benjy but now she went round the cottage, turning up radiators. Then she moved through to the kitchen and opened the back door. The garden was a picture, hedges and bushes plump with snow. It was impossible to tell where the path ended and the borders began and she picked her way carefully to the shed where the logs were stashed. She filled a stout bag with a mixture of logs and kindling and carried them back to the house, stamping her feet once more to avoid carrying snow into the kitchen. She whistled to Benjy who was cocking his leg, leaving a faint yellow trail in the snow and he came scampering back to the house. She soon had the fire going and she sat, perched on the edge of the sofa, warming her hands with Benjy at her feet. Once she was confident the fire had caught she added another log then switched on the sitting room lamps. Outside the sky was inky black and she drew the curtains across. The Christmas tree sat in the corner, reminding her for a moment of Alison Reid's house and she turned on the multicoloured lights, giving the room a festive glow. She had thought about taking the tree down that night but she decided she would enjoy it for one more evening.

She wondered if Neil had examined Alison's body or if he too had gone home early for fear of being snowed in at the mortuary. A glance at her phone told her there were no missed calls or messages. Tomorrow, then.

Clare ate another of her mother's frozen meals at the dining table, browsing through web pages on her laptop. Then she logged on to Facebook. She hadn't meant to look at DCI Gibson's page but somehow she found herself checking his timeline. She could see he was online and had just uploaded an album of photos which he'd called Innsbruck Ski Trip. So that was where he'd spent the Christmas break. She scrolled through the photos. They were like an advert for ski holidays. A group of them – six, she thought – three men and three women. All clad in brightly coloured ski jackets, goggles and, in some photos, helmets. They were tanned and attractive, full of happiness. There were photos of them standing on their skis, ready to go, others with skis propped up against their shoulders outside a wooden chalet. Some were taken in a bar with shots lined up on the table. There were no action photos but Clare had the impression the DCI was a confident skier. Something about the way he stood on the skis, as if impatient to be off. Not like her, with her one trip to Glenshee a few years ago, most of which she'd spent on her backside.

She flicked through the photos again, studying the group. Were they all friends? Or were these people he'd met out there? Or… had he gone out there with someone? As part of a couple – eating fondue and sipping glühwein in the evenings round a cosy fire? Clare put down her fork, her appetite gone. She rose from the table and went upstairs to her spare bedroom to fetch the Christmas decorations box. It was time to take the tree down.

Wednesday, 6th January

Chapter 12

The snow had stopped during the night but it was still dark when Clare forced herself out of bed. She pulled back her bedroom curtain but it was hard to see how thickly it had fallen. Downstairs, she opened the kitchen door to let Benjy out for a pee. The snow had blown against it and there was a cornice six inches high on the threshold. Benjy ran through it, scattering snow on the kitchen floor and launched himself at the garden, delighting in this new white world, almost disappearing up to his middle. He bounded along until he found his feet then cocked his leg.

In the kitchen Clare threw down a towel to mop up the melting snow and began making herself coffee and toast. Benjy reappeared, bringing more snow in with him and she stooped to wipe his paws with the towel. He began sniffing at the cupboard where his food was kept and Clare took the hint.

As she munched on toast she considered the day ahead, wondering if the DCI would return her call. There was something about the deaths of the two women that bothered her. Hopefully Neil would phone with the results of Alison's post-mortem and she'd have a better idea if there was a link. She had to hope not.

Her thoughts turned to Miles and Cheryl Sharp. Had they known Ingrid too? It seemed unlikely but she couldn't shake the feeling they were both hiding something.

The Rohypnol was another worrying factor. If there was someone in the town using the so-called date rape drug, she had to find the culprit before any more women were attacked.

As she drained her coffee mug it occurred to her there could have been other victims, perhaps too confused or ashamed to come forward. Maybe they should put out a message via social media. She tapped a note on her phone to speak to the press officer about that. They might have something ready-made they could share on Facebook and the like.

Thinking of Facebook reminded her of the DCI's skiing photos and, suddenly, she felt very lonely. She had ended things with Geoffrey. That had to be done, either way. But now it looked as if the DCI might have found himself a new partner.

And it was only January.

–

It took Clare a good ten minutes to clear the snow from around her car. As she worked, she heard the sound of a tractor approaching. She lifted her head as it passed her drive and was delighted to see the farmer had fixed a snow plough to the front of a red Massey Ferguson. A spray of dirty snow was thrown into her garden, but she didn't mind about that.

'God bless the farmers,' she muttered as she cleared the last of the snow at the entrance to her drive.

She drove along the newly ploughed road, thinking how beautiful the world was after a snowfall, the harsh edges smoothed out with a white blanket. Heading east she could see the sky beginning to grow light as sunrise approached and she was filled with a sudden longing for spring and for happier days.

With the roads newly cleared she was soon at the station. Someone had been out early, clearing a path to the front door again but the markings delineating the parking spaces were hidden. There were a few cars in the staff car park already and she lined hers up next to them. As she stepped out she saw the pink faux-fur coat approaching. Zoe was picking her way along Tom Morris Drive, an enormous pair of headphones clamped over her ears. She wore yellow fisherman's wellies on her feet and was carrying a Tupperware container. Clare waited to walk in with her.

'You're certainly dressed for the weather,' she said.

Zoe grinned. 'I love these wellies. You can keep your fancy expensive ones – I've had these for years and they're still going strong.'

'Is that your lunch?' Clare said, indicating the box.

Zoe laughed. 'I'd be some size if this was my lunchbox. No, I made a chocolate cherry cake last night. Just a thank-you to everyone for being so nice.'

'Oh Zoe! So much for my new year diet...' She held open the station door for Zoe.

'You don't have to eat it,' Zoe said, laughing again.

'Yeah, right.'

As Clare headed for her office her phone began to ring. She glanced at the display. The DCI. She tucked it under her ear and opened the office door flicking on the lights. 'Hi, Al. Happy new year.'

'Oh, yes. Um, happy new year, Clare. Hope you had a good break?'

'Yes, thanks. You?' She was about to mention his skiing trip then thought better of it. She didn't want him to think she was checking up on him.

'Yeah, it was great. I was away for a week. Just back last night so playing catch-up.' She thought she could hear a noise in the background, as if he was tapping at his keyboard while he spoke. 'Listen, Clare,' he went on, 'I got your message. Is it important? I've a hell of a lot to wade through today.'

She sat down in her chair, faintly nettled at this. He ought to know she wouldn't have called unless it was important. Or did he think it was a social call? 'Well...' She thought she heard him sigh. 'Just forget it, Al. I'll chat to Chris about it.'

'No, it's fine. I've got a couple of minutes.'

That's big of you, she thought but didn't say. Instead she related the events of the past twenty-four hours. 'I'm not even sure the two deaths are linked though...' she tailed off.

'Do you have a cause of death for either of them?'

'Nothing definite. I'm hoping to hear from Neil today.' She realised how lame the whole thing must have sounded. 'It's just, I have an odd feeling about these deaths.'

'Better to wait until you have something more concrete, Clare. Call me later if you want to chat again. Now, I really must go.' And, with that, he ended the call.

She sat for a minute, contemplating his reaction. He'd been terse, impatient to get off the phone. Was he really that busy? Or did he think Clare had more than work on her mind? And, if so, was he trying to put her off? She could hardly blame, him. She'd had her chance with him and she'd blown it. She sat back in her chair, staring at the phone. The call couldn't have been more than two minutes long.

Her office door opened and Chris looked in. 'Morning, boss. How's the snow out your way?'

She put the DCI to the back of her mind. 'Oh, you know. Pretty deep.' She indicated a chair. 'Come in and sit down, Chris. I could do with a chat.'

'Hold on…' He disappeared for a minute. When he returned he was carrying two pieces of Zoe's cake, wrapped in paper towels. 'Plates all gone,' he said, adding, 'greedy bastards.'

Clare eyed the cake. It did look lovely but it wasn't even nine o'clock. 'I'll save mine for later,' she said, putting it over on the filing cabinet.

'So, what's on your mind?' Chris said, breaking off a piece of cake and popping it in his mouth. He licked cherry jam off his fingers. 'Oh my God, this cake's amazing!'

'I had a phone call yesterday afternoon – not long before I went home.'

'Oh yeah?'

'Neil Grant.'

'That was quick.'

'No, it wasn't Alison Reid. Another sudden death – came in when I was on leave. Woman in her thirties, again – Ingrid McKinnie. Did you attend?'

Chris shook his head. 'Nope. I was off from Christmas Eve. Did Dundee not deal with it?'

'Yes they did. But Neil thinks it might be suspicious. Admittedly, she'd been drinking and was found in the Kinness Burn so it could have been a drunken accident. But the odd thing is there was Rohypnol in her system and no sign of sexual assault.'

'Washed away in the burn?'

'Neil doesn't think so. She wasn't fully submerged. And there were no trauma injuries.'

'Alcohol, though…'

'Yes, that's true.'

'And the Rohypnol would prevent her struggling so the absence of injuries doesn't mean she wasn't assaulted.'

'I suppose.'

'But you're not convinced?' Chris broke off another bit of cake. 'Oh, Clare,' he said, licking his lips, 'You really need to try this.'

'Maybe… I'm not sure.' She sat forward in her chair. 'Chris you remember the marks on Alison Reid's neck?'

'Yeah…'

'Well, according to Neil, there were marks on Ingrid McKinnie's neck too.'

'So, someone's picked her up in the pub, slipped her a tablet – walked her down to the burn meaning to assault her. Maybe had his hands round her neck then he's been disturbed – partygoers wandering past – he's left her and she's tumbled into the water.'

Clare considered this. 'Could be. But… if he'd been disturbed, would he have had time to strangle her?'

'You think she was strangled?'

'That's just it. I don't know. Neil was a bit reluctant to give me a cause of death. He's going to phone back today – ideally with Alison's results as well.'

'You're thinking they're linked?'

Clare shrugged. 'I'm just not sure.'

'No point in second-guessing it Clare. Wait till you've heard from Neil.' He rose, picking up the remains of his cake, and made to leave.

Clare's phone began to ring again. She glanced at the display. Diane Wallace from Tech Support. 'Hold on, Chris, it's Diane.'

After the exchange of new year greetings which Clare was starting to find tedious, Diane got straight to the point.

'We're swamped here, Clare, so I'll keep it short. The laptop wasn't password protected so I've downloaded all the data. It's in a folder on the network.'

'Brilliant. Thanks so much, Diane. Anything else on the laptop we should know about?'

'Nah. The usual social media apps. She wasn't logged in though and I've not got into them yet but I've got Craig, my boy wonder, running password crackers. Hopefully it won't take too long.'

'Okay, Diane. Let me know when you've got anything else, and let's catch up soon, yeah?'

She ended the call and turned to Chris. 'Alison's laptop. Diane's put the data on the network.' She picked up her mouse and navigated to the drive where Diane had uploaded the folder. She began with Alison's emails, sorting the messages by recipient. Then she glanced at Chris. 'Put that cake down and take a look at this.'

Chapter 13

'So, she was corresponding back and forth with Miles Sharp during December,' Chris said, sitting back in his seat.

'Looks like it. The question is why?'

'No idea. The earlier messages are all full of We need to meet and Time we talked but nothing concrete,' Chris said. 'And look at this one…'

Clare zoomed in to read the email Chris indicated. The subject was:

Think about it!

The message below the subject was simple:

Miles, it's a seriously bad idea.

Sorry, I know this isn't what you wanted to hear.

Alison

'What do you make of that?' Chris said.

'I'd say it's something neither of them wanted to be explicit about. And that makes me suspicious.'

'I wonder… do you think he might still have feelings for Alison?'

Clare shrugged. 'Goodness knows. Either way, they were both very careful about how they worded these emails. There's definitely something going on and it wouldn't surprise me if the lovely Cheryl knew nothing about it.'

'Want to pull him in for a chat?'

Clare considered this. 'Not yet, I think. Let's wait and see what Neil says about the cause of death.'

'Try a search for Cheryl.'

Clare began searching through the emails again but she couldn't see any between Alison and Cheryl or even any that mentioned Cheryl's name. 'Nothing.' She checked her watch. 'Let's give it till early afternoon and if Neil's not phoned, I'll call him. Then we can talk again. Meantime, we need to look into Ingrid McKinnie's background. Find out where she lived, who she lived with, next of kin – the usual. Can you get onto that please?'

Chris put the last of the chocolate cake into his mouth and wiped his fingers on the paper towel. 'Yeah,' he said through a mouthful of cake crumbs. 'I'll just get a coffee to wash this down, first.'

While Chris went to check up on Ingrid McKinnie, Clare called the press officer. Clare had worked with Suzi Bishop when she'd been stationed in Glasgow. By coincidence they had both moved east around the same time, Suzi to the large Bell Street office in Dundee and Clare to the smaller St Andrews station.

'So, what can I do for you, Clare?' Suzi asked, after initial pleasantries.

'I had a sudden death, over Christmas, Suzi. Woman in her thirties – Rohypnol in her system. Still waiting for a definite cause of death but there's no mistaking the drug. And then another body yesterday. I don't know yet if this one had been drugged – and there may be no connection – but I wondered if you could put something out on social media? You know the usual stuff – covering your drink, asking a friend to keep an eye on it – and if anyone thinks they've been the victim of this kind of thing...'

'Yeah, no problem. We did run a campaign before the party season began so it'll be easy enough to pull something out.'

'Thanks, Suzi. I appreciate it.'

'I'd suggest getting round the pubs to encourage them to use lids on their glasses.'

'I can try,' Clare said. 'But the punters don't like the paper straws so bars have stopped using the lids.'

'All the same...'

Clare ended the call with the usual We must catch up soon, reflecting that she'd been saying that rather a lot recently. Maybe she'd have a party at Daisy Cottage. A kind of January's miserable so let's party sort of thing. And then she remembered Chris and Sara's engagement ceilidh – the one Sara didn't know about. Maybe Chris would invite Diane and Suzi, and Clare could catch up with them both at the same time. She probably should make an effort to arrange something herself but it was freezing just now and it felt like a lot of bother. 'Oh for goodness sake, Clare,' she muttered. 'You're turning into an old woman!'

'I didn't like to say...' Chris said from the door, earning himself a look in return.

She glared at him. 'Did you actually want something?'

'Calm down, grandma. I just came to fill you in about Ingrid McKinnie.' He glanced at the filing cabinet. 'You going to eat that cake or what?'

Clare sighed. 'Go and make me a coffee and we'll share it.'

–

Over coffee and the cake, which Clare had to admit was delicious, Chris explained that Ingrid worked in an outdoor equipment shop.

'It's called Tradgear – on one of the lanes off South Street.'

Clare nodded. 'I know it. Some nice stuff.'

'According to the manager,' Chris went on, 'Ingrid was a keen climber. But she kept her private life to herself. He thought maybe she'd broken up with a boyfriend a while back but he didn't like to ask. She hadn't gone on the last two climbing wall outings with the rest of the staff.'

'Did he do anything about it?'

Chris shook his head. 'Said she was still a hard worker, good with customers and that's what mattered. And, as a climber, she knew her way round the equipment.'

'Fair enough.' Clare scooped up the last of the cake before Chris could beat her to it. 'How old was she?'

He checked his notebook. 'Thirty-three.'

Clare shook her mouse and scrolled to the report on Alison Reid. 'Same age as Alison.'

'You reckon they knew each other?'

'Maybe. If the PM comes back linking the two deaths I'll check with the Education Department. See if they were at school together. Who's the next of kin?'

'Parents are in Cupar. No siblings, though.'

'Who spoke to them?'

'Dundee Inspector. Can't remember which one off hand, but I could check.'

Clare shook her head. 'Leave it for now. At least until we have a cause of death.'

Chris rose from his seat. 'Okay. Want me to carry on with the December crime stats?'

Clare scrutinised his face. It wasn't like him to volunteer for such a tedious task. 'What are you up to, sergeant?'

He assumed an injured look. 'Nothing – just thought I'd lend a hand.'

'Then that would be much appreciated,' Clare said, turning back to her Inbox which was still bulging with unread emails.

'Only...'

'I knew there was a catch.'

'Is it okay if I nip off early tonight? I've an appointment.'

Clare looked at him. 'What sort of appointment?'

'Just an appointment.' He grinned and made for the door. 'Thank you, Inspector!' And he closed it behind him before Clare could interrogate him further.

Clare lifted her head from dealing with her Inbox and realised it was after midday. She emerged from her office, heading for the kitchen to retrieve her lunch from the fridge. Sara and Zoe were poring over a computer, Zoe with a doorstop of a sandwich in her hand. Clare wandered over and Sara immediately minimised the screen, guilt written all over her face.

'PC Stapleton,' Clare said, in a tone of mock horror, 'what are you up to?'

Sara flushed. 'Nothing, boss. Just a bit of fun.'

'Go on then,' Clare said. 'I can't have you calling me the station fun sponge.'

Sara glanced at Zoe who shrugged. 'Promise you won't laugh?' she said to Clare.

'Scout's honour. Just show me!'

Sara clicked and a brightly coloured web page headed Attracto appeared. Clare looked at it. The name sounded familiar but she couldn't place it.

'Is it…'

'It's a dating site,' Zoe said. 'Obviously Sara's fixed up but I'm fancy-free.'

And then Clare remembered. The dating site Alison Reid had signed up to. She thought immediately of the Rohypnol in Ingrid McKinnie's system. It must have shown in her face.

'Oh, you're horrified,' Sara said. 'Sorry, boss…'

'No,' Clare said, 'it's not that. It's just that… well, look, it's not official yet but I have reason to believe someone in the town is spiking drinks.'

Zoe stared. 'Date rape?'

'Afraid so.'

'Jeezo. Mind you,' Zoe went on, 'only an eejit would leave their drink unattended.'

Was that what Ingrid McKinnie had done, Clare wondered. She really needed to speak to Neil Grant – sooner rather than later. She looked back at the computer. Might the dating site be significant? 'Go on, then,' she said to Zoe. 'Show me.'

Zoe turned back to the computer and took the mouse. 'So, this is me – up here – my photo...'

Clare looked but it seemed to be Zoe's red curls from the back. 'The back of your head?' she said.

'Yeah. You don't have to do full face if you're not comfortable. So you put up your photo, a few facts about yourself then you can choose the categories you're interested in.'

'Like what?' This was a new experience for Clare.

'Oh, if you're outdoorsy, or if you like books, the gym and so on. Then it gives you a list of likely men.'

Clare pulled out a chair and sat down behind Zoe. 'Then what?'

'You can send a thumbs-up. That means you like them. They see that and they can ignore it or send you one back. It works the other way round, too. They can send you a thumbs-up and you can decide if you want to send one back – or not.'

Clare felt slightly sick at the thought of putting herself back out there again. Was this the only way to find someone these days? Surely she wouldn't have to go through this rigmarole to have someone in her life? 'And then what happens?' she asked.

'Well, if you both like each other you can send a private message or click to arrange a date. Then you get lots of advice about meeting in public, daytime better than night-time and all that. It's really well-organised. Once you've met on a date you can exchange contact information.'

'And what happens if you ask someone for a date and they don't want to go?'

Zoe shrugged. 'It's no biggie. They just say no thanks and that's it. You move onto the next one. Honestly, Clare, it's a lot safer than picking up a stranger in a pub.'

'Ooh, he's nice,' Sara said, taking the mouse from Zoe. 'You should send him a thumbs-up.'

Zoe peered at the photo. It showed an attractive man, dark-haired with designer stubble. It was hard to see from the thumbnail but he looked as if he might be athletic. 'Stoneman,' she said.

'Why is he called that?' Clare asked.

'Sometimes folk don't want to use their own names. See...' Zoe jabbed her profile picture at the top of the screen. 'I'm ZoeM. But I could have called myself anything.' She turned to Clare. 'I can sort you out with a profile, if you want? Get you fixed up in no time.'

Clare laughed. 'Nah, you're all right. I'll leave you to drool over... what's his name?'

'Stoneman,' they said, in unison.

'Happy drooling.'

Chapter 14

It was mid-afternoon by the time Neil Grant phoned.

'Okay, Clare. The first thing is that Alison Reid also had Rohypnol in her system.'

Clare swore under her breath. She'd been hoping the drug was a one-off. 'Any alcohol?'

'A little – not as much as the other one.'

'Did she drown?'

'I doubt it. There are none of the indicators I mentioned. And this is where it gets complicated.'

'Go on...'

'Have you heard of the vagus nerve, Clare?'

'In the neck? Yes but... oh...'

'See where I'm going?'

'I think so.'

'Applying the correct amount of pressure at the right spot on the neck can stop the heart for a short time. Now, ordinarily that wouldn't be sufficient to cause death. But if the airway is also constricted...'

'...as in strangulation...'

'...quite – the result would be a quicker death. The combination of what we call the vagal inhibition, coupled with compression of the airway, hastens collapse, then death. The result is less bruising round the neck. We also see less petechial haemorrhaging.'

'What about Ingrid McKinnie?'

'The same. To be honest, Clare, if I hadn't had the two deaths so close together I might not have picked it up. Drowning is often given as a cause of death in the absence of other indicators. But it can be difficult to be absolutely sure.'

'And the Rohypnol?'

'My guess is the killer administered it to make it easier to overpower the victims.'

'Would it have taken great strength? Big hands?'

'No. Not with the pressure on the vagus nerve. The combination of the drug plus interrupting the heartbeat would have made it easier to constrict the airway.'

Clare was silent for a moment, considering this. Then she said, 'Would it require medical knowledge?'

'Probably. If it was just one death I'd say it could be down to luck. A fluke. But two victims so close together – I reckon your killer knows what he's doing.'

'Or she.'

'Quite. Anyway, that's the gist of it, Clare. My report will be up on the system by the end of the day but I thought I'd give you a heads-up.'

Clare thanked Neil and ended the call. In the outer office Chris was tapping away at a computer, compiling the crime reports. 'Chris?'

Something in her tone made him look up. 'What's up?'

'Post-mortem for Alison Reid, that's what. Come into my office.'

Clare closed the door behind Chris and perched on the edge of her desk. 'We've a double murder on our hands.'

'Alison and Ingrid?'

'Yep.'

'So… were they drowned?'

'Nothing so straightforward.'

'Eh?'

'They were strangled.'

Chris's eyes narrowed. 'But there was hardly any bruising.'

'That's because the killer knew to press on the vagus nerve.'

'The what?'

'It's a nerve that can be stimulated to regulate the heartbeat, by pressing on the side of the neck.'

Chris's eyes flicked back and forward as he tried to process this. 'When you say regulate the heartbeat...'

'Our killer knew exactly where to press and how much pressure to use to stop the heart altogether. The victims would collapse within a few seconds allowing the killer to tighten their grip, constricting the airway.'

Chris stared. 'So... it's like a gentle way of strangling someone?'

'I suppose you could put it like that. And the Rohypnol would make it even easier.'

'So it could have been a woman.'

'That's a bit sexist, Chris. But, yes – it wouldn't have to be a six-foot rugby player. But it would have to be someone who knew exactly where to press.'

'So... someone with medical knowledge?'

'I think so. Neil said it's where you feel for the neck pulse. But you'd have to press a bit harder to stop the heart. I doubt anyone with basic first aid training would know that.'

Chris pulled out a chair and sank down. After a moment he said, 'Could it be accidental? The killer just happened to be at the right angle?'

'Once, maybe. But Neil says the two deaths coming so close together makes that unlikely. Plus, Alison Reid had Rohypnol in her system too.'

'Shit. I don't like the sound of this.'

'Nor me. So the first thing we have to do is to establish if the two women knew each other. They're local and the same age, so can you start with the council Education Department please? See if they went to the same schools? I'll check if we have Ingrid McKinnie's laptop and phone records. And we'll have to go over Ingrid's house too.'

'What about Miles Sharp?'

Clare considered this. 'I'm starting to think we jumped the gun there. Unless it turns out he knew Ingrid McKinnie as well.'

'Did you believe him when he said the last time he saw Alison was at the supermarket?'

Clare looked at Chris. 'Nope. Did you?'

'No. I reckon he's hiding something.'

Clare slipped off the edge of the desk. 'Right, then. Let's pay him a call.'

Chris checked his watch. 'You are remembering...'

'Your appointment, yes. I've not forgotten. So get moving and call the Education Department while I check if we have a laptop and phone for Ingrid.'

–

Sharp and Lafferty's offices were in Hope Street, part of an attractive Georgian Terrace. It was a side road so the snow plough hadn't been along but there had been enough traffic to break up the snow and Clare had little difficulty negotiating her way into a parking space opposite.

The pavement outside the offices had been cleared of snow and a sprinkling of grit from a nearby bin applied. As they crossed the road, Clare studied the building. It was built on four levels, including a basement which could be seen through the spear-topped railings bordering the property. She noticed it was one of the few in the street which still had windows with Georgian bars. From the pavement three shallow steps led up to a substantial front door which was newly painted, with gleaming brass fittings.

'Accountancy pays well,' Chris muttered as Clare pushed open the front door.

'Certainly raking in more than Crossford Financial.'

An inner etched-glass door was locked and Clare pressed a bell. There seemed to be no intercom or buzzer and after a few seconds a young woman in an immaculately cut suit appeared and ushered them in.

'Detective Inspector Clare Mackay and Detective Sergeant Chris West,' Clare said. 'We'd like to see Mr Sharp please.'

The young woman frowned. 'Do you have an appointment?'

'No, but we'd like to see him all the same.'

The woman hesitated then showed them to a waiting room. 'If you'd wait here, please.'

The contrast with Crossford Financial was even more stark on the inside. Instead of the posters about mortgages there were paintings by Scottish artists hung in deep wooden frames.

'Is that one of those Vettrianos?' Chris asked, peering at a portrait of a man in dark clothing, skating.

'No, you wally. That's a Raeburn. The Skating Minister. It's very famous.'

'Looks just like those beach paintings. Sara has one in her flat.'

Clare was prevented from answering by the reappearance of the woman. Her expression was not encouraging and Clare prepared to do battle.

'Mr Sharp can spare you five minutes,' she said. 'If you'd like to follow me…'

'Five minutes!' Clare said to Chris, her voice low. 'More like fifty-five minutes, by the time I've finished with him.'

'Remember I've got…'

'…an appointment – yes, you said!'

The woman led them down a broad hallway with more paintings dotted along the walls. Then she tapped softly on a door near the end of the hall. Clare heard a muffled 'Come in' and the woman held the door open to allow them to enter.

Miles Sharp rose to greet them. He was more formally dressed, in a fine grey suit and a dark maroon tie knotted tightly at the neck. His face, once again, was set in a smile, of sorts, but Clare thought he looked faintly rattled. Good, she thought. That's just how I want him.

He went through the pretence of offering them tea and coffee which Clare declined.

'I'll get straight to the point, Mr Sharp.' She paused for a minute, watching him closely, then said, 'I'm afraid to tell you we believe Alison Reid was murdered.'

Miles Sharp stared at them. He swallowed once or twice as he tried to compose himself and he reached for a glass of water. He sipped, then replaced it on the desk, dabbing at the corners of his mouth.

'Murdered? But how? Who would do that? Alison – she wouldn't hurt a fly.'

Clare paused for a few seconds to let this sink in then she went on. 'Mr Sharp. I'd like to ask you again when you last saw Alison.'

Miles sat up in his chair. 'Oh hold on a minute, Inspector. If I'm being accused of something then I'd like my solicitor present.'

'Of course, sir. If you feel you need legal representation then I'm happy to continue this at the station, on a more formal basis.' Clare hoped he wouldn't realise she was bluffing. The last thing she wanted was to question Miles formally at this stage. Better to save that for when they had something concrete to throw at him.

Miles looked down, silent for a few moments. Then he said, 'Ask what you wish, Inspector. But I reserve the right to end this if I feel the questioning is becoming oppressive.'

Clare saw Chris's expression cloud and she carried on before he could say something that might inflame the situation. 'Of course, Mr Sharp. And we're grateful for your co-operation. So, if you could think again when it was that you last saw Alison – please?'

Miles turned to a computer monitor on his desk and clicked the diary icon. But before he could consult it the door flew open and Cheryl burst in. She glared at Clare and Chris then went to stand beside her husband.

'What's all this about? We told you all we knew the other day.'

Chris rose and moved round the desk to stand beside Cheryl. 'Mrs Sharp, we would like to speak to your husband alone. If necessary we will also speak to you but, for now, you need to leave us.'

'I don't see why,' she said, her eyes flashing. 'No secrets between husband and wife, are there?'

Like when you were carrying on with Alison's husband? Clare wanted to say but didn't.

'They think Alison was murdered,' Miles said, his voice flat.

'Eh? And you're here questioning Miles… because?'

Chris indicated the door. 'If you'd just like to…'

Cheryl marched to the door. 'This,' she said, dramatically, 'is not over!'

Chris closed the door quietly behind her and resumed his seat.

'Sorry…' Miles said, '…she gets a bit…'

'It's understandable, Mr Sharp,' Clare said. 'I'm sure it's been a shock for you both.' She gave him a few moments to compose himself then said, 'You were going to check your diary.'

Miles turned back to his computer and scrolled to December. Chris moved his chair slightly, leaning over so he too could read the screen.

Miles glanced at him then he cleared his throat. 'It was, erm, the third of December. In the afternoon. We met for coffee.'

'Where was this?' Clare asked.

'Actually, it wasn't a café as such. I got a couple of take-out coffees and we sat in the car park at the Golf Museum. In my car…' He broke off, glancing at Clare. Then he said, 'Cheryl, you see – she wouldn't like it – if she thought I was seeing Alison.'

'Why did you meet?' Clare asked.

'Oh, just business, you know. Nothing much.'

'Mr Sharp – as I understand it, Sharp and Lafferty and Crossford Financial offer similar services. You are, in effect, business rivals. Now I don't wish to appear rude but I do find it a little… unlikely that you would be discussing business.'

Miles shrugged. 'I assure you, Inspector, that's all it was.'

Clare observed him for a moment then said, 'Mr Sharp, you should know that we have downloaded emails from Alison's laptop and we've found an exchange of messages between you. Maybe you could tell us the reason for these emails.'

Miles reached for the water again, taking a few sips. Clare thought he was playing for time; deciding what to say. And then he put down the glass.

'All right,' he said. 'It's like this: Alison – she was hoping to rekindle things between us. And, well, I was trying to let her down gently. In the end, I think she accepted it. She agreed with me it was a bad idea.'

He's trying to recall what was in those emails, Clare thought. And he's making a right mess of it.

'I'm sure you understand, officers,' Miles went on, 'that I don't wish to distress my wife with any of this. She would find it very hard…'

Clare could just imagine Cheryl's reaction to the news that her husband had met his ex-wife just a few weeks ago. She tried a few more questions but Miles seemed to have gathered his wits and they learned nothing further. As they turned to leave she said, 'Oh, one more thing, Mr Sharp…'

He stiffened. 'Yes?'

'Do you know an Ingrid McKinnie?'

Miles look genuinely surprised by the question. 'No, never heard the name. Why do you ask?'

Clare smiled. 'No reason. Thanks again for your help.'

As they walked back to the car Clare said, 'What do you reckon?'

'Ingrid? I'd say he's telling the truth.'

Clare fished in her pocket for the car key. 'I agree. I don't think he recognised the name.'

'I'm not so sure about Alison wanting to rekindle things, though,' Chris said.

'Yeah. I didn't believe that either. He was obviously trying to remember what was in the emails and making it up on the spot.' Clare clicked to unlock the car and they climbed in. 'And I'd very much like to know why they did meet.'

She started the engine and pulled away.

Chris glanced at his watch. 'Just drop me at the West Port, please.'

She flicked a glance at him as she turned into Abbotsford Crescent. 'What is this mysterious appointment?'

'Nothing. Just an appointment.'

'Hmm. Okay. Bright and early tomorrow, mind. We've a double murderer to find.'

Chapter 15

The station was quiet when Clare returned and she went straight to her office and sat down to think. She'd have to alert the DCI but, somehow, she wasn't keen to call him. He'd been so dismissive when they'd spoken earlier. Impatient, even. And then there was Miles Sharp. What was it he and Alison had been discussing that day in his car? And, if it wasn't connected to Alison's death, why was he being so evasive? She jotted down Ingrid's house on her notepad. They'd have to search that. Phone records too...

A tap at the door interrupted her thinking and Jim's head appeared. 'Looking for Chris... oh, are you all right, Clare?'

She glanced at him. 'We've a double murder to investigate, Jim.'

He came into the room and pulled out a chair. 'Those two lassies?'

Clare nodded. 'Alison Reid and the woman found in the Kinness Burn between Christmas and new year. Both were likely strangled but by someone who knew what they were doing – pressure on a particular point on the neck stops the heart. Leads to a quicker death. Oh, and both had been drugged with Rohypnol.'

'God almighty, Clare. You'll be needing extra troops, then, I'm guessing?'

'I will, Jim. Look, I need to call the DCI and work out our next steps. Could you give Dundee and Cupar a bell please? See who they can spare. I'll do a briefing at eight tomorrow morning.'

'Aye, no bother. Anything else I can do?'

Clare smiled. 'Thanks, Jim. It's a great help knowing you're in my corner. Once I've ordered my thoughts we'll talk again.'

As Jim made for the door Clare remembered he'd been looking for Chris. 'Sorry, Jim – you wanted Chris?'

'Just a phone message from Rothesay House.' He saw Clare's expression. 'The Education Department. He was asking about the two women?'

'Oh yes – of course. What did they say?'

'Both in the same year at school.'

'Really?'

'Yep. Primary school, at least. Different secondaries, though.'

'Got the details?'

Jim handed her a piece of paper. 'The phone number of the education officer's there if you need anything else.'

Clare smiled her thanks and Jim closed the door behind him. She sat looking at the paper wondering if this might be something – the school connection. Or was it just a coincidence?

She picked up the phone to call the DCI, half expecting it to go to voicemail but he answered within two rings.

'Clare, hi. How's things?'

'Not great, Al, to be honest.'

'Those two sudden deaths?'

'Afraid so. Both murders and probably by the same person.'

'Cause of death?'

Clare relayed Neil Grant's explanation.

'Were they sexually assaulted?'

'No, as far as Neil can tell. Admittedly both were found in water, although the first victim was only partly submerged but no traces of semen, no vaginal or anal trauma – it's as if the killer wanted the victims subdued so he or she could strangle them easily.'

'Anything to go on?'

'Other than a shifty ex-husband for the second victim, nothing yet.'

'Okay, it's the usual, then Clare. Workmates, friends, social media.'

Clare sighed. There was something that felt a bit off about these two killings. But she couldn't put her finger on it.

'Want me to come up?' the DCI said.

'I'm not sure.' And she wasn't. Did she want Al Gibson in the station, looking over her shoulder, taking over? Maybe better to keep him at arm's length – at least until she'd got used to thinking of him as nothing more than her boss. 'Al – let me put the wheels in motion. I'll get the team together first thing tomorrow. If I need your input I'll call again after the briefing.'

'Okay, Clare. Whatever you think. You want me to rustle up some extra bodies?'

'Jim's on the case. But thanks.'

'Good plan. Keep in touch, though.'

'Will do.'

'And, Clare…'

She hesitated then said, 'Yes?'

'You are okay, aren't you?'

'Yeah. I'm fine. Thanks, Al.'

She put down the phone and sat, thinking. Was she okay? Was it ending things with Geoff that was on her mind? 'I honestly don't know any more,' she said softly. Then she gave herself a shake and returned to making notes on her pad.

Ingrid's laptop

Phone

Social media

School connection?

She remembered Kathy, the receptionist at Crossford Financial. She'd struck Clare as the nosey type. 'And thank God for the nosey ones,' she muttered, adding Kathy's name to the list. She might know something about Alison's private life or even why she was in touch with her ex-husband. And there was one more thing Clare didn't understand. She studied the list, then wrote at the bottom:

Water

Chapter 16

As she drove home along the familiar roads, now largely clear of snow, Clare wondered if she'd covered everything. Jim had confirmed both Dundee and Cupar would be sending extra officers in the morning. She'd requested a SOCO team to go over Ingrid's house in Lamond Drive and had asked for copies of her phone records. Sara had been despatched to check Ingrid's house for a computer or laptop and to take them straight to Diane at Tech Support. As she turned into Bogward Road her headlights picked out a group of older schoolkids having a snowball fight on the road ahead. They stepped back onto both sides of the pavement, still firing their missiles across at each other. One of them hit Clare's car and the culprit raised his hands in apology.

Making the most of it, Clare thought. The sky, so blue earlier in the day, had clouded over now and there was rain forecast. It was as if the weather couldn't make up its mind. She left the residential streets and switched on her full beam. The trees either side of the road which had been laden with snow that morning were dripping steadily and, once more, the channels at the sides of the road were running with snow-melt. A drain outside Daisy Cottage had been overwhelmed and flood water was gathering now across the entrance to her drive.

Benjy was his usual excitable self, chasing his tail round and round, knocking into a side table, making the lamp that sat on it wobble ominously.

'Benjy,' Clare said, attempting the kind of stern tone that Isobel the dog trainer was trying to instil in her. Benjy stopped for a moment and looked at Clare then resumed chasing his tail. Clearly they were destined to have many more of the dreadful Sunday morning sessions. But that meant seeing Ralph and his owner so it wasn't all bad. She wondered again if he was married, or if he had a girlfriend. Or a boyfriend, even. He probably had someone. All the good-looking ones did.

In the kitchen, seized by a rare fit of domesticity, she poured some pasta into a pan and added boiling water. Then she chopped onions and peppers and sweated them in olive oil in another pan. The aroma of the onions filled the kitchen and she began to remember how much fun cooking was. She added a tin of passata, sloshing in a dash of the Chianti she had opened the other night. While this bubbled and reduced she tossed in a handful of oregano and the leftover vegetables that were languishing in the fridge.

A quarter of an hour later it was done. She set the table and arranged the pasta on one of her best plates, with the sauce in the centre. As a finishing touch she crumbled some of her mother's Stilton on top and stood back to admire her work. She began to understand why people on Facebook were constantly photographing their food and she took up her phone and snapped a photo.

Just to prove I do cook, sometimes! she typed, sending the photo to her mother and sister. She poured a glass of the Chianti and sat down to enjoy her meal. It was surprisingly good and it reminded her of how much she missed home-cooked food. As she ate, her phone pinged with triumphant messages from her mother and laughing emojis from her sister.

When she had cleared up dinner she took her wine glass through to the sitting room. She hadn't lit the fire and, now, it seemed too much effort so she turned up the radiators and switched on the TV. Flicking through the channels she found nothing to interest her and she switched it off again. She took up her laptop and opened Facebook. She was determined not to look at Al Gibson's page. It was time to stop obsessing about him. Whether she liked it or not, he was no more than a work colleague now.

And then she saw a Facebook advert for Attracto, the dating site Sara and Zoe had been browsing. Clare clicked on the advert and was taken immediately to Attracto's website. She wasn't logged in, of course, so she couldn't see any of the members. She sat looking at the home page and, as she did so, a pop-up appeared, offering a month's free registration. 'You're too old for this, Clare,' she told herself. But her hand hovered over the sign-up button. Alison Reid had been on Attracto too. Might she learn something useful if she joined?

'Oh why the hell not?' she said to Benjy, adding, 'It's research, after all.' She took a slug of Chianti for good measure and set about creating a profile. Her first attempt at a username, CM, was rejected as too short. She tried again with CMac but this was already taken. She thought about incorporating Daisy then decided she didn't want any clues that might lead an unwanted admirer to her front door. Finally, she settled on MercFan, a reference to her beloved Mercedes C-Class. The photo was more difficult. Like Zoe, she didn't want anything that showed her face. She'd like to have used something arty but, frankly, she knew she wasn't in the least arty. She scrolled through the photos on her laptop and found a favourite one of Benjy and she clicked to upload this. There were a few more questions on her preferred location, her hobbies, likes and dislikes. And then it was done. She hovered over the Go Live button and clicked. Her profile was online.

She had meant to search for Alison Reid but, as she learned more about how Attracto worked, she became distracted from that. She found she could add men she Liked to a Favourites list, without giving them the thumbs-up, and she began trawling through profiles. There were more than fifty men in her age range so she reduced the geographical area to within fifteen miles and scrolled through the results. Four results in and she saw him: Stoneman. She could see he had lots of thumbs-up clicks and she wondered if Zoe was among them. He was seriously attractive and Clare wondered why he was unattached. Maybe in the throes of a divorce. Or perhaps the photo was an old one – photoshopped, even, to improve his appearance. She added him to her Favourites but she stopped short of clicking to say she Liked him. She didn't want to step on Zoe's toes, after all. But maybe if Zoe wasn't interested...

As she scrolled through the photos of the men who lived around St Andrews she wondered if one of them might be the killer. Impossible to tell, of course, but it could be worth checking, depending on what they found out about Ingrid McKinnie.

Glancing up she saw it was almost ten o'clock. She'd an early start in the morning and decided to call it a night. She whistled to Benjy who was snoozing in front of the radiator and led him sleepily to the garden for a last pee before turning out the lights and going upstairs to bed.

Thursday, 7ᵗʰ January

Chapter 17

The incident room was a busy hum of chatter when Clare entered the following morning. The blinds were still closed against the early morning darkness, the artificial light glaring and harsh. She glanced round and saw that Cupar and Dundee had been obliging with extra staff and she threw Jim a smile of thanks. He'd pinned up photos of the two victims and Chris was helping him carry in a stack of laptops from the store room.

'Morning, everyone,' Clare said, taking up position in front of the whiteboard. 'Thanks for turning out so early and special thanks to the folks from Cupar and Dundee stations – your help is much appreciated.'

There was a murmur acknowledging this and Clare continued.

'What we have is two similar but unusual deaths.' She indicated the first photo. 'Ingrid McKinnie, thirty-three years old, lived alone in Lamond Drive which is a short walk from here. Found partly submerged in the Kinness Burn in the early hours of the twenty-ninth of December. Ingrid had been out in the town that night but, so far, we don't know where. She'd been drinking and also had Rohypnol in her system.'

Nita, a plain-clothes officer from Cupar raised her hand. 'Did she drown, Inspector?'

'Just Clare is fine, Nita – and no. She didn't drown. This is where it becomes a bit complicated.' For what felt like the umpteenth time, Clare explained how pressure had been applied to Ingrid's neck to stop her heart. 'After that, she could be quickly and easily strangled.'

'And that's why there was minimal bruising?' Nita asked.

'Precisely.'

'Was she sexually assaulted?'

'Difficult to tell, given she'd been in the water for a good few hours but the pathologist thinks not.'

Another officer raised her hand. 'Janey, from Bell Street station in Dundee, boss. So the Rohypnol was used to make it easier to strangle her?'

Clare spread her hands. 'It's the only reason I can think of. But I'm open to suggestions.'

'Anything on social media?' someone asked.

'We should have that and her phone records later today,' Clare said. 'I'd like volunteers to go round the pubs with Ingrid's photo. See if we can trace her movements on the twenty-eighth.'

Three hands went up at the back of the room and Clare nodded. 'Sara, will you organise that please?'

Sara nodded to the three volunteers and Clare carried on.

'As far as we know, Ingrid didn't have a significant other but Chris and I are seeing the parents this morning so we'll check that.' She glanced at Chris and he nodded but said nothing. Clare raised an eyebrow in question but he ignored this, directing his gaze instead at the photos of the two women. Thinking back to his appointment the day before she wondered briefly if he was okay. He hadn't been keen to talk about it. She hoped he wasn't ill. Her thoughts were interrupted by a question from Robbie.

'Where did she work, boss?'

'Tradgear. An outdoorsy kind of shop. Just off South Street. Chris spoke to the manager yesterday. Not much forthcoming other than she'd recently stopped socialising with the staff.'

She moved along to the photo of Alison and tapped it with her pen.

'Alison Reid. Also thirty-three. Found dead in her bath by the next-door neighbour on Monday the fourth of January.' She looked back round the room. 'Again, Alison had Rohypnol and a small amount of alcohol in her system. Like Ingrid, she had bruising to the neck, suggesting the same murder method.'

'Any sign of sexual assault?' Janey asked.

'The pathologist says not.'

Nita caught Clare's eye. 'Could she have been put in the bath to wash away evidence of an assault?'

Clare shrugged. 'It's possible, Nita. We may never know. Now, her clothes were left at the side of the bath but the SOCO report says the trousers were outside in...'

'As though someone pulled them off?' Nita said.

'Exactly.'

An older officer in an open-necked shirt raised his hand. 'Bill, also from Bell Street in Dundee,' he said by way of introduction.

'Yes, Bill?'

'Why would the killer go to the bother of undressing her and running a bath? It seems so contrived.'

'I agree. Maybe the killer meant to drown Alison in the bath once she was drugged but she fought back and he or she had to strangle her. At this stage we just don't know.'

'Don't forget the wine cork,' Chris mumbled.

Clare looked across at him. He seemed so subdued this morning. She made a mental note to have a chat with him before they headed out to see Ingrid's parents. 'Yeah, thanks Chris.' She turned back to the assembled officers. 'SOCO found a wine cork and a corkscrew in the kitchen but no sign of a bottle.'

'Checked the fridge?' Janey asked.

'Yep. Nothing there and no glasses sitting out either. Now we could have missed it when the house was checked so we need to go over it again.'

Janey indicated she would do this.

'Thanks, Janey. Take Robbie with you – he was first on the scene so he'll be able to fill you in.' Clare looked down at her notepad and went on. 'SOCO also said there was food in the oven – a dozen sausage rolls.'

'Oven still on?' Bill asked.

Clare shook her head. 'No. Either Alison or her guest – if she had one – must have turned it off. And I'd say a dozen sausage rolls is too much for one person.'

'I'd give it a go,' someone said but Clare ignored this.

'Anything amiss at Ingrid's house?' Nita asked.

'Not sure yet, Nita. Chris and I will go in after we've seen the parents.' Clare glanced back at Janey. 'Was there anything noted at the time, Janey?'

'Not that I recall. But I'll check the report.'

Gillian, one of the uniformed PCs, raised her hand. 'Boss, did the two women know each other?'

'It's possible. According to the Education Department both women attended Lamond Primary School in the town; but we don't know if they were in the same class. They went to different secondaries so the primary school link needs to be checked.'

'I'll call the school,' Gillian said, and Clare smiled her thanks.

'Now,' Clare went on, 'Alison Reid has an ex-husband. Name of Miles Sharp – he's a partner in Sharp and Lafferty, accountants in Hope Street. Alison worked there while they were married but Miles had an affair with the other partner, Cheryl Lafferty, now the new Mrs Sharp. They've been divorced five years but Miles admitted he and Alison met for a chat in his car on the third of December. His story is Alison was trying to rekindle their relationship. But we've seen an exchange of emails between them – all quite guarded – and it certainly doesn't read that way.'

'Does Cheryl Sharp know this?' Janey asked.

'He says not.' Clare paused for a minute then said, 'I'm not convinced Miles had anything to do with Alison's death. And he denies knowing Ingrid McKinnie. But he's definitely hiding something.'

Clare scanned the room to see if there were any questions then said, 'Okay, that's it.'

There were murmurs and the sound of chairs scraping back. Laptops were switched on and began humming to life.

Clare looked round for Chris. He was chatting to Janey who was relating a story, gesturing with her hands. As Clare approached, Janey delivered the punchline and Chris began to laugh. And then Clare saw why he'd been hanging back at the briefing.

'Bloody hell, Chris! There's a piano somewhere, missing a set of keys. What on earth have you done to your teeth?'

Janey snorted and Chris's hand went to his mouth.

'Just a scale and polish,' he muttered.

'Liar. You've had them whitened. I can feel your smile burning the backs of my eyes.'

'They're not that bad.'

'They are quite white, Chris. What does Sara say?'

'Not much. Suppose it'll fade.'

'In a few months! You'd better get start gargling with Pinot Noir.'

'You done?'

'For now. C'mon, then. Let's see how the McKinnies are bearing up.'

Chapter 18

Marie and Joe McKinnie lived in Cupar, a small but busy town ten miles west of St Andrews.

'Head for Tesco,' Chris said, peering at the map on his phone. 'Then take the left fork, signposted Ceres. After that, turn right at the primary school.'

'What's the name of the road?' Clare said, swinging the car up and round as they crossed a bridge over the railway line.

'Erm… Sandylands Road.'

'Okay, thanks.'

'Nice café, that,' Chris said, as they passed a modern building with what seemed to be a full-size vintage car on the roof. 'Plenty of parking too.'

'No promises.'

'I was only saying…'

Clare hesitated then said, 'Your teeth…'

Chris sighed audibly. 'Can we please change the subject?'

'It's a serious question!'

'Go on then.'

'Can you eat? I mean is there anything you can't have?'

'A list as long as your arm, Clare. But basically the advice is to avoid anything that might stain the teeth for the first forty-eight hours.'

'So no coffee then?'

'Aye right! I'm taking it with lots of milk. And anyway… if they got a bit less white… turn here.'

Clare indicated and turned right, past the entrance to the cemetery and began driving slowly up Sandylands Road.

'Stop,' Chris said. 'That's it – red door. Are they expecting us?'

Clare switched off the engine. 'Yeah, I phoned ahead.'

'Do they know?'

'About Ingrid being murdered? I didn't want to do it over the phone.'

'Oh hell.'

The McKinnies must have been watching out for Clare and Chris. As they walked up the path a tall man with a shock of silver hair appeared in the doorway. Clare held out her ID badge and he simply nodded in response, standing back to admit them. He introduced himself as Joe McKinnie. He looked the outdoors type, dressed in cargo pants and a Rab bodywarmer. His face and hands were tanned and Clare felt his hand was calloused when she shook it.

'My wife's just making some tea,' he said, indicating the sofa. 'Please, sit.'

It was a cheerful room full of light wood furniture and bright cushions. There were oil paintings too, similar in style and she wondered if one of the McKinnies was the artist. Or Ingrid, maybe. 'Lovely paintings,' she said, breaking the silence.

'My wife,' Joe McKinnie said, his voice tired. 'She's the artist.'

'She's very talented,' Clare said, and Joe simply nodded.

Her eye was drawn to one wall which was given over to a collection of photographs, fanning out from a central point. Portraits of the same child, by the looks of it, taken at different ages. Baby photos with a head full of curls, then gap-toothed school photos, gradually becoming older until the graduation shots, one a smiling Ingrid with a scroll and another flanked by Joe and Marie, clearly bursting with pride. How sad, Clare thought – their only child who now lay dead in the police mortuary.

The door opened and the small dark-haired woman from the graduation photo entered, carrying a tray with a teapot and mugs. Joe jumped up to take the tray from his wife. She was dressed in a thick grey jumper and jeans; her feet clad in pink furry slippers. Her face was attractive, her hair well cut but there were shadows below her dark eyes and her cheeks were tear stained. She sank down beside her husband, her shoulders sagging as though even the effort of sitting was too much. She seemed enveloped by her grief.

Clare introduced herself and Chris, and Marie looked from one to the other, her eyes full of fear.

'Thank you so much for seeing us,' Clare began. 'I'm so sorry to trouble you at a time like this.'

Joe McKinnie glanced at his wife. 'I er... I think we're both wondering why you've come, Inspector.' He took hold of his wife's hand, clasping it between both of his. 'We thought maybe... the funeral, you know – we'd like to begin making arrangements.'

'I'm afraid not quite yet,' Clare said. 'In fact, I have some news about the manner of Ingrid's death.'

Marie sat, unmoving, her eyes fixed on Clare's.

'Yes?' Joe said, after a few seconds.

'I'm so sorry to tell you that we think Ingrid's death is suspicious.'

'Suspicious?' Marie said. 'In what way? What do you mean?' Her voice was rising and her husband put his arm round her, rubbing her arm.

Clare hated this. The worst part of the job. The pain this couple had already endured must be immense and now she was about to make it so much worse. She took a deep breath. 'I'm afraid we believe Ingrid was deliberately killed.'

Joe opened his mouth to say something then seemed unable to form the words, his mouth resting in an O shape.

Clare went on. 'We think that Ingrid had been drinking somewhere that evening and that someone put a substance called Rohypnol in her drink.'

'Ohhh,' Marie gasped, her hand going to her mouth. 'You mean somebody...'

'We don't believe Ingrid was sexually assaulted,' Clare said quickly. 'We're not sure why someone chose to doctor her drink, but we think whoever it was followed her on her way home and killed her, leaving her to fall into the Kinness Burn.'

Marie began to cry, her shoulders shaking while her husband sat staring at Clare and Chris in disbelief.

'I think maybe we should have that tea,' Clare said, rising to lift the teapot. She stirred sugar into Marie's mug and put it down on a coaster. After a minute or two Marie lifted the mug and sipped, screwing up her face at the taste.

'I don't take sugar,' she said, putting the mug down.

'You've had a shock,' Clare said. 'It might help.' She glanced at Joe and saw his eyes flicking left and right, as he tried to order his thoughts.

'Inspector,' he said, after a moment, '…what happened to Ingrid? I mean, how did she die?'

'This is confidential at present, but she was asphyxiated.'

'You mean strangled?' Joe said, his voice sounding tight.

Marie emitted a loud sob and Joe pulled her in to his chest, both arms round her now.

'Our daughter – was strangled?' he said again.

'I'm afraid so,' Clare said. 'And, if you are up to it, we'd like to ask a few questions.' She indicated the mugs. 'Maybe we should drink these while they're hot?'

Joe lifted his mug and sipped but Marie pushed hers away. She rose. 'I'll get another mug. I can't drink that.'

Over tea and biscuits, Joe and Marie began to speak about Ingrid.

'She was so bright,' Joe said.

'Very bright,' Marie agreed. 'She studied English at university, you know, Inspector.' She indicated the graduation photos on the wall. 'First class honours.'

'She must have worked hard to be so successful,' Clare said, smiling.

'Oh, she did,' Marie said. 'Always a worker, our Ingrid. She won the English prize at school, you know.'

Clare steered the conversation round to Ingrid's workplace. 'Had she worked at Tradgear long?'

'About eight years,' Marie said. 'She'd tried to find something where she could use her degree. But there was nothing she fancied. And she'd always been a keen climber so Tradgear suited her.' Marie smiled at her husband. 'She was good with the customers, wasn't she?'

Joe nodded. 'We heard her, a couple of times – when we popped into the shop, you know. Very knowledgeable. Made us quite proud.'

Clare let them talk on for a bit then she said, 'Did Ingrid have a boyfriend?'

The couple looked at each other. 'Not that we knew about,' Joe said.

'Not for a few months now,' Marie agreed. 'There was a lad – Kelvin – but he went off to Canada. Just before the summer, Ingrid said.' She glanced at her husband. 'I think he's still there...'

Joe nodded.

'If we could have his details – just to check,' Clare said.

Marie rose. 'I'll get some paper.'

Clare waited while Marie jotted down what she knew of Kelvin then she carried on. 'Friends? We believe Ingrid had been out somewhere in St Andrews on the twenty-eighth. Would you know who she might have been with?'

Again, the McKinnies looked to each other. Clare wondered how much they'd known about their daughter's life.

'Just folk from work, I think,' Marie said, at last. 'I mean, with her having her own place, well, we didn't really know who her friends were.'

Clare asked a few more questions, then she said, 'Did Ingrid ever mention a friend called Alison Reid?'

Marie's brow creased as she considered this. 'I'm not sure... I mean, there was an Alison,' she said. 'Long time ago now

– when they were at primary school. I think she and Ingrid were friendly at the time.'

'Did they keep in touch?' Clare said, trying to keep her tone light.

Marie shook her head. 'I don't think so. If I remember correctly, Alison went on to Albany High and we sent Ingrid to Melville Academy.'

'Any particular reason?'

Joe frowned. 'Reason for what?'

'Sending Ingrid to Melville Academy?'

'It is allowed, you know, Inspector. We worked hard for our money and we can spend it how we like.'

Clare held up her hands in a gesture of apology. 'Oh, please – I wasn't suggesting anything by it. Melville Academy's a lovely school. I just wondered if there had been any problems – with Ingrid's classmates, I mean. Sometimes children are moved because of bullying and the like.'

Joe nodded. 'Yes, I see what you mean. Sorry for snapping. I don't remember anything like that.' He glanced at his wife. 'Marie?'

Marie shook her head. 'No, nothing like that. We just wanted Ingrid to have the best start in life.'

Clare smiled. 'Of course.' She glanced at Chris and they rose from the sofa. 'Thank you both so much for your time. We won't keep you any longer.'

Joe McKinnie saw them to the door. He put a hand on the Yale lock to open it then said, 'Alison – why were you asking? Do you think she's involved with Ingrid's death?'

Clare looked at his face, lined with worry and her heart went out to him. His worst nightmare had come true and here she was compounding the misery. 'I'm afraid Alison was also found dead.'

Joe's hand went to his face. 'Dead?' he whispered. 'Do you – I mean, do you think it's anything to do with what happened to Ingrid? Is there someone going round doing this?'

'At the moment, Mr McKinnie, we just don't know. So, if you do remember anything that might help us – anything at all – you will let us know?'

Joe nodded. 'Of course.' He looked at Clare for a moment then said, 'You'll catch him, won't you? This person – you will catch him?'

Chapter 19

Ingrid McKinnie lived in a compact semi-detached house with a dormer window built into the roof. The front garden had been tarmacked with a dropped kerb at the road to allow a car to be parked, although it didn't look as if Ingrid had a car. The snow had melted off most of the tarmac, other than where her neighbour's hedge had screened it from the winter sun.

A collection of different-coloured bins stood to the side of the house with a high wooden gate beyond leading, presumably, to a back garden. SOCO had closed the blinds against prying eyes, and the peeling paint on the front door made the house look rather forlorn.

The cold hit them as they stepped into the hall.

'I can see my breath,' Chris said, opening a door to the left. 'I hope someone's turned the water off so the pipes haven't burst.'

They walked into a small sitting room and stood taking it in. It was comfortably furnished with a black leather suite and a long oak sideboard on which sat a pair of graduation photos, identical to those in Joe and Marie McKinnie's house. Around the room were more framed photographs showing Ingrid in a variety of outdoor activities. One had caught her clinging to a rock face with an assortment of climbing gear hanging from a harness; another showed her standing on top of a snowy peak. Pride of place, over the gas fire, was given to a muddy but ecstatic Ingrid breasting the tape at a trail run. As Clare looked round she wondered why this vibrant woman had suddenly lost interest in climbing? Was it all down to her boyfriend going off to Canada? Clare stood on for a few moments, taking in this snapshot of Ingrid's life, and her resolve to find the killer strengthened.

The kitchen was tidy enough but bore little sign of domesticity. The fridge and freezer were loaded with microwave meals, not unlike her own, Clare realised, her conscience pricking her. She really should do more home cooking. That pasta meal hadn't taken long at all.

She pushed open the flap on the tall kitchen swing bin but found it empty. SOCO's doing, presumably.

Chris emerged from under the sink and rose, dusting off his hands. 'Water's off now, at least.'

The bedroom, upstairs, had little in the way of personal things. No make-up or hair products, the only piece of jewellery a plain gold chain still in the jeweller's box. Ingrid's clothes were practical and the other bedroom had been used to store her climbing equipment. There were boots, crampons, a couple of ice axes and a bookcase loaded with climbing books and pink-covered Ordnance Survey maps. A black wetsuit hung from a wardrobe door and the wardrobe itself was home to climbing helmets and boxes of gear, some of which Clare recognised from the photos in the sitting room. Looking at it all, Clare could imagine the woman in the photos full of life and vigour, tackling whatever the outdoors could throw at her, and she suddenly felt sad.

'Sometimes, Chris, I forget that the bodies we deal with are real people.' She turned and went out of the room and into the bathroom. Other than the usual toiletries there was nothing of note. The final room was a small study where there were two boxes of paperwork. Clare lifted one and indicated that Chris should take the other. 'Come on,' she said, with a last look round the study. 'There's nothing here. We'll go through this stuff back at the station.'

Chapter 20

It was quiet when they returned, most of the team out on enquiries. A message on Clare's desk confirmed Diane had downloaded Ingrid's laptop data and put it on the network for Clare to access. 'Let's do these boxes first,' Clare said, and they carried Ingrid's paperwork into the incident room.

'What are we looking for?' Chris said, tipping the contents of his box onto a desk.

'Anything that might indicate money worries, red bills, bank statements showing she's overdrawn, credit cards not paid off – oh, and anything that involves another person.'

They worked systematically for the next hour. Ingrid had been methodical and her papers were in a logical order.

'Nothing here,' Chris said, putting his hands up to massage his neck. 'You?'

'Not much. Looks like she was solvent, paid her bills, wasn't extravagant. A couple of old photos in an envelope. Might be useful.' She held them out for Chris to see. 'Any in your pile?'

Chris shook his head. 'Probably all digital now.'

Clare nodded. 'I suppose so. Speaking of digital...' she pulled a laptop across the desk and pressed the button to bring it to life. 'Let's have a look at her emails and social networking.' Clare moved the laptop to the centre of the table so they could both see the screen and she called up the files Diane had downloaded. Ingrid's emails ran into the thousands and Clare groaned as she saw how much data there was to trawl through. 'Let's limit it to the past six months,' she said. 'If that doesn't show up anything we can go further back.'

She sorted the emails by sender and began scrolling. A good few hundred of them were from online shops and she scrolled quickly through these. The Tradgear emails were mostly from the company's head office, relating to the usual employment matters. 'Nothing there,' she muttered, scrolling further down.

'Stop,' Chris said suddenly. 'Go back up – yep, there.'

He jabbed the screen. 'Isn't that a dating site?'

Clare looked and she felt her face redden. He was right. It was a dating site.

It was Attracto.

She searched for further emails from the site and found around twenty. There were some concerning Ingrid's registration, others with advice about staying safe and there were a few informing Ingrid that someone had Liked her profile.

'We need to follow these up,' Clare said, noting down the names.

'Might not be so easy,' Chris said. 'I mean, what if they've not given contact details? They could be using a disposable email address.'

Clare thought back to the registration process she had gone through. She hadn't been asked for her home address, only email and a mobile number. Anyone not wanting to be traced could even have had a pay-as-you-go mobile. She wondered if members received an email if they Liked someone else's profile. If not, how would they know who Ingrid herself had Liked. 'It would help if we had her login,' she said.

'Tell you what,' Chris said, pulling the laptop towards himself and opening up the Google search page. 'We might see more if one of us was a member.' He typed Attracto into the search box and clicked when the sign-up page appeared.

'Oh,' Clare said, wondering how to stop him. 'I wouldn't, Chris. I mean, Sara – she'd go mad if she...'

'Don't be daft. I'm only going to register for a look. I'll delete it after.'

'No,' Clare said. 'Leave it. We can get Diane onto cracking Ingrid's password.'

'Too late, I'm in. Ooh, look – it shows who's joined in the past twenty-four hours.' He began scrolling down then he stopped and stared at Clare.

She glanced at him quickly then looked away again. 'Think I'll just get us some coffee.'

'That's your Benjy, isn't it?' he said.

Clare scraped back her chair and walked from the room. Chris followed her into the staff kitchen and watched while she busied herself at the kettle, spooning coffee into mugs, all with her back towards him.

'Clare…'

'Just forget it, Chris. I'd had too much wine last night and it seemed like a good idea at the time. And anyway,' she added, making an effort to sound bright, 'I thought it might help us find out more about Alison.'

Chris was silent for a moment then said, 'But Geoff…'

She turned to face him, her hands on the sink behind her. 'What about him?'

'I thought…'

'Then you thought wrong.'

'Did he…'

'No. It was me. I decided it had gone on long enough. Him over there, thousands of miles away, me here – it's stupid. It was stopping both of us getting on with our lives.'

Chris stood for a minute, processing this while Clare poured boiling water into mugs. Then he said, 'Was he upset?'

She put down the kettle. 'Not so's you'd notice.' She stirred milk into the mugs and handed one to Chris. 'More surprised than anything else.'

'He didn't ask you to reconsider?'

'Nope. And that – that dating site, well it was part curiosity after Zoe going on about it and part…' she broke off, sipping her coffee as she thought, '…partly a feeling that life is passing me by, Chris. I'm not getting any younger and I don't think I want to be alone.'

'Think?'

She shrugged. 'Who knows. I like my house, my life – maybe things not working out with Geoff is down to me not wanting to compromise. Maybe I'm not marriage material.'

'And you'd like to be married?'

She shrugged. 'Dunno.' She met his eye and forced a smile.

'But… Attracto, Clare? I mean – with this investigation – you're not seriously going to…'

'No of course not,' she bit back. 'I just wanted to see who was on the site. And I really did think it might help with this case,' she added.

He didn't look convinced but said nothing further.

Clare smiled. 'So, enough introspection. Let's get back to Ingrid. Can you check through her social media accounts while I try to get hold of Diane?'

Chris headed back to the incident room while Clare called Diane's number. It went straight to voicemail so she left a message asking if Diane could find Ingrid's Attracto password. Then she joined Chris who was scanning Ingrid's Facebook data. 'Just over a hundred friends,' he said. 'Not too many.'

'Can you see Messenger?'

He scrolled again. 'Here you go.'

They read through the messages. 'Lots of photos,' Chris muttered. 'Mostly holiday snaps and friends with babies.'

'Okay. Let's try WhatsApp.'

Chris navigated to the WhatsApp data. 'Looks like she's in a few groups.'

'We'll have to go through them all. Ooh, look at this one…' Clare indicated a group which was called Schoolies. 'School pals, probably,' she said. 'See if Alison Reid's in the group.'

Chris scrolled through the names. 'Nope. Unless she's using a pseudonym.'

'Dammit. I was hoping there would be something linking them. Keep looking.'

There was a family group with Ingrid's parents and a Tradgear group for staff which seemed to be mainly about shift swaps and climbing trips. They scrolled through the other messages looking for possible connections with Alison Reid.

'What's this one?' Clare said, spotting a group called LPS.

Chris scrolled through the group data. There seemed to be a lot of members with different conversations going on. And then they saw a photo. It was of a school class in three rows, the first sitting cross-legged on the floor, the middle row sitting on a long bench and the back row standing. 'Looks like a school group,' Chris said. 'LPS...'

'Lamond Primary School,' Clare said. 'Check for Alison Reid.'

'She's there!'

'Great. Now we're getting somewhere.'

'Are we though?' Chris frowned. 'I'm not sure how this helps us. The McKinnies already told us Ingrid and Alison were at school together.'

Clare's face fell. 'Yes, of course. But it does look like they were in the same class. And it's pretty unusual for two murder victims to have been at school together. Even in a small town.' She sat forward in her seat. 'Let's look for conversations they both took part in.'

It took twenty minutes to sift through all the threads in the group but there seemed to be no direct interaction between Alison and Ingrid. There were suggestions of a school reunion in the spring but it didn't look as if it had gone beyond a discussion.

'Dammit,' Clare said. 'I was hoping for something there.'

'If it's not a link, Clare, we're as well finding out now.'

'Suppose. They were both on Attracto, though. That's quite a coincidence.' She sat back, thinking, then said, 'We need to compare any men – or women – both Alison and Ingrid had in common.'

'Want me to call Diane back? See if she can save us some time on that?'

Clare was about to answer when Janey and Robbie came into the room.

'Robbie thinks he has something,' Janey said. Her expression said otherwise but Robbie ignored this.

'It's in the kitchen, boss,' he said. 'Alison's.'

'What about it?'

'Well, everything's really tidy. Like the neighbour said. All the dishes and mugs neatly stacked. Even the mug handles turned the same way.'

'And?'

'The wine glasses. There's two missing.'

Clare looked at him. 'How can you tell?'

'She's got six of everything. Six dinner plates, six bowls, six matching mugs, even the cutlery. Six beer glasses, six champagne flutes... but only four wine glasses.'

'Maybe she only had four,' Chris said.

'That's what I told him,' Janey said, but Robbie shook his head.

'The cupboard where she keeps the glasses – there's space for six. You can see how she's arranged them.' He held out his phone. 'Flick through the photos.'

Clare took the phone and began swiping through photos of Alison Reid's kitchen cupboards. 'Mm. See what you mean, Robbie. I think if she'd only had four she'd have spaced them out more.'

'She could have broken them,' Chris said. 'Not had time to get replacements.'

'Yeah, I know,' Robbie went on, 'but remember that cork we never found a bottle for...'

'Checked the bin again?'

'Yep. Nothing there.'

'Bedroom?' Clare asked, although she doubted someone as tidy as Alison Reid would have left dirty wine glasses lying around.

'Nope.'

Clare motioned to them to sit down. 'So why would two wine glasses be missing? Let's think what we know.'

'She was at home,' Chris began. 'Drank some wine…'

'Must have had a visitor,' Janey said, 'for two glasses to be missing. And that food in the oven, remember. You don't eat a dozen sausage rolls yourself.'

Clare nodded. 'Go on, Janey.'

'Whoever it is comes in – maybe brings wine, they share a glass, visitor slips Rohypnol into Alison's glass then kills her.'

'But why take the bottle and glasses away?' Chris said.

'DNA, probably,' Clare said. 'Fingerprints too.'

Chris frowned. 'Seems a bit OTT, unless it's someone whose prints and DNA are already on the system.'

'Yeah, could be.' Clare sat, considering this. Then she glanced at her watch. 'Can you get everyone back here for two please, Chris?' She rose from her seat. 'I'm going to try Diane again. We need to get into these Attracto accounts. If there is someone on the dating site who's picking off women, we'd better find him – and quickly.'

Chapter 21

Clare was about to start the briefing when her mobile began to ring. A St Andrews number she didn't recognise.

'Oh, Inspector,' a familiar voice said. 'This is Tanya Sullivan. Alison Reid's neighbour.'

Clare sighed inwardly but she sank down in her chair and made an effort to sound bright. 'Yes, Mrs Sullivan. How can I help?'

'You asked me to let you know if I remembered anything else. Well, I have remembered something. I mean it might not be important. But what I always say is…'

'What is it you remembered?' Clare said quickly, cutting across Tanya's monologue.

'A car.'

'A car?'

'Yes. Outside Alison's house.'

'Was that unusual? Perhaps the street was busy.'

'Oh no, Inspector. In fact that's why I noticed it. Alison never had visitors. Or not very often, at least. And it was such a nice car, you see?'

Clare picked up a pen and pulled a notepad across the desk. 'When was this?'

'The twenty-third of December,' she said. 'Two days before Christmas.'

'How can you be so sure?' Clare asked.

'My turkey.'

'Pardon?'

'I was waiting for my Christmas turkey delivery. I order from a local farm you know and for an extra fiver they deliver to your door. My delivery slot was between 11 and 1 but they were late, you see, so I was looking out of the window.'

'And you're sure about that?'

'Oh yes. I've got the receipt somewhere, if you want to see it, Inspector?'

'No, that's fine Mrs Sullivan. I don't suppose you remember the time?'

'Well my turkey came about half past one and I was watching for it, off and on from about quarter to one so sometime around then.'

'And the car was where?'

'Right outside Alison's. I mean I didn't think much about it at the time. But it was a nice car so I noticed it. Somebody's got a bob or two, I said to myself.'

'And did you see the driver at all?'

Tanya shook her head. 'Sorry, no. Just the car. But I can tell you it was a Mazda. A red Mazda.'

Clare jotted this down on the pad. 'What made you notice that?'

'I had one myself. A few years ago now, but I still recognised the badge on the bonnet. Of course this one was a lot fancier than mine but a Mazda all the same. Good cars,' she added.

Clare ended the call and sat for a few minutes, mulling this over. A fancy car parked outside Alison Reid's house a week or so before she was killed. Unusual enough for her neighbour to remember it. She pushed back her chair and went in search of Jim.

'It's a long shot,' she said, 'but could you find out what Miles and Cheryl Sharp drive, please?'

A few minutes later Jim tapped on Clare's office door. 'Got the cars, Clare. Mrs Sharp has a silver Audi TT and he drives a dark red Mazda MX5.'

They filed into the incident room just after two, some still munching on sandwiches. Someone had ordered pizza and the smell of garlic hung in the air, the heat from the pizzas steaming up the windows.

'Okay,' Clare said. 'Let's make a start.' She looked round the room. 'Who wants to kick off?'

Chris raised his hand. 'Kelvin Black…'

'Ingrid McKinnie's boyfriend?'

'Yeah. He checks out, Clare. Still in Canada. He's working at a ski resort in Lake Louise. Been there right through December.'

'Lucky for some,' Bill said, glancing out at the grey January afternoon.

'Okay, thanks Chris.' Clare looked round the room again. 'Who was in touch with the school?'

Gillian raised her hand. 'I spoke to the secretary. She's only been there five years but she said she'd check with the head teacher and get back to me. Said it might be at the end of the school day, though.'

Clare clicked her tongue. 'You said it was a murder enquiry?'

'I did. But they have two staff off with flu so the head's teaching all day.' Gillian glanced at her watch. 'It's only another hour, boss. I'll call back after three.'

The phone in the outer office began to ring and Jim went to answer it.

Clare waited for him to leave then checked her notepad again. 'There might be two wine glasses missing from Alison Reid's house,' she went on. 'Add that to the cork in the kitchen that we couldn't find a bottle for and the snack food in the oven, and it looks like Alison had a guest. Pound to a penny, the guest drugged and killed her. But there's something else.'

She looked round the room to make sure they were all listening, then she went on. 'Both victims had signed up to a dating site called Attracto.' She noticed Sara stiffen and she quickly scribbled Zoe on her notepad to remind herself to warn Zoe about the site. 'Now it's possible the women were drugged and killed by someone they had arranged to meet through Attracto. But we can't assume that. It could be the school that's the link. Or – and this is the worst case scenario, guys – the killings could be entirely random.' She paused to let this sink in then said, 'If our killer is picking off victims on a whim then we really will struggle to find him.'

'Or her,' Chris added. 'Could be a woman.'

'Yes you're right, Chris. No reason it would have to be a man but remember most violent crimes against women are committed by men they know.'

Nita raised her hand. 'Boss, did either of the women have current boyfriends?'

'Not as far as we can tell, Nita. No extra toothbrushes or that kind of thing. Alison's work colleagues told us she'd recently updated her Attracto profile. But that doesn't mean she had a date. And there's nothing to suggest Ingrid was seeing anyone either.'

The door opened and Jim came back in. 'Diane,' he said. 'She's got into both women's Attracto accounts and she should have Alison's WhatsApp data up on the network shortly.'

'Okay, thanks Jim. Can you co-ordinate checking Attracto in the meantime, please? You're looking for common links between the two victims. Anyone they've both Liked or who's Liked them. Messages between them and other members – that sort of thing.'

Jim indicated he would do this and Clare pressed on.

'As far as WhatsApp goes, we know from Ingrid's phone that both victims are in a group called LPS. We think it's a primary school group. Chris and I had a quick look at the conversations but I need them checked thoroughly.'

She glanced round the room and her eye fell on two of the uniformed cops. 'Robbie and Gillian, I'd like you to help Jim with that. Okay?'

The pair nodded to Jim and Clare pressed on. 'I'm going back to Alison Reid's workplace to speak to the receptionist again. Her boss was present when we spoke to her on Tuesday and I get the feeling she might be more forthcoming if he wasn't there.' Clare glanced at Chris. 'I think I'll see her alone, Chris. She might say more if you're not with me.'

Chris shrugged and Clare looked back at the board, running over the notes she'd scribbled there earlier. And then she remembered Tanya's call. 'Just one more thing: Alison Reid's neighbour says there was a red Mazda parked outside Alison's house around lunchtime on December twenty-third. It seems Miles Sharp drives a red Mazda so...' she scanned the room, 'Chris, I'd like you to go back and ask him about that. And take Nita with you. Caution him if you have to but try to keep it relaxed.'

Chris rolled his eyes at this but Clare ignored it.

'Okay, that's it. Keep in touch.'

Jim returned as they filed out of the room. 'More shoplifting,' he said.

'Where is it this time?' Clare asked.

'Soldier Blue. Vintage clothing shop in Market Street.'

'Much taken?'

'They think a denim jacket and some earrings. Sounds like the same person from the last couple of reports. Long black padded coat, big scarf round her neck and a hat pulled down. Hard to see her face.'

Clare sighed. 'We just don't have time for it.'

'Want me to look in?'

She considered this. 'On balance, I'd rather you were here, Jim. It's important we find any possible links between the two victims. Can you ask Sara please? She'll be going round the pubs anyway.'

'Will do.'

Clare glanced at her watch. Quarter to three. She wondered how quickly the head teacher would return Gillian's call. And then she remembered Zoe. She looked over and saw Zoe's head was down, tapping at her keyboard. She turned back to Jim and lowered her voice. 'Could you get onto whoever's running that dating site, please, Jim? Let them know we might want to take it offline, until we get to the bottom of these killings.'

'Aye, no bother, Clare. I'll speak to them about making their safety advice more prominent too.'

'Thanks, Jim.' Clare glanced across at Zoe again. 'Zoe,' she said, 'spare me a minute?'

Zoe's expression clouded. 'Have I done something wrong?'

Clare smiled. 'No, nothing like that. It's just a quick thing.'

Zoe followed Clare into her office and sat on the edge of a chair.

'I wanted to give you a heads-up,' Clare said. 'About that dating site – Attracto.'

'What about it? It's just a bit of fun, Clare. No harm in it.'

Clare looked at Zoe and, for a second, an image of Alison Reid lying in a bath full of water flashed across her mind. She blinked it away. 'That's just the thing, Zoe. I think it might be dangerous. It's these two murders…'

Zoe stared.

'The victims – well, they were both on Attracto. Now I'm not saying that's how the killer found them but… well, just be careful, yeah? At least until we've caught him.'

'You're not serious?'

'I'm afraid so. I'm going to speak to the DCI about having the site taken offline. But meantime…'

'You do know I always meet them in a coffee bar or something like that?'

'I'm sure you're really careful, Zoe. Just – well, be extra careful. Don't leave your drink unattended or give out your home address – that sort of thing.'

'I'm not daft, Clare,' Zoe said, her face flushing. 'You don't have to tell me this.'

Clare smiled again. 'Okay, Zoe. I just wanted to be sure you were taking care.' She brightened. 'How are you getting on anyway? Everything okay?'

'Yeah, it's fine. I like it here.' She scraped back her chair and rose. 'And don't worry. I'm a big girl, Clare. I can look after myself.'

Clare sat on, after Zoe left, mulling this over. 'Can you, though?' she said softly. 'Can you?'

Chapter 22

It was after four o'clock when Gillian tapped on Clare's office door.

'No luck with the school,' she said. 'The headteacher now's a Mrs Curzon but she's only been at the school for twelve years and none of the current staff were there when our two victims were pupils.'

'They've no class records?'

Gillian shook her head. 'Only the year group, not who was in which class. But there is one person who might be able to help.'

'Yeah?'

'The previous head was a Celia Crawford. She's retired now but Mrs Curzon's going to try and contact her.'

Chris tapped on the door as Gillian left. He entered the office and sat down heavily.

Clare regarded him. 'I'm guessing our Mr Sharp didn't roll out the welcome mat for you.'

He exhaled. 'Not really. He denies visiting Alison at her house on the twenty-third, or on any other date for that matter and he's threatening to complain about us harassing him.'

'I'll give him harassment,' Clare muttered. 'Believe him?'

Chris shrugged. 'I think so. He claims he was in Glasgow all day. Showed me his diary.'

'Did you get a copy?'

He reached into his jacket pocket and took out a folded sheet of paper. 'Names, times, phone numbers – it's all there. He's either telling the truth or he's bloody good at covering his back.'

'We'll have to check it out,' Clare said.

'Yeah, I know. I'll just grab a coffee then I'll start phoning round. Mind you, he could have them primed to say he was there.'

'Check ANPR. If he had lunch anywhere, used his credit card – you know the drill, Chris.'

–

As Clare left the office it started to rain. The car park was ankle deep in slush and she could only hope the rain would shift it before the temperature plummeted again. It was dark now and she flicked on the headlights, turning the car towards the town. The Christmas lights which had been so bright and cheerful for the past month were still strung across the streets; but, as Twelfth Night had now passed they hung unlit, looking forlorn and tacky. Given the problems the weather was causing, Clare reckoned it could be weeks before they were taken down. Sending out a lorry with a hydraulic platform wasn't likely to be a priority for the council.

The rain grew heavier and her windscreen wipers switched to fast speed. She had to concentrate as pedestrians dashed across the road trying to escape the rain and she wondered if it was time to have her eyes tested. She blinked a couple of times and turned down the fan which was keeping the windscreen clear, focusing on the road ahead. She drove on past the West Port, its octagonal sandstone turrets darkened by the rain. She carried on along City Road until she saw the modest spire of Hope Park and Martyrs Church ahead and turned right into St Mary's Place, scanning the street for a vacant parking space. She found one opposite the university union building and pulled in before someone else could nab it. She checked her watch. It was just before five. Damn this rain and damn her umbrella, safely propped up by the front door in Daisy Cottage. She pulled her jacket hood up and stepped out in the rain. She should just make Crossford Financial as they were closing.

Kathy, the receptionist, had sounded curious when she'd called. 'After work, like?'

'If you don't mind,' Clare had said. 'There's a nice pub just round the corner; if you'll let me buy you a drink…'

Clare huddled in a shop doorway opposite Crossford's office and a few minutes later she saw the door open and Kathy emerge with a young man in a dark suit. They said their good-byes and the man dashed across the road towards Tesco while Kathy glanced round, uncertainly. Clare stepped out from her shelter and waved to Kathy who crossed the road to join her.

Whether it was the weather or the lack of money after Christmas Clare wasn't sure but she was glad to see the pub was quiet and she led Kathy to a table in the corner. 'Drink?'

'Bacardi and Coke, please.'

Clare ordered an alcohol-free lager for herself and carried the drinks back to the table. Kathy had taken off her coat and hung it over a spare seat and Clare did likewise. She thought Kathy seemed nervous and she wondered if she had cause.

'Kathy,' she began, 'thanks so much for meeting me here. I wanted us to have a proper chat when you weren't distracted by work.'

This seemed to relax Kathy and Clare pressed on. 'I thought you probably knew Alison better than anyone else. They do say the receptionist is the lynchpin of an organisation, don't they?' She thought Kathy looked pleased at this and she continued. 'I mean, you field all the calls, the mail and so on. If anyone would know what's going on, you would.'

'Oh,' Kathy said, 'I'm not a gossip, if that's what you think, Inspector.'

Clare hastened to reassure her. 'Of course not. And do call me Clare.'

Kathy's expression cleared. 'Well that's okay then. I mean you have to be discreet in my line of work, don't you?'

Clare smiled. 'I'm sure you do. The thing is, we're struggling to find out anything about Alison. She doesn't have much in the way of family – I suppose Crossford was her family, really. I'm sure she relied on you all more than you realised.'

Kathy smiled at this. 'Oh I'm not sure...'

'Take my word for it,' Clare said. 'I've just been given a new admin assistant and I'm starting to wonder how I managed without her.'

Kathy smiled and took a drink of her Bacardi.

'Did you ever meet her ex-husband?' Clare said, keeping her tone light.

Kathy made a face. 'I did and I'll tell you this much, Clare, I didn't think much of him at all. Alison was far too good for him if you ask me.' She took another drink of Bacardi then went on. 'He came in to the office to see Alison one day, you know. But Mr Crossford, well he told him to leave. Said he didn't want him in poaching any of our clients.'

'When was that?'

Kathy put down her glass and looked over Clare's head, as if trying to remember. 'November, I think it was,' she said eventually. 'I know it was after bonfire night because I was trying to book the Christmas lunch and we always do that right after the fireworks.'

'Do you know why he wanted to see Alison?'

Kathy moved closer to Clare and lowered her voice. 'Well, I'm not sure. But I think it was something to do with some scheme he was involved in. We had this client, you see...' she broke off. 'Oh, but I can't talk about clients, Clare. It wouldn't be ethical.' She nodded as if to emphasise this and sat back, taking another drink.

'Of course not,' Clare agreed. 'Do you think he was trying to pinch one of your clients, though?'

Kathy glanced left and right then leaned into Clare again. 'Well we did have this client. Restaurant owner, you know. Not that I'm naming names. But we've handled his business for years. And then one day he had a meeting with Alison. It was supposed to last an hour but he came out after fifteen minutes.

Not a word to me, and he marched straight out the door. Last we ever saw of him.'

Clare waited, not entirely sure where this was leading. She glanced at the Bacardi which was more than half gone by now.

'Well then my friend Linda — she works at Miles Sharp's office you know — well, Linda sends me a WhatsApp message. Says did we used to have a client called — well, I won't say his name — so I said yes we did, and she said, Not any more, you don't. I asked her what she meant and she said Miles had pinched him.'

'That sounds a bit unfair,' Clare said.

'I'll say. I mean, the boss, well he went ballistic. Said you just don't do these things. He wanted to go round there and have it out with Miles but Alison talked him out of it. Said what he — the restaurant man — what he wanted to do was unethical and we were better off without his custom.'

'Unethical?' Clare said.

'That's what she said, Clare. Her very words.'

'Do you know what she meant?'

Kathy shook her head. 'No. But nothing would surprise me about Miles Sharp.' She sat back, evidently pleased with that observation. 'And that's all I know.'

Clare considered this. 'Would Linda know, do you think?'

Kathy thought for a moment. 'She might. But then she might not want to say. I think she's afraid she'll get on the wrong side of that Cheryl. Right madam she is.'

Clare ordered another drink for Kathy then said, 'Have you met Cheryl Sharp?'

Kathy nodded. 'Just the once. She came into the office as well, you know. Swanned in like she owned the place. Demanding to see Alison.'

Clare sat forward. 'When was this?'

'Two days before Christmas.'

'The twenty-third?'

'That's right. I remember because it was our last day before the holiday and I was trying to get tidied up.'

'Did she say what she wanted?'

'Nope. She just said if Alison was busy she'd wait. And I told her she'd have a long wait 'cause Alison wouldn't be back that day.' Kathy took another sip of her Bacardi. 'She was working from home, you see?'

Clare recalled the WFH in Alison's diary and she nodded. 'And did you tell Cheryl that?'

Kathy shook her head. 'I wouldn't tell that one the time of day. No, I just said Alison was out of the office and that she wouldn't be back before the new year.'

'And what did Mrs Sharp say to that?'

'Nothing. She just stormed off, slamming the door, stroppy cow.'

Chapter 23

The heavy rain on top of melting snow had overwhelmed the drains and Clare drove carefully back to the station, negotiating several large floods. She pulled into the car park just as a familiar figure was going in the front door. She locked her car and hurried in after the man. Inside the front entrance the floor was becoming wetter and muddier as callers brought the melting slush in on their feet, and she felt for the cleaner who would be in soon to try and make the station presentable.

Charlie McAinsh had been a reporter with North News for the past twenty years and had a good nose for a story. He was trying his best to engage Jim in conversation without much luck. Clare tried slipping past as she made for her office but she wasn't quick enough.

'Inspector Mackay,' he called. 'Happy new year to you.'

Clare stopped in her tracks and turned. 'And the same to you too, Charlie. Good Christmas?'

'Ach yes. Same as usual. Ate too much, drank too much. But I hear you've a bit of a story developing.'

Clare prepared to fend him off, planning to say something about their enquiries being at an early stage; then she realised he wasn't talking about the murders.

'How many shops have been hit since the start of December?' he was saying. 'Has to be at least a dozen. Is St Andrews being targeted by a gang of shoplifters?'

Clare hoped the relief didn't show on her face. 'Rest assured, Charlie, I'm on top of it. We'll catch the culprits.'

Charlie tried engaging Clare in further conversation but she managed to deflect his questions and escaped into her office. She sent Jim a quick email asking him to let her know when the coast was clear and she sat back to consider what she'd learned from Kathy. It looked as if Miles had poached a client from Crossford. Hardly crime of the century but it might explain his covert meeting with Alison in the car park. Had Miles actually gone to Glasgow on the twenty-third? Maybe Tanya Sullivan was mistaken about the car. Hopefully Chris would be able to shed some light on that tomorrow.

Most important of all, if Miles was engaged in something illegal, and Alison had found out about it, was that enough of a motive for him to kill her? Clare shook her head. It didn't sound likely. Miles Sharp struck her as a weasely bastard, but a killer? She didn't think so.

She yawned and suddenly realised she'd been on the go for ten hours without a break. No wonder she felt done in. She shook the mouse to bring her computer to life and, scanning her Inbox quickly, saw that Jim had finally rid them of Charlie McAinsh. She logged off and shut down the computer.

Zoe had gone home and Jim was preparing to switch the phones through to the control room for the night.

'I'm heading home, Jim, if anyone's looking for me. Time you were away too.'

'Right behind you, Clare,' he said.

Outside, the rain was still heavy, the snow almost gone. She ran across the car park and jumped into her Mercedes, starting the engine. The automatic wipers came to life and the temperature display said it was five degrees. It looked as if it wasn't going to freeze tonight, after all. She hoped they'd seen an end to the snow – for now at least, and she pulled out of the car park, heading for home.

Ten minutes later she turned into her drive and saw that the Christmas card image of Daisy Cottage had gone. Even in the winter darkness she could see the trees were dripping with snow-melt, and a large puddle was forming at the front porch. Her Christmas tree, which she'd carried out and left by the side of the porch, had fallen over and was a forlorn sight. Moira, her dog walker, had said something about Christmas trees being used to shore up the dunes on the West Sands and she resolved to investigate this at the weekend. She stepped carefully over the puddle and into the house, shutting out the driving rain. As she kicked off her shoes and hung her coat on a hook by the door Benjy came rushing towards her, his tail wagging furiously. He had one of her slippers in his mouth which he was disinclined to yield. She tried imitating Isobel's stentorian tones and, to her surprise, he dropped it at her feet. Maybe the training was paying off after all.

The box of Christmas decorations was still in a corner of the sitting room and she knew she should take it up to the attic and tidy up the spot where the tree had stood. The furniture she had moved to accommodate it was still out of place and there was a scattering of pine needles on the carpet. It would take five minutes to put the decorations away and run the Hoover over the carpet. But somehow she hadn't the energy.

In the kitchen she retrieved a portion of her mother's turkey curry from the freezer and put it in the microwave to defrost. She glanced at the wine bottle then decided against it. The early evening glass of wine was turning into a bit of a habit, and on a wet dark January night it would be so easy to drink her way out of the doldrums. And, standing in her kitchen, watching the rain teem down against the window, Clare felt she was very much in the doldrums. Instead, she took a bottle of apple juice from the fridge and poured herself a glass.

While the curry defrosted she switched on her laptop. She decided against looking at Facebook. There were no notifications anyway and she wanted to avoid the temptation to look at Geoffrey's page. Or Al Gibson's, for that matter. Instead she went to her Favourites where she'd saved Attracto. She stopped for a moment, remembering her warning to Zoe to stay off the site. She should delete it from her laptop and forget about it. And then she told herself it would do no harm to look. Just to see…

Seconds later she'd logged in. A red number three was flashing in the top right-hand corner. She had three Likes. Clare felt a small frisson of excitement as she clicked to see who had Liked her profile.

It didn't last. She was pretty sure she'd arrested one of them last summer and the other two were no more inspiring. 'Is this what I'm reduced to?' she asked Benjy. 'Trawling the internet like a desperate teenager?'

Benjy jumped up beside her and put his paws on her shoulder, nuzzling her cheek. This simple act of love disarmed her and her throat grew tight. And as she felt his tongue, wet against her ear, she buried her face in his fur and began very quietly to weep.

Friday, 8ᵗʰ January

Chapter 24

The snow was largely gone by the time Clare drew into the police station car park. The rain had finally stopped too, allowing a watery sun to peep through an otherwise leaden sky. A Scottish Water van was parked further along Tom Morris Drive where flood water was threatening to cover the road.

Jim was at the front desk as she entered the station.

'Morning, Jim. Anything new?'

'A couple of things, Clare' He glanced towards the incident room. 'They're starting to gather next door. Want me to fill you in now? Or at the briefing? What time were you thinking?'

Clare checked her watch. 'Fifteen minutes suit you?'

'Aye. Zoe should be in by then.'

'Leave it till the briefing, then. How's Zoe shaping up, anyway?'

'Oh, she's grand,' Jim said. 'Picks things up really quickly. She's a huge help just now, with all this going on.'

In her office Clare switched her on computer and it began to hum as it came to life. She scanned her emails quickly and dealt with a few.

Chris put his head round the door. 'Anything doing?'

'Not much, Chris. Briefing in a few minutes.'

'Zoe's brought in lemon drizzle cake...'

'Oh God,' Clare said. 'I really shouldn't...'

'Want me to get you a slice?'

'Go on. Before the locusts descend on it.'

Five minutes later, the cake safely stashed in her office, she entered the incident room and called the briefing to order.

'Okay,' she began. 'Let's get the easy stuff out of the way first. Chris – anything on Miles Sharp's trip to Glasgow?'

Chris got to his feet. 'They all confirm he was there. First appointment was eleven then he took clients out to lunch and his last was at three.'

'Do we know where lunch was?'

Chris looked at his notepad. 'Aye. The Canny Drap. Pub out the west end.'

'Argyle Street?' Janey asked. 'I've been there. The food's pretty good.'

'Can anyone verify it?' Clare asked.

Chris nodded. 'Manager said there was a table booked in the name of Sharp.'

'CCTV?'

'I've not asked.'

'Do that, would you please?' Clare said. 'We have a sighting of a car that looks like Miles Sharp's outside Alison Reid's house that day. I want to be absolutely sure he was in Glasgow. See if the cops there can email it through.'

Chris scribbled this down and Clare went on. 'ANPR footage?'

He shook his head. 'Negative, Clare.'

'Did he take a train?'

'It's possible,' Chris said, 'but I doubt it. His appointments were scattered across the city. He'd have been in and out of taxis all day.'

'Let's check that,' Clare said.

'What about Cheryl's car?' Bill suggested. 'He could have taken that.'

'Good point, Bill. can you check that too please, Chris?'

Clare looked round for Jim and found him standing by the door. 'You said there were a couple of things, Jim…'

Jim moved further into the room. 'Aye. Diane's found another document on Alison's laptop. It was among her hidden files and it's password protected too.'

'Can she get into it?'

'She's trying. It really depends what kind of password Alison used. If it's just a word or two words, or even a word with a couple of numbers then she could crack it in a matter of days. But if it's more complex, or long, well that might take more time than we have.'

'Okay, noted, Jim. Is that it?'

'Just one more thing – on Ingrid McKinnie's WhatsApp.'

'Go on.'

'Well, first of all that LPS group were talking about a reunion. A get-together in April. Various suggestions of venues, activities, that sort of thing. So we tracked the conversation right back and it was started by someone called Jessica Peters. We then found Jessica had a private conversation going with Ingrid.'

'Okay...' Clare wondered where Jim was going with this.

'There was lots of chat about what they were doing now, that sort of thing and then it turned to Were they married? Ingrid said she was out of a long-term relationship – lad had gone to Canada – so this Jessica suggests Ingrid tries the dating site – Attracto.'

Clare was suddenly alert. 'How did the conversation go?'

'I can print it out, but basically Jessica said why not try Attracto. She'd tried it and had a few good dates. Ingrid said she might and Jessica said to let her know how it went.'

'And that's it?'

'More or less.'

'Okay, Jim. Let me know if Diane gets into that document.'

Jim said that he would and Clare carried on.

'Pubs – where are we with that, Sara?'

'Been round most of them, boss. One possible sighting of Ingrid but the barmaid wasn't sure. They had the Zumba class in for their Christmas meal. Pretty busy night for them.'

'Where?'

'Harvest Moon – pub in South Street.'

'CCTV?'

'Working on it, boss.'

'Sooner rather than later, then.' She looked round at the faces before her. 'To be honest, guys, we don't have much. We've two deaths, pretty similar modus operandi. The two women knew each other as children but, other than a school reunion group, they didn't have any contact – as far as we know. Do we know what they did after they left high school?'

Nita raised her hand again. 'Ingrid studied at Edinburgh Uni and Alison at Dundee.'

'Okay, Nita. Any other links?'

'Sorry, boss.'

'Right,' Clare went on. 'So the women were at primary school together but St Andrews isn't a big town so that wouldn't be unusual. Them both being the same age is, though. That's quite a coincidence. Any thoughts on that?'

'Someone who knew them from school?' Chris suggested. 'Someone they'd rubbed up the wrong way?'

Clare inclined her head. 'It's possible but school spats would be a pretty thin motive for murder, especially so many years later. All the same, it's unusual, them both being in the same WhatsApp group.'

'Is it worth going round the other members of the group?' Janey suggested.

'I think so, Janey. Can you, Robbie and Gillian get onto tracking them down please?'

'Will do.'

'And prioritise Jessica Peters – the one who suggested Ingrid try the dating website.' Clare looked round the room again. 'It's possible the answer does lie in that WhatsApp group but we can't forget about the Sharps – Miles and Cheryl. There was something going on between Miles and Alison Reid. So let's check their social media as well. See if either of them were friends with anyone else in the WhatsApp group. Let's find out where and when they went to school, university – and anything else about them. I want their shoe sizes and what they had for breakfast.' She glanced round the room again. 'Everyone clear?'

There were nods and murmurs of, 'Yes, boss.'

And then Clare remembered something else. 'I nearly forgot – we had another report of shoplifting yesterday – Soldier Blue – shop in Market Street. I've already had the press sniffing round so let's be as visible as we can in the town, for the next week at least. Pop into the shops, show face. If we do have a gang of shoplifters in the area I want them to know we're onto them. Okay, that's it, everyone. Keep in touch.'

There was a general scraping back of chairs and the hum of laptops coming to life. Sara and a few others went to collect their outdoor jackets.

'Quick coffee, before I get onto Glasgow?' Chris suggested.

'Yeah, bring yours into my office. Something I want you to do.'

–

'Go on, then,' Chris said, putting his mug down on Clare's desk and drawing up a chair.

'Well first of all there are a couple of things I need to tell you.'

'Yeah?'

'You remember I was meeting Kathy, yesterday? The receptionist at Crossford Financial?'

'While I was being shouted at by Miles Sharp – yes I remember.'

'Well she told me something interesting.'

'Go on…'

'You remember Alison was working from home on the twenty-third?'

Chris nodded. 'Yeah. The day Tanya saw the red Mazda?'

'That's it. Well Kathy said that Cheryl Sharp came storming into Crossford's office the very same day demanding to see

Alison. Kathy told her Alison was out of the office and she stomped off.'

'Any idea what she wanted?'

'Nope. But I intend to find out.'

Chris picked up his coffee and took a draught. 'That it?'

'No. Kathy also said she thought Miles had pinched one of Crossford's clients.'

'Not against the law...'

'No, it's not. But Alison had a meeting with this client a few weeks before. It was supposed to be for an hour but the client came out after fifteen minutes – not a word to Kathy – marched straight out the front door. A few days later Linda from Sharp and Lafferty told Kathy he was their client now.'

'I'm still not seeing...'

'That's because I've not told you yet. Apparently, Alison said they were better off without him. That the client wanted Alison to do something she considered unethical.'

Chris sat back, weighing this. 'So...' he began slowly, '...that would fit with the email from Alison saying it was a seriously bad idea.'

'Exactly. So what I'm thinking is this: client goes to Alison, asks her to do something borderline. Maybe not illegal but Alison's not keen.'

'Some sort of tax scheme...' Chris suggested. 'She is a tax accountant.'

'Yeah, something like that. So client marches out and goes down the road to Sharp and Lafferty. Miles Sharp welcomes him with open arms. He has no such scruples. Alison gets wind that the client has gone to Miles – maybe through Kathy talking to Linda – and she asks to meet him in the car park. Sends a few emails saying it's a bad idea. Maybe she even threatens to report him to... I dunno, whoever their regulatory body is.'

'Miles loses the nut and kills her?'

Clare rubbed her chin. 'As to whether he'd go that far, I'm not sure. It would have to be a huge amount of money for that. So, I'd say probably not. But it could be a factor.'

'Okay, you want to speak to them again?'

'That's where you come in.'

'Because…? Oh you do not want me to go back there again? You have to be joking, Clare.'

'Look, Chris, I'm thinking Miles Sharp maybe was in Glasgow on the twenty-third. Obviously you'll check out ANPR cameras and the footage from the pub where he claims he had lunch, but he's probably telling the truth.'

'So…' Chris said slowly, '…if it wasn't Miles who visited Alison that day…'

'…it could have been Cheryl,' Clare finished. 'Maybe they swapped cars for some reason – I don't know. But I want to ask Cheryl face-to-face and see her reaction.'

Chris shook his head. 'I still don't know why you need me.'

'I need you to find out about that client they pinched from Crossford. But I wouldn't put it past Cheryl to warn Linda against speaking to us. So I want to catch both of them off their guard.'

'We could bring them in here – different times.'

'I don't want to make it official. Minute we do that, Cheryl will call a solicitor and clam up. So… I was thinking…'

'I'm starting not to like the sound of this…'

'I'm going to try to get an appointment with Cheryl, this morning if I can.'

'What? Like an accountant's appointment?'

'She is an accountant, Sherlock.'

'Do you actually need an accountant?'

Clare shrugged. 'I could have money. You don't know.'

'Do you?'

'That's for me to know and you to wonder, Detective Sergeant.'

Chris sighed. 'Okay, where do I come in?'

'As soon as I go into the appointment I want you to swoop in and speak to Linda. I might not have long before the lovely Cheryl chucks me out so you'll have to be quick. I'll send a text when I'm heading in. That's your cue to get in and chat Linda up.'

'Saying what?'

'Ask her directly if she's taken on any new clients in the last two months. Especially restaurateurs.'

'She'll just tell me it's covered under GDPR.'

'And a clever detective would know that our shiny new data protection law doesn't apply in the case of a criminal investigation.'

Chris avoided her eye. 'Well, yeah. I knew that, obviously.'

'So go to it.'

'What if she demands a warrant? She looks the type.'

'Tell her she's obstructing a murder inquiry.'

Chris sighed heavily. 'Go on then.'

Clare picked up the phone to call Sharp and Lafferty. 'And, if all else fails,' she whispered, as she waited for the call to be answered, 'just flash her your gnashers. Dazzle her into submission.'

'Don't give up the day job, Inspector.'

Chapter 25

Cheryl Sharp agreed to see Ms Mackay when she pleaded her case to Linda. 'I'm only in town until this afternoon and Mrs Sharp comes highly recommended.'

'Well, you're in luck, as it happens,' Linda said, her voice curt. 'Mrs Sharp has a cancellation at ten thirty this morning. Can you make that?'

Clare said that she could and at ten twenty-nine she stepped out of the car, leaning back in to Chris. 'I've a text message ready to go. I'll send it when I'm going in to Cheryl's office. That's your cue.'

Chris looked unconvinced but he agreed to give it his best shot.

Linda answered the bell, opening the door for Clare. Her face fell when she recognised her. 'I'm afraid Mrs Sharp has an appointment in a few minutes.'

'I know,' Clare said, smiling. 'I'm Ms Mackay.'

Linda's lips thinned. 'If this is simply a pretext…'

'Oh I assure you it's not,' Clare said quickly. 'I really do want some financial advice. And,' she indicated her surroundings with a hand gesture, 'I was pretty impressed with the set-up here so I thought, why not.' She continued to smile. 'Your reputation precedes you.'

Linda raised an eyebrow but said nothing more, indicating Clare should take a seat while she buzzed through to Cheryl. Clare sat, phone in hand and, when the door opened and Cheryl appeared, she sent the text message to Chris.

Cheryl's face darkened when she saw Clare. 'I'm sorry, Inspector,' she said, a hard edge to her voice. 'If you want to interview me then I will arrange for my solicitor to be present.'

'Oh, no, Mrs Sharp,' Clare said quickly. 'I really am seeking your advice in a professional capacity.' Cheryl stood her ground. Out of the corner of her eye Clare saw Chris emerging from the car and making for the front door. 'I have a sum of money to invest, you see...' she said.

Cheryl raised an eyebrow then turned on her heel. 'If you'd like to follow me...'

She held a door open for Clare and led her down a short hall to her office. As the door to the reception area swung closed behind her she heard the front doorbell sound and she hoped Chris would carry it off okay.

Cheryl's office was tastefully decorated. Thinking back to the décor in the Buchanan Gardens house, Clare thought this hadn't been Cheryl's choice. The whole building had the hand of an interior designer. The carpet was oatmeal in colour, flecked with navy and the walls ochre with raw-silk curtains in cerulean blue. A striking seascape hung on the wall opposite Cheryl's desk, the blues and greens merging into each other, the water foamy as it bubbled onto silver sand.

'Harris,' Cheryl said, following Clare's eye. 'You been?'

'No. But, seeing that, I think I'd like to.'

'Yeah you should. Not in summer though. Anyway, what's this about? Do you actually have any money to invest?'

'I do,' Clare lied. 'An elderly relative. An aunt,' she added. 'A legacy.' She was starting to think she should have rehearsed this.

Cheryl fixed her with a steely gaze for a moment then pulled a notepad towards her and picked up a pen. 'Where is it now?'

'Oh,' Clare hadn't thought about this. 'I... I er don't have it yet. I don't think it's cleared probate.'

Cheryl put down her pen. 'We don't have probate in Scotland, Ms Mackay.' She emphasised the Ms no doubt to make it clear she was not treating Clare as a police officer. 'It's called confirmation up here. I'd have thought the executors would have told you that.'

Clare smiled. 'Oh they probably did. I've been busy, you know. Anyway, I thought I'd come and see what my options are – once I have the money, obviously.'

Cheryl picked up the pen again. 'Are you the sole beneficiary?'

'Erm, no. Other... cousins.'

'Any inheritance tax to pay?'

'No, I don't think so.'

'HMRC monies due?'

Clare spread her hands. 'As I said I'm not the executor.'

'And the sum you have inherited?'

'They've not been precise about that yet. But it's in the tens of thousands,' she said, deciding that sounded a likely amount.

'So, in short, you are expecting a legacy, you don't know when, you don't know how much, but you have decided to come here – to an office where you recently carried out inquiries – to ask for investment advice, yes?'

'Yes please.'

Cheryl put down the pen once more and sat back in her chair. 'Frankly, Ms Mackay, I don't believe a word of it. I think you are seeking to obtain information under false pretences.' She shook her head slightly. 'I mean, do you even have a recently-deceased aunt?'

Clare decided to appeal to Cheryl's ego. 'Okay, I'm sorry. I am thinking of sorting out my finances, but I don't actually have a legacy. Not at the moment, anyway. I didn't think you'd see through me so easily.'

'And you're the detective?' Cheryl snapped, her eyes flashing. She rose from her chair. 'I'd like you to leave now, Inspector Mackay.'

Clare stayed in her seat. 'Look, Mrs Sharp, hear me out, please? Just give me two minutes to explain and then, if you still want me to leave, I will.'

Cheryl sat down again and pushed her chair back. 'Go on, then.'

'It's like this: I don't want to keep bothering Mr Sharp. I think it must be difficult for him, with what's happened to his ex-wife. So I thought maybe you could help me.'

'Help you how?'

'Just one question: did you visit Alison Reid at home, two days before Christmas?'

And, in that second, Clare had her answer. A moment of confusion flashed across Cheryl's eyes and she ran her tongue round her lips.

'I think you did,' Clare went on. 'And that's fine. I just need to ask what the reason was. And, if it's not relevant to our investigations, it'll go no further. I promise.'

Cheryl still didn't speak. Clare wondered if she was running through options in her head. Trying to decide how little of the truth she could get away with revealing?

'I…' she began, then she reached for a bottle of sparkling water and poured some into a glass. She offered the bottle to Clare but Clare shook her head. Cheryl lifted the glass, the water still effervescent, and she sipped at it. Then she replaced it on her desk. 'Miles – he thinks I don't know this, but he met her. In December. It was lunchtime and they met in his car.'

'How did you find out?'

'Simple. I followed him. I knew he was up to something. He'd been shifty all morning. So, when he said he'd be out at lunchtime, I left the office a few minutes ahead of him. I had a taxi waiting and I sat in the cab until he came out. Then I followed him. Told the taxi driver to hang back. He went to the car park beside the Golf Museum. After a few minutes another car drew up alongside him and I saw her get out and get into his car.'

'How long were they in the car for?'

'About twenty minutes, I think.'

'And then?'

'She got back into her own car and drove away. Miles sat on for a bit then he went too. I let him leave then told the taxi driver to hang back for a few minutes. By the time I reached the office Miles was already there.'

'And you never asked him why they met?'

Cheryl shook her head. 'No. But I reckon she was trying to get him back. He's a catch, you see, Miles. Worth a bob or two now and he moves in the right circles. We have a nice life, Inspector. I think she missed the lifestyle. So when I knew Miles would be safely out of the way in Glasgow, I took my chance. Her office said she was out seeing clients but it was lunchtime so I thought it was worth checking the house.'

'You went to warn her off?'

'Something like that.'

'And how did she react?'

Cheryl shrugged. 'As you'd expect. Denied it all. Said it was just a professional discussion, that day in the car.'

'Did you believe her?'

'Frankly, I didn't care. I told her if she went anywhere near Miles again I'd break her face.'

'How did she react to that?'

'Didn't wait to find out.'

'And what about Miles – do you think he still cared for Alison?'

Cheryl picked up the water again and took a longer drink this time, avoiding Clare's eye. 'She's very different from me, Inspector. She's quiet – she was quiet I should say – mousey, you know? She's into reading, and orchestras, that sort of thing. Me? I'm not. I like going out for meals, West End shows, cocktail parties, casinos – I like a bit of fun. Miles does too but, now and then, I think he misses the mousey bit. The quiet life, you know?' She raised her eyes to meet Clare's. 'Not enough, of course. I wasn't about to hand him back, Inspector. Not to her, anyway. I'll make sure he stays with me.'

Clare could believe it. Cheryl had shown a chink in her armour but the steely side would always win out.

Clare rose from her chair. 'Thanks for your honesty, Mrs Sharp. I appreciate it. And I'm sorry to have taken up your time.'

Cheryl shrugged. 'It's fine. I'd say it was a fair fight, wouldn't you Inspector?'

'Well?' Chris asked, as he started the car and pulled out of the parking space.

'I don't think she had anything to do with Alison's killing,' Clare said, tugging on her seat belt. 'Can't be sure of course but she claims she went there to warn Alison off.'

'Off Miles?'

'That's what she said.'

'And you believe her?'

'Yeah, Chris. I think I do.'

Chris pulled out into the traffic. 'Back to the station?'

'Please. Any luck with Linda?'

'Nah. Not really. She admitted they had a client who had been with Crossford but she wouldn't tell me who it was.'

'Did you explain about GDPR not applying?'

'Yep, but she said Miles would sack her if she said anything. She suggested we get a warrant.'

'And you got nothing else out of her?'

'Only that it was a restaurant owner and that he'd been very generous with discount vouchers for the staff at Sharp and Lafferty.'

Clare considered this. 'Maybe worth looking her up on Facebook. See if she's Liked any restaurants in the town.'

'Good idea.'

They fell silent as Chris drove back to the station. They reached the car park a few minutes later and Clare saw the Scottish Water van pulling way, puddle dealt with.

'I could murder a coffee,' Chris said, as they walked towards the station door.

'Me too. You reckon my lemon drizzle cake will still be there?'

'Not a chance.'

Chapter 26

'We've had a call,' Jim said, as they entered the station. 'A shop just off North Street – Castle Gifts. They reckon there's a shoplifter in. One of the staff spotted the woman's bag had a foil lining. Sara's on her way there now.'

'Does it sound like the same woman?'

'Aye. Same kind of coat and hat. Hopefully Sara will get there before she leaves. The staff are keeping her talking.'

'Okay, Jim. Keep me posted.'

To Clare's amazement the lemon drizzle cake was still where she'd left it. Chris brought in two mugs of coffee and they sat down at Clare's computer. She logged on to Facebook and typed Sharp and Lafferty into the search box.

'There it is,' Chris said, pointing to the third result listed.

'Right.' Clare clicked to open the company's page and began scrolling down. It took a few minutes but then she found it. 'Here we go,' she said. 'Staff Christmas night out. And there's our Linda – kindly tagged in the post by Cheryl. Remind me to thank her.' Clare clicked on Linda's tag and was taken to her profile. 'Now, let's see if she's been at any restaurants in the town since early December...'

'You're thinking those discount vouchers the restaurant client gave her?'

'Exactly.'

The security settings allowed her to see photos and Likes but nothing else. She scrolled down to Linda's Likes and found several St Andrews restaurants were among her favourites.

'Go back up to the photos,' Chris said.

Clare did this and they began browsing the photo posts.

'Stop,' he said. 'Go back up to that photo where she's in a red top.'

Clare peered at it. 'Second of January,' she said. 'That could be the restaurant.' She glanced at Chris. 'Recognise it?'

'It's hard to see. The globe lights are quite distinctive. Maybe someone else will recognise it.'

Clare rose from her seat. 'I bet I know who to ask…'

'It's The Heron's Nest,' Zoe said. 'Know it anywhere.' She pointed to something on the wall above Linda's head. 'See that? It's one of the herons they have painted round the walls.' She indicated the computer mouse. 'Mind if I…?'

Clare moved back to let Zoe take the mouse and she blinked as she caught a whiff of her perfume. Something fruity and strong. She wheeled further back in her chair. 'On you go.'

Zoe came off Linda's page and opened her own Facebook page. She went to photos and clicked on an album. The screen filled with photos of Zoe and a group of friends at what looked like a twenty-first party. 'See?' she said, jabbing the screen. 'There's one of the herons – on the wall behind us, yeah? It's definitely The Heron's Nest.' She relinquished the mouse and stepped back. 'Nice food there,' she added.

When Zoe had gone Clare returned to perusing Linda's Facebook page. There weren't any restaurant photos after the second of January.

'Doesn't mean that's the one, Chris,' she said.

'True, but it's possible.'

'I'm not sure where it gets us, though,' Clare said. 'I mean, even if Alison did threaten to report Miles, I can't see it as a motive for murder. It's just too far-fetched.'

'Yeah, I agree. So where does that leave us?'

Before Clare could answer there was a tap at the door and Jim's head appeared.

'Sara's back with our shoplifter. I think she'd like a word.'

Chris rose to leave, holding the door open for Sara who came in and sat down. Her face was lined with worry.

'Sara?'

'It's our shoplifter, boss. There's something not right with her.'

Clare sat forward. 'In what way?'

Sara shook her head. 'I'm not sure. But she's odd. I mean, when we arrived, she almost seemed relieved. No arguments. Admitted it there and then...'

'You cautioned her?'

'Oh yes. All done by the book. And then she said she'd take us back to her house and give us the stuff.'

'Did you get it?'

'Couldn't carry it, boss. There was just too much.'

'Eh? What sort of stuff?'

'You name it, she had it. Mostly clothes, some ornaments, candles, books, CDs.' She fished out her mobile phone. 'See here – I took photos.'

Clare stared at the photos. 'Is this a... looks like a garage.'

'Yeah, that's right. The house is in Trinity Place. Near Hallow Hill. There's a garage to the side. She opened it for us and... well you can see for yourself.'

Clare flicked through the photos. It was like looking at a garage sale. A dozen or more coat hangers with blouses and jumpers dangled from metal shelving that ran along the side of the garage. Other shelves had CDs and DVDs stacked up sideways and there was an assortment of small boxes piled on top of each other. It was shoplifting on a grand scale and everything she could see was still in its packaging. 'Is she stealing to sell?' Clare said, handing the phone back to Sara.

'She says not. Some of the clothes are from last summer so I'd say she's probably telling the truth.'

'Then why? Why take all this? Nobody needs this much stuff.' Clare peered at the photos again. 'These look like men's trousers, for goodness sake.'

'She doesn't know why she takes them. That's what worries me, boss. I think it might be some sort of illness – like a compulsion to steal.'

Clare sat back, considering this. She'd arrested her share of shoplifters as a young officer in Glasgow but usually they were stealing to sell so they could buy drugs. Unrepentant and careless of the consequences. This sounded different.

'Is she using?'

'She says not. And she doesn't strike me as an addict. She's shown almost no emotion. I'm a bit worried about her, boss.'

Clare rose from her chair. 'I'll come and speak to her. Where is she?'

'Interview room two.'

'Solicitor?'

'Declined.'

'Okay, I'd like you to sit in, Sara. And let's get her a cup of tea.'

'Already done.'

–

Ruth Williams glanced up as Clare and Sara entered the room but she didn't speak. Clare pulled out two chairs for herself and Sara. As she did so she appraised Ruth. Thirty-ish, maybe slightly older. Clean and tidy, her clothes not the height of fashion but trendy enough. Her hair was well cut too but her face was white now, a hint of mascara below her eyes indicating a few tears. She sat, head down, twisting her hands, the cup of tea untouched on the table in front of her.

Sara was right. Ruth Williams did not look like a typical shoplifter. She looked – for want of a better word – a bit too respectable.

Clare introduced herself and Sara, and started recording the interview, delivering the standard caution. When she asked Ruth if she understood, she simply nodded.

'Could you speak for the benefit of the tape, please, Ruth?'

'Yes,' Ruth said, her voice little more than a whisper. 'I understand.'

Clare smiled. 'Thank you. Is it okay if I call you Ruth?'

Ruth glanced quickly at Clare then down at her hands again. 'Yes. Ruth's fine.'

'First of all, Ruth, I'd like to suggest once more that we call your solicitor. Or we could arrange the duty solicitor if you prefer?'

Ruth shook her head. 'No solicitor. I just want to get this over with.'

Clare watched her carefully. Was it embarrassment that was preventing her accepting legal help? 'Okay, then, Ruth. We'll make a start. Now PC Stapleton has told me that you admitted to taking a large number of items from shops in the town without paying for them. Is that correct?'

'Yes.'

'I believe also that you took PC Stapleton to the garage at your house in Trinity Place and showed her these items. Is that also correct?'

'Yes.'

'PS Stapleton formed the view that some of these items had been there for quite some time.'

Ruth nodded. Her face was flushed now but otherwise devoid of emotion.

'For the tape, please, Ruth.'

'Yes. I... I had some of them for a few months.'

'And the items in the garage — is that everything? Or are there more items, elsewhere?'

Ruth shook her head. 'No,' she said, her voice still small. 'Everything... I took, it's all in the garage.' She raised her eyes. 'I'll give it back,' she said. 'All of it. I... I don't really want it.'

Clare hesitated, then she said, 'Ruth, I'm afraid with such a large quantity of items, that this can't be dealt with by a fixed penalty. Even if you do return all the goods, unused, I'm afraid the scale of theft is just too great.'

Ruth's eyes flitted from Clare to Sara then back to Clare again. 'Do you mean... I could go... to prison?'

'Let's not look too far ahead,' Clare said. 'There are many options that the courts could consider. But maybe it would help if you told me why you took the items found in your garage.'

Ruth's brow creased. 'I... I don't know.' She cleared her throat then said, 'I suppose I just wanted them...'

'But you haven't used any of them,' Clare said, 'have you?'

'No.'

'Did you plan to sell them, perhaps?' Clare suggested. 'Or give them as gifts?'

Ruth's eyes filled with tears. 'No,' she said. 'I just took them.'

Clare passed a box of tissues across the desk to Ruth who, after hesitating, took one and dabbed at the corners of her eyes. 'I think, Ruth,' she said, 'that we'll break now.' She indicated the cup on the desk. 'Maybe get you a fresh cup of tea. And I'd like you to see our duty doctor.'

Ruth said nothing to this, and Clare suspended the interview.

'Back shortly,' she said, lifting the now-cold cup of tea and leaving the room.

'What do you reckon, boss?' Sara said, when they were back out in the office.

'I'm no expert, Sara, but I'd say she's not well. Could you make her a fresh cup of tea while I call the doctor?'

–

The duty doctor arrived an hour later and was shown into the interview room to speak to Ruth. He was with her for about twenty minutes when Jim tapped on Clare's office door.

'Doc would like a word, Clare.'

Clare indicated a chair and the doctor sat, putting his medical bag on the floor beside him.

'I think she ought to see a psychiatrist, Inspector.'

'But what's your view, doctor? Off the record, I mean.'

'In my view, she may be suffering from kleptomania. It's pretty uncommon but the guilt she's exhibiting, the theft of items she clearly has no use for – they seem classic symptoms to me. But, I'm not a specialist. If I were you, I'd have a psychiatrist examine her before preferring any charges.'

Clare thanked the doctor and sat on, mulling this over. Then she moved to her computer and began looking for the list of medical specialists they could call on. The duty psychiatrist for the area was a Dr Mateo Morales. Clare found his telephone number and dialled. A voicemail cut in stating Dr Morales was on annual leave until the eighteenth of January. Clare ended the call and found the number for the duty doctor who'd just attended.

'I'm afraid our psychiatric specialist is on annual leave, doc. Can you recommend anyone else who might be able to help?'

The doctor gave Clare the name of a colleague working in St Andrews. 'Dr Sandra Holt,' he said. 'She's excellent. And, if she can't call round she may be able to talk by phone.'

Clare thanked the doctor and dialled the number he'd given her. She left a message for Dr Holt and sat back to think. Was there really any merit in putting someone like Ruth Williams through the court system? They had all the goods she'd stolen, after all. Perhaps there was some other way of dealing with her. Whatever the solution was she had to find it quickly. She had a double murder investigation that was going nowhere fast.

Chapter 27

As Clare wandered into the incident room to check on progress she heard the front door open. Checking over her shoulder she saw the tall figure of DCI Alastair Gibson enter the station. Suddenly she felt a knot in her stomach. He was tanned and looked lean. He clearly didn't have an admin assistant baking cakes on a daily basis. Or perhaps the week's skiing had burned off the Christmas calories. He hadn't noticed her and he strode up to the desk. Clare watched as Zoe looked up from her computer then went to greet him. They exchanged a few words then Zoe glanced across to the incident room door. The DCI turned and he saw Clare. He smiled and Clare felt her cheeks flush. Then she gathered her wits and went to greet him.

'Al,' she said. 'Great to see you. Erm… coffee?'

Zoe appeared in the kitchen as they were making coffee. She smiled at the DCI and held out a plate. 'Thought you might like a bit of cake,' she said.

'What about me?' Clare said, trying not to laugh as Zoe made sheep's eyes at the DCI.

'You've had yours!'

'Thanks, er…' the DCI said.

'Zoe.'

'Thanks, Zoe.' He watched her as she walked off. 'She seems nice.'

'Hands off,' Clare said. 'She's my new admin assistant and she's excellent. You're not pinching her.'

They carried their coffees back to Clare's office and sat down. The DCI held out the cake. 'If you really want it…'

'Let's share it,' Clare said, breaking the cake in two. She hesitated then they both began speaking at once.

'I hope...' the DCI began then broke off.

'Go/on,' Clare said.

'I hope you had a good Christmas? You were with your family, weren't you?'

Clare nodded. 'Yes, thanks.' She hesitated, wondering if she should say something about Geoffrey but he went on.

'I was skiing.'

'Yes, I know,' Clare said, before she could stop herself. Dammit. Now he'd know she was looking at his Facebook page.

'Innsbruck,' he added.

'Nice. Good time?'

'It was lovely. Good snow. Do you ski, Clare? I can't remember if you said.'

'Not really. I mean I tried it once and I'd love to have another go but I'm pretty hopeless.'

'It's just practice. Maybe you should go more often. Or book a ski holiday, even.'

Clare considered this. 'Yes, maybe.' She sipped at her coffee then said, 'I saw your photos. Facebook,' she added. 'They... they came up on my timeline.'

He nodded. 'Seems a distant memory now.'

'It looked lovely.'

'Yes it was. Good friends, good craic.'

Clare waited to see if he would say anything about the friends, or if there was one special friend, but instead he took out his phone and began flicking through photos. 'Check out that view,' he said, clicking on one that showed a ski hut with a backdrop of snow-covered mountains.

Clare leaned in closer and, as she did, she caught a whiff of his cologne, earthy and aromatic. She remembered it and had a sudden flashback to the night they'd shared a curry in Daisy Cottage. He'd spilled sauce on his shirt and Clare had insisted on soaking it to remove the stain. She'd taken the shirt from him and carried it into the kitchen, feeling it warm in her hands, fragrant with his cologne. Then they'd carried on eating – eating and drinking until the coffee lay untouched and Clare had taken his hand and led him upstairs.

Her mouth was dry now, her stomach in knots.

'We skied this piste,' he was saying.

She recovered herself and smiled. 'Amazing.' And she handed the phone back to him.

They fell silent again, munching the cake. Then the DCI said, 'So, your double murder. Any progress?'

She began filling him in on Miles and Cheryl, and on the links between the two victims. 'Both went to the same school and they're in a WhatsApp group.'

'Coincidence,' he asked, 'or a connection?'

'I'm not sure yet. They were both also on the same dating website.'

'Now that sounds more promising. You found anyone they both connected with?'

'Tech Support managed to get into their dating site accounts and the team are going through the data now, checking for common links.'

'Good. You'll have to alert the dating site.'

'Jim's been onto them, giving them the heads-up. If we can establish a link I'll have the site taken offline. Thing is…'

'Yeah?'

'Well the dating site doesn't ask for contact details, just an email address. And, as you know, people use disposable addresses. So tracking down anyone they have in common could be tricky. Unless…'

'Unless what?'

'Unless one of us engineered a date with whoever it is.'

'Absolutely not, Clare. I won't hear of it. Quite apart from the danger it would put the officer in, it could be construed as entrapment. If you did manage to arrest the perpetrator a clever solicitor would have it thrown out before it reached court. And the papers would have a field day.'

'Suppose.'

'There's no suppose about it. Look, Clare, I'll try to rustle you up a few more officers. You're not exactly drowning in manpower here.'

'That would be great, Al.' Clare's phone began to ring. Glancing at the display she saw it was the number she'd dialled for Dr Holt. 'I have to take this,' she said.

The DCI nodded. 'I'll just finish my coffee and leave you in peace. But I'll be in touch daily. I'm down at Dunfermline now so I could be up here in an hour, if you need me.'

Clare smiled her thanks and clicked to answer the call, her eyes on the DCI's back as he moved to the door. 'Dr Holt, thanks so much for calling. Our duty doctor said you might be able to help.'

'I'll try.'

Clare related the story of Ruth's arrest, of the garage full of unused goods and Ruth's tearful interview. 'Would you be free to come and examine her?'

'Unfortunately not this week,' Dr Holt said. 'I could probably come on Monday, if I rearranged things a bit. Any good?'

Clare considered this. 'I could release her, pending your examination, I suppose. But I am concerned about her mental wellbeing in the meantime.'

'Okay, Inspector. From what you say, it does sound like a classic case. I can certainly examine her and report on my findings. But, for her own sake, she should be properly assessed and that has to be through her GP. Unfortunately the waiting list for adult psych services is lengthy. I presume you have to decide whether to charge her or not.'

'In a nutshell.'

'Right. Let's set up an appointment for Monday, then. Say… two thirty?'

'Perfect. I'll make sure she's here for you. And, in the meantime, I'll consider how best to support her.'

'Start by telephoning her GP,' Dr Holt advised. 'They're the gateway to the services she needs.'

-

Clare called Sara and told her what Dr Holt had recommended. 'I think we'll release her, pending further enquiries. We'll have her back at two o'clock on Monday and the doc'll see her at two thirty.'

Ruth was even more tearful when Clare said she wasn't going to charge her until she'd seen a psychiatrist. 'I don't deserve it,' she said. 'Please, just charge me now. I'd like it over and done with.'

'I can't do that, Ruth. In fact, I don't want to do it. If it turns out there is a medical reason for what you've done we may be able to give you a formal caution, especially as you still have all the goods.' She smiled. 'I'm sure we can sort this out. Now, I'm going to send an officer home with you to collect your garage keys. And we'll be round with a van as soon as possible to uplift the stolen items. I'm also going to call your GP so if you can give me the details I'll leave you with PC Stapleton to go through the formalities. And we'd like you back here at two o'clock on Monday afternoon.'

Ruth nodded. 'Okay, Inspector. Whatever you say.'

-

When Clare had spoken to Ruth Williams' GP she wandered through to the incident room to see if there was any news. Janey, Robbie and Gillian were bent over laptops trawling through the WhatsApp group's social media accounts.

'Any luck?'

'Nothing yet, boss,' Janey said. 'Most of them are on Facebook but, from the little we can see of their profiles, there's nothing out of the ordinary.'

'What about private conversations between members?'

'We can't actually see that, boss. Only conversations Alison and Ingrid had with other members.'

'Dammit, of course. And WhatsApp's encrypted too, isn't it.' She stood, considering this for a moment, then said, 'I think it would be an idea to track them all down and pay them a call in person. I'll get some of the others to help.'

'Thanks, boss,' Janey said and the other two nodded.

'And keep an eye out for anyone in the group who has a link to Miles or Cheryl Sharp. Anyone at all, I want to know about it.' She turned to leave then she remembered something. 'Janey, did you have time to look up Sharp and Lafferty in Companies House?'

Janey shook her head. 'Sorry, boss. Been head down at this.'

'Not to worry. I'll do it myself.' Clare left the room and found Chris chatting to Sara.

'I'm going to run Ruth Williams home,' Sara said. 'She's just in the loo.'

Clare smiled. 'Thanks, Sara. I appreciate it.'

'What's this?' Chris said. 'We running a taxi service for shoplifters now?'

Sara glared at him. 'If you'd seen her, you'd know,' she said.

Chris raised an eyebrow then followed Clare into her office. 'What's that about?'

'Our shoplifter. She's a poor soul.'

'She's a light-fingered thief.'

'Yes, she's that all right but it's not straightforward this time.'

'Whatever. So, what now?'

'We're going to have a look at Companies House.'

'Fascinating.'

Clare typed Sharp and Lafferty Companies House into her computer and clicked when the weblink appeared. 'Here we go,' she said. 'Now, let's look at their filing history...'

She began clicking and scrolling while Chris yawned.

'Okay. So, no accounts for last year yet but we can see the previous few years.'

She clicked to open the accounts files for the last three years and scrolled through, studying them. Then she jotted figures down on her notepad. Finally she sat back. 'They're doing okay,' she said. 'At a rough calculation I'd say their profit has increased by around 20 per cent each year. Seems a lot, don't you think?'

'Maybe,' Chris said. 'But they are accountants. If anyone knows how to turn a profit it'll be them.'

'Okay then. Let's do the same for Crossford Financial.'

Clare typed the name into the search box and she called up Crossford's accounts for the same years. 'So, the turnover's a lot less,' she said, 'and so's the profit.' She indicated the figures she'd jotted down for Crossford. 'I'd say it's up no more than a couple of per cent each year. Certainly nothing like Sharp and Lafferty.'

'Maybe they're just better at it.'

'Could be. But that office in Hope Street won't come cheap.' She sat back, considering this. 'The quicker Diane gets into that document on Alison's laptop, the better.'

Chapter 28

'They've both Liked a lot of men,' Jim said, holding up his notepad. 'I've jotted down the names here.'

Clare, standing behind him, peered at the Attracto webpage on the screen. 'What about men who've Liked them first, Jim? Any common to both?'

'Aye, three so far. And I'm not done yet.'

'Any private messages?'

'Just a couple. Both women have exchanged phone numbers with men they have Liked on the site.'

'Any of them the same?'

'I've not got that far, yet but I will check. Thing is, though, Clare, if someone on Attracto is a murderer they might have multiple profiles, different mobiles. If we really do have a determined serial killer he won't be daft.' He sat back and stretched, rubbing his neck.

'We have to hope not, Jim. Look, you take a break. You look done in. I'll get young Gary onto checking their mobile records for common numbers.'

Clare wandered back into her office. Something was niggling away in the back of her mind. She sat down at her computer. The webpage of Companies House was still up on the screen and she typed The Heron's Nest into the search box. There were several companies with similar names but finally she found the entry she was looking for. There was only one company officer listed, a Nicholas Hamilton. She clicked to view the filing history and saw that there were accounts for the past few years. Browsing through the PDFs it was clear the restaurant was doing well. She opened up Facebook again and searched for Nicholas Hamilton but there were too many entries returned. So she searched instead for the restaurant. The Heron's Nest Facebook page was busy – full of photos, including group shots of the management team. Nicholas Hamilton had been tagged in some and one click took Clare to his Facebook page. He had opted for the minimum security and she was able to browse his timeline and his photos. And there were plenty of them. She scrolled through photos of him, at the wheel of a black 4x4 vehicle, shots of him teeing off on The Old Course – the world-famous (and eye-wateringly expensive) golf club in St Andrews – and others taken at a glittering black-tie dinner. He was clearly enjoying the fruits of his labour.

On an impulse she picked up the phone and dialled Crossford Financial. Kathy answered and Clare introduced herself.

'Kathy, I don't want to put you in an awkward position but if I said that the client who marched out of that appointment with Alison after fifteen minutes was called Nicholas Hamilton, would I be correct?'

Kathy hesitated and Clare knew she'd guessed correctly. 'I… I mean…'

'So let's agree I'm not wrong then?' Clare suggested.

'You're… not wrong.'

'Thanks, Kathy.'

Clare put down the phone and mulled this over. If Nicholas Hamilton had wanted Alison to do something questionable and she had refused, and if he'd suspected Alison was trying to stop Miles Sharp doing it, would that be enough of a motive to kill her? It sounded very unlikely but then murder was rarely the product of a rational mind.

Her office door opened and Chris looked in. 'Seen the time?'

Clare glanced at her watch. Quarter to six. 'Where's the day gone?'

'I'm knocking off now, boss. I'm guessing the weekend…'

'Everyone in as usual, Chris. Except Zoe, of course. Briefing at eight. Pass the word round, would you?'

–

As she walked out to her car, Clare clicked her mobile phone. She scrolled to the Attracto app which she'd downloaded the night before and, while she waited for the fan to clear the windscreen, she viewed her profile. She was glad to see a pop-up reminding users of the Safe Dating advice. But they really needed the site taken down. A red number two was flashing, indicating she had another two Likes. She hovered over the icon to view them. Then her warning to Zoe came into her head. For all she knew, one of her two admirers could be the killer they were hunting.

The windscreen was almost clear now but it was dark outside. Sitting alone in her car in the deserted car park, Clare suddenly felt uneasy. How many men had viewed her profile since she'd created it – were viewing it right now? And was the killer among them? Was she so desperate to be part of a couple that she was browsing men on a website possibly connected to a double murder? She pressed a button on the dashboard and felt the reassuring clunk as her car doors locked. Then she put down her phone and pulled on her seat belt.

Maybe it was time to delete her Attracto profile.

Then again, as long as there was a killer out there, it might just come in handy.

–

Benjy's welcome was to chase his tail immediately in front of her, scattering the post across the hall. Clare bent to retrieve it and wandered into the kitchen, switching on lights as she went. There were the usual bills and junk flyers and there was one handwritten envelope.

She glanced at the wine bottle then, remembering she was trying to drink a bit less, flicked the switch on the kettle. She took a knife from the drawer and slit the letter, withdrawing a stiff card. It was bordered by garlands of pink roses and in the centre were the words Save The Date. She read on and saw that it was advance notice of a wedding.

Tom's wedding.

Clare thought back to that evening when Tom, her ex-boyfriend from Glasgow, had turned up at Daisy Cottage with his new fiancée, Gillian, in tow. Clare hadn't even known Tom was seeing anyone. It had only been a few months since Clare had ended their relationship and here he was, on the rebound with the golden-haired Gillian (Call me Gilly). And she had been so right for Tom. So completely perfect. They giggled and finished each other's sentences until Clare had wanted to vomit.

Geoff had been there that night and had helped her through an interminable evening. She'd watched Tom with this vision of loveliness and wondered if she'd ever really known him. How on earth could she have spent so many years in a relationship with this man who now seemed besotted with this woman? A woman so completely opposite to Clare? She'd been a dancer with Scottish ballet for a time and now was a PE teacher at an exclusive girls' school. She was perfect, of course, but somehow Clare would have had more respect for Tom if he'd settled for someone a little less perfect. A little more like Clare perhaps. Her good intentions evaporated and she ignored the steam pouring from the kettle. It was going to be a wine night after all.

She hadn't thought it would last – Tom and Gillian. Perhaps she'd hoped it wouldn't last. And, once more, she faced the unpalatable truth that, while she no longer wanted Tom, she'd quite enjoyed him still wanting her. She wondered idly what would happen if she clicked her fingers in Tom's direction. Would he come running? Cast off his perfect bride-to-be and throw his lot in with Clare again?

Glancing at the card she saw Tom had scrawled at the bottom.

Do come if you can, Clare.

We'd love to have you with us on our special day.

'Aye, that'll be right,' she told Benjy.

Outside the moon was rising. It wasn't freezing but it was going to be a clear night. 'Tell you what,' she said to the dog, 'I'll shove a pizza in the oven and we'll go for a quick walk. Clear our heads.'

Benjy was beside himself with joy at the sight of Clare picking up his lead and he followed her to the front door, almost on his hind legs as he jumped up at her.

'Sit,' she roared, channelling her inner Isobel. To her delight he obeyed and she ruffled his neck. His tail thumped against the floor and she clipped on the lead, stepping out into the January darkness. As she emerged from the garden onto the road, the moon lighting her way, she looked up and saw a carpet of stars across the sky; and the more she looked the more she saw. She stood gazing up at it for a few moments until Benjy gave a quiet wuff.

'Come on then,' she said and, turning her collar up against the cold evening, she began to walk briskly with the little dog at her heels.

Saturday, 9th January

Chapter 29

Jim and Sara were carrying another desk into the incident room when Clare arrived on Saturday morning.

'Two more up from Glenrothes,' Jim said, nodding towards a couple of uniformed officers chatting over mugs of coffee.

Clare recognised them and smiled over. 'Just let me dump my things and check emails then I'll be in to start the briefing.'

Five minutes later they had gathered in the incident room. Clare thanked Liv and Erin, the two Glenrothes officers, then asked for updates.

'Working through the WhatsApp group,' Janey said. 'A few are proving hard to find but we're getting there.'

'Okay, guys. Liv and Erin: can you help with that?'

The two officers indicated they would, and Clare turned to Jim. 'Any luck with those dating site matches?'

'Aye. It is just the three, Clare. But they're all using names that make it hard to identify them.'

'What about photos?' Clare asked.

'Yes, we've photos of their faces but...'

'Reverse image search.'

Jim's brow furrowed.

'I'll show you when we're done here,' Clare said. 'So, what else do we have?'

Gary raised his hand. 'Both victims have texted the same number. But, unfortunately...'

'It's a burner phone?'

'Yeah. Sorry, boss. No way of tracing it.'

'So, now we know the two women were in touch with the same person. Those of you checking WhatsApp, make sure you have that number when you speak to the group members. If anyone matches it, call me immediately.'

Clare glanced at the board again. 'Any luck with the CCTV from that pub, Sara?'

Sara shook her head. 'Sorry, boss. With the shoplifter yesterday, I didn't get back to speak to them about it.'

'Okay. Make that a priority,' Clare said, and Sara nodded.

'Our accounting couple,' Clare went on. 'The Sharps – have they matched with any of the WhatsApp group?'

Heads shook. 'Okay,' Clare said. 'Now I visited Cheryl Sharp yesterday and she admitted she had called at Alison Reid's house two days before Christmas. She claims it was to warn Alison off Miles – she implied Alison still had a thing for him.'

'Do you believe her, boss?' Janey asked.

'Yes I do,' Clare said. 'She admitted knowing that Miles and Alison had met at lunchtime on the third of December. She followed them there in a taxi and waited while Alison spent twenty minutes in Miles's car. So it wouldn't be unreasonable for her to be suspicious of Alison. I think she's mistaken but I do think she believes what she told me.'

Chris caught Clare's eye. 'The restaurant, Clare.'

She nodded then looked round the room. 'Now, this next bit is completely confidential. I don't have any proof yet and, until I do, I don't want any of this getting back to the Sharps. Okay?'

There were murmurs of, 'Yes boss,' and Clare went on.

'I've been looking into the proprietor of The Heron's Nest restaurant – one Nicholas Hamilton. He was, until recently, a client of Alison Reid's. He called in to Crossford a few weeks ago for an hour-long appointment and flew out the door after fifteen minutes. Alison later learned he'd moved his business to Sharp and Lafferty. It's possible Hamilton asked Alison to do something questionable – tax evasion, or something like that.

'Either way, my guess is that Alison refused. He walks out the door in a temper and finds his way to Miles Sharp's office. Miles, I think, would have no such scruples, particularly with a client of his ex-wife's.'

'Any idea what he wanted Alison to do?' Nita asked.

'Not yet, Nita. But Diane is working on accessing a password-protected document on Alison's laptop. We don't yet know what's in the document but there must be a reason she protected it.'

Gary raised his hand. 'Are you planning to interview Hamilton, boss?'

Clare considered this. 'At the moment I'm not keen. If he has some connection to Alison's death – however tenuous – I don't want him or Miles Sharp forewarned. So, as I said, not a word about it outside this room.'

Janey said, 'Funny thing, boss. That WhatsApp group – they were talking about a school reunion. This...' she checked her notepad and went on, 'this Jessica Peters, the one who mentioned Attracto – she was trying to book somewhere for a meal.'

'And?'

'She suggested The Heron's Nest.'

Clare looked round the room. 'Any thoughts on that?'

Sara said, 'It's a nice place, boss. Good food.'

'Town's full of good eateries, though,' Gary said.

Clare nodded. 'Fair point. Let's just bear it in mind. There might be no connection.' She glanced round. 'Right, that's it. Keep in touch.'

As the officers began to drift out of the room, Jim reminded Clare she'd promised to show him how to search images.

'I'd like to see that too,' Sara said, and Chris wandered over to see what Clare was about to do.

'Okay,' she said, sitting down at a computer. 'Have you saved images of the three men, Jim? What are their names, by the way?'

Jim took the mouse and clicked to open the file where he'd stored the photos. 'I've saved them with their usernames,' he said. 'So, there's SandyD, BikerBoy and Stoneman.'

'Right, then,' Clare said, pulling the keyboard towards her. 'Thankfully all three are front facing. That gives us a better chance of finding them online.' She began typing. 'So, first open up Google… then click up there, where it says Images.'

'Oh,' Sara said. 'There's a camera in the search box now.'

'Right,' Clare said, 'now click that and upload the image.' She demonstrated this with SandyD's photo. Two pages of results came up, including his Attracto picture. 'See here,' Clare said, 'we've got his Facebook page now. If I open that in a new tab you can see his name is Sandy Donaldson.' She clicked the mouse again. 'Go back to the results and there he is on holiday last year. I'd say that's where his profile pic was taken. And…' she moved the mouse to indicate another result, 'this is from his workplace. Looks like he was giving a seminar in Stirling last October. That should be enough to let you track him down.'

Clare repeated the process with BikerBoy and a screen of results appeared. But when she ran the search with Stoneman, there were pages and pages of results. 'Uh-oh,' she said, 'looks like this one's used a fake photo. Or his photo's been stolen.'

'Why would anyone steal it?' Sara asked. 'I can't see the point. If he arranged to meet someone, she'd know he wasn't the man in the photo as soon as she saw him.'

'Usually it's criminals trying to trick people into parting with information. They use an attractive photo to create a fake persona and seek out likely targets – anyone gullible enough to believe they're talking to the good-looking guy.'

'Hanging's too good for them,' Jim said, his voice gruff. 'Wee scumbags.'

'No argument there, Jim.' Clare glanced at Chris who was staring at the screen. 'Chris? You seen this photo before?'

'Er, no. Don't think so. I thought he was familiar but I'm wrong.'

Clare looked at him. She was about to press him further when her phone began to ring. Diane.

'I've got into your document, Clare. It's up on the network now.'

'Thanks so much, Diane. I'm really grateful.'

'You'll need the password. Got a pen?'

Clare scribbled down the password and went back to her office. She shook the mouse to bring her computer to life then navigated her way to the document. It was called In Case Required. She clicked the icon and entered the password. It opened to reveal a heading Sequence of Events, followed by a series of bullet points. Clare increased the font size and began to read.

26 Nov – appointment 11 a.m. with NH to discuss proposal for future status of restaurant. NH proposed the following:

Forming new company – Cliff Bay Consultancy – Cayman Isles – to use for general consultancy, periodic rebranding for restaurants etc.

Cliff Bay bank account to be in Zurich

NH to pay Zurich a/c for consultancy work

Possible future loans from Cliff Bay – interest free?

Serious concerns re legality. Suggested it's aggressive tax avoidance. Unethical. NH left office.

27 Nov – rumour that NH has taken his business to Sharp and Lafferty.

27 Nov – emailed Miles re inadvisability of NH's proposal. Miles unconcerned!

30 Nov – again emailed Miles. No response.

1 Dec – emailed Miles – asked to meet.

3 Dec – 20-minute conversation with Miles, face-to-face. Warned him HMRC will catch up eventually. Miles, as advisor, could be liable. Miles agreed to talk again to NH but stopped short of refusing to assist.

Miles now not taking my calls, no response to emails.

10 Dec – emailed AEGIS Union Rep – appointment on 6th Jan to discuss (nb check time). Need advice on my responsibilities here.

23 Dec – Cheryl Lafferty turned up at door! Suspicious about my contact with Miles. No mention of NH scheme. Suspect she doesn't know.

Clare sat back considering what she'd read. Then she read it again to make sure she understood it. The plan was simple enough. Nicholas Hamilton wanted to reduce the tax he paid on restaurant takings. To do this he would create a company based in the Cayman Islands to undertake consultancy work, paying their fee to the company's account in Switzerland. The clever part was he would own the consultancy company so, in effect, he was paying himself, creating a business expense which wasn't taxable.

No wonder Alison Reid hadn't been keen. Clare wasn't even sure it was legal, never mind ethical. But it looked as if Miles Sharp was willing to give it a go. Clare had no doubt Miles would have it sewn up tightly with nothing in writing. No documentary evidence that he'd assisted Nicholas Hamilton with this. No doubt he'd tell him exactly what to do and how to do it but none of it would be written down. And, if HMRC did catch up with Hamilton, it would be his word against Miles's. Chances are Miles would wriggle out of any blame. He was just the type.

Alison had stopped short of naming Nicholas Hamilton in her document but Clare was in no doubt he was the architect of the scheme. But was it enough to challenge him? There was no actual proof. Only this document which, Clare guessed, wouldn't stand up in court.

She rose from her desk and went to her office door. Chris was tapping away at a keyboard. He glanced up and she motioned to him to come into her office. 'Have a look at this.'

She waited while Chris read through Alison's document.

'So, we've got him,' he said, looking up from the screen.

'Miles or Hamilton? At the moment there's no proof that either of them has done anything illegal. And we can't prove what Alison's written here is actually true.'

'Well she'd hardly have written it…'

'Yeah I know that. But this,' she jabbed the screen, 'it's not enough by itself. It's not illegal to think about doing something. I think about murdering you at least twice a week but the important thing is I haven't done it. Not yet…'

'Cheers for that.'

'Chris, what was the name of that officer from Dundee? The one who helped us with the money laundering.'

'Corinne. Corinne Sim. Want me to give her a call?'

'It's okay. I'll speak to her myself. Might be the best we can do is to flag it up to the Fraud lot and leave them to it. I could be wrong but I don't think this is what got Alison Reid killed.'

'Yeah, probably not.'

Clare sat back in her chair and yawned. 'How's it going out there?'

'Not bad. The team have got round most of the WhatsApp group. Still a few to track down.'

'Any phone numbers match with the burner phone Alison and Ingrid were texting?'

'Nope. Not yet at least. Tell you what though…'

'What?'

'One of the people they can't get hold of is Jessica Peters – you know, the one who was trying to organise a reunion?'

'And the one who suggested Attracto. Now that worries me, Chris.'

'You think she's something to do with the killings?'

'Let's just say I'll be happier when we've tracked her down. And, when we do, I want to interview her myself – face-to-face. There's something about her involvement in this that I don't like.'

Chapter 30

Clare was about to pack up for the night and hand over to the Dundee Inspector when she suddenly remembered Chris's reaction to one of the Attracto photos. She found him in the kitchen, washing his coffee mug.

'What's this? You suddenly become domesticated?'

'Sara said if I didn't start washing my own mug she'd wrap it round the back of my head.'

'Good girl!'

'Did you actually want something? Or is it Have-a-go-at-Chris Day?'

Clare closed the kitchen door.

Chris looked up, his face a study. 'Detective Inspector, are you about to importune me?'

'In your dreams, sonny. No. But there was something I wanted to ask you.'

'Go on, then.'

'That photo from Attracto. That guy, Stoneman – you recognised him, didn't you?'

Chris took a moment to answer. 'I think so,' he said. 'I think I've seen him before.'

'Where?'

He glanced at the kitchen door then lowered his voice. 'You know I've got this party arranged for next Saturday? The surprise one – for our engagement?'

'Yeah. The Kenlybank, isn't it?'

He nodded. 'I think I've seen him there. At the hotel.'

Clare frowned. 'A guest?'

'No. On the staff. I was chatting to the events manager about the party. Making arrangements, you know? And he went past carrying a tray of drinks. I mean, the hotel was busy. Christmas parties and the like. But I noticed him because, well – I'm not in the market for a bloke, Clare but, if I was – he's bloody good-looking! I was almost tempted to ask the manager to make sure he wasn't on duty at the party.'

Clare laughed. 'I wouldn't worry. I'm sure Sara only has eyes for you. But all the same, that's interesting.'

'I mean, if this Stoneman character's our murderer, he'd hardly be using his own photo. I reckon this poor guy's picture's been nicked. Well I know it has, judging by all the photos on the internet.'

'We should probably call round, anyway. Make sure he's legit.'

Chris's face fell. 'Tonight? I've not stopped since half seven this morning.'

Clare thought about this. 'I suppose it can wait. I mean I doubt he's our man. But we do need to rule him out. Tomorrow, then. And could you ask Jim to check the other two out please? SandyD and… whatever the other one was called.'

'BikerBoy, I think,' Chris said. 'Will do.'

'Come on then. Dry your mug and let's get out of here. Fresh start in the morning.'

–

It was only when she'd lit the fire and flopped down on the sofa watching Ant and Dec on TV that Clare remembered the next day was Sunday. There was no way she could take the morning off for dog training and she felt something approaching relief at having a genuine excuse. It was quite exhausting being the owner of the worst behaved dog in the field – except for Ralph of course. He always managed to outdo Benjy, thank goodness. And then there was Ralph's owner…

Maybe she could spare a few hours, after all.

She lifted the phone and dialled Chris's number.

He answered immediately. 'Please tell me there's not another body,' he said. 'I've just ordered a Chinese.'

'No, you're okay. What are you having?'

'Chicken fried rice.'

Although Clare was now full of her mother's cottage pie she had a sudden longing for a Chinese takeaway. 'I'm jealous,' she said. 'Enjoy.'

'So, if it's not a body...'

'It's tomorrow, Chris. Could you let the team know I'll be in a bit late – say midday? There's something I need to do in the morning.'

'I thought you hated that dog training?'

Dammit, Clare thought. She'd forgotten Chris knew about it. It wasn't really on, taking time off to go and stand in a field to be boomed at by the redoubtable Isobel. But she'd been working flat out since Alison's body was discovered on... she couldn't even remember which day it was now. No, it would probably do her good to have a couple of hours off. 'It's the trainer,' she said. 'She'll make me stand in a corner if I miss a week!'

'Aye, go on then. I'll cover for you.'

'Cheers Chris. Enjoy your chicken.'

Clare put down the phone and sank back into her sofa. Benjy jumped up and snuggled into her legs. On the TV Ant and Dec were dressed as traffic wardens, pretending to clamp some celebrity's car. Clare couldn't think who the celeb was but it was easy TV and just what she needed. After a few minutes Benjy began to snore softly and Clare, too, closed her eyes, letting the cares of the day drift away.

Sunday, 10ᵗʰ January

Chapter 31

Clare could see that the fields opposite Daisy Cottage were flooded and she elected to put on her wellies, rather than her usual trail shoes. She had a new pair of dark jeans which fitted beautifully but they looked wrong against her well-worn anorak, with its pockets full of dog treats and poop bags. There was a new red Holland Cooper coat with a soft furry hood in her wardrobe. She'd hardly worn it, having bought it in the January sales last year. Even the sale price was far above what Clare would normally spend but she found the coat irresistible. She turned round, admiring it in her bedroom mirror then grabbed a new scarf – a Christmas gift from her sister – and whistled to Benjy.

It was a lovely morning. The sun was struggling above the horizon but the sky was blue and the wind light. As Clare drove along Bogward Road, swerving round puddles, she saw the first shoots of winter jasmine brightening house walls. It wouldn't be long before the snowdrops were showing too. It had been a cold start to the year but every day that passed was a day nearer spring. As she left the town the road began to rise up and she glimpsed the North Sea. The sun was glinting off the tips of the waves which sparkled and danced in the breeze. She drove on, passing rows of green-coloured holiday homes in the St Andrews Holiday Park set high on Kinkell Braes. The road moved inland and after another mile or two she approached the field and signalled to pull in.

She was one of the first to arrive, earning a nod of approval from Isobel who was setting out marker cones.

'Criss-cross walking today,' she announced and Clare's heart sank. Benjy could never manage to pass another dog without barking and jumping at it, and it was Clare's most hated of all the activities. But at least she had Ralph's owner to look forward to. She took up position with her back to the sun so she could see him approach. And then another woman arrived with a husky straining at the leash and Clare's attention was taken up with trying to keep Benjy calm.

It was Benjy who spotted Ralph first. Clare was chatting to the husky's owner who was admiring her red coat when she felt Benjy's tail beating against her legs. She looked up and saw Ralph racing down towards the training area on an extendable lead. But it wasn't the good-looking man who held the other end. It was an even better-looking woman. She was olive-skinned, with good hair. The kind Clare had seen in magazines like Country Living. Dark, shiny and thick, it hung down past her shoulders, the wind catching her French-girl fringe as she staggered after an ebullient Ralph. In contrast to Clare she wore a battered waxed jacket and faded blue jeans tucked into an old pair of riding boots and suddenly Clare felt ridiculously overdressed.

She had an easy smile and seemed full of fun, and Clare's heart sank to her boots. To add insult to injury, Benjy seemed to sense her disquiet and he jumped up to lick her hand, placing a pair of muddy front paws on her new red coat. She couldn't remember off-hand if it was washable but, somehow, she doubted it. Maybe people who wore these coats didn't have to worry about such things.

The woman came over to Clare, smiling broadly, her hair blowing softly in the wind. Clare's own hair, she remembered, needed washing and was scraped back roughly with an old hair tie.

'This must be Benjy,' she said, bending to rub him behind the ears. Benjy responded by wagging his tail furiously and licking her on the hand.

Traitor, Clare thought, forcing a smile. 'Hi,' she said, 'I'm Clare.'

'Lesley,' the woman said, passing the dog lead behind her back as Ralph made to investigate the husky. She glanced at Isobel who was herding a couple of German Shepherd owners into the ring then turned back to Clare. 'It's usually my husband who brings Ralph but he's working today.' She inclined her head slightly towards Isobel. 'I think she's a bit scary.'

'Very,' Clare said.

Lesley laughed. 'We can be bottom of the class together, then.'

It was the longest dog training session Clare could remember and she escaped quickly at the end, the first to reach the car park. For once she made no attempt to clean Benjy's muddy paws. He jumped up to the front seat, smearing it with mud and grass, and stood patiently while Clare strapped him into his harness.

At home she settled him by the radiator and ran upstairs to change. Her red coat was streaked with muddy paw marks and she saw from the label that it would have to be dry-cleaned. 'Maybe it'll brush off when it's dry,' she said, more in hope than expectation. Then she changed into a work suit and, taking a bag of crisps from the kitchen, she headed for the station.

–

'Nearly finished checking the WhatsApp group,' Chris said, as she shrugged off her coat.

'Any likely suspects?'

'Nope. And no sign of Jessica Peters, either.'

'We have to find her, Chris. It's important.'

'Yeah, they are trying, Clare.'

'Surely one of the group members is still in touch with her – or knows something about her?'

'Good point,' Chris said. 'I'll get the guys to ring back round and see if any of them can help.'

'Fancy a trip into town?'

'To do… what?'

'I'd like to call in on our restaurateur. See what he has to say for himself.'

'You're not going to call him out on the Cayman Islands thing?'

'Not yet. I just want to see what he says about that appointment.'

Chapter 32

The Heron's Nest was at the far end of South Street, not far from the ruined cathedral. Clare pulled into one of the diagonal parking spaces near the close that led to the town's Byre Theatre. They emerged from the car and stood looking across at the restaurant. It looked busy, from what they could see. There were a few aluminium bistro-type tables outside where the smokers sat chatting, cradling coffees.

'Come on,' Clare said. 'Let's see what he has to say for himself.'

She pushed open the glass front door and a ding alerted a young man in dark trousers and a green shirt.

'Bit of a wait for a table, guys,' he said.

Clare took out her warrant card. 'Just a word with Mr Hamilton, please.'

The young man looked at the card then back and Clare and Chris.

'If you could let him know...' Clare said.

The man stood back to let a waiter with a tray pass then he turned and headed to the back of the restaurant. Clare took the chance to look round. The trademark herons were painted right round the walls and she wondered which of the tables Linda from Sharp and Lafferty had dined at. It was hard to say. There must be easily twenty tables, possibly more, and they were all full. A small bench to the side of the front door was occupied by a family of four, waiting to be seated. Looking round, it seemed as if everyone was having meals, not just coffee and cake. There was a specials board which was advertising smoked venison for twenty pounds a head and, as Clare read further down the board, a waitress in a black tunic rubbed the venison off. Another waiter went past bearing a large tray filled with plates of steak and hand-cut chips. The credit card machine was being passed from table to table and it was clear that The Heron's Nest was doing very well indeed.

A man appeared at Clare's arm. 'Detective Inspector Mackay?'

Clare took in Nicholas Hamilton. He wasn't tall, about the same height as she was. A bit overweight, his trousers straining at the waist, but he was otherwise neatly dressed. Unlike the waiting staff, he was wearing a crisp white shirt, open at the neck. Clare formed her lips into a smile. 'Is there somewhere we could talk, sir?'

He hesitated. 'As you see, Inspector, this is our busiest time. Maybe...'

'I appreciate that, sir, but we're investigating a murder so if we could go somewhere quiet...'

His face gave nothing away. He motioned to the green-shirted man who had greeted Clare and Chris. He spoke quietly into his ear and the young man nodded. Then he turned back to Clare. 'If you'd like to follow me.'

He led them through the restaurant then held open a side door before walking down a short corridor to another door. 'My office,' he said. 'Bit messy but you know how it is.'

It was a small room, dominated by a cantilever desk with a melamine top, scuffed here and there with a ring where a coffee mug obviously sat. A white MacBook was open on the desk and he closed this, moving it to the side. He stepped round the back of his desk and indicated two chairs in the corner of the room. Then he sat down and waited while Chris pulled the chairs over to the desk. When they were seated he looked from Clare to Chris and back to Clare again. 'So?'

Clare decided she didn't much like Nicholas Hamilton. She studied him for a few seconds, taking her time before she spoke. Then she said, 'We're investigating the murder of Alison Reid.'

The colour drained from his cheeks and Clare wondered if it was shock or could it be guilt?

'I... er, I didn't know.'

'I'm afraid so, Mr Hamilton. So I'd like to ask when you last saw Alison?'

'Oh wait a minute,' he said, sitting forward in his seat. 'You surely don't think I had anything to do with it?'

'We're just trying to find out as much as we can about Alison. I understand you were a client.'

'Yes that's right.'

'Although,' Clare went on, 'I gather this is no longer the case.'

Nicholas Hamilton's hand went to his face and he rubbed his chin. 'Well, no.'

'Can I ask why?'

He shifted in his chair and straightened his back. 'Professional differences.' He was recovering himself, Clare thought.

'Can you tell me about the last time you saw Alison, please?'

'Well I didn't bloody kill her, if that's what you're suggesting.'

Clare smiled. 'Of course not, sir. We're simply trying to build up a picture of Alison's life in the last few weeks. Personal and professional. So, if you could—'

'At her office,' he said, cutting across Clare. 'I had an appointment, then I left. That's all.'

'Would I be correct in thinking the appointment ended early?'

'Erm, probably.'

'After fifteen minutes, I understand. And it was supposed to be an hour.'

He shrugged. 'I've no idea how long her appointments are. I'm a busy man, Inspector. I said what I had to say, she made some comments and I left.'

'So there's no suggestion of an argument between you?'

He paused for a moment, as though choosing his words. 'If you insist on knowing, I wanted Alison to arrange some investments for me. She disagreed. Said they were risky and not a good move in the current financial climate. I told her it was my money and she said I was at liberty to take it elsewhere. So I did.' He glared at them, his mouth set, defying them to challenge him.

Clare, her eyes still fixed on Hamilton, sensed Chris sit forward and she reached out her foot to tap his ankle gently. She didn't want to give away the contents of Alison Reid's document. Not yet. Instead, she said, 'Did you find another accountant?'

'Yep.'

'Name?'

'Is that relevant?'

'Probably not. But it might save us disturbing you on another occasion.'

'I really don't see why…'

'It's entirely up to you, of course, sir. But if we find it has no relevance to our investigations then the information will be disregarded. Or is there some reason you prefer not to tell us?'

He looked at Clare for a minute, his gaze stony.

She stared right back, waiting.

Finally, he broke the awkward silence. 'Sharp and Lafferty, if you really want to know. And, now, Inspector, if there's nothing else, I've a restaurant full of hungry punters to feed.' He rose from his chair, indicating that the interview was at an end.

Clare sat on. 'Actually, Mr Hamilton, there is something else you might be able to help us with.'

He sighed and sat down again. 'I very much doubt it, Inspector. But go on.'

'I wonder if you might have had an approach from a customer. A potential booking for a school reunion.'

'I suppose this has to do with your enquiries as well?'

'It does.'

'We are governed here by GDPR, Inspector. I'm obliged to respect customer confidentiality.'

Clare nodded. 'I do realise that, sir. But, in the case of a murder enquiry, GDPR doesn't apply. We could of course get a warrant for the information. But it would mean a further visit...'

Nicholas Hamilton opened the laptop and wiggled a wireless mouse. 'Name?'

'Jessica Peters.'

'Any idea when the booking's for?'

'Not really. But I'd guess sometime in the spring. Easter, maybe.'

He began typing into the search box then clicked with the mouse. 'Got it.'

Clare glanced at Chris. Was this it? Had they tracked Jessica Peters down at last? 'I don't suppose you have a phone number for her?'

He peered at the screen. 'No,' he said, 'she sent a couple of emails. One to ask for menus, the other to say she'd be in touch.' He looked up from the MacBook. 'No firm date yet.'

Chris leaned forward. 'Could we see the emails please?'

Nicholas Hamilton raised an eyebrow. 'Is this really necessary?'

'I'm afraid so,' Clare said. 'And we will be back with a warrant, if you don't feel able to let us see them today.'

He turned the laptop round to face them. 'Go on, then. I've nothing to hide. But if she raises hell because I've shown you...'

'Don't worry, sir,' Chris said. 'We won't mention it – unless of course it's germane to our enquiries.'

Chris took hold of the mouse and began scrutinising the first email. Clare watched as he clicked and the screen filled with what seemed to be random strings of text.

'Header info,' he muttered. 'Is there a printer I can use?' he asked Nicholas.

'Sure. It's switched on.'

Chris took a screenshot then sent it to the printer. Then he repeated the process with the second email and the printer came to life once more. He turned the laptop back round and returned the mouse. 'Obviously, if Miss Peters gets back in touch you'll let us know?'

'Mind if I ask why?'

'Just routine.' Chris rose to retrieve the printouts and Clare followed suit.

'Thanks, Mr Hamilton,' she said. 'We appreciate your help.'

As they walked back down the short corridor, Clare said, 'Business is booming, then?'

'Sunday's always busy.'

'Well, good luck with those investments.'

'Eh?'

'Those risky investments. I'm sure Sharp and Lafferty will look after you.' And before he could reply Clare opened the door which led back into the restaurant area. The hubbub prevented him from replying and they made their way quickly to the front door and back out to South Street.

'You enjoyed that, didn't you?' Chris said as they walked back over to the car.

'It's always fun to put the wind up a smug bastard.'

'And you do it so prettily.'

Clare clicked to unlock the car. 'So, what's with the emails? What's all that...' she waved a hand at the printouts Chris was holding, '...that stuff?'

'Header info, like I said.'

'Which is?'

Chris climbed into the car and turned to pull on his seat belt. 'I'm buggered if I know. But what I do know is that near the bottom, somewhere, it'll show Jessica Peters' IP address.'

'So we can find out her location?'

'Yep.'

'Detective Sergeant West, sometimes I remember why we pay you.'

'I do my best.'

As she pulled out of the parking space, Clare said, 'Germane to our enquiries? You swallowed a dictionary or something?'

'English is a beautiful language, Detective Inspector. You oughta try it sometime.'

Clare was prevented from replying by her phone ringing. She glanced at the display and saw it was Sara.

'Boss, I'm at The Harvest Moon pub. Checking the CCTV. Looks like Ingrid was there on the twenty-eighth, right enough. Clear footage of her at the bar and heading into the loos.'

Clare pulled the car into the side to focus on the call. 'What about the door, Sara? Do they have a camera there?'

'Yeah but it's not too clear. The bar was busy and I can't find a clear shot of her arriving or leaving. There was a steady stream of folk going in and out. Smokers, probably. But the barmaid remembers her now. Once I pointed her out on the CCTV.'

'Are you still there, Sara?'

'Yes. Just about to leave.'

'We're just along the street. Can you hold on?'

Chapter 33

The Harvest Moon wasn't busy, compared to The Heron's Nest. There were a few tables occupied by people having sandwiches and toasties, and a couple of barflies nursing half pints. Sara introduced Clare and Chris and the barmaid indicated the office.

'Help yourself,' she said. 'Just shout if you need anything.'

Sara led them into a small room at the back and closed the door behind them. Clare looked at her surroundings without enthusiasm. The room was badly in need of decorating. A grubby net curtain hung limply over the window and the walls were yellowed, perhaps with age but, judging by the musty atmosphere, more likely from years of cigarette smoke. The carpet on the floor was worn and the skirting board was coming away from the wall. Having seen how quiet the pub was on a Sunday Clare wasn't surprised there was no money to spend on the back rooms.

An old office desk stood against one wall with a typist's chair in front. The fabric on the seat was worn and the foam padding was starting to escape. A bulky monitor sat on the desk alongside a computer tower which was humming loud enough for Clare to be concerned it might be overheating.

Sara sat down on the typist's chair and took hold of the mouse. 'I've taken some stills,' she said, clicking to bring up the files. 'So this,' she pointed at the screen, 'is Ingrid at the bar, ordering drinks.'

'Drinks?' Clare said, 'As in for more than one person?'

'Yep. If I click on a few frames… see there? She has a wine glass in one hand and a tall glass in the other.'

'Does she sip from either at all?' Clare asked.

'Not that I can see.'

'So we don't know which glass was her drink?'

Sara shook her head. 'And here she is again, at the Ladies. See, she goes in and…' Sara clicked the mouse again, '…she comes out five minutes later.'

'Hold on,' Clare said, and she went back through to the bar where the barmaid was polishing glasses.

'Think I might die of boredom today,' the barmaid said, indicating the now almost empty bar.

'Can I ask you about the woman in the CCTV please?'

The barmaid shrugged. 'I don't remember much…'

'It looks like she was buying her drinks two at a time,' Clare said. 'She'd a wine in one hand and a tall glass in the other. Was she with someone?'

The barmaid's forehead creased as she tried to remember. 'It's so long ago now,' she said.

Clare waited and then the barmaid's face cleared. 'Now I come to think about it, she was drinking white burgundy. I remember that because I couldn't find the bottle at first. Somebody put it behind the Chardonnay.'

'And the other drink?'

'I think, to start with, she was only buying single drinks. I'm sure I served her a couple of times and she was drinking by herself. I got the impression she'd been stood up, poor thing. Embarrassing, you know. Especially with the place so busy.'

Clare nodded. 'But later she buys two drinks?'

'Yes, I think so. In fact, I'm sure of it. I think she met a friend. She said something about her night turning out better than expected.'

'Did you see this friend? What he looked like?'

'Oh, it was a woman,' the barmaid said.

Clare glanced at Chris then back at the barmaid. 'Are you sure?'

'Yes, pretty sure. A blonde woman.'

Clare took out her phone and typed in the web address of Sharp and Lafferty. She found a photo of Cheryl and, obscuring the name, held it out for the barmaid to see. 'Was it this woman?'

The barmaid took the phone from Clare and scrutinised the photo. Then she handed it back. 'I can't be sure,' she said. 'But I don't think so.' She jabbed the phone screen. 'She's quite striking. I'd have remembered her.'

Clare took her phone back. 'Okay, thanks so much. Do you mind if PC Stapleton stays on to look through the footage again?'

'Sure, no problem.'

Sara's face fell but Clare steered her back into the office. 'I want you to go through it again and take stills of any other blonde women who arrive alone. I want this woman found.'

Chapter 34

Back at the station, Chris went to check the IP addresses while Clare made herself a coffee. Minutes later he appeared at the staff kitchen door.

'There's something funny about those IP addresses,' he said. 'Jessica Peters?'

'Yeah. From the emails she sent to The Heron's Nest.'

'Funny, how?'

'They're different.'

'Meaning she's sent the emails from different places? Could be work and home, Chris.'

'Yeah, it could be. But the locations…'

'Which are?' She began spooning coffee into mugs.

'The first one came from France.'

Clare looked up, spoon in hand. 'France? That might explain why we can't find her – if she's living abroad now.'

'Well it might, except that the next email the following day, was sent from San Francisco.'

Clare frowned. 'That's a bit of a schlep from France. Could she have gone on holiday after sending the first email?'

'Yeah, it's possible, although she'd be a bit jet-lagged. There was only eighteen hours between the times they were sent.'

Clare began opening cupboard doors. 'Any biscuits? I'm starving.'

'Nope.'

'What? Not even a Wagon Wheel?'

Chris shook his head. 'I have to fit into my kilt for the party,' he whispered.

'Then you'd better stop eating Zoe's... wait – you have a kilt?' Clare gaped.

'What self-respecting Scotsman doesn't?'

Clare thought of Geoffrey Dark, over in Boston now. She'd never seen him in a kilt. Come to that, she couldn't imagine him in one either. And then she gave herself a shake. No point in thinking about him now. That chapter was over. She returned to her perusal of the cupboards and found a pack of Twix biscuits. 'I promise I'll replace this,' she said, taking one out of the pack and peeling off the wrapper. She bit into the Twix and stood considering what Chris had found. Then she said, 'Jessica – could she be – what's the word, spoofing her email address? Trying to make it look as if it came from elsewhere?'

'I wondered that. So I called Diane.'

'Was she in on a Sunday?'

'No. But her wunderkind Craig was.'

'And?'

He shook his head. 'Craig reckons not. The point of spoofing is to make it seem as if someone else has sent the email. If she'd done that, and Nicholas Hamilton had replied, it would have gone to the email address she was pretending it came from.'

'Not much good for booking a restaurant, then.'

'Not really.'

'So?'

'Craig reckons she's probably using a VPN.'

'Virtual Private Network?'

'Yeah. He says if you sign up with a VPN company you can choose from thousands of locations, all over the world. What's more, you can chop and change. So...'

'France one day, San Francisco the next,' Clare finished for him.

'Exactly.'

Clare lifted the mug to her lips and sipped at her coffee. 'But why would she bother? I suppose, if you're ultra-conscious about internet security, a VPN makes sense. But why keep changing your location?'

Chris shrugged. 'Beats me. But there's nothing illegal about it. Maybe she just likes to keep one step ahead of spammers and hackers.'

'Or maybe she has a reason to hide her location,' Clare said. 'Maybe she wants it to look like she's in another country...'

'...but she's here all the time?'

Clare's lips tightened. 'Well, if she is here,' she said, 'why would she want us to think she isn't?'

Chris saw what she was thinking. 'So we don't connect her to the murder of two of her classmates.'

Clare shoved the last of the Twix into her mouth and dropped the wrapper into the bin. 'And if that is the case,' she said through a mouthful of crumbs, 'then we really need to get hold of her. And fast.'

The kitchen door opened and Sara looked in. 'I've checked up on those blondes, boss.'

'And?'

'Probably four of them, although the pub was so busy it's hard to be sure. And some folk came in with hoods up so the camera at the door didn't pick up their hair colour. Must have been raining.'

'Okay, Sara. Print them out and stick them up on the board in the incident room. And do a Google search on the images, please. Remember how to do it?'

Sara said she did and went off to pin up the photos. Clare picked up her mug. 'Fancy a chat, Chris? Help me get this straight in my head.'

Chris followed her through to her office and they sat down on either side of the desk.

'Let's recap what we know,' Clare said.

'Okay. Ingrid McKinnie goes to The Harvest Moon on the night of the twenty-eighth,' Chris began.

'We think for a date,' Clare added. 'Someone from Attracto – possibly one of the three men who also connected with Alison. Did you ask Jim to check them out?'

'Yeah. Want me to see if he's had any luck?'

'Please.'

Chris went to find Jim, and Clare sat mulling over Stoneman. As Sara pointed out, there wasn't much point in using a fake photo on a dating site. Could he be their killer? Posing as an attractive man to trick women into meeting him? If they'd followed the advice on Attracto, they'd have met somewhere public. And would a quiet-living accountant like Alison Reid have been naive enough to invite a man with a fake photo into her home?

'No go,' Chris said, coming back into the room. 'BikerBoy went to Australia for Christmas and new year. He's not actually due back here until this Saturday.'

'Definitely?'

'Yeah. Jim checked with the police in Adelaide.'

'Okay, and the other one – Sandy something?'

'SandyD.'

'Yeah – any luck with him?'

'He checked out too. Works at a call centre in Dundee. He was working a late shift on the twenty-eighth. Didn't finish until two in the morning.'

'By which time, Ingrid was probably dead.'

'Yeah. The Harvest Moon shut at midnight and the call centre's at least half an hour's drive away, so I'm pretty sure we can rule him out.'

'Which just leaves Stoneman,' Clare said. She picked up her cup and sipped from it again. 'I think it's time we popped into the hotel and checked out the man in the photo.'

Chris checked his watch. 'Want to go now?'

'In a bit. Let's get back to where we were.'

'Okay, Ingrid has a date,' Chris said. 'Either she's stood up and meets a friend or the date arrives late.'

'Now it's possible whoever she met is her killer.'

'Yeah. But, if not…'

'Then it's either a random attack or someone was waiting for her. Maybe someone's been watching her, knows where she lives, picks her up on her way home. Easy to do if she'd had a few drinks.'

'You're forgetting the Rohypnol,' Chris reminded her.

'Dammit, so I was. That must have happened in the pub, Chris. So it was either her date – if he turned up – or the friend she met by chance.'

'Jessica Peters?'

'It could be. I wonder if there was something between them. Something at primary school.' Clare suddenly remembered the photos found among Ingrid's paperwork. 'Those boxes from Ingrid's house – are they still in the incident room?'

'Think so. Want me to grab them?'

'Please. I want another look at those photos.'

Chris returned a minute later bearing the two boxes.

'That one,' Clare said, indicating the one she'd found the photos in. She began sifting through the contents again until she came to the envelope of photos. 'Right, let's have a proper look.'

Chris pulled his chair round to Clare's side of the desk. 'What are you looking for?'

'Friends, boyfriends… or anyone who might be Jessica Peters.'

There were just two photos, one of two little girls aged nine or ten, and another of the same two girls standing with another three children.

'Taken on the same day, judging by the clothes,' she said studying them. 'I reckon that's Ingrid. Look at the curls.'

Chris nodded. 'Think that's Jessica next to her?'

Clare turned the photo over but there was nothing on the back. 'Could be,' she muttered. 'What about the other one?'

Chris turned over the other photo. 'Something written here.'

Clare reached across and drew her desk lamp towards her, holding the photo under the glow from the bulb. 'Ingrid with Alison. So they were friends, despite what Ingrid's mother said.'

Chris nodded. 'Looks like it. What about the other names?'

Clare screwed up her eyes. 'Looks like John...' she turned the photo over again. 'Yeah, that one's a boy.' She turned it back, peering at the other names. 'I think that says Lexy,' she said, 'but I'm struggling with the last one.' There was a smudge over it but it looked like...

'Ruth,' Chris said. 'That says Ruth.'

There was a tap on the door and Sara's face appeared. 'Boss, funny thing,' she said.

Clare glanced up. 'Well?'

'I had to check the name to be sure,' Sara began.

'Spit it out, Sara!'

'Remember the shoplifter? The one we picked up the other day?'

Clare looked at her. 'Ruth Williams...' she said slowly.

'Yeah, that's her.'

Clare glanced back at the photo. It did say Ruth. Surely it was a coincidence.

'Well, she's in that WhatsApp group as well,' Sara said. 'She must have been at school with our two victims.'

Clare glanced at Chris, trying to work out what this might mean. Ruth Williams, recently brought in for shoplifting. The same Ruth Williams who was in a WhatsApp group with the two murdered women; and now Clare was holding a photo that included Alison, Ingrid and someone called Ruth.

Chapter 35

The house in Trinity Place was in darkness. It was a single-storey bungalow, finished in a pebbledash render which was coming away from the walls, here and there. The windows with their white PVC frames were newer, though. There was a garage to the side with a dark red up-and-over door and Clare thought back to the photos Sara had taken of the stolen goods. But that wasn't important just now.

'Go round to the back door,' she said to Sara and Robbie, and she waited for them to make their way down the side of the house before she rang the bell.

As she pressed it she heard the soft tones of a Westminster chime but there was no sound from within. She knocked firmly on the door but, again, there was no response. Stepping back, she scanned the house. There were two rooms to the front, one either side of the door. The curtains were drawn on one window and she moved to the other and peered in. But it was growing dark, making it difficult to see anything other than a small red light which she presumed was coming from a television left on standby.

Sara came back round the side of the house. 'No sign of life, boss. Curtains drawn on the rooms at the back.'

A neighbour appeared on her doorstep and looked across.

'We're looking for Ruth Williams,' Clare called.

'Not seen her for a couple of days,' the neighbour said.

Clare thanked the neighbour and waited for her to go back inside. Then she turned again to the front door and crouched to look through the letterbox. There was a vestibule and an inner glass door which had been left open. Squinting against the darkness, Clare could just make out a hall running towards the back of the house with doors off, left and right. Then she pressed her face up against the letterbox and looked down towards the floor. A copy of the Sunday Times lay on the mat and she guessed it had been delivered that morning. There were letters too which must have been there since Saturday at least. Was it likely Ruth had gone away, overnight? After the upset over the shoplifting, Clare didn't think so. An uneasy feeling began to form in her stomach. 'Any glass doors?' she asked Sara and Robbie.

'Yeah, boss,' Robbie said. 'The back door's half glass.'

'Open it.'

The lock on the back door wasn't particularly sturdy and Robbie elected to force it with a chisel, rather than smash the glass. The door swung open and they stepped into a utility room that ran along the back of the house. Clare felt for a switch and the room was bathed in light. Clothes hung from a pulley mounted on the ceiling and she put up a hand to touch a pair of jeans. They were bone dry. A light was flashing on a washing machine, next to the door, indicating it had completed its cycle. In front of them was another door which led to a kitchen. Again, Clare found a switch and a bank of downlighters lit the room. There was little evidence of life in the kitchen. The sink was empty of dishes, the surfaces clean and tidy. A walk-in larder cupboard to the side revealed shelves of store cupboard items, neatly stacked.

A door to the hall stood open. Sara and Robbie went ahead to explore the other rooms while Clare and Chris poked about the kitchen.

'There's nothing here,' she said to Chris. 'Come on – let's see the rest of the house.'

'Boss…'

Clare's heart sank. Something in Sara's tone. The bathroom light was on, Sara standing just outside the door. Clare moved past her to go into the room and saw Robbie standing by the sink. A dining chair which had been placed in front of it was occupied by the figure of a woman. Ruth Williams.

Her arms hung limply down while her head was bent forward, submerged in the sink which was full of water.

Clare glanced at Robbie. 'Dead?'

He nodded. 'She's cold, boss.'

She moved round to take a closer look. Ruth's head was turned slightly and through strands of hair which had settled on the surface of the water she could see that her eyes were still open. She longed to close them but resisted the temptation. She glanced at Chris who was standing next to Sara. 'Get SOCO and a pathologist out, Chris. And better get a locksmith for that door while you're at it. And I'll need someone on the door tonight.'

Chris dialled the number for SOCO and Clare took out her phone.

Jim answered immediately. 'Clare?'

'Another death, Jim. Ruth Williams, our shoplifter from Friday. Look, I really need to get hold of Jessica Peters. Get every spare body onto that WhatsApp group. Anyone who went to the same school and who's local is to be visited in person. See what they know about her. Check our databases, try the voters' roll, the phone book, even – anything else you can think of.'

'I can speak to the Registrar General when they open in the morning,' Jim said.

'Yeah, we may need to do that. But let's see if we can find her tonight.'

Clare turned to Sara and Robbie who were hovering just outside the bathroom. 'We can't touch anything until SOCO have been so I want you two back at the station, helping with that WhatsApp group.'

Sara's face was a picture of misery. 'Boss, if she's done this to herself...'

Clare shook her head. 'Sara, if you're worrying about her arrest yesterday then don't. You did everything by the book and she was treated with compassion.' She glanced back at Ruth Williams. 'If this is a suicide – and frankly, I doubt it – it probably would have happened anyway. It's certainly nothing to do with the way you handled Ruth yesterday.'

Sara's gaze strayed back to the sink and Clare put a hand on her shoulder.

'Go on, now. I need you to help find Jessica Peters. Okay?'

Clare watched Sara leave with Robbie then she took a last look round the bathroom. 'Better retrace our steps, Chris. Come on. We'll wait for SOCO in the car.'

–

It was almost nine when Clare and Chris finally returned to the station.

'You get off home,' she said to Chris. 'Not much more we can do tonight. And take Sara with you. Pour her a big glass of wine.'

'What about these?' He held out a large brown evidence bag containing Ruth Williams' laptop and a smaller one which held her mobile phone.

'Jim said he'd get one of the cops to take them down to Tech Support first thing tomorrow.'

'I'll leave them on his desk then,' he said. 'You coming?'

She shook her head. 'I'll have to update the DCI.'

'Good luck with that.'

DCI Gibson sounded as if he was in a pub when he finally answered her call. 'Hold on,' he said. 'I'll just get out of here.' Clare could hear background chatter and music playing, then suddenly it was quiet. 'Okay, what's up?' he said.

'Sorry to interrupt your night, Al. But we've another death.'

'Murder?'

'Hard to say at this stage. But if it's suicide then it's a bit of an odd one.'

'Odd?'

Clare explained how they'd found Ruth Williams. 'I mean she could have been drunk, a bit unsteady and decided to sit at the sink to wash her face. But that doesn't seem likely.'

'No, I agree,' Al Gibson said. 'And water again.'

'I know. Alison Reid found in the bath, Ingrid in the Kinness Burn and now Ruth Williams in her own bathroom sink.'

'Any connection between the women?'

'Oh yes.'

There was a silence then he said, 'I'll be up in the morning. We can chat about it then.'

'Okay, thanks Al. I'm… er, I'm sorry to have interrupted your night.'

'Don't worry. Just a few drinks with a friend.'

–

As Clare drove home she mulled over that last remark. A few drinks with a friend. Was it one of the glamorous women in the skiing photos? Or someone else? Maybe he too had been on Attracto, but with more success than Clare.

She had ended things with Geoffrey Dark because it was going nowhere. They were on different paths. At least that's what she'd told herself. But was that the only reason? Or, had she ended her relationship – such as it was – in the hope of rekindling things with Al Gibson? And, if so, had she left it too late? Had the DCI found someone to fill the gap left by his ex-wife? Perhaps she was better off not knowing.

As she turned left at the roundabout and began driving along the country road she flicked on her full beam, catching a startled rabbit in the headlights. She slowed as the rabbit ran this way and that until, finally, it chose a side and disappeared into the verge.

She approached the wood that bordered Daisy Cottage and stifled a yawn. It had been a long day. A long week, in fact. All she wanted was to get indoors, have some food and maybe soak in a bath. But then thinking of the bath reminded Clare she was hunting a killer of two – or maybe three – women. Who on earth was killing these women – and why?

Monday, 11th January

Chapter 36

'Anything new?' Clare asked as she entered the station.

'Couple of things,' Jim said. He picked up a sheet of paper from his desk. 'Janey managed to find one of the WhatsApp group still living in the town. The rest seem to be further afield.' He squinted at the paper. 'It's a Michelle Delaney.'

'Address?'

'It's down there. But she works at Razor, top end of North Street.'

'Hair salon?' Clare said. 'Think I know it.'

'Yeah, that's the one. They claim to have cut Prince William's hair, but then half the shops in town claim he was a customer.'

Clare shrugged off her coat and went to hang it on a hook. 'I'd forgotten he was a student here. How long ago was that?'

'Oh, now you're asking, Clare.' Jim rubbed his chin. 'Must be fifteen or twenty years ago I reckon.'

'Okay. Anyone spoken to her yet?'

Jim shook his head. 'I thought we'd wait and see how you wanted to play it.'

'Good. I'll call into the salon myself. I'm guessing it'll open at nine?'

'Suppose so.'

'And the other thing?'

'A DS from Dundee called for you.'

'Corinne Sim?'

'Aye, that's her. Said she'd be in all morning if you want to call back.'

222

'Great, thanks Jim. I've been trying to get hold of her. Erm…' she stood, trying to collect her thoughts. 'Any luck with those blondes? The photos Sara printed out from The Harvest Moon?'

'Not yet. But I can chase it with the team.'

'Thanks, Jim. Could you ask Chris to give me a shout when he arrives. And let the team know I'd like a quick catch-up before I head out.'

Jim nodded and Clare went into her office. She switched on her computer then sat down to telephone Corinne.

'It's a familiar story,' Corinne said when Clare had related the contents of the document on Alison Reid's laptop. 'If you email me over the details we'll have a look at it.'

'Could you sit on it for a bit, Corinne? It may be related to a murder investigation. I'm just not sure yet.'

'No problem, Clare. Just let me know when we can move on it.'

The door opened and Chris entered. He hovered in the doorway, shifting on his feet.

Clare put down her phone and regarded him. 'Something up?'

He came into the room and closed the door behind him. 'Don't suppose you could have a word with Sara? She's in a bit of a state. Thinking Ruth Williams killed herself because of her arrest. If you could maybe just reassure her…'

Clare glanced at her watch. She had emails to check, the team to brief and the hair salon would be open soon. 'I'd rather leave it till this afternoon, Chris. One of the WhatsApp group works in a hairdresser's in North Street. I'd like to be there when it opens.'

Chris stood his ground. 'It'll take two minutes, Clare.'

She sighed. 'I must be going soft in my old age. Go on, then. Wheel her in.'

A few minutes later there was a tap on the door and a white-faced Sara looked in.

'In you come,' Clare said, giving her what she hoped was a reassuring smile. She waited until Sara had sat down then said, 'Chris tells me you're still worrying about Ruth.'

Sara nodded but said nothing.

'Look, Sara. I'm a bit pushed this morning and, when I have more time, we will talk properly. But, for now, let me say that, in my view, you treated Ruth with kindness and compassion. You probably don't want to hear this but I'm glad it was you who arrested her. You were exactly the right person to deal with it. You didn't make a fuss, brought her here and alerted me to your concerns. It was a textbook arrest.'

'But then...'

'Sara, I'm very much afraid that Ruth will turn out to be our third murder victim. I'd love to be wrong, but I'd bet money she was killed in the same way as the other two. But, even if she did choose to end her life, it probably would have happened anyway.'

'You really think so?' Sara's voice was little more than a whisper.

'I know so. Ruth's shoplifting was a symptom of an illness. Her arrest was traumatic for her, but I think there was a bit of relief in there too. I believe she was glad we found out about it.'

'You mean like a cry for help?'

'Maybe. Obviously I'm not a doctor but I have met a lot of shoplifters in my time and Ruth certainly didn't fit the profile.' She smiled at Sara. 'Does that help?'

Sara's face cleared; the relief evident. 'Thanks, boss,' she said. 'It helps a lot.' Her eyes were bright and Clare thought she looked near to tears.

'Go and get yourself a coffee. Get one for Chris too, and pass the word round – briefing in ten minutes.'

Sara escaped and Clare turned to check her Inbox. As the messages loaded she considered calling Neil Grant to see if the post-mortem on Ruth had been done yet; but it was unlikely. He'd said it would be late Monday or early Tuesday. All the same, she'd be happier once she knew how Ruth had died.

Her office door opened and DCI Alastair Gibson came in. He closed the door behind him and hesitated for a moment. Then he smiled and pulled out a chair and Clare was momentarily thrown. He was wearing a charcoal grey suit she hadn't seen before and a pale blue shirt that seemed to set off his eyes. Those eyes. There was something disarming in their expression. Her mouth was suddenly dry and she reached down into her bag for a bottle of water. He was watching her and she held out the water, offering it to him.

'Or a coffee?' she said but he waved this away.

'Maybe later, Clare. I... er, how are things?'

She could feel the colour rising in her face. Godsake – she really needed to get a grip. She was behaving like a teenager. 'Yeah, fine, Al. You?'

He smiled again, and she found herself watching him. Studying his face. Thinking of what might have been – if only she hadn't chosen Geoff.

'Yes, thanks,' he was saying.

She gave herself a shake and tried to focus on the case. 'Sorry about disturbing you last night,' she said. 'You were out...' she added, before she could stop herself.

There was a tiny hesitation – a flicker of something. Then he said, 'Yes. Just catching up with a friend. A few drinks. Erm, maybe we should...'

A friend. The glamorous skiing friend? Or someone else? Was he on a date? She saw him watching her and she made an effort to push thoughts of him and his skiing companion out of her head.

'Yes, sorry, Al. The murders.'

'So...'

'The PM's not been done on the woman we found last night but I am expecting her to be our third murder victim.'

'And you said they were connected.'

She nodded. 'They were all at primary school together.'

'Okay. And leads?'

'Actually, Al, I'm about to have a briefing with the team. If you sat in it would save me going through everything twice.' She glanced at him. 'If that's okay…'

He looked at her and smiled. Those eyes again. 'Of course.'

'And if there's anything you're concerned about we could have a chat after the briefing.'

He scraped back his chair. 'Sure – let's get on with it then.'

As they walked through to the incident room, he said, 'Been to any parkruns lately?'

Clare shook her head. 'Not since last month. But I could do with shifting the Christmas weight.'

'Clare! You always look great. I didn't mean it to sound like that.' He stopped just outside the incident room, his expression warm.

She flicked a glance at him, but now wasn't the time. Stuck for something to say she muttered thanks and pushed open the door. The room was stiflingly hot, even allowing for the growing number of officers and laptops, and she made a mental note to ask Jim about the thermostat.

'Morning all,' she called and gradually the chatter subsided as they turned to face her. 'For those of you who don't know him, this is DCI Alastair Gibson. He's overseeing our investigation so expect to see him from time to time.' She paused for a moment and the DCI nodded to the officers. Then she carried on. 'We had another suspicious death last night.' She glanced at the board and saw that Ruth Williams's photo had been pinned up next to Alison and Ingrid.

'Same MO, boss?' Janey asked.

'Still waiting for the PM report, Janey. Probably tomorrow but the victim was found sitting at the bathroom sink, her head submerged.'

'Weird,' someone said.

'I know.'

'Like it was staged?' Janey asked.

'Possibly. I certainly don't think it's an efficient way to drown yourself. I'm not even sure it's possible. So,' she glanced back at the photos, 'for now, we treat Ruth's death as if it is connected to the other two.'

'Rohypnol?' someone asked.

Clare spread her hands. 'Too early to say. But she was found fully clothed so I doubt she's been sexually assaulted.'

'Wasn't she in here the other day?' Erin, one of the officers from Glenrothes, asked.

Clare glanced at Sara who was staring at the floor. 'She was, Erin. On suspicion of shoplifting but we hadn't charged her at that point.'

'Any intel from her phone?' Janey asked.

'Diane has her phone and laptop and she's prioritising them this morning. So, if anyone takes a call from her, I want it buzzed through to me immediately.' She glanced round the room and Bill caught her eye. 'Bill?'

'Next of kin?' he asked.

Clare scanned the room. 'Who was on that?'

Nita raised her hand. 'Me, boss. There's a daughter – Megan. I spoke to her late last night. Understandably upset. Wants to know when she can go to the mortuary. I'm keeping in touch with her.'

'Thanks, Nita. So, all three women were in that school WhatsApp group. Alison and Ingrid both had private messages from Jessica Peters suggesting they join the dating website. Once Diane gets into Ruth's laptop, we'll know if she too had a message from Jessica.'

'Don't forget the reunion,' Chris said, and Clare nodded.

'As we know, Jessica Peters was trying to arrange a class reunion. And the restaurant she had contacted was The Heron's Nest. The proprietor, remember, had been a client of Alison Reid's then moved his business to Sharp and Lafferty. Now, Chris and I visited the restaurant yesterday and the owner showed us two emails from Jessica enquiring about a booking. Chris had a look at the header info in the emails and she's either jetting around the world or she's using a VPN to disguise her location. And that makes me suspicious.'

Erin raised her hand. 'Is Jessica Peters a suspect, boss?'

Clare shook her head. 'Not at this point, Erin. But she is a person of interest so if anyone does manage to track her down bring her in, please.'

Bill raised a hand. 'Did you get the message about Michelle Delaney, boss?'

'Yes, thanks Bill.' She glanced at the DCI. 'Michelle Delaney is also in the WhatsApp group and still lives in the town. Chris and I will see her this morning as soon as we're done here.'

DCI Gibson nodded at this but didn't speak.

Out in the main office the phone began to ring and Jim slipped out of the room to take the call.

'Could this Jessica have a grudge against the others?' Bill asked. 'Some long-held resentment?'

Clare considered this for a moment then said, 'It's possible; and it would explain why she's at pains to disguise her location. But even a bad case of school bullying would be a pretty thin motive for murder, particularly twenty-odd years later.'

'Remember the photo,' Chris said, and Clare nodded.

'There was an old photo Chris and I found in Ingrid McKinnie's house. It's of five children aged around nine or ten. Four girls and a boy.'

'Any idea who they are?' Nita asked.

'Yes, I think so. Names are written on the back.' She hesitated, then said, 'three of the names are Alison, Ingrid and... Ruth.'

'Do we know if it's our victims?' Bill said.

Clare shrugged. 'I'd be surprised if it wasn't.'

'What about the other two?' Janey asked.

'According to what's written on the back, a boy called John and a girl called Lexy. Now, the friendship between our three victims might have nothing to do with the murders but it needs looking at.'

DCI Gibson eased himself off the desk he'd been perching on. 'If it is the same Ruth, then finding John and Lexy is a priority. Have you been onto the school?'

'Yes,' Clare said. 'They're trying to put me in touch with a retired head teacher but nothing so far.'

'Better get back onto them then,' he said. 'Before we have another victim.'

'Michelle Delaney might recognise the kids in the photo,' Chris said.

'Let's hope so.' Clare broke off and stood thinking for a moment. 'Anything else? Or is that it?'

'Stoneman,' Bill said. 'Still trying to track him down.'

Clare turned to the DCI. 'Our first two victims have links to the same three men on the dating site. Two of them have checked out but the one who calls himself Stoneman is using someone else's photo.'

'Any idea whose photo?' DCI Gibson asked.

Clare saw Chris try to catch her eye and shake his head and she realised he wouldn't want Sara to know he'd been to the hotel. She'd probably want to know why he was there, Clare thought. She gave him a slight nod then turned back to the DCI. 'Yes, I think so. I'm going to check it out today.' She looked round the room again. 'Meantime, I want as many of you as possible doing house-to-house. Start with the streets where our victims lived and spread out from there.'

The door opened and Jim came back in, holding a notepad. 'Diane,' he said.

'And?'

'Ruth's laptop wasn't password protected and she was logged into WhatsApp.'

'Anything significant?'

'Only this: she also had a message from Jessica Peters suggesting she join Attracto.'

'And did she?'

Jim shook his head. 'No. She replied saying it wasn't her thing, that she was fine on her own. Diane's gone through Attracto and she can't see anyone using Ruth's email address – or anyone who might be her. She's uploaded all the private chats from Messenger and WhatsApp to the network. But she said the school group seems to be the only thing that connected Ruth with the others.'

'Pretty significant connection,' Chris said.

'I agree,' Clare said. 'Let's hope Michelle Delaney can shed some light on it.'

Chapter 37

Razor was at the top end of North Street and Clare drove slowly along, eyes flicking left and right for someplace to park.

'Here,' Chris said, indicating a diagonal space just in front of the Younger Hall, the town's concert hall and graduation venue.

'I've always liked this building,' she said, admiring the high neo-Classical columns and tiered side sections. 'It's an odd mix of styles. Geoff said…' and then she stopped herself. She turned her back on the building and stepped out into the road, waiting for a gap in the traffic.

'Clare…' Chris hesitated.

She waited while a taxi whizzed past then began walking smartly across. 'Razor's about fifty yards further along.'

He caught up with her. 'You sure you did the right thing, finishing with Geoff?'

She stopped for a moment, not meeting his eye. Then she said, 'Yes, Chris. I am sure. It's just going to take a bit of time…'

'Okay. As long as…'

'Chris, I said it's fine!' And she began walking along. 'So Michelle Delaney – any thoughts?'

He shrugged. 'Not really. I mean there's nothing to suggest she's involved in this.'

'Except that, of all the members in that group, she's the only one we can find who still stays in the town.'

'So, what you thinking?'

'I think,' Clare slowed her pace as they approached Razor. 'I think we show her the photo first and see what she has to say – before we mention the murders.'

'Fair enough.'

They stopped short of the salon and regarded it. 'Sort of place my dad would go,' Clare said, taking in the barber's pole with its helix of stripes. The shop front had recently been painted in blue, similar to the shade found on the doors of university buildings and Clare suspected they were trying to cash in on the brand. A poster in the window announced they had been Barbers to Prince William. She glanced at Chris.

'Fancy a trim to go with the new teeth?'

'Shut up.'

The windows were steamed up making it difficult to see how busy it was. Clare pushed open the door and immediately their ears were assailed by the hum of hairdryers. A faint chemical odour hung in the air: hairspray, maybe. An elderly lady sat under a hood-type dryer, reading a copy of My Weekly. Next to her a toddler was perched on a high stool, swathed in a black gown while a woman with a neat blonde bob trimmed his hair, exchanging a steady stream of chatter with the boy's mother. Clare caught sight of herself and Chris in the mirror opposite and she thought how nice it would be to have her own hair cut. It always seemed to be at the bottom of her list of priorities. When had she last had it done? Was it October – or before that, even?

'Morning,' a woman with a silver-grey pixie cut said. 'Can I help?'

Clare noticed she had lilac highlights threaded through and she wondered briefly if it was time to add some colour to her own hair. Something fun to brighten up the winter days. Then she dragged her thoughts back to the investigation and took out her warrant card. 'We were hoping to have a word with Michelle Delaney.'

The woman frowned at Clare's card then glanced across to where the child was now having a soft brush flicked over his neck. He was giggling and said that it tickled, and the woman said how good he'd been. The gown was whipped off and the boy was lifted down from the stool by his mother.

'That's Michelle. She'll just be a minute or two. If you'd like to wait here…' She indicated a bench seat with a padded cushion that reminded Clare of the pews in the church her parents still attended, back in Glasgow. She sat down and felt the cushion move. There was a table to the side with a pile of magazines. Opposite the bench was a set of shelves stacked high with bottles of shampoo, conditioner, hair dyes and a clear tub of liquid in which sat a comb and two pairs of scissors. The toddler skipped past, holding his mother's hand and Clare felt a draught round her feet as they opened the door to leave.

'Hi,' a voice said, and Clare turned to see the blonde woman. 'What was it you wanted?'

Clare glanced round. The pixie-cut woman was hovering, and the My Weekly reader had set down her magazine and was now openly observing them. 'Is there somewhere we can talk?'

The woman turned on her heel and led them up the salon, past the checkout and through a beaded curtain. A door beyond led to what appeared to be a staff room. There was a sink against the wall and a table with an electric kettle and mugs next to it. A stack of chairs stood in the corner. 'Seat?' the blonde asked.

Clare waved this away. 'We'll try not to keep you. You are Michelle Delaney? Is that right?'

Michelle glanced at Clare and Chris then said, 'Yes, that's me. What's this about?'

Clare smiled. 'Nothing to worry about, Miss Delaney. We'd just like some information – about people you were at school with.'

Michelle's eyes widened. 'Must be fifteen years since I left school.'

'Actually, it's further back than that. Primary school.' She fished in her pocket and took out the photo of the five children. 'I wonder if I could ask you about this please?'

Michelle took the photo and stared at it. 'How old is this?'

Clare ignored the question. 'Do you recognise anyone?'

Michelle studied it for a few moments then said, 'That's Alison. Alison Reid.' She looked up. 'I read about her in the paper. That she died.' She glanced from Clare to Chris then back to Clare. 'What's this about?' she asked again.

'We're just trying to identify everyone in the photo. So… the others?'

Michelle looked back at the photo. 'Well Ingrid, of course. And I think that's Ruth next to her.'

'Do you remember their surnames?' Chris asked.

Michelle's brow furrowed. 'I think Ingrid was Mc… something.'

'McKinnie?' Chris said.

Her brow cleared. 'Yes, that's it. McKinnie. And Ruth was Ruth Williams.' She smiled. 'I remember now. Goodness, it takes me back.'

'And the boy?'

'John,' Michelle said. 'But I can't remember his surname. Sorry. The other girl…'

'Could it be Lexy?' Clare prompted.

'Yes! God you're taking me right back. It is Lexy. Lexy Harris.'

'Did you keep in touch with anyone in the photo?'

Michelle shook her head. 'Not really. Matter of fact, one of the girls – Jessica – she's trying to get up a class reunion. But I don't think many folk are interested.' She handed the photo back to Clare. 'Too long ago now.'

'Would that be Jessica Peters?' Clare asked.

She nodded. 'Yeah. That's her. Honestly, I don't know why she's bothering.'

'Have you had any other messages from Jessica? I mean, just between the two of you?'

Michelle stared. 'What? Like private messages?'

'Yeah. Either WhatsApp or Messenger – anything like that.'

Michelle shook her head. 'No. I mean it's not like we were pals at school. Why do you ask?'

'She didn't suggest you join a dating site?'

Michelle laughed. 'Think my boyfriend would have something to say about that.'

The door opened a little and the pixie cut looked in. 'That's your ten thirty, Michelle.'

'Be right out.' Michelle put a hand on the door. 'Was there anything else? Only I've a busy day today.'

'Nearly done,' Clare said. 'We do need to speak to Jessica Peters. Would you know where she's living now?'

Michelle shrugged. 'No idea. I mean, I think she went off to France.'

Clare glanced at Chris. France was one of the places Jessica had emailed from. 'When was this?' she asked Michelle.

Michelle frowned. 'Probably when we were all about fourteen. I can't honestly remember. She wasn't in my classes at Albany High. So I didn't see much of her once we left primary school.'

'And, as far as you know, she's still in France?'

'Yeah, I think so. When she was talking about the reunion I'm sure she said something about coming back for it. So she must still be there, mustn't she?'

Clare turned for the door but Chris stood his ground.

'Just one more thing,' he said, and Clare stopped, keen to hear what he was going to say. 'Can you remember what colour Jessica's hair was?'

Michelle patted her neat bob. 'Blonde, like me. Only hers didn't come out of a bottle. Lovely blonde hair, she had.'

Chapter 38

They walked back to the car, dodging past a clutch of tourists who were listening to a guide pointing out a line of swagged urns over the entrance to the Younger Hall. As they cleared the group Clare said, 'What do you reckon?'

'Jessica Peters? Probably still in France.'

'And San Francisco? Remember one of the emails looked like it came from there.'

'Yeah, that's true. I mean she could have been on holiday – sent the first email before she left.'

Clare glanced over her shoulder then stepped into the road to cross. 'Yeah, but the two emails were sent pretty close together, remember.'

'Maybe she was on a plane, heading for the USA – realised she'd forgotten something and typed the email. As soon as she landed and picked up Wi-Fi it would send.'

'Suppose. Interesting about the blonde hair, though.'

'Doesn't mean anything,' Chris said, 'although, statistically, less than twenty per cent of Scots are blonde. So it's worth noting.'

'Sometimes, Detective Sergeant, I remember why I let you stay.'

'I keep up.'

'So it seems.' She threw the keys to Chris. 'You drive – I want to phone the DCI.'

Chris clicked to unlock the car. 'About the DCI...'

'Yeah?' Clare took out her phone and typed in the passcode.

'Did you and he not...'

'Just stop right there, Chris.'

'If you ask me, Clare,' he said, ignoring her, 'he had a thing for you at one time.'

'Maybe he did, maybe he didn't. It's academic now. Geoff came back and whatever there was with the DCI... well, it went away.'

'Sure?'

She didn't look at him. 'Sure.'

Chris put the key in the ignition and pulled on his seat belt. 'Just checking.'

The DCI was driving back to his office in Dunfermline, some forty miles south-west of St Andrews. 'Go ahead, Clare.'

'Al, I need a favour. I'm trying to track down Jessica Peters – remember, the one from the WhatsApp group? The one pushing the school reunion?'

'Okay...'

'I think she may be in France and I need to get hold of her.'

'You want a Europol request?'

'Please.'

'How urgent?'

'Pretty urgent. Next couple of days if you can. As far as we know, she moved there about twenty years ago.'

'Okay, Clare. Email me the details and I'll get onto it. I'll check with border control too. See if she's come back into the country recently.'

'Cheers, Al.'

Clare ended the call and directed Chris to carry on up North Street.

'Where are we heading?'

'The Kenlybank Hotel. I want to speak to your photo man.'

–

Clare had hoped to find Pawel Nowicki on duty at reception. He'd helped Clare with enquiries in the past and she had come to think of him as a friend. She asked for him when they arrived but the young woman behind the desk shook her head.

'Sorry,' she said. 'Pawel's on paternity leave.'

Clare was surprised. For some reason she hadn't thought of Pawel as having a home life. He always seemed to be at the hotel. 'Oh, how lovely,' she said. 'Please give him my congratulations.'

The receptionist took out her phone and flicked until she found a photo. She held the phone out for Clare to see. 'Paulina,' she said. 'Isn't she gorgeous? Pawel's besotted.'

Clare looked at the baby. A little girl with a shock of dark hair, fast asleep, one hand curled up beside her face. 'She's beautiful,' she said, handing the phone back.

'So,' the receptionist went on, 'if it's Pawel you want...'

'Actually, no,' Clare said. 'It's a member of your staff we'd like to see.'

Chris took out his mobile phone and navigated to the photo he'd saved of Stoneman. 'Do you recognise this man?'

The receptionist glanced at the phone and nodded. 'Oh yeah. That's Donny. Donny Cohen. He's one of the staff. In the cocktail bar.'

'Could we see him, please?' Chris asked.

The receptionist frowned. 'I'm not sure if he's in today. I don't think I've seen him.' She moved to a computer behind the desk. 'I'll just check...' She shook the mouse to bring the screen to life then began tapping at the keyboard. 'No,' she said, after a minute. 'Looks like it's his day off. But he's on early shift tomorrow if that helps.'

Clare thought for a moment. She really needed to speak to Donny Cohen. See him face-to-face. If he was Stoneman she wanted to see how he would react to questioning. 'Could we have his home address?'

The receptionist looked at Clare. 'We don't normally...'

'It is important,' Clare said, not keen to say more than that.

The receptionist hesitated then turned back to the computer and tapped the keyboard again. Then she took up a pen and began writing on a notepad. She tore a sheet off and handed it to Clare. 'There you go. I hope everything's okay...'

Clare smiled. 'Just routine,' she said. 'Nothing to worry about.'

'Early lunch?' Chris asked, as they walked back to the car.

'You're joking. It's only just gone eleven. And we need to get hold of Donny Cohen.' She put a hand in her pocket and brought out the paper the receptionist had given her. 'Kingsbarns,' she said.

'I know it. Want me to drive?'

'Go on then. Twice in one day, Sergeant. What a treat!'

Clare settled back in the passenger seat to enjoy the drive. Kingsbarns was only about six miles south of the hotel, through flat farmland. The flooding was gradually drying up and she could see fields of winter crops greening up. Further on, a bright blue tractor was pulling a plough. It was still the depths of winter, particularly in Scotland, but she felt heartened at the promise of spring in a few months.

Chris slowed as he approached the village. 'Which street?'

Clare scanned the paper. 'Back Stile.'

'I know it. It's at the end of the village. Leads down to the beach.'

He drove on slowly as Clare took in the village. It was an attractive collection of houses and low cottages, some built in a rough, honey-coloured stone with pantile roofs, others newer, finished in a white render. They passed a church with graveyard attached and an inn which had a board outside advertising meals. Clare's breakfast seemed a distant memory now, but she couldn't stop for a pub lunch in the middle of a murder investigation.

As they neared the end of the village she saw fields ahead. Chris slowed further, signalling, then turned left down the quaintly named Back Stile. It was a narrow road and fifty yards on he had to pull into the side to allow a campervan to pass.

'There's a car park at the beach,' he explained.

'Oh I know this,' she said. 'I've been down here with Benjy. The Cheesy Toast Shack have a shed down here.'

Chris smiled. 'I know. It'd be a quick lunch, too.'

'Let's just see how we get on with Donny Cohen.'

But, again, they were out of luck. There was no answer at Donny's cottage. Clare walked round to the side and opened a gate that led to a small square of garden. There was another door, newer than the cottage, and she rapped on it but there was no reply. A neighbour was out in the garden next door, feeding chickens.

'They're out,' he volunteered. 'Away about seven this morning.'

'They?'

'Donny and Lin.'

'Any idea when they'll be back?'

The neighbour shook his head. 'They had skis on top of the car. Probably gone up to Glenshee.'

Clare thanked the neighbour and headed back round to the front. 'Gone skiing, apparently,' she told Chris. 'The neighbour thinks Glenshee.'

They climbed back into the car. 'That's the best part of a two-hour drive from here,' Chris said. 'So, if they came off the slopes no later than four they'd be lucky to be back here for six. Maybe later if they stopped somewhere to eat.'

'Speaking of eating…' Clare said.

'Great idea, Inspector.' And he pulled away down the narrow road again. It carried on with a smattering of cottages to the north and tree-lined fields to the south. The trees were bare and Clare could see the North Sea in the distance, sparkling in the midday sun. As they neared the beach the road crossed a golf course. A couple of golfers in padded jackets were walking along, golf bags on their shoulders. It was windier here and she admired their hardiness. And then the car park came into view, its blaze surface peppered with potholes.

'Just watch the car,' Clare warned. 'Some of those look deep,'

He swerved past them and parked in a spot overlooking the sea. The Cheesy Toast Shack Open sign was propped up beside a gate. 'Thank God for that,' Chris said. 'I wasn't sure it would be open today.'

'What you having?' Clare said as they walked across to the gate.

'Red Leicester and chorizo,' he said without hesitation.

'Ooh that does sound good. Make that two.'

'I'm paying, am I?'

'It's your turn.'

'I'm honestly not sure it is…'

Five minutes later they were munching hot toasties. 'Oh my God this is good,' Clare said. 'I don't come here often enough.'

'Me neither,' Chris mumbled, through a mouthful of chorizo.

'So Veganuary's going well then?'

Chris shook his head. 'Honest to God, Clare, I never want to eat tofu again. Not as long as I live.'

'Ach, there's only another three weeks to go.'

'Don't remind me.'

Chapter 39

Clare's phone was ringing as they pulled into the car park back at the station. She glanced at the display. Sara.

'I'm just outside, Sara. Be in shortly.'

'Okay, boss. Um, there's a woman here to see you. She said you were expecting her.'

Clare racked her brains as she walked into the station. As she entered the public enquiry area she saw the woman. She was tall, warmly dressed in a long herringbone patterned coat with polished brown boots. She wore a brown felt cloche hat and was carrying a calf-coloured briefcase.

Clare approached her with a smile. She was pretty sure she'd never seen the woman before so why was she asking for her? 'DI Clare Mackay,' she said.

The woman smiled. 'I'm Dr Holt. Sandra Holt.'

And then Clare remembered. Her heart sank. 'Oh, Dr Holt – I'm so sorry. You've come to examine Ruth Williams.'

She nodded. 'That's right. Did you forget I was coming?'

Clare glanced round. The station was quite busy. 'If you'd like to come into my office...'

In the privacy of her office Clare explained that Ruth had been found dead on Sunday. 'I'm so sorry,' she said again. 'I should have called to cancel. I'm afraid I've wasted your time.'

Dr Holt looked shocked. 'Oh, how dreadful. Do you know... I mean, what happened? Was she ill?'

Clare hesitated. They still didn't know officially. The PM report wouldn't be out until the end of the day or even tomorrow. 'We don't have a cause of death yet but we are treating it as unexplained at this stage.'

Dr Holt said, 'Then I imagine you'll be busy. I'll not keep you any longer, Inspector.'

'Actually...'

'Yes?'

'I can't tell you how we found Ruth but, until we have a cause of death, I did wonder...'

'You're thinking that the balance of her mind could have been disturbed by her arrest?'

Clare was grateful for the doctor's directness. 'Frankly, yes. If there is a chance that the arrest contributed to her death we need to learn from that.'

'I'd have thought not, Inspector. But maybe if you could tell me a little about the circumstances...'

'Can I offer you something to drink first?'

Dr Holt smiled. 'I'd love a cup of tea, if you have time. No milk.'

Over mugs of tea – Clare couldn't find any cups and saucers – she related the story of Ruth's arrest. As she mentioned the garage full of stolen goods Dr Holt interrupted her.

'How did she seem, when she opened the garage? Was there any sense of pride? Were the goods arranged in any order?'

Clare rose from her seat. 'Hold on. I'll fetch Sara.'

Sara trailed in after Clare, twisting her hands.

'Dr Holt's keen to learn how Ruth reacted when she opened the garage,' Clare explained.

'Can you remember what she said?' Dr Holt added. 'At the garage.'

Sara's brow creased and she stood thinking for a minute. 'I think she said something like It's all here. And she stood back to let me go in.'

'You didn't see her face?'

'I did,' Sara said. 'She wouldn't meet my eye, though. Just looked away.'

'Her body language – was it defensive? Arms crossed, that sort of thing.'

Sara shook her head. 'Oh no.' She half closed her eyes, as if recalling the scene. 'I think her shoulders were down. She'd sort of slumped, if that makes sense.'

Dr Holt nodded. 'And the garage? How were the goods arranged? Any order or method?'

'No, nothing like that. A bit like a jumble sale, to be honest. Some of the clothes were dusty and the things on the floor were just a mixture. No order at all.'

'And did she attempt to show you anything? Point anything out?'

'No. In fact, I think she was desperate to close the door again. She seemed ashamed of it.'

Dr Holt smiled her thanks and Sara escaped with obvious relief.

When the door was closed again, Clare said, 'Well, doctor?'

'It certainly sounds as if she was crushed by the experience, Inspector. But, from what your officer said, I think her problems pre-date her arrest. That kind of random, disorganised shoplifting, with no apparent benefit to the thief, no sign that she's using the stolen goods to improve her life, well, it's a kind of compulsion. Rather like an alcoholic who drinks, not because he enjoys it, but because he must. He fears the alternative more than the drink itself. I'd say Ruth Williams stole because it made her briefly happy. The guilt she demonstrated at her garage is typical. It's not particularly common but is a recognised mental health condition.'

Clare hesitated and Dr Holt seemed to guess what she was thinking.

'Put your mind at rest, Inspector. If Ruth Williams did kill herself – and, from what you say, I think you have your doubts – the root cause goes further back than her arrest on Friday. I'm just sorry I wasn't able to see her then. I might have been able to recommend the types of therapy that could have helped.'

Clare smiled. 'Thank you. I'll relay that to Sara. She's been terribly worried.'

Dr Holt rose and began to pull on her coat. 'Please do reassure her. Whatever the outcome of the post-mortem, I'm sure your officer wasn't to blame.'

–

Jim was waiting for Clare when she showed Dr Holt out. 'I've been on to the Registrar General – about Jessica Peters.'

'Any luck?'

He shook his head. 'Nope. All they have is her birth certificate. No record of a marriage or anything like that. I've been through our own records and the voters' roll. She's not on either.'

Clare nodded. 'That figures. When we spoke to Michelle Delaney this morning...' She saw Jim's face cloud. 'From the WhatsApp group – hairdresser, still lives in the town – she said she thought Jessica had moved to France when she was about fourteen.'

'Ah. That makes sense,' Jim said. 'Thought about Europol?'

'Thanks for the reminder, Jim. I promised to send the details to the DCI. He's agreed to process a request. Better do that now.' She turned to head back to her office then stopped. 'Any luck with the house-to-house yet?'

'Not that I've heard. They'll phone in if there is anything.'

Chapter 40

Clare was contemplating calling Neil Grant to ask if he'd carried out the post-mortem on Ruth when her phone began to ring. Oh please, not another victim, she thought clicking to take the call.

'Inspector, this is Maureen Curzon. I'm the headteacher at Lamond Primary School.'

At last, Clare thought, but didn't say. 'Mrs Curzon – thank you for calling.'

'I'm just sorry it's taken me so long to come back to you. So many staff off sick, you know. But, then, you don't want to hear about that…'

Clare waited for Maureen to draw breath then said, 'Have you managed to track down your predecessor?'

'Well, yes and no,' Maureen said. 'The headteacher before me was Celia Crawford and I have her mobile number, but I only heard about her yesterday.'

Clare didn't like the sound of this. 'Heard?'

'Oh, it's fine,' she said. 'I gather she's going to be fine. But she had a heart attack just after Christmas and she's been in intensive care since then. That's why I've not been able to get hold of her.'

Clare tried not to let the disappointment show in her voice. 'I don't suppose we'll be able to visit then.'

'Well, that's why I'm calling now,' Maureen said. 'I've spoken to her daughter and they think she might be well enough for a short visit tomorrow, if that helps.'

'Oh, tomorrow would be fine,' Clare said. 'If Mrs Crawford's daughter can give us a time, we'll be there.'

'Then I'll give you her number and you can sort it out between you.'

–

It was almost six by the time Clare remembered she hadn't phoned Celia Crawford's daughter. She keyed in the number Maureen Curzon had given her and switched the speaker on, setting the phone down on her desk. It went to voicemail.

'Dammit,' she muttered, waiting for the beep. She left a message asking Celia's daughter to call her back and ended the call. As she did so an email popped up. Al Gibson. The DCI. Just one word.

Europol?

She'd forgotten that too. She clicked to reply, typed Sorry and began keying in what the Education Department had told her about Jessica Peters. She sent the message then leaned back in her chair, stretching out her legs. She was tired now and longing for home. Benjy would have been well walked by Moira but would still be excited to see her. She watched her Inbox to see if the DCI would send a reply but, after five minutes, she gave up and shut down her computer. As she locked her desk and turned out the lights she remembered what he'd said earlier that day. Clare, you always look great. Had he meant it? Or was it just one of those things you say when someone makes a remark about their weight – or their hair? Did he feel anything at all for Clare? Maybe she should ask him. Get it out into the open.

And then she knew she wouldn't. She wasn't the kind to chase after men. Not her style. 'You'll end up an old maid, Clare,' she told herself. And then she thought there might be worse things.

When she'd fed Benjy and eaten another of her mother's meals, she lay on the sofa with the dog at her feet scrolling through Facebook on her laptop. Inevitably she found herself browsing through photos on Geoffrey Dark's timeline. As usual he was pictured smiling, always with friends and colleagues, all smiling too.

And then she saw one photo that was like a knife in her heart. There was snow on the ground and the sky was a deep blue. It looked like a city park, she thought, noting the skyscrapers in the background. There were six or seven of them in the group, plus whoever was taking the photo. They weren't looking at the camera but at something beyond the photographer. They were all facing the same way, except for Geoff. He had his arm round a petite girl with a heart-shaped face. She wore a pale grey beanie hat decorated with a line of red and yellow chickens. Her hair, a rich coppery brown, lay over her shoulders in thick wavy hanks; Clare couldn't help comparing it with her own poker-straight hair. The girl was gazing beyond the camera in the same direction as the others, apparently not heeding the fact that Geoff's eyes were fixed on her upturned face. Clare studied his expression. She'd seen it before – when he'd looked at her, sometimes. Usually when he was about to say he loved her. And now, it was trained on someone else. A petite girl with good hair and a heart-shaped face.

'Didn't take you long, Geoff,' she muttered, closing Facebook. She wondered idly if he'd only just met the girl. Or had there been something all along…

She hovered over the shortcut to Attracto and then, seized by an impulse, she opened it up, navigated to Settings and clicked Delete Profile. A pop-up asked if she was sure and she clicked to confirm this. She wasn't going to learn anything about Stoneman through the dating site anyway. Jessica Peters was the key to this case. She was sure of that now.

Clare watched the progress bar fill up and felt something approaching relief as her profile disappeared from the site. Attracto wasn't for her. But maybe there were other sites...

She opened up Google and began searching. After a few minutes scrolling past the usual sites she had heard Zoe mention, she found one aimed at professionals. She wasn't really sure about that. It sounded a bit self-important. But then the photo of Geoff gazing at that girl came into her head and she thought she had nothing to lose. As with Attracto she had to create a profile before she could browse through the thumbnails and, again, she used the photo of Benjy. It took a good half hour to complete the registration process but eventually she was able to browse the men who met her criteria.

The profile photo was taken from behind, but the tall athletic figure in the black wetsuit with the blue flashes on the legs was unmistakable. Clare had seen it before on his Facebook page – DCI Alastair Gibson.

She scanned his profile to see if he'd been active recently. One hour ago. And suddenly Clare's mouth felt dry. Whatever had gone on between him and the woman in the ski photos, he was on a dating website now and he'd been active that evening. Just an hour ago. She hovered over his profile to give it a thumbs-up and then decided against it. Surely if he was available and interested in Clare he would have said something.

And then she knew he wouldn't have. Of course he wouldn't. After all it was Clare who'd chosen Geoff over him when she had come out of hospital the previous year. She'd almost died. And he'd arrived at the hospital, ready to take her home and look after her. But then Geoff had come striding in, straight from the airport. He had breezed into her life once more, ready to nurse her back to full health. And she had let him.

And Al Gibson had melted into the background taking their burgeoning relationship with him. At the time Clare had wondered if she'd made the right decision. Now she knew she hadn't.

Tuesday, 12ᵗʰ January

Chapter 41

A dense fog had rolled in from the North Sea overnight and Clare drove slowly, the sound of her tyres on the damp road breaking the stillness that comes with thick mist. She'd switched off the car radio, trying to order her thoughts for the day ahead, but she couldn't seem to make any sense of this case.

Her phone began to ring as she reached the station car park. An unfamiliar number. She killed the engine and clicked to take the call.

'Detective Inspector?' a woman's voice said. 'I'm Carolyn Joseph. You called me last night.'

It took Clare a moment then the penny dropped. Celia Crawford's daughter. 'Oh, yes,' she said. 'Thank you so much for calling.'

'Not at all. I'm sorry it wasn't last night. We were up at the hospital until quite late.'

'Can I ask how your mother is?'

'Oh, thank you. She's recovering, albeit slowly. They had to operate, you see. She was very woozy last night. But I'm hoping to find her a bit better today.'

Clare hesitated. Clearly her investigation wasn't going to be a priority for Carolyn Joseph. But she had to find out more about her three victims, assuming Ruth's PM confirmed she was victim number three. 'I wonder if it might be possible to speak to your mother,' she said. 'I wouldn't ask but it is important.'

'I doubt she'll be fit today, Inspector. But I can ask the doctors. Maybe Wednesday or Thursday...'

'Wednesday would be better, if it's at all possible. I would prefer not to trouble your mother but it is a murder inquiry.'

'I'll plead your case, Inspector. Leave it with me.'

Clare thanked Carolyn and ended the call. She emerged from her car and saw Chris and Sara heading for the door. They held back and waited for her.

'Morning, boss,' Chris said. 'Any news?'

'Celia Crawford's had heart surgery,' Clare said. 'Won't be able to speak to her today, that's for sure. I've asked her daughter to press for an interview tomorrow.'

They walked into the station which was stiflingly hot and Clare made a beeline for Jim. 'I don't suppose you can do anything with this heating?'

'Tried, Clare. The thermostat's stuck again. I'll give maintenance a call.'

In her office Clare hung up her coat and switched on the computer. She opened her emails and went through to the kitchen to put her lunch in the fridge. By the time she came back her Inbox had loaded and her eye went immediately to one from Neil Grant. The post-mortem for Ruth Williams. As usual it was a comprehensive document so she scrolled to the summary information which she read quickly. She took a couple of minutes to skim the rest of the report then rose from her seat.

Chris and Sara were in the kitchen making coffees.

'Pass the word round, would you,' she said. 'Briefing in five minutes.'

Chris raised an eyebrow but Clare turned and headed back to her office.

She sat at her desk, thinking for a moment. So now they knew. She lifted her phone and called Diane's number but it went straight to voicemail so she left a message, scribbling some notes on her pad. There was another email that caught her interest and she read it quickly. It had an attachment labelled Kiosk Manual and she flagged the message to read properly when she had time.

As Clare entered the incident room the hum of chatter died down, as though they sensed that something was coming.

'Thanks, everyone,' she began. Then she scanned the faces. They were all there, even Jim, standing by the door in case the phone went. 'I've just had confirmation that Ruth Williams was killed in the same way as the other two victims. The cause of death was constriction of the airway and the pathologist believes death was hastened by applying pressure to the vagus nerve. Again, there was a small amount of alcohol in her system and, crucially, traces of Rohypnol.'

A hum went round the room and Clare waited for it to die down.

'So, there's no doubt, guys, we're dealing with a serial killer. Someone who is systematically picking off women who were at primary school together.'

'Any idea why, boss?' someone asked.

Clare spread her hands. 'At the moment, no. But at least we have the school as a link.'

'And Attracto,' Janey said.

'Well yes. Our first two victims were contacted by the same man – Stoneman – but so far we've not been able to track him down. And Ruth Williams wasn't on Attracto, although Jessica Peters did try to persuade her to join.'

Chris raised his hand. 'Are we thinking that Jessica Peters could be Stoneman?'

'It's certainly a possibility,' Clare said. 'We've been working on the assumption that our killer is a man. But Neil Grant said the Rohypnol would make it easier to strangle the victims. So our killer – whether it's Stoneman or someone else – could easily be a woman.'

Sara frowned. 'But if it was this Stoneman, how would it work?'

'Pretty straightforward, I'd say, Sara. Jessica Peters persuades the women to join Attracto. She creates a profile for a man, username Stoneman, and she starts flirting with her chosen victims. She persuades them to go on a date and, when Stoneman doesn't show up, she does.'

'So,' Janey began, '...you're saying Jessica sets up a date, knowing Stoneman won't turn up...'

'...because he doesn't exist,' Chris added.

Janey nodded. 'Exactly. Then Jessica herself just happens to be in the pub, or wherever the date is, and moves in offering sympathy.'

'That would certainly work for Ingrid,' Clare said. 'But not for Alison or Ruth. Both were found at home and Ruth wasn't even on Attracto.'

Janey fell silent, considering this.

'But it is a link,' Clare said. 'It's possible that's what happened to Ingrid but, if Jessica – or Stoneman – couldn't persuade Alison to go on a date she could have found Alison's address some other way. Maybe she asked where everybody worked in the WhatsApp chat. Then she just happens to be passing Crossford at the end of the day and bumps into Alison. She engineers an invitation to Alison's house and turns up bearing wine. She probably chose red to disguise the Rohypnol tablet. Let's not forget the sausage rolls in the oven. That suggests Alison had a guest.'

'So Jessica turns up,' Chris said, taking up the thread. 'Alison asks her in and, when she's distracted, Jessica slips the Rohypnol into her glass. Half an hour later, when it's taken effect, she strangles Alison putting pressure on the vagus nerve to make it quicker and easier.'

'And, if she couldn't get Ruth to join Attracto,' Nita went on, 'maybe she used the same trick on her.'

This was met with silence while they digested this new development.

Then Janey said, 'We still don't know where Jessica Peters is, boss?'

'Well, we think she was in France, at least until recently. The DCI has put in a Europol request to find her and he's checking with border control, too. If she's entered the country in the past few weeks we'll soon know.' Clare went on. 'So we now have a triple murder hunt and I don't have to tell you how important it is we make progress before we're looking at victim number four.'

Chris was the first to speak. 'How do you want to play it, Clare?'

'Well for a start, you and I will interview Donny Cohen as soon as we've finished here.' She looked round the room. 'Donny Cohen is the man whose photo Stoneman is using,' she explained. 'Given how many times his image appears on the internet I doubt he is Stoneman but we do need to rule him out.'

Chris acknowledged this and Clare went on. 'So back to basics. Anything from the house-to-house?'

Janey said, 'Nothing much, boss. No one noticed anything unusual and no blondes around the times the women were thought to have died.'

'Okay, thanks Janey. So the blondes from the pub CCTV...' Clare indicated the photos from The Harvest Moon pinned up on the board. 'Anything from Google?'

Janey shook her head. 'One of the photos was too grainy for any results. The others only returned their Facebook photos.'

Clare nodded. 'What about the WhatsApp group – how many are blonde, do we know?'

'A few,' Janey said. 'But none living in the area, apart from Michelle, the hairdresser.'

Clare nodded. 'Okay. I'm going to ask the press office to put out a statement about the murders. No details at this stage, just that we're linking three recent deaths. But we need to make sure everyone in that WhatsApp group is warned about the danger. They need to know about the murders and to be on their guard. Advise them no visitors, meet no one from school, no activity on dating sites and to phone us immediately if they suspect something's wrong. And if any of them lives alone, see if they can have someone to stay, at least until we've caught our killer.'

'What about Attracto?' Nita asked.

'I've been on to Diane this morning. She's trying to get it taken offline. We can't stop messages between members who've already made contact but we should be able to stop new folk getting sucked in.' She glanced down at her notepad. 'I've also asked Diane to check Attracto for anyone who has mentioned a medical background in their profile: doctors, nurses, anyone with a science degree. The average man – or woman – in the street is unlikely to know about the vagus nerve. But our killer does.'

Jim cleared his throat. 'Clare, is it possible some of the classmates aren't in that WhatsApp group?'

'Definitely. Good point, Jim. And some of those might have medical qualifications. So,' she scanned the room. 'Who was dealing with the school?'

Gillian raised her hand. 'Me, boss.'

'Can you get back onto the Education Department and get a full class list please? Let's go for the last year they were at primary school – primary seven. And any who aren't in that group, we need contact details asap. Also, find out what did they did post-secondary school. If anyone went into anything scientific or medical, I want to know about it. Okay?'

Gillian indicated she would do this and began scribbling on her notepad.

'And while we're talking about the school,' Clare went on, 'I hope to speak to the head teacher who was in post at the time the girls were pupils. Unfortunately she's had heart surgery but, with luck, I should be able to see her tomorrow.' She glanced at Chris. 'Have I forgotten anything?'

'Just that pair at Sharp and Lafferty.'

'Miles and Cheryl? Much as I'd love to see them behind bars, Chris, I don't think there's anything to link them with Ingrid or Ruth. But it is worth keeping them in mind. If they do turn up in any other connection, let me know.'

She looked round the room. 'Okay, guys. That's it. Get me on my phone if you find anything.'

They began to shift off desks and boot up laptops. A few headed to the kitchen to make drinks while others sat down to telephone the WhatsApp group members again.

Clare watched them to make sure everyone knew what they were doing then she turned to Chris. 'Come on,' she said. 'Let's see what Donny Cohen has to say for himself.'

Chapter 42

The Kenlybank Hotel was busier than Clare expected for a Tuesday morning. As they walked into reception they saw a large board to the side of the desk bearing the words,

Welcome to our delegates

from

Cassells Insurance & Investment

A long trestle table, covered with a pristine white linen cloth, bore rows of delegate lanyards and a smiling woman behind the desk was handing them out to sharp-suited men and women. A pair of double doors to a function room stood open and Clare could see another long table set out with cups and saucers just inside the door. A small group of delegates stood at the table, pouring themselves hot drinks from flasks.

The receptionist recognised Clare and Chris from the day before and asked them to wait while she fetched Donny.

'Is that where your party is?' she asked Chris, indicating the function room.

'No,' he said. 'Other side of reception. Nice room.'

'Don't suppose you've invited Diane and Suzi?'

'Suzi Bishop? Press Officer? I hadn't planned to. Diane's coming though.'

'That'll be nice. I never get the chance to see these guys.'

'I would invite Suzi but Sara doesn't really know her.'

'No problem.' Out of the corner of her eye Clare saw Donny Cohen approaching. He was missing the designer stubble from

Stoneman's profile photo but there was no mistaking it was him. He was tall and lean, with good hair – thick and dark, swept back from his forehead. He had the kind of face that smiled easily but, this morning, as he approached Clare and Chris, he looked wary.

'I'm Donny Cohen,' he said. 'I gather you were looking for me yesterday.'

'That's right,' Clare said. 'Is there somewhere we could talk?'

Donny glanced around, as if concerned they would be overheard. Then he said, 'This way.'

He led them past the reception desk, through a heavy wooden door that gave onto a corridor. At the end of it a woman in a dark blue tunic was filling a wheeled hamper with bed sheets while the trolley next to it held piles of freshly folded linen.

'In here,' Donny said, pushing open another door marked Staff Only. They followed him into a small windowless room, simply furnished with a desk, chairs and a telephone. He indicated the chairs. 'Would you like to sit?'

Clare and Chris sat down and Donny followed suit, moving his chair to the other side of the desk.

'So, what's this about?'

'We're investigating the murder of three women in the town,' Clare said, watching him carefully.

There was no mistaking his reaction. His eyes widened and for a moment he didn't speak, as though trying to process this. Then he said, 'You're not here to ask me...' he tailed off.

'Thing is, Donny, we believe there could be a link with a dating website, and we've found your photo on that site.'

He stared and then he started to laugh. 'I'm not on a dating site,' he said. 'I'm married, Inspector.' He indicated a gold band on his wedding finger. 'You've got the wrong guy.'

Chris took out his phone and opened up his photos where he'd stored a screenshot of Stoneman's profile. He handed the phone to Donny.

Donny stared at it for a moment, reading the description below the photo. He shook his head. 'I don't understand,' he said. 'This isn't me.' He looked up at Clare. 'Inspector, I am not on this dating site. I don't know if this is one of my mates doing it for a laugh but this is not me.' The colour was rising from his neck and Clare saw beads of perspiration starting to form on his brow. He shook his head again. 'It really isn't me. I swear.' He handed the phone back to Chris.

'Can you tell us your shifts at the hotel between Christmas and new year please?' Clare said.

'Five to one, every night,' he shot back.

'Night off?'

'Twenty-seventh.'

'We'll have to check that,' Clare said. 'I'd also like your permission to check your phone records.'

'I'm telling you I'm not that... that Stone-guy – whatever he's called.' He ran a hand through his hair. 'I don't know how else to say it.'

Clare smiled. 'I'm sure you're not, Donny. But we do need to check everything. We have three dead bodies in the mortuary so I am sorry, but it has to be done. You are, of course, within your rights to refuse to let us have your phone records. But we'll apply for a warrant so it's only a matter of time.'

He hesitated then took his phone out of his pocket. 'Sorry,' he said. 'But if I could just...'

They waited.

'Well, it's like this: you might find some messages, back and forward – one of the waitresses, you see. We sort of text each other...' he tailed off.

'Name?' Clare asked.

'Maddie. Sorry, Madeleine White.'

Clare wrote this down then gave him a smile. 'Rest assured, Donny, if it has no bearing on our case we won't be pursuing it.'

'Won't even mention it to your wife,' Chris added.

Donny looked stricken and Clare kicked Chris's ankle under the desk.

'It's unlikely we'll have to talk to her,' Clare reassured him. 'Providing none of the numbers on your phone match with those we're interested in.'

'I can't be without my phone, though,' Donny said. 'I use it all the time.'

Clare considered this. 'I think we can work round that.' She checked her watch. 'What time do you get off?'

'Two.'

'Can you call into the station as soon as you finish?'

He nodded. 'Suppose. Only…'

'Yes?'

'Well, my photo – how did it get onto that site?'

Chris took out his phone again. 'You on Facebook, Donny?'

Donny shrugged. 'Yeah. Course I am.'

Chris began tapping at his phone and a few seconds later held it out to show Donny. 'Now we're not friends on Facebook but see how much of your data I can see? Your security settings are pretty loose. Someone's stolen your photo.' Chris then copied Donny's photo and pasted it into a Google search. He handed the phone to Donny. 'This is a search on your photo.'

Donny gaped at the results of the search. Then he looked back at Chris. 'Why the hell are all these people using my photo?'

'Spammers or hackers, usually. Trying to trick someone into giving away personal information. You're a good-looking guy. Might attract a lot of women online. Your photo's a hacker's dream. If I were you, Donny, I'd tighten up my security settings.'

They watched him walk briskly back to his duties. When he was out of earshot Clare said, 'That was a bit cruel.'

'What, mentioning his wife? Serves him right. I can't be doing with guys like him.'

'The good-looking ones?'

'Shut up.'

At the front desk, they waited while the receptionist dealt with a phone call. When she'd finished Clare said, 'Could I see your duty rota please? For the week between Christmas and new year.'

The receptionist was doubtful. 'I'm not sure...'

Clare sighed. 'We can ask for a warrant and it will be granted. But it'll hold up our enquiries. Now I don't plan to copy any of the data. I just need to check something.'

The receptionist relented and, after a few minutes, a printer behind the desk began to whirr. Seconds later the receptionist handed two sheets to Clare and Chris and they bent over them.

Then Chris noticed the receptionist hovering and he nudged Clare. 'Let's take this over to one of these tables,' he said. 'Save disturbing this lady at her work.'

The receptionist gave a thin smile and turned back to her computer.

Clare and Chris sat down at a small round mahogany table. A single rose in a narrow vase stood in the centre next to a menu offering morning coffees and pastries. Clare moved the vase to the side to make room for the printouts but Chris was studying the menu.

'You've a kilt to fit into,' she told him, moving the menu out of the way, 'and you've had far too many of Zoe's cakes.' She ignored his injured look and spread the sheets of paper out on the table. 'Now let's see... so here's Christmas Day.' She ran a finger down a list of names stopping at D Cohen. 'There he is. So let's check all his shifts.'

As Donny had said, he was working from five until one in the morning every day except for the twenty-seventh.

'And Ingrid was definitely killed on the twenty-eighth,' Chris said. 'Or the early hours of the twenty-ninth at the latest.'

Clare nodded. 'So that lets him out of the frame,' she said. 'The Harvest Moon shut at midnight. Even if Ingrid was drunk it would have taken her less than twenty minutes to reach her house in Lamond Drive.'

'Yeah, I doubt he's involved.'

'All the same, we'll check his phone this afternoon.'

'Check for his waitress girlfriend,' Chris said. 'Probably a long shot but I'd like to know if she was off on the twenty-eighth.'

Clare scanned the rota again. 'No. Looks like she was working the same shifts as Donny.'

They rose from the table, Chris casting a last wistful glance at the menu. Clare handed the printed rota back to the receptionist and, dodging past a clutch of conference delegates, they headed for the main door. As they walked, Clare said, 'I had an email this morning. We're getting a Cyber Kiosk.'

'Which is?'

'A device that lets us download phone data in minutes. It's on a trial basis and the legalities are still a bit up in the air. Strict instructions not to store anything without a warrant but it'll let us download the data from Donny Cohen's phone without having to hang onto it.'

'Should we not have taken him back with us? In case he starts deleting stuff.'

'Doesn't matter. It'll show deleted stuff too.'

Chris considered this. 'I'm struggling to see the downside, Clare. It sounds brilliant. Think how much time that'll save us running stuff down to Tech Support.'

'Yeah, although it is better if we can use their expertise. But for a quick job like this I think it'll be ideal.'

'If it works.'

'There is that.'

Chapter 43

There was an email from Diane waiting for Clare when she arrived back. There was also a padded bag on her desk next to a cupcake with bright pink icing. Evidently Zoe had been baking again.

'Came in the internal mail,' Jim said, indicating the parcel, a hint of curiosity in his voice.

Clare took a bite out of the cupcake and wiped the crumbs off her face. 'Jim, any of those spare phones kicking about? The ones we hand out to victims when we've taken their phone for analysis?'

'Aye. Want one?'

'Please. Bring it into my office. I've something to show you.'

Clare bit into the cupcake again then took a pair of scissors to the padded bag. It was sealed with layers of thick tape and it took a few minutes to open. She felt inside and withdrew a small console, peeling off the bubble wrap. The Cyber Kiosk. She plugged it in and waited while it came to life. Chris and Jim crowded round.

'What is it?' Jim asked.

'It's a device that lets us download phone data in minutes,' Clare said, shaking her computer mouse to bring the screen to life. 'There's a manual attached to the email.'

'But that would save us hours,' Jim said.

'That's the idea. Got that phone?'

Jim handed over an old Nokia. Clare attached the cable and plugged it into the Cyber Kiosk.

'Now, if I can just remember...'

'You seen one of these before?' Chris asked.

'Yeah. Back end of last year. Remember that training day I had, over at Gartcosh?'

'The Crime Campus? Yeah.'

'This was part of the day. We have it on a trial basis and I'm the only one authorised to operate it for now. So it stays in my office.'

The screen lit up as it began to extract data from the phone. 'See this?' Clare said, indicating a menu down the side of the screen. 'We can choose which data we want to interrogate. So, let's look at text messages.' She pointed to the display and it began to fill with screen after screen of text messages. 'So, we can see the other number, name too, if the person is stored as a contact, and the content of the message.'

'Date and time too,' Chris said, peering at it.

Clare unplugged the burner phone from the Kiosk and handed it back to Jim. 'Chris and I interviewed Donny Cohen this morning. He's definitely the man in Stoneman's photo but he denies being on Attracto.'

'Believe him?' Jim asked.

'Yeah, I think so,' Clare said, and Chris nodded in agreement. 'He's bringing his phone in this afternoon,' Clare went on. 'So I'll check his contacts against the WhatsApp group and hopefully rule him out.'

–

Donny Cohen arrived at the station just after quarter past two. Clare took his phone and asked him to wait in the public enquiry area.

'Shouldn't be too long,' she said.

He waved this away. 'I'm in no rush.'

Chris brought the list of contacts from the WhatsApp group into Clare's office and they sat down to compare them with the data from Donny's phone. They weren't really surprised when there were no matches. As she unplugged his phone from the

Kiosk Clare's own phone began to ring. Diane. 'Could you give this back to Donny please, Chris? Thank him for his co-operation – the usual. I need to take this call.'

Clare waited until he'd closed the door then switched the phone to speaker. 'Diane, hi. Thanks for calling.'

'No problem, Clare. How's tricks?'

'Not bad,' Clare said. 'I've just been playing with my new toy.'

'Ahh. They've sent you a Cyber Kiosk. Good, aren't they?'

'Yup. Hopefully save us bothering you guys so much.'

'Ach, it's what we're here for, Clare. And speaking of that.'

'Got anything?'

'Yeah, maybe. So first of all, Attracto should be down by the end of the day. They're being a bit sticky but they have agreed.'

'I'll give them sticky,' Clare said.

'It's fine. Your DCI's already done it. Now I could have got it taken down right away but...'

'You got something else?'

'Maybe. You wanted to know about anyone on Attracto with a medical background?'

'You've got someone?'

'Two actually.'

Clare grabbed a pen and notepad. 'Okay, tell me...'

'Dr Helen Armstrong. GP in Cupar. I've got her username on the site and managed to get her contact details too.'

Clare scribbled down Dr Armstrong's details then said, 'And the other?'

'Finn McDonald. He's a lab technician over in Dundee. Out at the Technology Park.'

Clare noted this too and thanked Diane. She rose and went to her office door to find Chris about to come back in.

'That's Donny Cohen away, heartily relieved.'

'Never mind him. Diane's come up with a couple of Attracto members with a medical background.' She squinted at her notepad. 'Dr Helen Armstrong,' she said. 'GP in Cupar. Diane says she's in the forty to fifty age bracket. Her interests are classical concerts and art galleries.'

'Doesn't sound like our murderer,' Chris said.

'All the same, we'll need her checked out.'

'Is that it?'

'No.' Clare tapped her notepad. 'There's another one. Lab technician across in Dundee. Finn McDonald. Twenty to thirty age group. Interests are rugby, curling... curling? Where the hell does he go curling round here?'

Chris shrugged. 'Dunno. Perth maybe. Rink in Dundee, too, isn't there?'

'Suppose. Anyway, I've got contact details for them both. So we need to cross-check their phone numbers with the WhatsApp group members. I want to know where they went to school and when. See if they have any siblings who might have been in the same class as our victims. Previous employment – anything at all. Can you see to that, please?'

Chris scraped back his chair. 'Sure. Want someone to call on them?'

'Not at this stage. Let's see what the team can come up with first.'

–

A man in dark green overalls was unscrewing the thermostat from the wall when Clare emerged from her office.

'I hope it's a quick fix,' she said to him. 'We've been sweltering here.'

'Just replacing it, hen,' the man said, his accent suggesting he hailed from south-west Fife. 'Cheaper than trying to fix it, ye ken?'

Clare thanked him and wandered into the incident room. 'Any progress?' she said.

A few heads shook but Janey looked up. 'We've pretty much got round the WhatsApp group,' she said. 'All warned not to go on dates, not to be on their own – the usual.'

'Great, thanks Janey. What about that class list?' She scanned the room for Gillian.

'Got it, boss,' Gillian said. 'It's a full list of everyone who started primary seven that year. I'll print you off a copy.'

'Thanks Gillian. Can you liaise with Janey, please? I need anyone on the list who's not on the WhatsApp group spoken to.'

'What if one of them's our killer, though?' Janey asked.

It was a good point.

'If we warn them to be careful they'll know we're onto the school connection,' Janey went on.

Clare considered this. 'How many are there?'

'Just the four,' Gillian said. 'I'm checking on them now.'

'Okay. See what you can find out first then we'll rethink. But I'd rather risk letting a killer know we're on to them than have another victim.'

Clare went back to her office with the intention of calling the DCI to update him on their progress – or lack of it – when her phone rang again. She recognised the number this time. It was Celia Crawford's daughter.

'Mrs Joseph,' she said. 'How is your mother?'

'Much better, Inspector. She's a real tough cookie. Sitting up in bed, joking with the nurses.'

'I'm so glad to hear that,' Clare said. She hesitated and Carolyn went on.

'I've asked the medical staff and they say you can have a short visit tomorrow morning after rounds. But only if she's not too tired.'

'Perfect,' Clare said. 'I'm so grateful. So what time?'

'They said about eleven. I'm sorry it couldn't be today but I think another day will make all the difference – if you can wait.'

'I can wait,' Clare said. 'And thank you. I really do appreciate it.'

An alert sounded from Clare's phone when she was settling down to look at the class list Gillian had printed off. A reminder that Moira, her neighbour, had a hospital appointment that day and wouldn't be able to do a second dog walk with Benjy. She gathered up her things and headed for the door. 'I need to go home early tonight, Jim,' she said. 'But I'll have my phone. Keep me updated.'

The fog had lifted but the light was going as Clare pulled into the drive at Daisy Cottage. She could hear a delighted Benjy barking from within the house and she hurried in with promises of a walk before it was fully dark.

It was only later, when she was sprawled out on the sofa, channel-hopping that she remembered Gillian's printout and she took it up to read. Most of the names were known to her by now, she'd been through that WhatsApp group so many times. But, as Gillian had said, four of the pupils weren't in the group. There were two girls: Gemma Golden and Alexandra Harris. Clare realised Alexandra must be Lexy and she wondered why Lexy wasn't part of the group. Maybe Celia Crawford would shed some light on that. The two boys were John Mason and Ben McEwan. John must be the boy from the photo, she thought. Another one to ask Celia about.

With luck Gillian would have found contact details for all four by tomorrow. She looked again at the list and couldn't put her finger on what was bothering her.

And then she saw it.

Or rather she didn't.

Ingrid McKinnie's name was missing.

Wednesday, 13th January

Chapter 44

'I'm seeing Celia Crawford at eleven this morning,' Clare said to Chris as she entered the station. 'I'd like you with me.'

'Yeah, sure.'

'Any progress overnight?'

'Kind of. The primary seven classmates who weren't in the WhatsApp group – Gemma Golden checks out but they're still trying to locate Lexy Harris and the two men.'

Clare pushed open her office door and held it for Chris. 'Maybe Celia Crawford will know something.' She shrugged off her coat and threw it over an empty chair then sat down at her desk. 'I discovered something odd last night.'

'Yeah?'

'That class list Gillian gave me – Ingrid McKinnie's not on it.'

'Eh?'

'That's what I thought.'

'Want to speak to the parents again?'

'Not at this stage. There could be a reasonable explanation. Again, I'm hoping Celia will know.'

'Bit of a long shot, Clare. Must be almost twenty years since that class left primary school.'

'Yeah, I know. If Celia doesn't come up with anything useful I will speak to the parents. But I don't want to add to their distress if I can help it.'

–

There was a queue for car park number nine at Ninewells Hospital in Dundee. It was set on an elevated site looking across the River Tay to Fife and had a number of car parks dotted around the grounds. Number nine, the furthest from the building, was always the last to fill up and today there was a queue for the remaining spaces. Chris drummed his fingers impatiently on the side of the car as the barrier admitted one car at a time – slowly.

Eventually they were through the barrier and Clare crawled along until she found a space. She backed in then killed the engine, clicking off her belt. 'Come on,' she said. 'We're late enough already.'

'We could wait for the courtesy bus,' Chris said, indicating the sign where a minibus stopped every fifteen minutes.

'Ach, the walk'll do you good,' Clare said, setting a brisk pace. 'Think of that kilt.'

The Coronary Care Unit was located three floors below the entrance and they followed the signs through the concourse and down to the ward. Clare showed her warrant card at the nurses' station and was directed to Celia's bed.

'She's quite bright this morning,' the nurse said, 'but please don't tire her out.'

Clare nodded at this and approached the elderly lady. She was sitting, propped up in bed, reading a newspaper while, on either side of her, machines and monitors flashed silently. Her face was lined with age and the soft hair snowy-white, but her eyes looked quick and intelligent. As they approached she folded the newspaper and laid it down, greeting them with a smile.

'Detective Inspector Mackay?' she asked. Clare smiled and introduced Chris. He went to fetch two chairs from a stack at the window.

'I'm so sorry to greet you in these surroundings,' Celia said. 'It's not as if I can offer you a cup of tea.'

Clare smiled. 'We're the ones who should be sorry – for disturbing you so soon after your surgery. But we do have some urgent enquiries we hoped you could assist with.'

'So my daughter said. I'll be happy to help, if I can.'

Chris returned with the chairs and they sat down.

'We're investigating the deaths of some young women who were pupils at Lamond Primary School when you were headteacher.'

Celia's brow clouded but she said nothing.

'We'd like to find out as much as possible about the women so we can work out if the school is the connection. I'm afraid, if we don't discover why they are being killed, there may be more deaths.'

Celia looked grave. 'Then, please, ask me anything you wish, Inspector.'

Clare took out the photo she had found among Ingrid's papers and handed it to Celia. She studied it for some minutes then said, 'That was a long time ago. But I do remember the girls.' She tapped the photo. 'Alison, of course. And Ingrid.' She began to smile at the memory. 'Great friends, they were.' She studied the photo again. 'Oh, that's Lexy,' she said, a note of surprise in her voice. 'And Ruth next to her. And, of course...'

'You sounded surprised at Lexy being in the photo,' Clare said, cutting across Celia. 'Was she not friendly with the others?'

Celia leaned back on her pillows considering this. Then she said, 'I think three of the girls were particular friends – Alison, Ruth and Ingrid. They were quite a trio. They used to walk about the playground, arms linked, and woe betide anyone who got in their way. Not that anyone did. They were popular, you know, Inspector. Everyone wanted to be their friend. I suppose, to the other children, they must have seemed as if they had it all. They were quick and clever, good at sports, invited to all the parties. I think they might have included Lexy sometimes, but not always. Just when they felt charitable.'

'Were they unkind to the others in the class?' Clare asked.

'Hm... not especially,' Celia said. 'But they doled their favours out sparingly. I would say they knew their worth.' She glanced at the photo again. 'And that's John,' she said. She closed her eyes for a moment, as if trying to recall, then she said, 'John Mason, I think. A bit of a poor soul, really. He clung on to the girls, almost for protection. He didn't have many friends in the class and they rather took him under their wing.'

Clare reached into her pocket and took out the class list Gillian had printed off, running her eye down the names. 'You have a good memory,' she said. 'There is a John Mason.'

Celia smiled. 'No doubt, Inspector, you have heard that the elderly can't recall what they had for breakfast but they can remember things which happened fifty years ago. I'm afraid it's absolutely true.'

Clare laughed then said, 'Could I ask you about another pupil, please?'

'Of course. It's enjoyable thinking back to those days.'

'Jessica Peters.'

Celia pressed her hands together while she thought and Clare couldn't help noticing a large bruise spreading out from a bandage, where a drip needle had been inserted through her papery skin. After a few moments she said, 'I don't recall anything special about Jessica. She wasn't particular friends with the girls in the photo. Just an ordinary girl, I suppose. Nice enough, but unremarkable.'

'Did she have any arguments with her classmates? Any fighting or bullying?'

Celia shook her head. 'Not that I recall. Mind you, often it doesn't come to the attention of staff. But I wasn't aware of anything like that.' Her brow furrowed and then she said, 'I think she went abroad a few years after leaving Lamond.'

'She did,' Clare said. 'To France.'

'Ah yes. That's right. Is she still there?'

'We think so. Having a bit of trouble getting in touch with her.'

The nurse reappeared and scanned the monitors around Celia. 'Maybe just another few minutes, Inspector,' she suggested, and Clare nodded.

Celia cast a glance at the nurse. 'I'm perfectly fine, nurse. I'm enjoying talking about the old days.'

The nurse walked away again and Clare said, 'There is one more thing, Mrs Crawford, if you feel up to it.'

Celia smiled. 'Of course.'

'Ingrid McKinnie – for some reason her name's not on this list. But I'm pretty sure she was at Lamond Primary. Could she have been in another class?'

Celia's brow furrowed again and she was silent for a minute. And then her expression cleared. 'I remember now,' she said. 'Ingrid left Lamond a year early. Her parents put her to Melville Academy. You know, the private school south of the town.'

Clare nodded. The list they were working from showed all the pupils who'd started their final year together at Lamond Primary. But the McKinnies hadn't told Clare that Ingrid had left the school a year before the others.

'Usually,' Celia went on, 'the parents wait until the child has completed their primary education, but I think Ingrid's parents wanted her away from the school. There was an accident, you see...'

Chapter 45

They packed into the incident room, conscious that Clare had something significant to impart. The DCI had driven up from his office in Dunfermline and, as he entered the room, the buzz of chatter died away.

When there was absolute quiet, Clare began. 'First of all, thanks to DCI Gibson for coming up at short notice.' She glanced at him. 'Can I ask if you've heard back from Europol?'

He shook his head. 'Hopefully in the next forty-eight hours,' he said. 'But I've escalated it to urgent so we might hear sooner.'

Clare smiled. 'Thanks, Al. Meantime, I spoke to Celia Crawford this morning. She's the former headteacher at Lamond Primary School and was in charge at the time our victims were pupils. She's currently in the Coronary Care Unit at Ninewells Hospital, following heart surgery so we couldn't stay long; but she has given us some quite significant background information.' She paused to ensure they were all attending then went on.

'As you know, our three victims were at school together. It seems they were popular – everyone wanted to be their friend.'

'The in-crowd,' someone said.

'Precisely. Now that continued until the end of primary six when Ingrid was moved to Melville Academy, a year before the end of primary school.'

'Any idea why, boss?' Janey asked.

'Oh yes.' She paused for a moment then said, 'There was an incident at a birthday party – Lexy Harris's birthday. Lexy's younger brother Sam, aged three, managed to escape from the garden. It was a long garden, lots of trees with a gate at the bottom. Easy for him to wander off, unnoticed. Most of the children were playing outside while Lexy's mum set out the party food in the kitchen. Somehow – and Celia doesn't know the details – Sam Harris managed to open the gate. Beyond the gate was a steep embankment that led to a fast-flowing stream. Sam must have missed his footing and tumbled down the bank. He fell into the stream and Celia thinks he hit his head, knocking him unconscious. By the time they found him he was dead. Drowned.'

'Shit,' someone said.

'Quite.'

'When was this?' the DCI asked.

'In the summer holidays. Between primaries six and seven. Ingrid's parents took her out of the school immediately. They had planned to send her to Melville Academy after primary seven anyway but, with the upset over the little boy's death, they brought the move forward a year.'

'Were we involved?' Janey asked.

'Only initially. It was logged as a tragic accident. Now, Lexy's name is on that class list so we know she started primary seven with the rest of the class. But, as far as Celia can recall the family moved away a few months later. Just before Christmas, she thought.'

'Ah, so that's why she's on that class list and Ingrid's not,' Chris said.

Clare nodded. 'The list was compiled at the start of the academic year.'

'Where is Lexy now?' the DCI asked.

'Not sure,' Clare said. 'Has anyone managed to track her down?'

Heads shook. 'Got Ben McEwan, though,' Gary said.

Clare nodded. 'So it's just Lexy Harris and John Mason we're looking for.'

'Lexy is your priority,' the DCI said. 'It's her brother who died at that party. If there's any link with the deaths, we have to start with her.'

They fell silent for a moment then Janey said, 'So where do we go from here, boss?'

'We need to find everyone who was at that birthday party. I'm not exactly sure how but I'm afraid it means going back to the WhatsApp group again.'

'Jesus,' Bill said. 'They'll be sick of the sight of us.'

'Better than putting a tag on their toes,' Clare said. 'As DCI Gibson says, Lexy Harris is your number one priority. We need to speak to her parents too. So, the usual please. Voters' roll, phone book – you know the drill.'

'Is that all she said, boss?' Sara asked.

Clare hesitated. 'That lad in the photo – John Mason – she said he was a bit of a loner. Not many friends but the girls took him under their wing. She actually used the words poor soul about him. I'm not sure it's significant but there was something about the way she said it...'

'No luck tracking him down so far,' Janey said. 'If he is a bit vulnerable, maybe he's just opted out of society.'

Clare nodded. 'Could be.' She looked round the room and spotted Gillian. 'Gill, would you get back onto the Education Department please? See if their records show if Lexy and John went on to college or uni. Or if they found jobs. I'm pretty sure the Scottish Government collects data on school leavers so it should be recorded. It might point us in the right direction.'

Clare glanced at the DCI to see if he had anything further to say but he shook his head. 'Right,' she said, starting for the door. 'That's it for now. But keep in touch.'

They turned back to their laptops and phones and began their enquiries. Clare, Chris and the DCI headed for her office.

'What's your gut feeling, Clare?' he asked.

'I just don't know. But something about the way Celia said John Mason was a poor soul worries me.' She fell silent for a moment then said, 'Chris, could you dig out the press reports of Sam Harris's death please?'

'Sure. Any idea how long ago?'

'Let's think… the murdered women were all thirty-three and it was the summer between primary six and seven, so they'd have been, what, eleven?' She counted back in her head. 'Better start from twenty-three years ago and work forward.'

'Okay,' Chris said.

'That lad,' the DCI began.

'John Mason?'

'Yes, him. Bit odd, a lad of that age, hanging about with girls.'

'What are you thinking?'

The DCI sat back in his chair as if trying to order his thoughts. Then he said, 'I'm just wondering… if he was at that party, maybe he did something to Sam Harris – maybe he was a bit disturbed.'

'Would that not have come out at the time?'

'Not if there were no witnesses. That head teacher said there were lots of trees in the garden. Could be he found a spot where no one could see him.'

Clare began to see what he was saying. 'And, if he did, maybe he's worried those girls know something…'

'…and he's making sure they don't talk?' Chris added.

Clare thought for a moment then shook her head. 'I don't buy it. I mean I can see that might have happened, but why now? Why wait twenty-odd years to silence them?'

–

It was almost six o'clock when Sara tapped on Clare's office door. 'Those two medical folk from Attracto, boss…'

Clare was reading Ruth Williams's post-mortem report again, in the hope of finding something – some clue to the mind of the killer. But the more she read it the more muddled she became. She looked up and yawned. 'Tell me some good news, Sara – please?'

Sara shook her head. 'Sorry. I mean it's progress of a sort but it doesn't help.'

'Go on, then.'

'The doctor and the lab technician – they were the two on Attracto with a medical background.'

'Both checked out?'

'Yeah. Finn Macdonald was in Ireland for two weeks over Christmas. So he definitely couldn't have killed Alison or Ingrid.'

'And our doctor?'

'Helen Armstrong. She was away last weekend, when Ruth Williams died. She was at a medical conference in Sheffield. Checked into the hotel on Friday night, gave a speech on the Saturday and took part in focus groups on the Sunday. She didn't travel back up until Monday morning.'

Clare sighed. 'Okay, thanks Sara.' She glanced at her watch. 'Tell the team to pack it in for tonight. I'll do a handover to the Inspector in Dundee. Back in sharp tomorrow morning.'

–

Clare's resolve to do more home cooking weakened in the face of weariness and she phoned for a pizza delivery. Moira's husband Bill had dropped off a load of logs and she filled a stout bag with these and knelt down to light the fire. With her back to the sofa and Benjy's head on her knee she sat on the rug, feeling the heat from the fire on her face as the kindling sparked and spat. She'd opened a bottle of red wine too, not even stopping to check the label, and she set her glass down on the hearth as she munched on pizza. Sometimes, she thought, it was good to have a treat. Her laptop lay discarded on the sofa and she heard a ping from it. She wiped her hands on a piece of kitchen roll and turned it round. A message from the DCI.

She shook Benjy off her knee and lifted the pizza box out of his reach, putting it on the dining table. Then she sat down on the sofa and clicked to open the message.

> Hi Clare.
>
> Hope you're not still at work?

She looked for the tell-tale dots, indicating he was typing but there were none. She typed back,

> Hi Al.
>
> Home now, thank goodness.
>
> Sitting, having pizza by the fire. You?

The dots appeared and she waited while he typed. Then she read,

> Fire? Lucky you.
>
> I've been waiting on a guy installing a wood burner for weeks now.
>
> Supposed to be in before Christmas.
>
> Just had a stir-fry though.

Clare was about to type a reply but she saw the dots again so she waited. And then the message appeared.

> Just wanted to check you're okay.
>
> You seemed tired today.
>
> I know this case is a huge strain but we'll get there.
>
> We'll get him.

She read this over twice. It wasn't the kind of message she was used to having from a DCI – from her boss. Admittedly they'd come close to being more than that at one time. But, since then he'd been, well, more distant. And here he was now, wanting to check she was okay. Was this simply the act of a caring boss, or was there more to it than that? Suddenly her appetite deserted her. She reached for the wine glass and took a long drink. There were no more dots now. He was waiting for her to reply. But what to say? Was she reading too much into it? Or was he waiting for some small sign from her. And then the dots started again. But this time the message said,

Hold on – email from Europol.

Clare held her breath. Was this it? News of Jessica Peters? The woman who'd tried to persuade the three victims to sign up for a dating site – a site where two of them had been contacted by a man called Stoneman? A man who was using someone else's photo. Was Jessica behind it all? And had the police in France found her? If they hadn't, might that mean she was here in St Andrews, orchestrating the murders of her classmates?

The wait seemed endless, her eyes fixed on the message, waiting for the dots to indicate he was typing again. A spark from a log startled her. Benjy, disturbed from his sleep, gave a low growl. And then the trill from her phone cut through the air and she snatched it up, glancing at the display. Al Gibson.

'Al?'

There was a moment's hesitation, then he said, 'Clare, I'm sorry.'

She waited, not daring to breathe.

'Jessica Peters died five years ago.'

Thursday, 14th January

Chapter 46

'They're absolutely sure?' Chris said as they waited for the incident room to fill up.

'Yep. They emailed over a copy of the death certificate. She died in hospital in Perpignan.'

'Cause of death?'

'From what I can gather, some kind of cancer.'

'So, who knew about that, I wonder?'

Clare nodded. 'Yep. Whoever took over her identity must have known she was dead – and banked on no one else finding out about it, with her being in France.'

'Bit of a risk.'

'Maybe. Not impossible, though. Send out a few messages to former classmates saying you're trying to get in touch with her. You'd soon find out if anyone knew she'd died.'

Sara entered the room and made for a desk near the back. She settled on the edge of it and gave Chris a shy smile. He beamed back.

'All set for Saturday?' Clare whispered.

'I reckon so. She thinks she's going out with her friends. They've said a posh restaurant so she's bought a new dress.'

'She's going to wonder why you're putting your kilt on, though.'

'It's fine. One of the friends has said they'll have prosecco at her house so she'll be out by six. Plenty of time for me to change and get over to the hotel.'

Clare smiled at him. 'Chris, I think it's a lovely thing to do. She'll be thrilled.'

'Hope so.' He glanced at the door. They were nearly all in. 'DCI coming up?'

Clare shook her head. 'Not this morning. I'm updating him by phone.'

Chris raised an eyebrow but Clare ignored it.

'Did you check up on Sam Harris's death?'

He was about to reply when the hubbub in the room died away and they all turned to face Clare. She moved to stand in front of the board.

'Right, everyone. I'll make this as short as I can. The DCI heard from Europol last night.' She paused, knowing the impact her words would have, then went on. 'Jessica Peters died in France five years ago.'

'Eh?' someone said.

'I'm afraid it's true. So someone is posing as Jessica, using a VPN to disguise her location...'

'Or his,' Janey said.

'Indeed.'

Bill raised his hand. 'Why not ask one of the WhatsApp group to message her? Draw her out.'

Clare considered this. It was worth a shot. She glanced at Chris. 'What do you think?'

'We could ask the hairdresser.'

'Michelle Delaney? Yes, I suppose. She might not want to, though. Doesn't seem fair, involving her.'

Nita raised her hand. 'Boss, I know it's not exactly ethical but, since we can't get hold of Lexy Harris, could one of us...'

'Stop right there, Nita,' Clare said. 'If you're suggesting we send messages impersonating Lexy, then it's out.'

'But Lexy does appear to be connected to this case,' Nita persisted.

Clare shook her head. 'We'd be breaking the law. I'm sorry guys but it has to be no.'

'What if it's the only way to find out who's behind the messages?' Chris said.

Clare hesitated. It was a good point. But she couldn't take the risk. Even if they did find the person sending the messages, it would come out in court and she'd be lucky to keep her job. 'I know,' she said, 'I know. But we can't do it. At least, it's way above my pay grade.'

There were a few murmurs round the room. Chris was looking at her and even Sara was frowning.

'Look, if we exhaust all other avenues I'll speak to the DCI. But, in the meantime, Sam Harris's death, Chris?'

Chris got to his feet. 'Nothing much more than the headteacher told us. Police attended, found Sam face down in the burn, unresponsive. He was taken to Ninewells Hospital where he was pronounced dead on arrival. Parents distraught. Gate was normally kept latched. They weren't sure if someone had lifted the latch out of curiosity, but no further action was taken.'

'Thanks, Chris.' Clare looked back at the team. 'What about Lexy and her parents? Anyone tracked them down?'

Nita took up her notepad. 'They moved to England, boss. Bristol. Stayed there for a couple of years. Then the parents split up. Father stayed in the family home, mother and Lexy moved out.'

'Do we know where they went?'

'No. Father died a few years later. Local cops have been round to speak to the neighbours. One of them said Lexy's mother was talking about changing her name. Apparently a local paper had run a feature on Sam's death and it had renewed interest in the case.'

'Okay, Nita. We should be able to trace her, then. Got her new name?'

'Sorry, boss. Not so far, and, from what I can gather, you can change your name by deed poll but you don't have to register the new name.'

Clare gaped. 'Seriously?'

'Yep. They recommend it but it's not mandatory.'

'Ideal if you do want to drop off the radar,' Chris said.

Clare frowned. 'Is that it, Nita? Nothing else?'

'I've maybe got something, boss. The mother worked for a hotel chain...' Nita glanced down at her notepad again. 'Stelling Hotels. So she could have moved about with them.'

'I know it,' Clare said. 'There's one in Glasgow. Out the west end. Can we find her through that, please?'

'I'm on it,' Nita said.

'Okay. If not, try HMRC. They should be able to check her National Insurance number.' She looked round the room again. 'What about Lexy – any luck?'

Erin shook her head. 'Nothing yet, boss. But if we do find the mother, there's a good chance of finding Lexy.'

Clare nodded. 'Okay. Classmates – Gillian, you were phoning the Education Department again. Did you find anyone who went into medicine or science?'

Gillian nodded. 'Yeah, they pulled it off the database. But they could only tell me what the pupils' plans were at the time they left the school.'

'And?'

'Only two went down medical routes. One's an ambulance driver in Manchester now...'

'Checked him out?'

'Yeah. Been on regular shifts for the past couple of weeks. I doubt he's involved.'

'And the other?'

'John Mason.'

'What?' It was out before Clare could stop herself. Surely this was the break they'd been waiting for. 'Tell me?'

'Left school and started a nursing degree at Dundee uni. But he's not registered with the Nursing and Midwifery Council so I spoke to the uni. Seems he dropped out after first year.'

'Where is he now?'

'Still trying to find him. Should have an address this morning, boss.'

'Get hold of me when you do. We need to pick him up.'

As they filed out of the incident room Chris said, 'What do you want to do first, Clare?'

She hesitated. 'Look, I'm not willing to send messages impersonating Lexy.'

'Yeah, I get that.'

'But maybe we could persuade Michelle Delaney to send Jessica Peters a message.'

'Definitely worth a shot. Want to head along there now?'

–

Michelle Delaney was brushing colour on a client's hair then wrapping it in foils when Clare and Chris arrived at Razor. A young girl with jet black hair was at the counter and she eyed them nervously. But, before she could speak, Michelle glanced across.

'Give me five minutes,' she said, and Clare smiled her thanks. They sat down on the bench watching Michelle expertly applying the colour while the pixie-cut woman backwashed a man's hair at one of the sinks. Eventually Michelle finished and she passed the woman a magazine and wheeled her trolley over to Clare and Chris. 'Pretty busy today,' she said.

'Can you spare us five minutes?' Clare asked and Michelle nodded.

They followed her through to the back room again. Michelle closed the door and turned to face them.

Clare had decided not to let Michelle know that Jessica Peters was dead. 'Michelle, we really need to get in touch with Jessica Peters, but we can't track her down.'

Michelle frowned. 'You think she's keeping a low profile?'

Clare was grateful for the suggestion. 'Yes, we think so. Thing is, she might have a reason for not wanting to contact us.'

'Some folk can be funny with the police,' Chris suggested, continuing the theme.

'Yeah, I can see that,' Michelle said. 'So you want me to message her?'

'Would you mind? Even if we had some clue as to where she was it would be a huge help.'

Michelle shrugged. 'Suppose. It's not like we were that friendly, though.' She reached in a pocket for her phone. 'Want me to do it now?'

'Please.'

'Okay. You'll need to tell me what to say, though.'

Clare thought for a minute, then she said, 'How about...'

Hi Jessica

Hope you're well.

I could do with some help, if you have time. If you're back from France just now, could I pick your brains pls? I've a cousin wanting to find work out there.

Any pointers would be a huge help. I'll stand you a drink in return.

Cheers for now,

Michelle

Michelle tapped as Clare spoke then she held out her phone. 'Look okay?' she asked.

Clare nodded. 'Thanks Michelle. I really appreciate it. Obviously if she gets in touch let me know without delay. Don't open or answer the message. Just call me and I'll come right over.'

–

Janey looked up as Clare put her head round the incident room door. 'John Mason,' she said.

'You've got him?'

'Got an address and a workplace. It's a care home.'

'Good work, Janey! Give me the details.'

Janey handed Clare a sheet of paper.

'Pitlethie Care Home,' Clare read. It rang a vague bell, then she remembered it was the home where Alison Reid's mother was.

'I know it,' Chris said. 'It's in Leuchars.'

Clare grabbed her coat. 'Right. We'll try the care home first. I want you to follow us, Janey. Get someone else with you and another couple of bodies too. Chris and I will lead the way.'

They raced outside and jumped into cars, Clare and Chris in the first, Janey and Gary with another two uniforms in the second.

'Blues and twos,' Clare told Chris and he flicked the switch to turn on the siren and lights. At the roundabout in Guard-bridge the traffic from other directions came to a standstill to let the police cars through. As they neared Leuchars Chris killed the siren and lights and they slowed their approach to avoid alerting John Mason.

The care home was a low, modern building in red brick. It sat on a flat, windy site with Tentsmuir Forest to the east and the Eden Estuary beyond. Chris pulled into the car park, followed by the second car. They jumped out and Clare directed the others to go round the side of the building. 'There must be a few entrances. Fire doors and the like,' she said, her voice low. 'Look for the kitchen door too. Staff might nip out for a smoke so it would be an easy exit.'

Once they were all in place Clare pressed the buzzer and asked for the matron.

They were buzzed in and greeted by a smiling woman in a blue dress. Clare thought she was maybe fifty, but a young fifty. There was a youthful energy about her but the light brown hair was threaded with silver here and there and her eyes had crinkled into crows' feet. She held out a hand. 'I'm Maria Wilkins. How can I help?'

'Can we speak in your office?' Clare said, her voice low.

Maria led them into her office and stood, waiting for an explanation.

'I don't want any fuss,' Clare said, 'but I need to speak to a member of your staff urgently. John Mason. I understand he works here as a care assistant. Could you ask him to come here please, but don't tell him the reason.'

Maria spread her hands. 'I wish I could help, Inspector. But John isn't working today.' She moved to a chart on the wall. 'I'll have to check but it looks like he's not due back until Saturday. Late shift so he'll be here about two, if that helps?' Her brow clouded. 'I do hope he's not in any trouble. He's an excellent worker and so good with the residents.'

Clare shook her head. 'Nothing to worry about,' she said, hoping she sounded convincing. 'But if you do hear from him before Saturday would you let me know please? It is important.'

Maria nodded. 'Of course. And I'm guessing you don't want me to tell him you're looking for him.'

Clare smiled. 'That's correct. We'll try his house now. But thank you for your time.'

Chapter 47

John Mason lived in Fern Place at the north end of Leuchars, just half a mile from Pitlethie. The street was a short cul-de-sac of narrow two-storey houses with single pitched roofs. Chris pulled up outside the address they'd been given, Janey nosing in behind him.

Clare surveyed the house. There was a side gate leading to a back garden and she directed Janey and two of her party round there while she, Chris and the other uniformed officer went to the front door. The curtains on a window near the door were drawn back and as Clare rapped on the door, Chris peered inside.

'No sign of life,' he said.

Clare put an ear to the door but could hear nothing. There seemed to be no bell to press so she rattled the letterbox. Again, there was no sound from within. 'Must be out,' she said.

'To be honest, Clare, there's not much sign of life at all,' Chris said. 'Have a look.' He indicated the window.

Clare shielded the sunlight with her hands and squinted through the glass. 'See what you mean,' she said. 'Furniture, but no bits and pieces lying around.'

'You looking for John?' a voice said and they turned to see a neighbour standing on the doorstep of the next house.

'Yes. Any idea where we might find him?'

'Sorry, hen. He moved out last week. Think he has a flat in St Andrews now.' The neighbour jerked her head towards John's house. 'Landlord wants to sell this so John had to find somewhere else. Going on the market next week, I hear.'

'You wouldn't know where in St Andrews?'

The neighbour shook her head. 'Sorry.'

Clare took out a card from her pocket. 'If he does come back, could you ask him to give me a call please? It is important.'

The neighbour took the card and looked at it. 'Police, eh? He in a bit of bother?'

Clare smiled. 'Nothing like that. We just need to speak to him.'

Janey and the others appeared from the side of the house and Clare nodded them across to the cars, away from the neighbour's gaze.

'Seems he's moved on. Just last week. Obviously not had time to tell his employer.'

'Dammit,' Janey said. 'Any idea where?'

'Neighbour thinks St Andrews.'

'Rental Central,' Janey muttered.

'Quite. So we need to get back to the station and get onto every solicitor, estate agent and rental agency in the town. Anyone moved into a property since Christmas, check them out, even if the name's different. If he's trying to slip under the radar he might have given a different name.'

'Hold on, though, Clare,' Chris said. 'Any reputable agency would want to know he was employed before giving him the keys so they'd be onto the employer.'

'Not if he'd rented from them before,' Janey said.

Chris nodded. 'That's true.'

'Right,' Clare said. 'There are a few things we can try. Check the rental agencies anyway. If he's an existing tenant they probably didn't contact the care home. Next, try Gumtree, Facebook pages – what's it called?'

'Facebay?' Chris said.

'Yeah. All that. And the local papers. We need backdated adverts for flats to rent. Go back a month.'

'What about vans?' Janey said. 'To shift his stuff.'

'Good point. Given it's a furnished let he probably didn't have much but he might have hired a van. So let's get onto car rental companies. See if anyone hired one with this address. And while we're at it, let's try DVLA. If he has a driving licence he might have his own vehicle. That could help.'

Chris exhaled. 'It's a helluva lot of work, Clare.'

'Yeah, I know Chris. Tell you what, let's ask women to stop being murdered. That'll keep the work down.'

'Okay. Just saying.'

'Just don't.'

–

Chris drove while Clare called the DCI. 'I want to go public, Al,' she said. 'John Mason wanted for questioning in connection with murder.'

'You got something concrete?'

'I wouldn't put it as strongly as that. But he's one of the few in that class who has some medical training. Plus he was at Lexy's party the day Sam Harris died. And the headteacher described him as being a bit of a loner and a poor soul.'

'It's a bit thin, Clare. You sure?'

'Not really. But I'd rather be wrong than end up with another corpse. We've been to his work and to his house and he's nowhere to be seen. Work are not expecting him until Saturday afternoon and his neighbour says he moved out a week ago. We don't have his new address and I really can't risk him being at large any longer.'

'Fair enough, Clare. I'm happy to trust your judgement. I'll get it across to the press office. Got a photo?'

Clare swore under her breath. She should have asked Maria Wilkins for a copy of his ID badge photo. 'Not yet but I'll get onto the matron of the care home where he works and get her to email it over.'

It was almost three in the afternoon by the time Clare saw the press statement on a local news website. It wouldn't be long before the nationals picked it up. She studied the photo of John Mason. Sandy hair and eyebrows, pale blue eyes. But, from the head and shoulders photo, Clare thought he looked thick-set, possibly quite powerful – certainly strong enough to overwhelm a half-drugged woman.

She wandered into the incident room. 'Any luck on those flat rentals?'

Heads shook.

'Got DVLA, though,' Janey said. 'He has a licence and a car.'

'Got the reg?'

'Yep. It's a Skoda Fabia.'

'Big enough for a flitting?'

Janey considered this. 'Depends how much stuff he has. Might need two trips.'

'Okay. Let's cross-check van hires against his licence number. And run the Skoda reg through the ANPR database. Anything in the last two days. Plus, I want his photo out to every officer in the town. You never know. It might help.'

–

It was just after five when Clare emerged from her office to make a cup of tea. She noticed Zoe's chair was empty, her computer screen blank.

'Zoe away?' she asked Jim.

'Aye. She'd built up a couple of flexi hours and asked if she could take them.'

'I think she's got a date,' Sara said, rising from her computer and rubbing the back of her neck.

'Let's hope it's no one from Attracto,' Clare said.

Sara said nothing.

'Sara, you are joking? Please tell me she's not gone out with someone from that site?'

Sara hesitated. 'She said they'd made contact before the site was shut down. She also said her pal's going along to sit in the bar to keep an eye on her.'

An image of John Mason's face flashed across Clare's mind. Thickset, she had thought. A man who'd almost certainly over-powered and killed three women. Zoe wasn't tall. She was slim, too. Suddenly Clare's mouth felt dry. She ran her tongue round her lips. 'Who's she meeting?'

Sara shrugged. 'Not sure. Want me to text her, boss?'

'Yes. Do it now. And find out where she's gone.'

Clare stood while Sara sent the message. A few minutes later the phone buzzed with the reply. Sara held it out for Clare to see.

> Just arrived.
>
> Bluesie Bar on Market St. Don't tell the boss but it's that guy Stoneman. He sounds great. I sent him a message today. No reply but hopefully he'll be here.
>
> Anyway, Becca keeping an eye from across the bar.
>
> Wish me luck!
>
> Z xx

Whether it was seeing the name typed out on Sara's phone, or the fact that they'd been hunting John Mason all afternoon, she wasn't sure; but it was suddenly as if someone had turned the lights on and Clare saw what had been in front of her nose all this time.

'Get Chris,' she said, her voice level, 'and as many officers as you can. Then text Zoe back and tell her not to drink anything – nothing at all! And get onto the bar. Describe Zoe and tell the bar staff to keep an eye on her. She is not to leave that pub, understood?'

'Clare?' Jim said, his expression clouded.

'John Mason,' she said, heading for her office to fetch her coat. 'Think, Jim. Mason – the name. Where does it come from?' She pushed open her office door, Jim trailing in her wake.

'Well, I suppose from stone masons, originally... oh God.'

'Stoneman. John Mason. It's too much of a coincidence.' She slammed her office door shut, heading for the exit. Chris was waiting, pulling on his jacket. 'Come on, Chris. Let's hope we reach the bar before Stoneman does.'

Chapter 48

'I don't know what all the fuss is about,' Zoe said, her face flushed. 'I know how to look after my drink and, anyway, Becca was over there watching me like a hawk.'

Clare glanced across the bar at a slightly built girl of about nineteen and thought she wouldn't have been much of a match for John Mason.

'He didn't turn up,' Zoe went on. 'But, even if he had, I'd have been perfectly safe.'

The officers were drifting away now, heading back to the station but the other customers were still watching the proceedings with interest. Clare and Chris steered Zoe and Becca over to a corner and sat them down at a table.

'Zoe, listen to me,' Clare said, trying to keep her voice calm. 'This man could be our killer. He's already killed three woman, older and more experienced than you. There's any number of ways he could have diverted you – and Becca – and slipped something into your drink. He might have suggested going onto another pub, having some food, walking you home. Even if you'd got into a taxi without him, he could have followed you in another car then turned up at your door. Surprised you with flowers or asked if you'd picked up his keys by mistake. Then you'd go looking in your handbag and he'd be in your flat. These people are clever.'

Zoe said nothing, her expression mulish. 'I'd have known,' she said, sounding less certain than before. 'I'm not stupid.'

Clare looked at Zoe. She'd taken such care with her appearance. Her dark red jersey dress and black Doc Martens went perfectly with her ruby lips and dark eyes. She'd tied a matching scarf in her hair and her ear was studded with pink earrings. She must have looked stunning when she'd entered the bar but now she was close to tears. 'Look, Zoe,' she said, softening her tone. 'It's okay. You're fine and no harm done. But, please, no more dates until we've caught this man. Promise?'

Zoe nodded. 'Suppose.'

Clare smiled. 'Now, Chris will run you two ladies home if you've had enough excitement for one night.'

–

At quarter past eight Clare stood the officers down. 'With luck the news reports will throw up John Mason's whereabouts. Meantime, I doubt there's much more we can do tonight.'

'Why do you reckon he didn't turn up to Zoe's date?' Sara asked.

Clare shook her head. 'I've no idea although, from what Zoe said at the bar, it sounds like it was her making all the running. Maybe she said something like See you there if I don't hear from you and he didn't bother to reply.'

'Do you still think he's our killer?' Chris asked.

'John Mason? Yes. I'm convinced of that. But I'm starting to wonder if he is Stoneman. The similarity in the two names might just be a coincidence. I'm probably overthinking it.' She yawned. 'I need to go home. Come on, guys. We'll review things in the morning.'

As if on cue the phone began to ring. Jim moved to answer it and Clare wandered into her office. She wondered idly when she might have a day off. Not until this killer had been caught, that was for sure. Thankfully, Moira was happy to step in with extra walks for Benjy. She glanced at her phone and saw that Moira had been round to Daisy Cottage and had fed Benjy for her. She really was a godsend. Maybe she would pick her up some...

'Clare!' Jim's voice broke across her thoughts. '999 call.'

She stared at him. 'Is it...'

'Think so. Chris has gone to start the car.'

She grabbed her coat and ran for the door, not stopping for an explanation. Out in the car park she could see exhaust fumes coming out the back of the car, cutting through the still night air. She skidded on a patch of early frost but regained her footing and reached the car. She jumped in and Chris roared away out of the car park, not even waiting for her to pull on her seat belt. She checked over her shoulder and saw another three cars following, blue lights flashing. As Chris raced past a car that had pulled into the side of the road, Clare wondered where they were going – and what they would find when they got there.

–

'It's an old farmhouse, on the way to Dunino,' he said, over-taking a taxi. 'South of the town. The control room said the caller was incoherent so we don't really know what we're going to. She kept saying The man on the news, over and over again. That, and the address, is all they could get out of her.'

Clare felt sick at the thought of what they might find when they reached Dunmerry Farmhouse. She lurched forward as Chris hit the brakes, swinging the car round and up a farm track. The house stood at the top of the track, silhouetted against the night sky. It was a two-storey, solid block of a house with stout chimney stacks at either end. Lights burned in the ground floor windows and the front door stood open. As they neared the entrance Clare saw the figure of a woman, bent over, her arms clutched round herself. She could see the woman was sobbing uncontrollably and when they leapt out of the car they heard her cries cutting through the air like an animal caught in a trap. Clare raced towards her as the cars behind disgorged officers. The woman fell into Clare's arms, her body convulsed with sobs.

'Get an ambulance,' she said softly to Chris, 'and make sure you have overshoes on before you go inside.'

Sara and Gillian rushed up and Clare handed the woman to them then followed Chris into the farmhouse, pulling the overshoes from her pocket. As they stepped inside she felt a stillness as the sound of the sobs receded.

'In here,' Chris said, from a doorway further up the hall. Clare followed him in and stood surveying the room. It was a large dining kitchen, probably formed from two smaller rooms. To one end there was a wall of kitchen units finished in sage green with deep Belfast sinks under the window. The room was dominated by a large island with a gas hob in the centre, an orange Le Creuset casserole standing on one of the rings. To the left was a round oak table with four matching chairs and at the other end of the room a brick-red sofa faced a wall-mounted TV. A side table held a bottle of wine and two glasses and in front of the sofa was a brightly patterned rug covering what seemed to be original flagstones.

And on top of the rug, the life draining out of him, lay the figure of John Mason.

Chapter 49

'Ambulance is on its way,' Sara said.

Clare glanced across to where Gillian was comforting the woman. 'Better make that two,' she said.

Sara took out her radio to summon another ambulance while Clare walked across to Gillian and the woman. Her sobs had eased and she sat now on a garden bench, shaking violently.

Clare was about to suggest they moved her into a police car for warmth when the woman raised a mascara-streaked face. It took Clare a moment to recognise her. The face was contorted into an expression of pain but suddenly she saw that the woman John Mason had chosen for his fourth victim was Dr Sandra Holt, the psychiatrist she'd asked to examine Ruth Williams.

'Dr Holt!'

The woman frowned as though wondering how Clare knew her name. And then there was a spark of recognition in her eyes. 'Inspector Mackay?'

Clare sat down beside her and nodded. 'Yes, it's me.' She took Dr Holt's hand. 'You're safe now.'

The blanket Gillian had put round Sandra Holt's shoulders was slipping off and Clare pulled it back round. 'It's cold,' she said. 'I think we should get you into one of the cars.'

As they rose Clare saw the sky towards St Andrews light up and heard an approaching siren.

'That'll be the ambulance. We'll get you warmed up in there. But, are you able to tell me anything at all about what happened tonight?'

Dr Holt began to shiver again. She opened her mouth then shook her head.

'The man in the house, did he attack you?'

She wrapped her arms across her chest and nodded vigorously.

'And did you cause his injuries?'

She met Clare's eye and nodded again. 'Knife,' she mumbled.

'One of yours? Or did he have a knife with him?'

'Mine.'

The ambulance rumbled up the farm track and came to a halt in front of the entrance. Two green-clad men jumped out and approached Clare and Dr Holt. Clare gave a brief summary of what she'd learned then directed the men inside where Chris had been attempting CPR on John Mason. A second ambulance could be heard approaching and Clare put an arm round Sandra Holt.

'Soon have you in the warm,' she said, and Dr Holt nodded mutely.

Clare handed her over to the paramedics, promising to follow her across to Ninewells Hospital in Dundee. Then she went back to the farmhouse door. Chris was coming out, peeling off a pair of blood-soaked disposable gloves. As he saw Clare he shook his head.

'Dead?'

'Afraid so. Massive blood loss. He arrested in front of me. Didn't know whether to try and stem the blood or give him CPR.'

Janey appeared at Clare's shoulder. 'SOCO heading over. Should be here within the hour.'

'Thanks, Janey. Chris and I will follow the ambulance to Ninewells. I want to speak to her as soon as they'll allow it. Could you stay here till SOCO arrive?'

'Sure, boss.'

'And I'll need a couple of cops on duty overnight,' Clare added, 'plus one at Ninewells to keep an eye on Dr Holt.' She glanced back at the farmhouse. 'We'll have to find someone to identify the deceased formally. And we'll need a warrant to search his house, wherever it is. See if there's anything on the body that will help with an address.'

The paramedics were leading Sandra Holt into the ambulance to assess her and Clare steered Chris down the path where they couldn't be overheard.

'What do you reckon?' she said.

He considered. 'Stab wounds in his side. Not your usual site for a defensive wound. Unless...'

'Yeah?'

'If he had her from behind, she might have managed to grab a kitchen knife – swung it behind her – she'd have caught him in the side.'

'So he's attacked her, she's grabbed the knife and hit lucky.'

'Looks that way.'

Clare closed her eyes, picturing the scene again. Then she said, 'There was wine, wasn't there?'

'Didn't notice, to be honest, Clare.'

'There was. I'll mention it to Janey. I want to know if it's drugged. If it is...'

'We've got our man.'

'Let's hope so, Chris.'

—

The Accident & Emergency Department at Ninewells was buzzing with drunks, and men in sports kit clutching their shoulders.

'She's gone up to the Short Stay ward,' the receptionist told them.

Clare and Chris made their way through the corridors and up one floor to the ward. Clare showed her warrant card and explained they hoped to interview Dr Sandra Holt.

'The doctor's with her now,' a nurse in a blue tunic told her. 'If you could wait here...'

They sat on hard chairs at the end of the ward while a steady stream of medical staff in different-coloured uniforms flew back and forth, wheeling monitors and scribbling on charts. After twenty minutes, Clare again approached a nurse.

'Hold on, I'll check…'

The nurse returned a few minutes later and led them to one of the rooms. 'Not too long, if you don't mind. She's pretty shaken up.'

Sandra Holt lay, still clothed, on top of the bed, her head resting on a pile of pillows. She'd kicked off her shoes and pulled a honeycomb blanket up round herself. Beside her on the bed lay a buzzer and a grey cardboard sick bowl. There was a small tear in the neck of her jumper and Clare's eyes were drawn to her throat and the slight scratching at either side. She reckoned it was probably self-inflicted as Sandra struggled to remove John Mason's hands from her neck. She tried to see if there was bruising around the vagus nerve but Sandra's hair had fallen forward. As Clare approached the bed she saw Sandra's eyes fill with tears.

'Is… is he dead?' she asked, her voice little more than a whisper, doubtless hoarse from the attempt at strangulation.

Clare nodded. 'It's not official yet but, yes. I'm afraid he died at the scene.'

Sandra closed her eyes and a tear began to roll down her cheek. 'I didn't mean to…'

Clare interrupted. 'Dr Holt, I don't want to prejudge your version of this evening's events but, in light of what's happened, I must caution you formally. I hope you understand.'

Sandra wiped away the tear and Clare delivered the standard caution. When Sandra had acknowledged this, Clare carried on. 'If you feel up to it, I'd like to ask what happened tonight. Could you manage that?'

Sandra ran her tongue round her lips then said, 'Yes. I'll try.' She put her hands down on the bed to lift herself up and glanced across at a jug of water on the cabinet. Chris rose and walked round the bed to pour her a drink.

When Sandra had sipped the water, Clare said, 'Dr Holt...'

'Call me Sandra.'

'Sandra,' Clare began again, 'if you could tell us what you remember – maybe start with how the man came to be in your house.'

She swallowed and put a hand to her throat. Then she said, 'John Mason works at Pitlethie Care Home.' She took another sip of water then continued. 'I've met him a couple of times when I was seeing a patient. He always struck me as perfectly pleasant and very good with the residents.' She shook her head. 'I liked him.'

She closed her eyes for a moment, took a deep breath in and out, then she opened them again. 'One day – last week – I was leaving the hospital in Cupar. I do a clinic there once a week – and I saw him parked just outside. He was holding a fuel can so I rolled down my window and asked if he'd run out of petrol.' She stopped to clear her throat then went on. 'I offered to run him to the petrol station in my car but he said I shouldn't be offering men lifts.' She stopped again, cleared her throat and took another sip of water.

'Take all the time you need,' Clare said, smiling.

Sandra nodded and, after a moment, she continued. 'So I said I'd drive along, fill the can and bring it back which I did. He offered to pay but I said not to bother and I went on my way.'

'When was this?' Clare asked.

Sandra's brow creased for a moment then she said, 'Tuesday. It was Tuesday, about four thirty.'

Clare jotted this down in her notebook.

'Then, last night, my doorbell rang.'

'Time?'

Sandra took a moment, then she said, 'Seven, I think. Or a bit after.'

Clare continued scribbling in her notebook.

'I went to the door and was surprised to see him there. He had a bottle of wine and said it was to thank me. I said there

308

was no need but he said it was the least he could do. He told me he'd be on holiday the next time I came to Pitlethie so he wanted me to have it before he went.'

'Did you ask how he knew your address?'

Sandra nodded. 'He said I'd talked about the farmhouse on one of my visits to the home.'

'Had you?'

Sandra shrugged. 'I've no idea. I chat to the staff – you know how these things are. Small talk. Anyway, it was pretty cold. Clear sky. I could see frost already on the garden so I said did he want to come in for a few minutes.' She eyed Clare and Chris. 'Stupid, I know. But I'd met him through work, you see? I never thought...'

Clare gave her a reassuring smile, then asked, 'Did you offer him a drink?'

'Yes. I meant tea or coffee. But he said why not open the bottle he'd brought. And he picked it up and opened it there and then. Before I could stop him. It was a screwcap, you see. He... he just opened it.'

Clare could visualise it clearly. 'Who poured the wine?'

'He did. I fetched glasses from the cupboard and he poured. And then he said could he have a glass of water too. He'd left his car at the end of the track and didn't want to be over the limit. So I went to the sink and poured him a glass of water.'

Clare glanced at Chris. Had this been a diversion? An opportunity for him to slip a tablet into Sandra's glass? He'd only have had a few seconds but, in red wine, the Rohypnol would be invisible.

Sandra seemed to read her thoughts. 'I thought I saw his hand draw back as I turned round from the sink. And, well, I'm a naturally cautious person. I wondered if he might have done something to my drink. So I said I was just about to have a sandwich and would he like one. He said that would be nice so I took my wine glass with me, pretending to drink. I opened the fridge to get out some cheese. There's a sort of half wall at that end of the kitchen – blocks the view from the sofa so I tipped the wine into a bowl of chilli in the fridge and pretended I'd drunk it. I made the sandwich and brought it through, saying what lovely wine it was.'

Sandra stopped for a moment, her eyes closed. Then she took a deep breath in and out and carried on. 'After half an hour he asked if I was feeling all right.' She shivered, then said, 'That convinced me something was wrong. I guessed he'd tried to drug me so I played along. Said I was feeling drowsy.' She closed her eyes again, as if trying to remember. 'I thought maybe I could hit him with something so I got up from the sofa and walked back to the kitchen, pretending to be wobbly. I was looking for something I could use to defend myself.' She opened her eyes and met Clare's. 'But he was too quick. He was there, behind me, hands round my neck.'

Tears started to course down Sandra's cheeks and she reached for a box of tissues next to the glass of water. She dabbed at her eyes. 'I'm sorry,' she said, between sobs. 'It's just…'

Clare took hold of her hand in both of hers. 'Sandra, you're doing so well. Nearly there. If you could just tell us what happened next.'

She nodded and blew her nose. 'It's a bit of a blur. He said something about my time having come and how he would enjoy arranging my body. Something about the shower, I think.' She flicked a glance at them. 'Like the others.'

From the corner of her eye Clare saw Chris move forward in his seat and, holding Sandra's gaze, she tapped his knee lightly, warning him not to interrupt.

'I put out my hand,' Sandra went on. 'I was grabbing at air then suddenly a drawer flew open and I felt something. I didn't know what it was but I grabbed it and tried to hit him with it. But I couldn't get past his arms – he was so strong, you know? So I swung it behind me. I tried and I tried and then I heard this noise – this horrible noise and I couldn't pull it back. He shouted something and I felt the strength go out of his hands.

I realised I must have grabbed a knife. So I mustered all my strength and pulled it out and I dashed it behind me again. This time I didn't pull it out and he staggered back.'

'What did you do next?' Clare said, her voice gentle.

Sandra's eyes flicked left and right as if she was trying to remember. Then suddenly she said, 'My phone! I saw my phone so I grabbed it and ran outside. I pressed the emergency button and I must have dialled 999...' she tailed off then she looked from Clare to Chris. 'Will I go to prison?'

'I'd say almost certainly not, Sandra. We will investigate but if we find evidence to support what you've told us you can claim self-defence.'

The door opened and a nurse entered, wheeling a blood pressure monitor. 'Is it all right if I do this now?'

Clare rose from her seat and Chris followed suit. 'You've done brilliantly, Sandra,' she said. 'We'll leave you now but, once you're out of here, we'll take a formal statement. And I'll post an officer on your door overnight.'

Sandra forced a smile. 'Thank you,' she said. 'Thank you for understanding.'

As the nurse wrapped a blood pressure cuff round Sandra's arm Clare said, 'Is there someone we can call for you?'

Sandra shook her head. 'No thanks, Inspector. There's no one.'

As they walked back through the corridors, dimmed with the night lights, Chris said, 'Reckon she'll get off okay?'

'Yeah. Pretty clear case of self-defence. With his hands round her throat her life was in danger, not much chance of escape. I'd have done the same in her shoes.'

Chris eyed his boss. 'I bet you would, too!'

They emerged into the fresh air, bitterly cold after the stifling heat of the hospital. The car had begun to ice up and Clare reached into the well of the door for a scraper. She threw this to Chris. 'I'll get the engine going. You scrape.'

He sighed. 'I'm sure it's your turn to do the scraping.'

'But you do it so beautifully...'

Friday, 15th January

Chapter 50

Clare sat at her kitchen table, chewing on a slice of toast while Benjy demolished the contents of his bowl. It was the first morning she'd lingered over breakfast since the discovery of Alison Reid's body. She couldn't even think how long ago that was. A week? Ten days? Longer, probably. But now she felt she could relax a bit. Go in an hour later. There was still a lot to do. Sandra Holt's story would have to be checked closely and John Mason's phone and laptop records retrieved, hopefully confirming he was Stoneman.

Clare finished the last of her toast and rose, carrying her plate to the dishwasher. An image of John Mason, lying on Sandra Holt's floor, bleeding out, came into her mind and she shivered. Could they have saved him? Probably not. But at least he wasn't at large now.

It wasn't the result she'd wanted, though. The death of a suspect never was. No. Clare had wanted John Mason sitting in an interview room, explaining why he had killed three women and attempted to kill a fourth. She wanted to understand what had driven this man to such lengths, to drug and kill these women then to leave them in water. She particularly wanted to know about that. Had some experience in his past given him a fear of water? With John Mason lying in a mortuary fridge they'd probably never know.

She put a tablet in the dishwasher compartment and pressed it closed, switching it on. It began to hum and fill with water and she whistled to Benjy. 'Quick walk,' she told him, dangling the lead. As she clipped it on she wondered if Sandra Holt might be able to shed some light on John Mason's state of mind – on his obsession with water. She was a psychiatrist, after all…

–

Michelle Delaney phoned as Clare was backing the car into her usual space.

'Sorry, Inspector. Not heard anything from Jessica. The message was delivered but it's not been read.'

Clare thanked her and ended the call. It wasn't surprising, really. She was pretty sure, by now, that John Mason was both Stoneman and Jessica Peters. He wouldn't be reading any more messages.

'Positive ID on the victim,' Jim said as she approached the public enquiry desk. 'It is John Mason.'

'Who ID'd him?'

'Matron at the care home, plus another staff member. Still trying to trace his family but it seems he lived alone.'

'You found his house then?'

'Aye. One of the flats up by the swimming pool. Lads went in this morning and picked up his laptop. It's down with Tech Support now.'

'Okay, thanks Jim. What about his phone?'

'No sign. Wasn't on the body and the lads couldn't see it in the house. Still to get into the car but that's back up at the farmhouse.'

'Okay, Jim. What about SOCO?'

'They finished at the house just after midnight. I've left Gary up there, meantime.'

'Can she go back, then – Dr Holt?'

'Yeah. Should be okay.'

Clare nodded and went into her office. She felt oddly tired, today. Maybe the strain of the investigation was catching up with her. The Christmas holidays seemed weeks ago, now. She hung her coat on a hook and switched on the computer. While it booted up she took out her phone and called the DCI to update him on events.

'Want me to come up for the interview?'

'Sandra Holt? No, I think Chris and I will be fine. She told us most of it last night anyway.'

'Make sure she has a solicitor,' he said. 'We need to be absolutely sure her actions were the only possible ones in the circumstances.'

'Yeah, I know.'

There was a pause and Clare was about to end the call when he said, 'You'll be relieved to have this one tied up, Clare. Maybe take a few days off when it's done.'

She wondered about this. It was the second time he'd said something like that. Was she starting to look her age? She opened her bag and took out a small mirror and peered at it. Her face did look drawn. Maybe she needed...

Her thoughts were interrupted by a tap at the door and Zoe's face appeared. Clare motioned her to come in. She came slowly into the room and she seemed to be grasping for the right words.

'Just wanted to say sorry, boss – all that fuss last night.'

Clare smiled. 'No harm done, Zoe. You are okay?'

Zoe smiled. 'Definitely. I was going to make a cake to say thanks, you know? But Becca came home with me and we opened a bottle...'

'Best thing you could have done. But mind you steer clear of Attracto.'

Zoe nodded. 'No danger. I'm done with that site. Matter of fact, I might not need it...'

'Oh?' Clare was intrigued.

'Got a message last night. Facebook. Lad I was at college with.' She grinned. 'I'm seeing him tonight.'

Clare smiled. 'Oh, that's lovely, Zoe. I am glad. Just remember, though...'

'Guard my drink, yeah, I know.' She hovered as if unsure what else to say, then, 'Better get to work, or I'll have Jimbo on my back.'

Clare laughed, wondering if Jim knew what Zoe called him. Left alone, she sat thinking. They were all pairing off now. But maybe she wasn't meant to be part of a couple. Maybe it was time to start looking after herself. On an impulse she rose and went in search of Zoe who had just started tapping at her keyboard. 'Zoe?'

'Yes, boss?'

'Your hair – where do you go? To have it done, I mean?'

'McArthur's in South Street,' she said. She studied Clare. 'You fancying a new look?'

Clare shrugged. 'Maybe. Not red, though.'

'No. Not your colour. Don't go to my girl, then. See if you can get an appointment with Greta. She's great with colour. Not too whacky.'

—

Clare's next call was to Raymond Curtice.

'Hi, Clare.' He sounded as perky as usual and she could just imagine him busily piecing together the events of last night. 'Just working on your case now. Bit of a messy scene, though.'

'It was. Anything so far?'

'Yes, hold on…'

She waited and then a moment later he was back.

'Okay. First of all, he had a strip of tablets in his pocket.'

'Rohypnol?'

'Yep. Now we analysed the wine bottle and both glasses. There were no drugs in the bottle itself and, initially, both glasses tested negative.'

'Initially?'

'Once we got them back to the lab we examined what was left in the glasses under a UV spectrometer. Definitely Rohypnol in one of them.'

This matched with Sandra's story that she thought he'd slipped a tablet into her glass.

'Manage to get anything from the chilli in the fridge?'

'Sadly no. The wine would have soaked in. Shame, really. It smelled lovely.'

Clare had to smile. Only Raymond could be faced with such a scene of horror and think how appetising a bowl of chilli smelled. 'What about the knife?'

'Dr Holt's prints only. Pretty expensive knife, though. Sabatier. Probably saved her life. It had to be sharp to get through his clothes, given she must have been stabbing wildly behind her.'

'Okay, thanks Raymond. Anything else, give me a buzz.'

Chris appeared at the door. 'Gillian's just phoned from the hospital. They've released Sandra Holt. She's bringing her in now for interview.'

'Solicitor?'

'On his way.'

'Good. I'll be glad to put this one to bed. If we can just get hold of John Mason's phone and laptop records...'

'What about your fancy new cyber thing?'

'Need the phone for that, genius. I suppose it's still not been found?'

Chris shook his head. 'Want a couple of lads up there to have another look? SOCO could have missed it.'

Clare considered this. SOCO were thorough. She knew that. But it was worth another look. 'Go on, then. See who's available. But I want you in with me when I take Sandra's statement.'

–

Sandra Holt was white-faced but calm when she arrived at the station. Her solicitor, a serious man in his fifties, was at pains to stress that Sandra was the victim. Clare reassured him on that point.

'We'll keep your client as short a time as possible. My sergeant and I already spoke to her last night, under caution, but I can assure you that was simply a formality. Once we have her statement she'll be free to go.'

They filed into the largest interview room, Sandra's eyes flicking left and right as she took in her surroundings. Clare offered them drinks and Sara was despatched to make a pot of coffee. 'See if you can find any biscuits,' Clare whispered, and Sara nodded.

The interview began with the usual preamble. Sandra's voice, while quiet, seemed less hoarse than last night and she managed to give her statement with only a couple of pauses. Her version of events was unchanged from what she had told them at the hospital and within an hour it was all done.

'I have a couple of officers still at your house,' Clare said. 'Just checking things over.'

Sandra's shoulders sagged at this. 'I just want to go home.'

The solicitor said, 'I'll take you for lunch, Sandra. We can stretch it out for a few hours. Then I'll run you back.'

Clare smiled her thanks to the solicitor and the pair departed.

'All done?' Jim asked when they emerged from the interview room.

'Yeah, pretty much,' Clare said. She couldn't shake the feeling that she'd forgotten something but it wouldn't come. She'd probably remember it in the middle of the night.

Jim lifted his notepad. 'I'm not sure if it's relevant any more but I've managed to find Lexy Harris's mother.' He tore off the top sheet and handed it to Clare. 'Address and phone number all there – if you want to speak to her.'

Clare stood looking at the piece of paper. Stepps – an attractive town on the outskirts of Glasgow, for years the main route into the city from the east. Then the motorway had opened and the town had become much quieter. In fact, Clare couldn't remember the last time she'd been through Stepps. And now that John Mason was dead and Sandra Holt had given her statement, did she need to speak to Lexy Harris's mother? Probably not. All the same…

She tapped the address into Google Maps on her phone. One hour, thirty-five minutes away. She caught Chris's eye. 'Fancy a road trip?'

Chapter 51

Clare was so used to bypassing Stepps on the new motorway that she only just saw the turnoff. She signalled and pulled over, earning herself a blast on the horn from the car behind. The road layout was unfamiliar, but she soon saw the distinctive Buchanan Tower standing out against the skyline and knew she was heading in the right direction. Despite the sad nature of their visit, her spirits rose as she drove past rows of houses built in the red sandstone, so redolent of Glasgow. Her home town but no longer her home.

Chris was looking out of the passenger window as they drove along. 'Nice town,' he said.

'I imagine it's a lot nicer without the motorway traffic.'

'Take a right here,' he said, eyes trained on his phone. Then he looked up. 'This is the street. It should be just along here on the left.'

Clare slowed the car as Chris checked house numbers and finally they saw the house and pulled into the kerb. Clare thought she saw a figure at the window but it vanished seconds later.

They stepped out of the car and surveyed the street. There were houses along one side and what seemed to be a park, bordered by trees on the other.

'Think it's a tennis club,' Chris said.

'Never mind that. Remind me of their names.'

'Andrews. Roy and Irene.'

'Interesting that Lexy kept Harris as her surname when her mum remarried,' Clare said. 'I wonder if she didn't get on with her stepfather...'

Chris shrugged. 'Maybe. So... how do you want to play it?'

'Not a clue.' Clare began walking towards a gap in the hedge. A long monobloc drive led to a wooden garage and to the right of this sat the house. It was a two-storey villa in blonde sandstone with dormer windows built into the roof. A neat square of grass was surrounded on two sides with a narrow earth border and a path led off the drive to the front door. As they approached, the door was opened by a man who looked to be in his sixties. He was about the same height as Clare, with receding hair so black it had to be dyed. He wore dark grey trousers and a navy ribbed pullover.

'Inspector Mackay?' he said, not moving from the threshold.

Clare smiled. 'And Sergeant Chris West. Thanks for agreeing to see us.'

He stood his ground. 'I'm not sure,' he said. 'My wife – well, she's struggled for years to put things behind her. It's not good for her, you see.'

'We'll keep her as short a time as possible,' Clare said. 'If we could maybe come in...'

Roy Andrews hesitated then stood back, just enough to allow Clare and Chris to pass through the door. He led them into a square sitting room. It was pleasant enough, Clare thought, with an off-pink carpet and a beige velour suite but it lacked personality, somehow.

Irene Andrews was standing by a living flame electric fire. She was spare, dressed simply in dark trousers and a purple sweatshirt. Clare's overriding sense was of someone who was tired. Not sleepy-tired, but tired of life, of going through the motions day after day. She recalled some of the fitter-looking residents she had seen on her brief visit to Pitlethie Care Home and thought how much more life they had about them than this woman.

She introduced herself and Chris, and Irene invited them to sit. As Clare moved to the sofa she took the chance to scan the room for family photos. But she could only see a small one in a silver frame showing a white-haired boy of about two. Sam Harris, she guessed. There didn't seem to be any of Lexy and she wondered about that. Had there been a rift?

Irene waited until they had sat then she perched on the edge of a dining chair pulled out from a small gateleg table.

'You should have a comfy seat,' Roy Andrews said, but she waved this away.

'I'm fine here.' She glanced at her husband. 'Maybe you could make us some tea, Roy? I'm sure the officers would appreciate that after their long drive.'

Roy Andrews stood for a moment, clearly unwilling to leave his wife.

She inclined her head towards the door. 'Go on,' she said. 'I'll be fine.'

He left the room and Irene rose from her seat to close the door. Then she turned back to face them. 'He fusses,' she said. 'Thinks it's not good for me to dwell in the past.' Then she lowered her voice. 'What he doesn't realise is I like dwelling in the past. It helps, you know?'

Clare smiled. 'I understand. And we're so grateful to you for seeing us, Mrs Andrews.'

'Irene, please.' She resumed her seat then said, 'What is it you wish to know?'

Clare cleared her throat then began. 'If it's not too painful, I'd like to ask you about the day your son Sam died. I understand it was your daughter's birthday party.'

'Lexy, that's right. She was eleven. Actually her birthday was the day before but it was easier to have the party on a Saturday.'

'Were there many children there?'

Irene nodded. 'Quite a few. Probably a dozen girls, plus Lexy and Sam, of course.'

Clare took out the photo she had taken from Ingrid McKinnie's house. 'I think some of the children in this photo were there. Is that correct?'

Irene took the photo and studied it. A smile spread over her face. 'I don't think I've seen this before. I don't suppose...'

'I can have a copy made for you,' Clare said. 'Once our enquiries are complete.'

Irene smiled then she looked back at the photo. 'These three girls...' she broke off for a minute then she said, 'I always wondered – Lexy – when she said she wanted them to come to the party – I wasn't sure. They hadn't always been kind to her, you see, and I didn't want her party to be spoiled. But she assured me they were friends. So I relented.' She squinted at the photo again then said, 'And that's John, I think.' Then she looked up at Clare. 'I hope it doesn't sound unkind but I always thought he was quite an odd boy.'

And how, Clare thought but didn't say. Instead, she asked, 'Odd in what way?'

Irene sat back, considering this. 'Oh, I don't know – just a bit strange. Not very talkative but always hanging about the girls. I suppose he lacked confidence and those girls, well, they were the in-crowd, you see.'

Clare smiled. 'Was the party going well? Before your son went missing, I mean.'

Irene's gaze dropped and she seemed to be running through the events in her mind. Then she nodded, slowly. 'I think so. We'd had some games in the garden and then we were making pizzas.' She smiled. 'Lexy loved pizza and she'd asked if the party guests could add their own toppings. So, I was in the kitchen doing that with the children, a few at a time. Lexy was there too, supervising – that's what she told me. She was quite a shy child. I think she enjoyed feeling she was in charge.' Irene paused for a minute and her brow furrowed. Then she continued.

'It was only when the last four came in and their pizzas went into the oven that I realised Sam was missing. I asked

324

the children and they said he'd been playing on the climbing frame. So I sent Lexy out to bring him in. And that's when we realised...' Irene reached into her sleeve and pulled out a tissue. She dabbed her eyes then said, 'We realised Sam wasn't in the garden.' She swallowed.

'Would you like a break?' Clare asked but she shook her head.

'No, I want to tell you. To talk about it. Roy...' she gestured towards the kitchen. 'I can't talk to him about it. He won't...' She blew her nose on the tissue then carried on.

'We searched everywhere. It was quite a big garden, you see. Lots of trees. But I think I knew from the start. Knew he wasn't there. I ran – ran for the gate. And I saw his shorts. They were red, you know. And his hair, his lovely blonde hair – almost white...' she nodded, as if to emphasise this. 'Lovely hair. Anyway, I ran down the bank. I fell. Nearly ended up in the water myself. And I picked him up.' She broke off again, reliving the moment. Then she said, her voice barely above a whisper, 'He was heavy, you know? A dead weight. There was a noise. An awful wailing. I didn't know it was me. Then someone tried to take him but I wouldn't – wouldn't let go. And then Dan – he was Sam and Lexy's dad, you know – Dan, he said it was the ambulance and I had to let them have him. But I knew, if I did, they wouldn't give him back.'

The tears were coursing down Irene's face now and she wiped them away with the sleeve of her sweatshirt. Then she turned a tear-stained face towards Clare. 'I knew he was gone, you see. I had known Sam since the moment he was conceived. I knew every inch of his perfect little body. I knew his personality and how his eyes would light up when he was happy. And I knew – I knew that the light had gone from his eyes for the last time.'

The door opened and Roy Andrews came in bearing a tea tray. He looked at his wife and set the tray down on the gateleg table. 'I told you she wasn't to be upset. You shouldn't have come.'

Suddenly, Irene seemed to snap. 'I want to talk about it,' she cried. 'Don't you understand, Roy? I want to talk about it!'

Roy stood for a moment, stunned into silence, then he picked up a cup and saucer from the tray and handed it to her. 'Here,' he said, his voice lower. 'This will help.'

She took the cup and gave him a smile. 'Thanks, love.' The teaspoon rattled on the saucer as her hand shook and she set the cup and saucer down on a side table.

As they drank their tea, Clare asked, 'Are you in touch with Lexy? We weren't able to make contact with her.'

Irene shook her head. 'She's not had it easy, Lexy. What with Sam, then us moving. She never really settled in Bristol, you know. Then her dad and I separated, and he died a few years later. I thought, maybe, if we changed our name, moved back to Scotland, she might be happier.'

'And was she?'

Irene shrugged. 'Not really. She did well at school, though. She's a clever girl. Then she took a couple of years out and never moved home again. She went off to university but she always managed to have a holiday job. I helped her as much as I could, financially. But, until I met Roy,' she threw her husband a smile, 'it was a bit of a struggle – bills and so on.'

'Did she finish university?' Clare asked, wondering at the lack of a graduation photo. Irene seemed so proud of her daughter. The absence of a photo seemed odd.

She beamed. 'Oh yes. She did really well. First class honours. But she didn't want a graduation celebration. Said she had a job lined up in Manchester and off she went.'

'Does she come home much?'

Irene glanced quickly at Roy then away again and she shook her head. 'We've kind of lost touch.'

Clare drained her cup then said, 'We won't keep you much longer. If I could just ask one more thing?'

Irene looked at her. Waiting for the question.

'You said when the last four came in. For the pizzas, I mean. Can you remember who they were?'

Irene nodded. 'The girls in the photo. Those three girls: Alison, Ingrid and – oh, I've forgotten the other one's name.'

Chris seemed about to prompt her but Clare nudged him.

'Ruth,' Irene said at last. 'Ruth Williams.'

'And the fourth?'

'That lad John. As I said, always hanging about the popular girls. I think maybe he felt safe with them...'

–

They made their way back through the streets towards the motorway in silence. But once they were on the M80 Clare set cruise control to sixty and relaxed back into her seat.

'What do you reckon?'

Chris sighed. 'Sad.'

'Isn't it. One child dead, another estranged. And I'm not even sure she's happy with that man.'

'He does seem a bit – it's hard to say what he is.'

'He's like a bloody mother hen,' Clare said. 'The poor woman probably didn't have any counselling at the time. And the first chance she gets it all comes tumbling out.'

'Yeah. Not sure where it gets us, though.'

'It makes you wonder,' Clare went on, easing the car into the left lane to take the road to Kincardine, 'whether John Mason was responsible for little Sam's death.'

'Why would he be?'

'Well, that's two people who've said he was a bit odd. What if he had caused Sam's death and those girls were the only ones to witness it?'

Chris shook his head. 'No. Doesn't work.'

'Why not?'

'Well for a start, if he did kill Sam then he killed the three girls to shut them up, why wait until now? Twenty years later?'

'Suppose.'

'And then there's Sandra Holt,' Chris went on. 'It doesn't explain why he would attack her. Unless...' he broke off.

327

Clare glanced at him. 'Unless what?'

'Unless he's not our killer. Unless the attack on Sandra's unconnected to the other killings.'

Clare groaned. 'Don't say that, Chris. We've nearly got this case wrapped up. Anyway, the Rohypnol. And Sandra told us he said something about how he would arrange her body – in the shower...'

Suddenly there was a blast from a car horn and Chris grabbed the steering wheel. 'Christsake, Clare! You nearly drifted into that car.'

'Sorry,' she said. 'Sorry.' And she raised a hand to wave to the driver of the other car. They were almost at Kincardine now and she indicated left at a sign for a service station.

'Clare?' Chris said. 'You feeling okay?'

'Chris, I need to think,' she said, slowing her speed and following the Services sign. She drove on towards the car park and drew into a space in front of a Premier Inn. She switched off the engine and rubbed her temple.

'You want to catch me up?'

'The shower,' she said. 'In Sandra's statement. She said that John Mason planned to arrange her in the shower.'

'Yes, you said.'

'Then she said like the others.'

Chris was silent, thinking this through.

'You noticed it at the time,' Clare said. 'I saw you react but we were still trying to find out what had happened, I think we kind of forgot.'

Chris looked at her. 'Are you saying...'

'Chris, it doesn't fit. Sandra Holt. It's not the same as the others. She's not on Attracto...'

'Nor was Ruth Williams.'

'No, that's true. But Jessica Peters tried to get Ruth to join. Sandra Holt wasn't in that WhatsApp group either. We don't know where she went to school. She didn't even know the other women. She's an outlier.'

'Oh God...' Chris said.

'So John Mason might not be our killer. He or she might still be out there.'

Chris rubbed his head. 'But the shower, Clare – how does that fit? Oh wait, she must have heard it on the news.'

'That's just the point, Chris. We didn't give that information out. Nothing was released about Alison Reid being found in the bath, or Ruth Williams with her head in the sink.'

'Alison's neighbour might have said something about it.'

'But who to? It's not been in the papers and I doubt Sandra Holt would have heard it from Alison's neighbour. So how did she know about the water?'

Chapter 52

Chris drove while Clare made phone calls. Roy Andrews hadn't been keen to put his wife on the phone but Clare was insistent.

'Sorry to trouble you again,' Clare said, when Irene finally came to the phone. 'I wondered if I could just check something?'

'Of course, Inspector. What is it?'

'Lexy – can you tell me what she studied at university?'

Clare could hear the pride in Irene's voice as she said, 'Medicine. She studied to be a doctor.'

Clare's stomach was in knots now. 'And the job in Manchester?'

'Junior doctor. And then she specialised in psychiatry. I was so proud of her, Inspector. She'd had such a rough time after – you know – but she came through it.'

Clare thanked Irene Andrews for her help and ended the call.

'Lexy Harris trained as a psychiatrist.'

Chris glanced at her then back at the road ahead.

'And I'll tell you something else,' she went on. 'The 999 call handler said she kept saying The man on the news.'

'Yeah, so?'

'She told us she knew John Mason. She'd met him at Pitlethie. Now we named him that afternoon. It was on the news about three. If she'd heard the news and recognised his name, surely she'd have phoned in, knowing where he worked? And do you really think she'd have invited him in when he appeared on the doorstep? More likely she'd have made an

330

excuse. Said she had to go out or was expecting guests. She could have hit the emergency button on her mobile and left the call open.'

'Maybe he barged his way in.'

Clare shook her head. 'No, think back. She said it was a frosty night and she asked if he wanted to come in for a few minutes. Chris, there was nothing in her statement that indicated she was fearful of him at that point. Only when she thought he'd slipped something into her wine.'

'And that call will be recorded. Reckon we've got her?'

She shook her head. 'It's not enough, Chris. We need more.'

Clare's next call was to Neil Grant, the pathologist. 'Neil, I need a favour – straight away, if you can.'

They were crossing the Clackmannanshire Bridge now, just outside Kincardine. An hour away from St Andrews.

'Go on, then,' Neil said. 'But it'd better be good.'

'Can you look at the photos of the woman who fought off our killer last night, please? I need her injuries compared with the other three victims. I'm concerned her attacker might not have killed the other women.'

'Give me ten minutes,' Neil said. 'Twenty tops.'

Clare ended the call and dialled the station.

Jim answered on the first ring. 'Clare?'

'Jim, can you see what background you can find on Lexy Harris please? Her first job after uni was in Manchester then she specialised in psychiatry. See if you can find where she went after that. Where she lived, relationships – anything at all. Soon as you can, please. I'll be with you in an hour.'

It was almost half an hour later by the time Neil Grant called Clare back. She flicked it onto speaker so Chris could hear. 'Go ahead, Neil.'

'Sorry for the delay, Clare, but I wanted to be sure.'

'Go on.'

'The injuries are less pronounced on Sandra Holt.'

'Could they have been self-inflicted?'

'How the hell did you know that?'

'Just tell me.'

'Well the fingernail marks are consistent with trying to prise someone's hands off her throat. But there's a massive clue in the bruising round the neck. The person who strangled the first three victims wore a distinctive ring – a crossover pattern – one band overlapping another. It left an imprint on the victims' necks on the left-hand side.'

Suddenly she remembered. They had been leaving Sandra Holt's hospital room as the nurse prepared to take her blood pressure. Her right arm was extended as the nurse wrapped the cuff round it. Sandra's hand lay face-up on the bed, a rose gold ring on her fourth finger. At the time Clare had noticed it was quite a chunky ring. But now she realised it wasn't chunky at all. It had only seemed thicker because it was made up of several bands arranged in a crossover pattern.

She closed her eyes, visualising the attacks. 'So the assailant wore the ring on the right hand.'

'Correct. In the case of Sandra Holt, there is a mark but it's on the right side of her neck, and further back.'

'Can you be sure it's the same ring?'

'If it's not, it's one very like it. Now, if you wanted to create the kind of bruising that occurs in strangulation your thumbs would be to the front, fingers to the back. It's too awkward doing it the other way round. So the position of the ring would be towards the back of the right-hand side.'

Clare put her hands up to her neck and saw what Neil meant. 'Okay, Neil. In your opinion, the marks on Sandra Holt's neck were self-inflicted?'

'It's a very strong possibility.'

'What about the stab wounds?'

'She's been a bit more careful, there. I'd say she's contrived to have him behind her in the kitchen and she's grabbed the knife, slashing back at him. Maybe he thought she was inviting him to kiss her and, as he moved in, she picked up the knife.

She'd only need one stab to disorientate him. Then she could turn round, keeping the knife carefully in the same position and finish the job. If I were you I'd pick her up, Clare.'

She ended the call. 'Talk about cunning.'

Her phone rang. Jim. She snatched it up and switched the speaker on. 'Go ahead, Jim.'

'It's Lexy Harris, Clare…'

'Go on.'

'Right. The mother seems to have changed the family name from Harris before she married Roy Andrews,' Jim said, 'but the change was never registered.'

'It's Holt, isn't it, Jim?'

'It is, Clare. I'm guessing when the mother remarried, Lexy decided to stick with Holt. But she kept her first name the same. She goes by Sandra now but her name is actually Alexandra.'

'Alexandra,' Chris said, shaking his head. 'Of course. It works with Lexy and with Sandra.' They'd reached the motorway at Kinross now and he accelerated down the slip road to join the M90.

'There's more,' Jim went on. 'We got John Mason's phone number from the care home and the phone company were pretty quick with his records. There are text messages from an unlisted number, inviting him round on Thursday evening about seven.'

'What about his phone? It wasn't on the body, was it?'

'Nope.'

She heard the triumph in his voice. 'You've got it, haven't you?'

'We have. Buried under a load of rubbish in Sandra Holt's wheelie bin.'

'Pick her up, Jim.'

Chapter 53

'There's just one more thing I want to do,' Clare said, as Chris slowed for the thirty miles an hour sign entering St Andrews. 'Can you head for The Harvest Moon, please?'

South Street was quiet for mid-afternoon and Chris nosed the car into a space just outside the bar. Inside two women sat drinking coffees, a clutch of shopping bags at their feet. A man in a checked shirt was behind the bar restocking bottles of mixers and, as they approached, he rose and gave them a smile.

Clare flashed her warrant card. 'I was hoping to see the other lady who works here.' She described the barmaid who'd shown Sara the CCTV footage.

'Sounds like Ella,' he said. 'Afraid she's gone now. Only temporary for Christmas. I might have an address…'

Clare shook her head. 'We're in a bit of a hurry,' she said. She took out her phone and typed Dr Sandra Holt into Google. An array of images flashed up and Clare clicked on the clearest. 'Do you recognise this woman?' she said, holding out her phone.

The barman shook his head. 'Sorry.'

Clare racked her brains. It wasn't going to be easy to link Sandra Holt to Ingrid McKinnie's murder. Then she said, 'Can you remember the twenty-eighth of December? I gather the bar was busy that night.'

'Hold on.' He reached under the bar and produced a large desk diary. The dark blue cover was well worn and the pages dog-eared from being thumbed through. He flicked back through the pages until he reached the last week in December.

'Mm, that was the night we had the ladies' Zumba class in.' He turned the diary to show Clare.

There was a name next to the entry. 'Kirsten Hayes,' Clare observed. 'Is that the person who made the booking?'

He shrugged. 'Suppose so.'

Clare opened Facebook on her phone and typed in Kirsten Hayes. A string of entries appeared and she added St Andrews to limit the results. A dark-haired woman wearing a lime green running vest with a London Marathon number pinned to it was the only profile returned. 'Is that her?' She held out her phone.

He studied the photo then his face cleared. 'Yeah, that's her. I remember her coming in to pay the deposit. Nice woman.' He handed the phone back.

Clare clicked to view Kirsten's profile, praying she didn't have maximum privacy. Kirsten's page appeared with a link to the Zumba group. She followed this and clicked to view the group photos. And there it was. An album called Christmas Night Out. She opened it and began to scroll through, looking to see if Sandra Holt had been caught in any of them.

It was a video clip, in the end, that gave Clare the evidence she needed. Kirsten Hayes was up on her feet, in the middle of the bar announcing a series of prizes. The clip was just over six minutes long and Clare and Chris stood watching each of the winners wriggling out from behind their tables to collect their prize from Kirsten.

'Stop!' Chris said, suddenly. 'Go back.'

It was the prize for the fastest 5K and, as the camera panned round to the winner's table, Clare paused the video. At the next table were two women. She recognised Ingrid McKinnie's curls from her photos and there was no mistaking the woman who sat opposite her. Dr Sandra Holt.

'Got you,' Clare said, tucking the phone back in her pocket. It began ringing again as they headed back to the car. Jim again. She swiped to take the call.

'No joy at the farmhouse,' he said. 'She's gone and so's her car.'

'Dammit. Okay, Jim. I'll be back in five minutes. Can you alert Traffic Control, please? Give them the car reg.'

'Done, Clare.'

'Any idea how much of a head start she had?'

'Fortunately not that much. Our lads only left the house about an hour ago. Just after you called. She was there waiting to get in when they packed up.'

Chris started the engine and began backing out of the space.

'Get her phone tracked as well, Jim,' Clare said as Chris roared away. 'And track that burner phone too – the number used to invite John Mason to her house last night. She may still have it on her. We'll be there shortly.'

—

'We've a traffic car sitting on all the main roads out of Fife,' Jim said as they entered the station. 'Unless we've missed her they should spot her soon.'

'That's great, Jim. Thanks.'

'What now?' Chris asked.

Clare shrugged. 'I honestly have no idea. If we pick her up we can check her DNA against Ruth and Alison's houses. John Mason's phone, too. But we have to find her first.'

They wandered into the kitchen and Clare flicked the switch on the kettle.

'What I don't get,' Chris said, taking mugs out of the cupboard, 'is why she killed them in the first place.'

'My money's on her blaming the four of them for Sam's death,' Clare said. 'Remember, Irene Andrews said the three girls and John were the last to come in from the garden for their pizzas. Maybe Sandra decided they must have been responsible for her brother's drowning.'

'Yeah I get that,' Chris said, 'but why now? Why all these years later?'

Clare nodded. 'It's a good point. And I doubt she'll tell us.'

They fell silent then Clare said, 'Hold on… she told us she bumped into John Mason in Cupar, didn't she?'

'Yes, she did,' Chris said. 'He'd run out of petrol.'

'And she works there one day a week.'

Chris frowned. 'So?'

'Well it's a long shot, Chris, but we might find out something from her colleagues. Where she's likely to have gone.'

'I dunno, Clare. Remember at the hospital she said there was no one she wanted us to call.'

'Chris, if we're right, she's responsible for four murders. We have to try everything we can to find her.'

The kettle came to the boil and he looked at it hopefully.

'Sorry,' Clare said. 'Get your coat. – we're going to Cupar.'

–

'I don't know why we couldn't do this by phone,' Chris grumbled as they waited to be buzzed into the hospital.

'Because you get a lot more, face-to-face,' Clare said. 'And besides they might try and quote data protection at us and we haven't time for that.'

'Fair enough.'

A buzzer sounded and they were admitted to the hospital. At the reception desk Clare showed her warrant card and explained she'd like to speak to any of the staff who were friendly with Dr Holt. The receptionist looked doubtful but turned to her computer and began typing. Then she lifted a phone and spoke into it.

A few minutes later a woman of about forty came tapping along the corridor. She introduced herself as Dr Geraldine Colvin then said she wasn't sure how she could help them.

Clare, with one eye on the receptionist who appeared to be reading something on her notepad, asked if they could speak somewhere more private. Dr Colvin hesitated then led them back along the corridor. She pushed open the door to a small room and flicked on the light. It was simply furnished with a desk, bearing a computer tower and monitor. To the side of the desk were four easy chairs arranged round a small coffee table. Dr Colvin indicated the chairs. 'Please, sit,' she said. She waited until they had sat then she perched on a chair opposite, her back ramrod straight.

Clare smiled, hoping to put her at her ease. 'We're trying to contact Dr Holt as a matter of urgency. She's not at home and we wondered if you – or any of her other colleagues – might know where she could have gone.'

Dr Colvin's face cleared, evidently relieved at such a straight-forward question. 'As a matter of fact, you've just missed her. She came in to say she had to take some compassionate leave. Some crisis with her parents I think. I said I'd sort out her case load and she left.' She frowned. 'I'm not sure I have their number but it might be on her record, as an emergency contact.'

Clare glanced at Chris. 'When was this?'

'Literally five minutes before you arrived.'

'Did she say where she was going?' Clare asked, getting to her feet.

'No, sorry.'

Clare put her hand on the door handle. 'Thanks so much for your time, Dr Colvin.' She took a card out of her pocket. 'If Dr Holt does contact you would you give me a call, please?'

She took the card. 'Of course. Do you want me to ask her to call you herself?'

Clare shook her head. 'No, in fact, don't mention it to her. Just let me know.'

They ran for the car, Clare calling Jim as they went.

'Jim, she's been in Cupar. Left about twenty minutes ago.'

'Direction?'

'Sorry – no idea. Better get someone onto the A91 and A92 – both directions. And sit a car at the Fife end of the Tay Road Bridge. We'll be back soon.'

Chris put his foot to the floor, siren blaring and headed back towards St Andrews. They were just entering Guardbridge, nearing the roundabout when Jim called again.

'They've spotted the car. It's on the A92, heading towards the Tay Road Bridge.'

'Gotcha,' Clare said into the phone. 'Chris, take a left at the roundabout. She's heading for the bridge.' Then she spoke into the phone again. 'What kind of car is it, Jim?'

'Subaru Impreza – bright blue.'

'Give me the reg…'

Clare wrote down the registration number, leaning on the dashboard as Chris took the Guardbridge roundabout at speed. With the siren and lights going, the traffic parted and he was soon driving through Leuchars.

'We should be at the bridge in ten minutes,' Clare said into her phone.

'Five,' Chris said, picking up speed.

'Are you in contact with the traffic car at the bridge, Jim?' Clare asked.

'Yeah. They've got it blocked off. Should see the car soon.'

As they approached the Forgan roundabout, the last one before the bridge, Clare told Chris to kill the siren and lights. 'We don't want her alerted.'

And then they saw the car a quarter of a mile ahead. The traffic cops were standing on the verge with their fluorescent jackets, checking cars then waving them on. The Subaru's brake lights came on then it swung across to the outside lane. The traffic car was parked broadside across both lanes and one of the officers stepped out into the road, his hand held up to stop the Subaru.

'There's nowhere for her to go,' Clare said. 'We've got her.'

But, as the road neared the roundabout the crash barrier which ran along the centre of the dual carriageway sloped down to ground level and stopped just short of a grass verge that bordered the roundabout. Suddenly the Subaru's wheels spun, kicking up gravel and dust and bumped onto the grass. It emerged onto the road opposite, taking the slip road that led to Tayport.

'Shit!' Clare said. 'Can you follow her?'

'Too right,' Chris said. He switched the siren and lights back on and they followed the Subaru over the grass and down the slip road. They heard the screeching of brakes as it reached the junction, turning right towards Tayport without stopping.

'Jim, get a car to the other end of Tayport as soon as you can. We're tailing her.'

The road wasn't wide and Chris weaved in and out of parked cars, causing oncoming traffic to screech to a halt to allow him through. But when they approached a bend in the road, Clare leaning to the left saw a bus heading straight for the Subaru as it overtook parked cars. Instinctively she stuck out her feet to brace herself for the inevitable impact but the bus pulled up short and the Subaru swung left and down Castle Road which was even narrower than the main street. It was a twenty-miles-an-hour zone but the Subaru careered down at easily double that.

'Careful, Chris,' Clare said, one hand on the door to steady herself. 'We want her, but not at any cost.'

The street came to a T-junction at the end and a car was sitting to the right, waiting to turn up. The Subaru turned left, causing a woman with a black Labrador to jump back from the edge of the pavement. It roared down the road, towards the Harbour Café. A large yellow grit lorry was moving slowly along the road to the right and a learner driver was approaching from the left. With nowhere else to go the Subaru went straight ahead into the harbour area.

Whether it was the speed, the sudden braking or a patch of icy ground, Clare wasn't sure, but she watched in horror as the car skidded through a gap in the fence and plunged headlong into the icy cold waters of the River Tay.

Chapter 54

Chris only just managed to stop the car from following the Subaru into the water. Clare clicked off her seatbelt and jumped out. The Subaru was sinking, fast. The light was fading now but it was still clear enough for her to see a panic-stricken Sandra Holt struggling with the door. Clare ran round to the back of their car and opened the boot, taking out a tow rope while Chris called for an ambulance and fire engine.

He jumped out of the car, phone clamped to his ear and Clare threw the end of the rope to him, kicking off her shoes. 'Here,' she shouted. 'Tie this to the tow hook.'

She took off her jacket and threw it behind her. The tide was in and the Subaru was more than half submerged now. It was starting to move round with the sway of the tide and Clare could see Sandra's desperate face at the window.

'Clare,' Chris yelled. 'You can't…'

'I have to. Now tie it and I'll attach the other end to the drive shaft.'

Chris reached down to the front of the bonnet and pressed desperately at the flap which concealed the tow hook. But it wouldn't budge.

'Use the key,' Clare shouted.

He ran back to the driver's door and snatched the key out, using it to lever the flap open. Then he lashed the tow rope round the hook, knotting it tightly. 'Okay,' he shouted.

'Get ready to back up,' Clare called and she slipped off the harbour wall, easing herself down into the freezing waters. She gasped as if she'd been hit in the chest as the icy cold spread through her body and she took a few seconds to control her breathing. She could only just see the top half of Sandra's head as she continued struggling with the door.

'Stay inside,' Clare shouted, gasping for breath. 'Stay inside.'

The car was sinking lower and lower and she couldn't put it off any longer. She took a few deep lungfuls in and out then one final huge breath. She plunged beneath the surface, feeling for the front wheel. The water was grimy and she could see nothing through the silt and sand kicked up by the car. Her hair wrapped itself round her eyes but she carried on, feeling her way round the front of the car. She found the number plate and moved left and under until she could feel the drive shaft where it connected to the wheel. The car was bobbing around, gradually sinking lower and she struggled to keep a grip on it. Her fingers were starting to seize with the cold and she felt her lungs bursting for air. She would have to surface soon if she couldn't get the rope round.

And then, finally, her fingers found the gap and she forced the rope round and out again. Terrified it would slip back she gripped tightly as if her life depended on it and tried to recall her uncle teaching her how to tie a bowline when she was just twelve.

It was a sunny Saturday afternoon and she was practising for a Guides badge. Her uncle, endlessly patient, was taking her through a series of knots. Make a loop, she could hear him saying and she forced her frozen fingers to form a loop. Now pass the end through the loop, the voice in her head said, and she tried to forget the car, forget the ice that was spreading through her body. Remember the bowline, he said when she'd finally mastered half a dozen different knots. It's the strongest knot you'll ever need. And now, in this grimy freezing water, with the Subaru and its occupant sinking fast, she thought if ever she needed a strong knot, it was now. But doing it blind, submerged in freezing water. I can't do it, she thought.

Then Sandra Holt's terrified eyes came back into her mind and she forced herself to recall the knot. The rope was through the loop now and she felt her way round the back of the rope and through the loop again. And suddenly it was done. She pulled as tightly as she could and tugged at the rope to check it was secure. Then she let go of the car and rose to the surface, gasping as she reached fresh air.

She tried to speak but the cold of the water was drawing the breath from her body. She gestured with her hand for the car to reverse. Chris was already in the driving seat, the door lying open, exhaust fumes condensing in the cold air. She heard the revs increase and the car began to move slowly back, taking up the slack on the rope.

Suddenly Clare felt strong arms lifting her up and she was hoisted into a boat which had come up behind her. The boatman then lifted a long pole and began steering the Subaru round until the front of it was facing the harbour wall and Chris's car. As Chris reversed further back trying to raise the front end high enough up to keep Sandra's head above water, the wheels began to spin. He eased off the revs and this time the wheels bit and the car began moving again. But it wasn't enough. The rope caught in the harbour wall and stuck. Then Clare saw men and women appearing from every direction. Word must have spread. They formed a line, as if preparing for a tug-o-war, and dug their heels in. And suddenly the front end of the car began to lift. Clare's heart rose as Sandra's head once more came into view. Shivering violently, she brushed hair off her face and saw Sandra's eyes meet hers.

The boatman threw a coat round Clare's shoulders and she clutched it round herself. He began steering his way back to the wooden pontoon. 'Soon have you warm, lass,' he said, and Clare nodded. In the distance she could hear sirens coming closer and she bent forward, hugging her knees, wondering if the cold would ever leave her body.

Chapter 55

A woman appeared on the pontoon, clutching a hot water bottle which Clare took then immediately dropped as the heat connected with her icy fingers. The boatman retrieved an oily rag from the cabin and wrapped it round the hot water bottle, handing it back to Clare. A young lad with a flask ran from the Harbour Café and he stood waiting for Clare to step out of the boat, pouring hot coffee into a plastic cup.

'Haud on, son,' the boatman said and he went back to the cabin for a water bottle. 'Don't want it too hot.' He poured some water into the plastic cup then held it to Clare's mouth. Even cooled by the water, it felt burning hot and she spat it out involuntarily. 'Sip it, hen,' the man said, and Clare tried again, spilling coffee as she shook with the cold. 'Blankets!' the man barked and the hot water bottle woman ran back towards her house.

Clare allowed herself to be hoisted up onto the pontoon by another two men but her legs wouldn't support her and she fell into their arms. Suddenly a siren which had been distant split the air as an ambulance appeared in the harbour car park. Chris waved it over as close as it could get to the pontoon, running with the paramedics as they wheeled a stretcher trolley out of the back.

She eyed the trolley and opened her mouth to protest but she couldn't speak.

'Hypothermic,' the boatman said, and the paramedics nodded.

'We've heated blankets,' they said and they eased Clare onto the trolley. 'Soon have you warmed up.'

The sky lit up with more blue flashing lights as a fire engine, siren blaring, drove into the car park. As the sound died Clare heard the puttering of a boat engine. Out of the corner of her eye she saw the distinctive orange lifeboat moving slowly into the harbour.

Chris was running alongside the paramedics as they wheeled Clare towards the ambulance. 'Lifeboat's here now, Clare. They'll get her out.'

Clare eyed him, then he was there no longer as she was wheeled up a ramp into the ambulance. She felt the heat of warm blankets then a jolt as the doors were slammed and it began its journey back to Ninewells Hospital.

–

Two hours later Clare was sitting up in bed, hooked up to an IV drip, drinking endless cups of tea. She was wearing a printed hospital gown and swathed in honeycomb blankets. She managed a smile as Chris approached her bed.

'What the hell are you like?' he joked, although his expression couldn't conceal how worried he was.

Clare shrugged. 'I know. Can't turn your back for a minute.'

He pulled up a chair and sat down at her bedside. 'What's in that?' he asked, indicating the drip.

'Just warm fluids. I can't tell you how lovely it feels.' She examined her fingers, still white. 'I'm gradually starting to feel my fingers again. I don't think I've ever been so cold.'

A nurse appeared with some tablets in a cup. 'Antibiotics,' she explained. 'In case you picked up any parasites in the water. Short course, just to be on the safe side.'

Clare tipped the tablets into her mouth and washed them down with tea. The nurse stuck a digital thermometer in Clare's ear then nodded.

'Coming up nicely.'

'When can I go home?' Clare asked.

'Probably another couple of hours,' the nurse said, writing on the chart at the end of Clare's bed. 'But I'll check with the duty doctor.'

The nurse moved away, and Clare lay back on her pillows. 'What happened after I left?'

'The lifeboat got her out. Car's still there but it's pretty much stuck in the silt, now the tide's gone out. The harbourmaster said it was bad luck. The harbour's just been dredged and it was fully high tide. Otherwise, the car might have settled on the bottom without putting her in danger. She wasn't actually as cold as you, apparently. She hadn't been fully submerged. But she's here, somewhere.'

'Tell me you've got her under guard?'

'Oh yes. Two officers on the door.'

'She's to be arrested the minute she's fit to leave,' Clare said, reaching across for the tea and taking another sip.

'Clare, I do know that,' Chris said, shaking his head. 'Can you just concentrate on recovering, please?'

She rolled her eyes. 'I'm absolutely fine. Just need to warm up a bit. I'll be right as rain in a few hours.'

'The DCI says you've not to darken the station door until Monday at the earliest.'

Clare's lips thinned. 'We'll see about that.'

'Seriously, Clare, you do need to make sure you're okay.'

'Yeah, I know. Thanks, Chris. I appreciate it. I don't suppose someone could fetch me some clean clothes?' She glanced down at a large white plastic bag beside the bed, knotted at the neck. 'That lot's going straight in the bin.'

He laughed. 'Way ahead of you. Sara's on her way up with something. Time you had some new clothes anyway.'

'I hope they fit,' she said, thinking of all the cakes she'd eaten over the past two weeks, thanks to Zoe.

'It's okay. I told her to bring something from her fat ward-robe.'

Clare closed her eyes. 'I don't even have the energy to scold you.'

'And I've phoned Moira – your neighbour? She's taking Benjy overnight. Just to give you time to recover.'

Clare smiled. 'I might just have a nap.' And she closed her eyes and drifted off to sleep.

–

It was almost nine o'clock when the doctor gave Clare the go-ahead to leave. 'See you keep taking these,' he said, handing her two packs of antibiotics. 'Some nasty parasites in those waters.'

Clare assured him she would. As she headed out of the ward she was surprised at how weak her legs felt and she allowed Chris to give her an arm. Sara walked behind, carrying the white bag of Clare's filthy clothes. As they reached the end of the ward she saw the two officers standing outside the door to a small room. 'She in there?' she asked, and they nodded.

'Clare, I don't think...' Chris began, but she paid him no heed, pushing open the door.

Sandra Holt lay, like Clare, hooked up to a drip, her face white and waxy. Her blonde hair was matted on the pillow and Clare wondered suddenly what her own hair was like. Sandra opened her eyes and she took a moment to register who they were.

'How are you?' Clare asked.

Sandra looked away. She didn't speak for a moment, then she said, 'I'll live.'

Clare nodded. 'I'm not going to say anything now but, once you feel better, you should call your solicitor.'

Sandra flicked a glance at Clare but said nothing.

Clare turned away and Chris moved to open the door.

Then Sandra said, 'You saved my life.'

Clare shrugged but she made no reply.

Sandra ran a tongue round her lips then she said, 'Thank you.'

Clare acknowledged this with a nod then she glanced at Chris. He opened the door for her and they left the room.

As they walked through the concourse Clare said, 'I want her DNA taken then a SOCO team to take swabs from the bathrooms at Ruth and Alison's houses. Also John Mason's phone.'

Chris stopped in his tracks. 'Clare, will you stop this? Take a bit of time, for God's sake! You could have died tonight, if they hadn't warmed you up quickly enough. You could even have drowned in that harbour. Who knows what's below the water level. So, for once in your life, will you let Sara and me take up the slack? You've an excellent team back at the station. For the love of God, trust us to do our jobs.'

Clare stared at him. 'Okay, calm down, Sergeant.'

'He's right,' Sara said. 'You need to take it easy for a few days.'

Clare shook her head. 'It's just as well you two are getting married. No one else would put up with you.'

–

Moira had switched the heating on full blast and it hit Clare as she opened the door to Daisy Cottage. She thanked Chris and Sara, promising to return Sara's clothes, duly laundered, then she closed the door on them, so glad to be home. She would never have admitted how wobbly she felt and the enormity of what had happened just a few hours ago at the harbour was beginning to dawn on her. She was too tired to switch the heating off and she climbed the stairs, weary to her very bones, hot tears pricking at her eyes. In the bathroom she switched on the shower and began removing the unfamiliar clothes. Then she submitted herself to the stream of hot water, head bowed, and she watched as the mud washed off her skin and down towards the drain. And as the tension began to leave her body she sank down into the corner of the shower, clutching her knees. The tears she had held back since being hauled out of the water began to course down her cheeks and she gave way to choking, convulsing sobs.

Saturday, 16th January

Chapter 56

Clare wakened to a long message from the DCI. She glanced at it then put her phone down. The fluids that had been pumped through her body meant she was bursting for a pee and she rose unsteadily from her bed and padded through to the bathroom. Sara's clothes lay in a heap on the bathroom floor where she'd stepped out of them and she saw that the bottom of the shower tray had traces of silt from her shower the previous night. She examined her face in the bathroom mirror and noticed a bruise on her forehead. She'd no idea how that had happened. Maybe she'd collided with the car as she fought to secure it with the tow rope. She had colour back in her cheeks though and she was suddenly aware of how warm the house was. Then she remembered the heating had been left on all night. Probably not a bad idea, given how cold she'd been.

She went back to the bedroom, missing Benjy but also glad that she didn't have to deal with him. She still felt curiously tired and sank back into her bed, taking up her phone to read the DCI's message. Sandra Holt had been released from hospital not long after Clare. She'd been taken back to the station in St Andrews and arrested. Her solicitor had arrived and after consulting with him she had agreed to her DNA being taken but had exercised her right to silence.

She's been sent to the cells at Methil, the message said.

Going in to interview her this morning.

It's likely we'll charge her.

She'll be up in court on Monday and we'll oppose
bail. Given the seriousness of the charges I reckon
she'll be remanded in custody.

Clare felt a vague sense of disappointment. She'd like to have
been in at the end, been the one to charge her with the murder
of John Mason. But, with luck, they'd amass enough evidence
for Clare to charge her with the other three murders too. She
wondered if Sandra might talk – might tell them why. Was it to
do with her young brother's death? It surely had to be. But, in
Clare's experience, defendants like Sandra never talked. She'd
go to trial, pleading self-defence against John Mason. Probably
contrive some story about being in touch with the other three
women for old times' sake, thus explaining away her DNA in
their houses. Clare wanted justice for the three women too. But
she might have to settle for John's murder. Her phone buzzed
with another message. Chris.

Hi Clare.

Hope you slept well and feeling better.

Just to say, don't worry about the party tonight.
Not expecting you to come. Will fill you in later.
My dad's going to video Sara when she arrives so
I'll show you that.

Take care.

Maybe see you next week.

C x

The party! She'd forgotten all about it. The problem with
working on a major investigation was that one day merged
into another. Weekends became meaningless. Tonight was the
surprise engagement party for Sara. A smile spread across her
face when she thought of them. Her joke last night about them

being suited was quite true. They were a perfect couple – just enough differences for them to complement each other.

A second message from Chris arrived and she clicked to read it.

> PS the guys searching Sandra's house found another mobile hidden in a wardrobe.
>
> I'm guessing she forgot about it in her rush to leave.
>
> Hoping it'll be the one she used to pose as Jessica Peters.

Clare hoped so too. If it was the same phone it might be enough to charge her with all four murders. She stretched her legs and yawned, thinking again about Chris and Sara. She decided then that she'd make an effort to attend the party. Maybe not stay late but she wanted to be there to see her young PC's face when she walked into that function room. And it would be a chance to catch up with some of her colleagues without the stress of the investigation.

Downstairs, she made breakfast, amazed at how hungry she was. It was odd not having Benjy to feed and walk and she wondered what she might do with her day. Moira had texted again to say she was taking Benjy down to Elie, a popular seaside town south of St Andrews. It had a broad sweep of beach and Benjy loved it. Give you a proper break, Moira had said.

Clare rose from the table and washed up her breakfast things. She felt better for the long sleep and the food. She switched the boiler back to its normal setting and went to dress. The sun was up now and the frost from last night was starting to melt. It would be a lovely day for a walk but she was vaguely unsettled. She'd worked this investigation for the past two weeks and now she felt as if it had all been taken away from her. Like leading a race from the start only to be overtaken at the finish line. She stood looking out of her bedroom window across the fields opposite, still frosty in places where the sun hadn't penetrated. And she thought about the case, about all the hours she and Chris had put in – the whole team.

'I'm damned if I'm going to be edged out now, just as it's all coming together,' she said aloud.

Fired with an energy she hadn't felt for some days she opened her wardrobe and took out the first work suit she could see.

–

'Clare!' Jim's face broke into smiles as she pushed open the station door. 'I wasn't expecting to see you.' He came out from behind the public inquiry desk and, unusually, held out his arms, to embrace her in a hug. She allowed herself to be hugged then pulled gently back.

'You scared the bejesus out of young Chris,' he said. 'How are you? The DCI warned us not to let you over the door. But I'm guessing...'

'Just you try and stop me, Jim. And I'm fine – thanks so much for asking.'

'Coffee?'

'Go on then.'

As they wandered towards the kitchen Clare asked, 'Anything doing?'

'Not much. Sara's off today. Chris is doing a half day. He's around somewhere.'

They made their coffees and Jim indicated a Tupperware box next to the fridge. 'Mary's sister brought us some homemade shortbread.'

Clare took a piece and bit into it, licking the sugar off her lips. It was buttery and delicious. 'Oh Jim,' she said. 'This is wonderful.'

'Aye. She makes good shortbread.'

'Fancy taking these into the incident room?' Clare said. 'See who's around.'

Jim hesitated. 'I – er, I wouldn't, Clare...'

She scrutinised his face. 'Eh? What's up? What's going on in there?'

'Clare…'

But she had gone, walking quickly towards the room. She pushed open the door to find them all gathered round the whiteboard. Chris was standing in the centre of the group, pinning a pair of bright orange water wings to a large poster for Finding Nemo. As she drew nearer she saw that Nemo's face had been replaced with Clare's photo. The group broke apart and Chris glanced round. His expression changed from mirth to horror as Clare slowly approached the board. The laughter had died and the room was silent now, no one daring to speak. Clare stood, looking at the board, at the water wings, then she spun round to face them.

'You bunch of bastards,' she said, and she started to laugh. They joined in, doubtless relieved at the break in tension and she was glad to see it. They'd been working so hard without a break for two weeks now and it was good to see them relaxing, even if it was at her expense. 'But if anyone starts addressing me as Inspector Nemo…'

Chapter 57

Clare wandered through to her office and switched on the computer. As she began typing in her password the door opened and Jim came in. She glanced at him. He seemed to be struggling for the right words.

'Jim?'

He came right into the room and sat down opposite her. 'Bit awkward, Clare...'

'Go on. It can't be that bad.'

'Sandra Holt's just arrived...'

Clare pushed back her chair and made to stand but Jim put a hand out.

'Wait – please. Just hear me out.'

Clare relaxed back into her seat again. 'This had better be good.'

Jim sighed. 'It's like this: the DCI has said, if you are in the station when Sandra Holt's being interviewed, you are not to go near her. He wants Chris and Janey to conduct the interview.'

'Just let him try and stop me.'

Jim shook his head. 'He's concerned that her solicitor might view your presence in the room as putting additional pressure on his client, with you saving her life, you know? And he doesn't want to lose her at this stage.'

Clare was silent for a moment. She'd seen enough defendants wriggle out of a conviction, thanks to a clever advocate, to recognise that the DCI was right. She didn't want to lose the case either. But she also wanted to see Sandra Holt put through the mill.

Jim went on. 'I was thinking… maybe if you briefed them on the important points then you could watch it by video link. And, if it's not going the way you want, let me know and I'll interrupt the interview.'

She glanced at Jim then away again.

'Trust your officers,' he said. 'They know what's needed for a conviction. And it would be great experience for them.'

Clare shook her head. 'Do I even have a choice?'

'Not really.'

'Go on, then. Stick them in Room One and I'll watch by video link.'

—

The interview began half an hour later. Clare and Jim watched as Chris repeated the caution which Sandra acknowledged. Clare sat forward and studied her. There wasn't a trace of emotion on her face and, as Chris began running through the evidence against her, she either made no response or muttered, 'No comment.'

It was only when Chris mentioned Sandra's little brother, Sam, that her demeanour changed. Her shoulders seemed to sag and her head drooped a little.

'I'm going to suggest to you, Dr Holt,' Chris went on, 'that you recently learned your classmates were responsible for the death of your little brother.'

Clare moved closer to the screen, watching Sandra for any sign of a reaction. Sandra's eyes flicked left and right.

'She's weighing up her options,' Clare said softly, and Jim nodded. 'She knows we'll find enough prints and DNA, and she's probably realised she left that mobile phone in her wardrobe. She's trying to decide how to play it.'

'Dr Holt?' Chris prompted.

'Perhaps I might have a few minutes with my client?' the solicitor said.

But Sandra waved this away. She raised her eyes to meet Chris's. 'I recognised him straight away,' she said. 'John Mason. When I walked into Pitlethie. He hadn't changed much over the years. Still the same dullard.' She shook her head. 'He didn't know me, of course. But I knew him all right.'

'Did you make yourself known to him?' Janey asked.

Sandra shook her head. 'No. I didn't. He'd avoided me at school. After the party. Never came near me again. Nor did the other three. Little bitches,' she spat, suddenly.

'Did you believe John Mason to be responsible for Sam's death?'

She was quiet for a moment, brushing an imaginary speck of dust off her sleeve. Then her face softened and she raised her eyes to meet Chris's. 'He was so little – Sam. And such a sweet boy.' Her eyes were bright now and she seemed to be trying to compose herself.

'Let her talk,' Clare whispered, her eyes on Chris and Janey and Janey flicked a glance in the direction of the camera, as though she understood.

After a few moments, Sandra gave a slight nod. 'I always knew there was something, you know?' She nodded again. 'The way they were at school, when I went back – after the funeral.'

'How were they, Sandra?' Chris said, a gentle note to his voice.

Clare felt a lump in her throat. This was so important and he was handling it beautifully. He could be gruff and tactless at times but she'd never been more proud of her DS than she was right now.

Sandra's brow creased, as though she was trying to remember. Then she said, 'They wouldn't look at me. Everyone else was kind, you know? Really kind, but the four of them – John and those girls – well they avoided me.' She shook her head slowly. 'My mum said it was because they were too young to understand. That's why they didn't know what to say. But I wasn't sure. And then, one day, Ruth came up to me in the school cloakroom and said she was sorry.'

'Did you ask what she meant?' Chris said.

Sandra shrugged. 'I didn't care, to be honest. Not at the time. But later, I started thinking about it. And then I remembered their faces that day. When Sam was found.' Sandra's eyes narrowed. 'All the other party guests, well, they were shocked, you know? Some of the girls were crying. But those four, they looked guilty. At the time I didn't understand. Not really. But it must have lodged in the back of my mind.'

'Did you tell anyone?'

She shook her head. 'I couldn't think how to explain it. And then Mum and Dad were talking about moving away. They had pictures of new houses and it was something to look forward to. I think I sort of forgot.'

'And then?' Chris asked.

'And then I met John Mason at Pitlethie Care Home. And, as soon as I saw him, it all came flooding back.'

'Did you ask him about it?'

'Not at first,' Sandra said. 'Not directly. But it didn't take much to get it out of him.' She nodded, as if recalling. 'I'm a psychiatrist, you see? I know how to work people. And I wanted to know the truth. So I started making an effort to speak to him, anytime I was at the home. Sought him out, you might say. Asked how he was, struck up a friendship, that sort of thing.' She leaned forward and picked up a cup of water, drinking from it. Then she went on. 'A few stray remarks about childhood trauma, the importance of adults revisiting past events and he was singing like a canary.'

'To be clear, Dr Holt,' Janey said, 'John Mason admitted to you that he was responsible for Sam's death?'

She nodded. 'Him and those girls. Obviously it took a few chats before he trusted me enough to tell the whole story. I fed him a line about not being able to reveal anything he told me, even in court. Stupid man believed it.' She smiled again. 'So I took him for a coffee. Said it sounded like he really needed a counsellor but that the waiting lists were so long. I said I'd do it as a friend.' She shook her head. 'He was pathetically grateful.'

'And what did he tell you?' Janey asked.

Sandra Holt looked down for a moment and Clare held her breath. Then she raised her head and Clare saw her expression had changed. Hardened.

'They didn't much like me, those girls: Alison, Ruth and Ingrid. I knew that. But they were popular, you see? And I wanted to be their friend. So I asked them to the party. They said John had to come too so I asked him as well.

'They came, of course, and they loved the garden.' She nodded. 'We had a great garden. Lots of grass and trees. Places to hide, you know? Anyway, they were the last to come in for their pizzas. My mum called us but they said they wanted to play a bit longer.' She shrugged. 'I didn't care. They were at my party and they were enjoying themselves. And I thought maybe they'd like me a bit more after that. Pathetic, really.'

She paused for a moment then went on. 'We had a swing on one of the trees. Near the gate. Just a couple of ropes and a wooden seat my dad made. He put it there because the ground sloped down and you could get a better swing. Anyway, John Mason told me he'd put Sam up on the swing and told him to hold on tight. Sam was laughing and laughing and John began to push him. Gently at first then more and more. The girls were urging him on. Push him harder, they were saying. And then Sam started to cry and said he wanted down but John just kept on pushing and pushing. Suddenly, Sam wasn't there.' She broke off, swallowing again.

Janey glanced at Chris, and Clare willed them not to interrupt. Chris gave a slight shake of his head.

'Good lad,' Clare whispered. 'Let her talk.'

Sandra cleared her throat then continued. 'The swing had taken him over the gate, and he must have fallen down the bank. John said they thought they'd get into trouble if they told anyone about putting Sam on the swing. My mum and dad had warned us that Sam was too little for it. But I think John was showing off – to impress the girls. And then the girls warned him not to tell or they'd put all the blame on him.' She shook her head again. 'He wasn't the sharpest lad, John. So he did what they said and went into the kitchen to make his pizza.'

Chris sat forward. 'You're saying that John Mason admitted responsibility for Sam's death, egged on by Alison Reid, Ingrid McKinnie and Ruth Williams? And that, after Sam had tumbled down the bank, they left him so they wouldn't get into trouble?'

Sandra nodded. 'Yes,' she said, her voice husky. 'They left my little brother to drown while they put cheese on their pizzas.' She reached across the desk and took a tissue from a box, blowing her nose. Then she said, 'I think they thought Sam would come back up himself and they were going to say he was lying about being on the swing. But he never came...'

The room was silent for a moment then Sandra cleared her throat. 'I can still hear my mother screaming.'

There was a pause then Chris said, 'Dr Holt, did you kill John Mason, Alison Reid, Ingrid McKinnie and Ruth Williams because they were responsible for your brother's death?'

Sandra looked at Chris for a few seconds then she looked away and shrugged. 'No comment.'

–

If she was tired before she watched the interview, Clare felt utterly wrung out after it. She congratulated Chris and Janey on a job well done and went back to her office stifling a yawn. She looked without enthusiasm at her computer and decided there was nothing that couldn't wait. She had a couple of things to do in town before she could go home so she shut the computer down and turned out the light. She emerged from her office and found Jim in his usual place at the front desk. 'Think I'll head off, Jim.'

'Aye,' he said. 'You do look weary, Clare, if you don't mind me saying.'

She nodded. 'I am a bit. But I'll see you tonight, yeah?'

His face creased. 'You're not thinking of coming to the party, are you? You're bound to be tired after your dip in the Tay.'

'Tired I certainly am, but I wouldn't miss that party for the world, Jim.'

He smiled. 'You're fond of the lad, aren't you?'

'I am. He's a lazy bugger at times but he and Sara are perfect for each other. And I want to see her face tonight.'

'Aye. It'll be a good night.'

She headed out to her car, stopping only to put her work bag into the boot. Then she turned and began walking along Pipeland Road towards the town. The sun had melted the frost and there was a hint of warmth in its rays. As she walked along she spotted clumps of snowdrops poking through the frozen earth and the pale yellow of a winter jasmine bursting with delicate blooms. Perhaps spring wasn't quite on its way but today it seemed a little bit closer.

South Street was bustling, as it always was on a Saturday, its broad south pavement outside the Madras College building dotted with buskers and red-gowned students, back now from their Christmas break. She made her way over one of the many zebra crossings, so numerous in the town that they drove motorists mad, and she found the shop she wanted. It was a furniture shop she knew Sara loved.

But it's always so expensive, Sara had said. Clare thought a voucher for the shop would be the perfect engagement gift and she paid for her purchase, tucking it into her handbag.

Her next call was two doors down, a shop she'd not visited before. The door dinged as she pushed it open and she was faced with a sea of baby clothes in pink, blue and every other colour imaginable. To the side were shelves of baby memento books, board books for toddlers, toys, rattles and a selection of Beatrix Potter baby dishes. It was a dazzling array and she scarcely knew where to start.

An assistant approached and asked if she could help.

'I'd like a gift for a baby girl,' Clare said.

'Age?'

'Very new.'

The assistant smiled. 'Sometimes the parents are overwhelmed with gifts in the new-born size. I'd suggest maybe a summer frock, say six to nine months?'

That sounded sensible and the assistant helped Clare pick out a dress in a tiny print with smocking across the front.

'We have little socks to match,' the assistant said and these were duly added to Clare's order.

She was just paying for her purchases which the assistant had offered to gift wrap when her phone sounded. A text message. Her heart sank. Surely not something else? She was longing to go home and put her feet up for an hour or two; but she couldn't risk anything going wrong at this stage. As the assistant tied ribbon round the parcel, Clare took her phone out and opened the message. It was from someone called Greta. Clare couldn't think who Greta was and she clicked to read it.

Don't forget your appointment with Greta this afternoon at two o'clock.

McArthur's Salon, South Street

'Shit!' Clare said and the assistant looked up in alarm. 'Oh, sorry. Just realised I've forgotten an appointment.' She checked her watch. Ten to two. She would just make it.

Ten minutes later she was sitting in a comfortable black chair at McArthur's Salon being scrutinised by Greta.

'Been a while, then,' Greta commented, lifting hanks of Clare's hair and examining it.

'Yeah. Work, you know?'

Greta let Clare's hair fall and studied her in the mirror. 'What you thinking?'

Clare spread her hands. 'I've absolutely no idea.'

'Okay. I think you need some layers to give it a better shape and definitely a colour to lift it. It'll give it some body. But we'd need to do a patch test first so I couldn't do a full colour today. You going anywhere special tonight?'

'Engagement party.'

'Yours?'

For a split second Clare thought of Geoffrey, then she put him out of her mind. 'No. Just some friends.'

'Tell you what, then,' Greta said. 'I'll put a natural colour through it for today – it'll wash out though. And I'll do a little patch test. If you react okay to that you could make another appointment for next week and I'll do a proper colour then.'

Clare smiled. 'Sounds great.'

Two hours later, Clare emerged from McArthur's, feeling her new haircut swishing round her face. She had to admit Zoe had been right to recommend Greta. The new layers were flattering and she loved the warmer brown tone from the temporary colour. She had an appointment for Thursday after work to have a proper colour done and, for the first time since she'd called Geoff to end their relationship, she was starting to feel positive. She walked quickly, heading down Queens Terrace and took the footbridge across the Kinness Burn. She was soon back at the car and on her way to Daisy Cottage. The sun had set now but it didn't look as if it was going to freeze tonight.

As she drove home she wondered about Sandra Holt. It was quite a coincidence, her being around when John Mason had run out of petrol, just outside the hospital where Sandra worked. How on earth had she engineered that?

And then she gave herself a shake. 'You're losing your touch, Clare,' she said. Of course he hadn't run out of petrol and of course she hadn't met him in Cupar. She'd made the whole thing up so she could explain John turning up on her doorstep. And poor John Mason, seeing a message from her asking him to call round, had walked right into an ambush.

Clare turned the car into her drive and jumped out, leaving the baby gift on the passenger seat to take with her later.

Indoors she dropped her handbag at the door and went through to the sitting room. She lit the lamps then lay down on the sofa and was asleep within minutes.

Chapter 58

In the end she arrived at the party after Sara.

She had wakened, to her horror, at ten to six and real-ised she'd missed lunch. She quickly put a cottage pie in the microwave to heat and went for a shower, feeling the grit from the river still on the tray. She stood half out of the stream of water, guarding her new hairdo, then turned the shower off and stepped out and towelled herself dry.

In the bedroom she hunted through her wardrobe to find something suitable for a ceilidh. It was still January so it might be cold but then she'd be hot if she was up dancing. She found a dogtooth checked dress and elected for flat-soled boots.

'Not that I feel much like dancing,' she said to herself.

The aroma of the pie drifted upstairs and she ran back down to spoon it onto a plate. She ate quickly and loaded the dish-washer then ran back upstairs again to apply some make-up, admiring her new haircut as she did so. She really did like it. There was no sign of Moira dropping Benjy off and she sent a quick text to say she would be out for the evening but to feel free to leave Benjy in the cottage. Moira replied immediately saying they were just back from Elie, that Benjy had been swimming in the sea and was now fast asleep in front of their fire. She offered to keep him until morning and Clare sent back a heartfelt thank-you. The next morning, of course, would be dog training, a thought that filled her with dread. But that was tomorrow's problem. She ran back downstairs and, picking up her handbag from where she'd dropped it at the door, she went out into the night to celebrate Chris and Sara's engagement.

The Kenlybank Hotel was an impressive building, one Clare had always admired, and it looked particularly handsome at night with lights burning in the front windows. She crunched up the drive slowly, following the signs to the car park behind the building. Then she walked back round to the front entrance and in through the revolving door.

She stopped at reception and was delighted to see Pawel Nowicki back in his usual place behind the desk. He had dark circles beneath his eyes but otherwise he was unchanged, in his usual dark grey suit, tie knotted neatly at the neck. His face broke into a smile when he saw Clare.

'Inspector, how lovely. You are here for the party?'

Clare smiled back. 'I am, Pawel, but first, may I congratulate you? I gather you have a little girl.'

Pawel beamed and he reached for his phone. 'Paulina,' he said, holding the phone out for Clare to flick through the photos. She gazed at the tiny baby, dark eyes staring back at the camera. In some photos Pawel was holding her close as she nuzzled into his neck and in others a small dark-haired woman held the bundle. 'She is perfect, Inspector. I know everyone says that about their baby but she really is.'

Clare handed the phone back and pushed her gift across the desk. 'Just something small to welcome her to the world.'

Pawel looked as if he might cry and Clare wondered if that was what parenthood did to you. She seemed to recall her sister, Jude, and husband Frank, being misty-eyed over their toddler James on many an occasion.

'You are so kind, Inspector. Thank you so much.'

Clare smiled again. 'Give her a kiss from me.' And she headed for the function room Chris had indicated on their last visit.

Sara was already inside, full of excitement at the surprise party. Clare stopped to take her in. She was utterly beautiful, in a red velvet dress, a tiny string of pearls round her neck.

'Boss! You knew about this?'

Clare shrugged. 'I admit nothing.' And she took Sara in her arms and gave her a hug. Then she fished in her handbag and took out the voucher. 'Have fun with this,' she said, and it was Sara's turn to look as if she might cry.

'No crying!' Clare ordered her young PC. 'This is a happy day.'

Sara laughed and dragged Clare off to meet her parents. And then she saw Chris, a sturdy figure in a dark green and blue kilt and a black Prince Charlie jacket. She had to admit he wore it well and the waistband didn't look too tight, either. He turned, saw her and came striding over, one of the laces on his kilt shoes unravelling.

'Your lace is out,' she told him.

'Can't get the damn things to stay in. But I've brought a pair of trainers – for the dancing, later.'

'Good plan.' She looked round at the party which was buzzing. Zoe was across the room, chatting to a group of officers, and Clare gave them a wave. The band was setting up on a dais at the end of the room and there were circular tables dotted round the edge with guests sitting behind them. 'So you pulled it off then? Was she pleased?'

'Absolutely gobsmacked, Clare. So surprised and...' he turned to look at Sara who was greeting a clutch of perma-tanned girlfriends, '... she's so happy.'

Clare slapped him on the back. 'Well done you. Now go and greet your guests.'

Chris indicated a table in the corner. 'Jim and Mary are over there. And Diane arrived a minute ago.'

She smiled. 'Thanks, Chris.' She made her way across to where Jim was sitting with his invalid wife Mary. She was in her wheelchair but she looked happy to be there and greeted Clare warmly, admiring her new haircut. Diane was sitting next to Jim and she opened her mouth to speak to Clare when the band announced that the first dance would be a Gay Gordons.

Clare went to the bar and ordered a round of drinks. The barman produced a tray and she carried them back to the table, dodging the dancers as she went.

'I hear you had a bit of excitement,' Diane shouted over the band and Clare tried her best to explain what had happened at Tayport Harbour.

The dance came to an end and Clare moved her chair round so she had a view of the floor. The Gay Gordons was succeeded by a Virginia Reel, then another dance Clare wasn't familiar with. And then the band announced a waltz and the dancers began drifting back to their tables for a well-earned rest.

As the lilting music filled the room the door opened again. Clare glanced absently to see who had come in then her mouth dried. DCI Alastair Gibson was walking uncertainly up the room towards their table. He too was wearing a kilt, a brightly coloured tartan of red, green and yellow with a dark blue open-necked shirt and dark kilt socks. If Chris wore his kilt well, Clare had to admit the DCI wore his extremely well. He cut a handsome figure as he moved through the dancers, his kilt swinging gently as he walked. As he approached their table she caught a glimpse of his chest hair, nestling under the shirt. He looked a little uneasy and Jim rose to greet him, introducing him to Mary. He made polite noises and smiled at Diane.

And then he turned to Clare. With a nod to the band he said, 'May I have this dance?'

Clare rose from her seat and took his hand. He led her onto the dance floor and put an arm round her back, offering his hand for hers. She put her other hand on his shoulder and he pulled her in towards him. She could smell his cologne, so familiar now, and she became suddenly aware of her own heartbeat. He led off and they began to dance.

For a minute he said nothing. And then they both spoke awkwardly together.

'Sorry, Al,' Clare said. 'I interrupted.'

'Nice hair,' he said.

'Thanks. Time I had a change.'

They fell silent again then he said, 'I was going to say I'm so glad to see you, Clare. You gave us such a fright yesterday.'

She smiled. 'Gave myself a fright, to be honest, Al. But it turned out okay in the end.'

He shook his head. 'Will you never stop doing these things?'

She laughed. 'Probably not.' Then she said, 'I didn't expect to see you here.'

This seemed to disarm him and he moved awkwardly, stepping on her foot. 'Look,' he said, 'do you desperately want to waltz?'

'Not really.'

'Then come with me.' Still holding her hand, he led her through the dancers and out of the function room into the reception area. 'Drink?'

'Oh, I've a drink back in the room.'

'Forget it. I'll get you another.'

'Erm, lime and soda please.'

He shook his head 'Clare, you can get a taxi home tonight. Let's have a proper drink.'

'You're not driving back?'

He shook his head. 'Thought I'd treat myself. Booked a room for tonight.'

'Lucky you. Go on, then. I'll have a gin and tonic.'

Clare sat down at one of the tables to await the drinks. A few minutes later he returned with two tall glasses, damp with condensation, bobbing with ice and lemon. He placed these down on the table and sat opposite. Then he said, 'I wasn't really invited here tonight.'

'Oh?'

'Young Chris,' he said. 'After you were taken away in the ambulance he phoned me. Told me what had happened. I said I'd come up straight away but he said to leave it until you were home. And then he told me something that gave me a little bit of hope.'

Clare watched him, waiting to hear what he was going to say, a lump forming in her throat. She picked up her drink and sipped at it, enjoying the coolness in her mouth.

'He told me you had ended your relationship with Geoffrey. And that, as far as he could tell, you weren't seeing anyone else.' He took Clare's hand in both of his and began gently stroking her fingers. She looked down and watched this, enjoying the sensation. She hadn't noticed his hands before. They were long, tanned, possibly from his skiing trip, and she decided she liked them. Her own fingers seemed pale and slender by comparison.

'And that gave me hope,' he was saying. 'Hope that perhaps...'

'Al,' she said, cutting across him. 'I have to say this. I... can't forget how I treated you. That time in the hospital – when they said I could go home and you and Geoff turned up together. I can't forget that I chose him over you. I don't deserve...' She broke off, not knowing what else to say.

He smiled. 'That's what's so lovely about you, Clare. You always think of others. Of course you would choose Geoffrey. He'd just flown three thousand miles to be with you. And you were in a kind of relationship with him. It would have been unkind to have sent him away.' He stopped feeling her fingers and gripped her hand more tightly. 'And you couldn't be unkind, Clare. You simply don't have it in you.'

She raised her eyes to meet his. 'Al...'

'What I'm saying, Clare, is... I think we missed our moment. Last year. That night in your cottage, with the curry and my shirt – we shared something then. You know we did. But I let you slip through my fingers. And now, well, I don't want to make the same mistake again. Miss another moment.'

Clare's mouth was suddenly dry and she eyed her drink.

'I can't stop thinking about you, Clare,' he went on. 'Even the bloody-minded bit that makes you jump into freezing rivers to save murderers.'

She laughed at this but didn't know what to say.

'So, can we?' he asked. 'Can we try again?'

He was still gripping her hand and she squeezed his back. 'I'd like that, Al. I'd like that very much.'

He put his hand up to her face and gently pulled her towards him. And then he kissed her on the lips. A long, lingering kiss that she didn't want to end.

Then he pulled back and she saw his eyes, so blue, alight with love, and she thought that maybe, just maybe, she wouldn't go to dog training in the morning.

Acknowledgements

I'm seldom more than half a chapter into a book before seeking help from a wonderful group of friends who are ever-ready with answers to the most obscure questions, and What They Knew was no exception. Special thanks go to Liz and David Anderson, Angela and Gavin Nurse, Alan Rankin, Richard Renwick, Professor Frank Carey, Dr Julie Curran, Heleen Kist and my very good friend Isabel S. And to my three amigos, Ally, Euan and Alicia, and my wonderful partner Peter, my love and thanks for always being there.

I'm so grateful to my outstanding editors, Louise Cullen and Siân Heap. I don't know how you do it, ladies, but please keep doing it! I'm so lucky to have Deborah Blake's eagle eye as a copy editor and Abbie Headon as proofreader – thank you both for your astonishing attention to detail. And to Stephen Mulcahey for a quite exceptional cover design, a huge thank you. To the whole team at Canelo, my special thanks for believing in me and for working so hard to bring this book to print.

My agent Hannah Weatherill is, as ever, the most wonderful support and I feel very lucky to be in such excellent hands – thanks so much for everything, Hannah.

To Police Scotland and the good people of north-east Fife, my thanks for allowing me once more to bring crime to your streets. I hope you'll agree that DI Mackay's clear-up rate more than makes up for it.

Finally, to the booksellers and readers who have taken Clare to their hearts, a very special thank-you for making the hard graft of writing so very worthwhile.

Do you love crime fiction and are always on the lookout for brilliant authors?

Canelo Crime is home to some of the most exciting novels around. Thousands of readers are already enjoying our compulsive stories. Are you ready to find your new favourite writer?

Find out more and sign up to our newsletter at canelocrime.com